Praise for Sam Peters

'A first-class SF thriller. Even though Peters wrapped up the case, I still wanted to know more about the universe of Magenta'
Peter F. Hamilton

'Not only a gripping SF crime thriller but a moving investigation into the limitations and capabilities of artificial intelligence'
Guardian

'A masterly piece of writing and plotting that manages to merge classy space-opera with a police procedural as twisty as a Christie'
Joanne Harris, *Sunday Times* bestselling author of *The Strawberry Thief*

'Immersive SF, full of world-building detail, with a twisted love story at its heart'
Financial Times

'Interesting and powerful'
SFX

'It's easy to see why *From Darkest Skies* has already been optioned for TV, what with its cinematic action and fast-paced plot, but the real strength lies in the humanity of its characters'
SciFiNow

'Peters' convincing world-building and a tense plot mean that this is a debut destined to make waves'
The Morning Star

'Crime noir in the style of *Blade Runner*'
The Book Bag

'Outstanding s
Crime Time

By Sam Peters from Gollancz:

From Darkest Skies
From Distant Stars
From Divergent Suns

FROM DIVERGENT SUNS

SAM PETERS

This edition first published in Great Britain in 2020 by Gollancz

First published in Great Britain in 2019 by Gollancz
an imprint of The Orion Publishing Group Ltd
Carmelite House, 50 Victoria Embankment
London EC4Y 0DZ

An Hachette UK Company

1 3 5 7 9 10 8 6 4 2

A CIP catalogue record for this book
is available from the British Library.

ISBN (Mass Market Paperback) 978 1 473 21482 8
ISBN (eBook) 978 1 473 21483 5

Typeset by Deltatype Ltd, Birkenhead, Merseyside

Printed in Great Britain by Clays Ltd, Elcograf S.p.A.

MIX
Paper from
responsible sources
FSC® C104740

www.gollancz.co.uk

For my dad.
Rest in Peace.

INSTANTIATION ONE

Agent Laura Patterson of the Magentan Investigation Bureau – the Tesseract, as everyone calls it these days – sits in a quiet office. She's alone and it's late. Everyone else has long since gone home.

Summary Progress Report: Suspect: Chase Hunt

Case notes. Nothing official. A report in progress. Unseen, Instantiation One watches her read.

Primary suspect in the killing of Walter Becker outside Mercy hospital. Associated data theft from Mercy. Arson. Abduction, assault and imprisonment of Kamaljit Kaur. Post-mortem mutilation of Doctor Nicholas Steadman (bullet in the head several hours after death – same gun as Becker).

On the desk beside her is a small, sealed evidence bag. Inside is a single hair. Attached is a DNA analysis.

Evidence suggests a well-resourced and experienced professional intelligence operative with excellent fieldcraft and marksmanship. Intimate familiarity with operational practices and procedures of the Tesseract and with the Firstfall surveillance network. Clear connection to Darius Vishakh: recommend bringing this up in Vishakh's questioning.

Query: Becker fits for the Steadman and Kettler murders. Sadly too dead to interrogate. Did Becker do it or did Hunt set him up?

Query: Is Chase Hunt a real person or a shell?

Patterson deletes the last line and types new words in its place.

Query: Chase Hunt is one of us? Or was?

She pauses and thinks, looks at the evidence bag and hisses between her teeth.

'Alysha Rause.' But everyone knows that Alysha Rause died six years ago.

Agent Patterson files the report in her personal workspace where no one else will find it, pockets the evidence bag and goes home. Through the cameras in the Tesseract, through the Servant in her apartment, Instantiation One watches.

1

THE GHOST

There's a woman by the door, half turned away and barely visible in the dark. Her hair is in a style I don't recognise but I know her. I'd know her anywhere.

'Liss?'

I'm dreaming. I have to be.

She freezes. 'Keon?'

I know that voice but it isn't real. It can't be real because she's dead; but then she turns to face me and blood roars in my head. I see her, and on her face is a look of grief and joy and love and despair and tragedy that no shell could ever feign.

Not a shell. Real. Real and human and alive.

'Hey, Keys,' she says.

Alysha. My Alysha. Flesh and blood and back from the dead. She comes to me and I feel the touch of her fingers on my face, gentle as silk. I feel her lips brush mine as she kisses me. I smell her, a touch of Xen and seaweed laid over something far more familiar. *Her* smell.

Alysha. My dead lover. The part of my soul I thought I'd

lost. I inhale her scent as she leans over me, a silhouette in the darkness of my hospital room. Her hair hangs over her face like a shroud. She has it cut shorter that I remember, but I recognise her even if her features are lost in shadow. I know her smell and her touch and her voice. I know the shape of her and the way she moves. I know all of these things as surely as I know how to breathe.

'Alysha?'

It's the night after Esh's funeral, a night for the dead to be restless. I've longed for this for so many years, longed for it so much that I made a shell and filled it with Alysha's memories and her persona and called it Liss ... but Liss isn't real, isn't right, isn't Alysha, isn't *her*.

I must be dreaming.

I feel tears well up. I start to rise but Alysha puts a hand on my chest and eases me back.

'Hush.'

'Why did you leave?'

'I'm so sorry.'

'Where did you go?'

She leans into me, her face over mine. I feel a drop of something warm and wet that tastes of salt on my tongue. A tear, and again that smell of her, a hint of the sea and a whisper of Xen.

'I need you to do something,' she whispers, and presses an object into my hand.

'Who did this to us?' I ask.

'*October*.'

She slips away, gone like a ghost.

Six years ago, Alysha sent a covert extraction team to the corporate enclave Settlement 64. She sent them to pull an Earther scientist, Anja Gersh, who was tinkering with Magenta's unique xenoflora in the hope of curing a rare genetic disorder; but what Gersh found was something wild, something her experimental strains of Xen unlocked in her test subjects. Telekinesis. Uncontrolled, random, invariably and quickly fatal, and impossible to explain. Something Gersh's masters were willing to kill to protect, and so they did, again and again and again until Alysha was the last, and she ran, but they got her anyway ...

Or so I thought.

I tell myself again that she was a dream, that it has to be, but in the morning I have two memory slivers clutched in my hand.

I've never seen them before.

No.

It isn't possible. I can't let myself think she somehow survived.

Alysha ...?

Is it possible?

Laura tried to tell me. After Esh's funeral. She tried to tell me what she'd found ...

No!

The extraction team that snatched Anja Gersh got out and promptly flew straight into a Magentan storm because someone hacked their weather feeds. Everyone died. Against all reason or procedure, only Alysha knew they were even there. Two weeks later – the day before it came out – she cashed in a favour with a Fleet intelligence agent, Darius Vishakh. He gave her an exit and smuggled her onto the overnight mag-lev from Firstfall to Disappointment. He was supposed to pick her up at the other end, only Vishakh also hired a lunatic with a bomb. The train exploded at a thousand miles an hour halfway between Firstfall and Disappointment, and all they ever found of Alysha were her tags. I know this because Darius Vishakh told me while I had my fingers round his throat. He set her up to die because someone in the Tesseract wanted her gone.

He's in a Tesseract cell now, awaiting trial. Like everyone else, he thinks Alysha is dead.

But I remember the words Liss wrote across my lenses as Vishakh and I struggled to kill one another. Liss, the copy of Alysha that I made, as close as can be done – every trace Alysha left behind, every word she spoke or gesture she made, everything of her ever captured or recorded, crushed into an AI core ...

Alysha isn't dead.

They were just words, just something she said to keep me alive after Vishakh and I were done with each other. We should both be dead but we're not. Someone came after us. Someone came and saved me.

They were just words.

Weren't they?

I can't bring myself to look at the slivers in my hand. There's a roaring in my head, a pressure too much to take. She *can't* be alive. Not after all this time. It can't be real. Six years ... but what then? Who was that last night? Vishakh? A last cruel trick played from inside whatever cell the Tesseract has given him ... I can't think why or how but this can't be real. It *can't* be ...

The first sliver is addressed to Doctor Elizabeth Jacksmith at the Magenta Institute. It contains a complex decryption key and nothing more. I don't know what it means or what it's for and I don't know what to do with it. Give it to Jacksmith? I don't think so.

The second holds three short video clips. I project the first to my lenses and see ...

... Alysha looking back at me. She sits in a corner of the Magenta Institute cafeteria. A screen in the background displays the breaking news: an explosion in the mag-lev tunnel between Firstfall and Disappointment, an automated freight train annihilated in the blast, no casualties but the tunnel will be closed for at least two months. It's the day after the bomb and the report is wrong on both counts. It took three months, not

6

two, before the tunnel opened again, and later that same day we discovered four stowaways had been aboard, their bodies vaporised by the explosion ...

The thought catches in my throat: all they ever found were Alysha's dog tags.

All they ever found ...

I'm sinking. Sinking into believing that maybe, just *maybe*, this could be real ...

Liss?

I reach for her, the shell, the recreation of the Alysha I loved, so nearly perfect and yet not quite.

Liss, why did you tell me that Alysha isn't dead?

My knuckles are white, my fingers digging into my palm. I can't let myself go there. I can't let that hope come back into me, not until I know for sure. I can't let it be possible that she's alive only to discover I'm wrong and lose her all over again ...

The clip is short. She stares into the lens. Her face is hollow with horror, with bleak despair.

'I'm sorry, Keon,' she says. 'I don't know what else to do. One day ... I hope it won't be for long. Weeks. A few months, maybe, but if you find this then it's because I can't stop them, because ... because I couldn't get back to you ... The Earthers did this to us, Keon. They're inside us, inside the bureau, inside Fleet. I ... I don't know how else to do this but it's better that everyone thinks I'm gone. I didn't want it to be this way. I love you.'

She looks haunted. Desolate, a face saying goodbye to everything it knows, even to itself.

A few months? Try six years.

Liss?

But Liss doesn't answer.

The next clip is from the morning before the bomb: a visit to an old friend, Doctor Elizabeth Jacksmith. The clip is short, a small handful of seconds: Alysha staring at a picture on the wall showing Jacksmith with the crew of the *Fearless* from twenty-six years ago, Darius Vishakh beside her. The start of all this.

'Darius Vishakh is a snake,' says Jacksmith to Alysha.

The last clip is more recent and again brutally short. The Alysha from my dream that wasn't a dream.

'Yours forever, Keon. I'll find you again when I can. It'll be soon now, I promise. I can't pretend any more. Destroy these when you're done with them. Please.'

Destroy them? I lock the videos into my Servant under as much encryption as I can manage and watch them again, burning them into my memory. Destroy them? I can't.

And again ... and I hardly notice the tears, the sobs that shake me.

And again ... and why she didn't tell anyone about Anja Gersh? *Why?*

And again ... and the last six years have been a lie, and I don't know what to do but find her, but I don't know where to even start.

ONE

UNE MEELOSH

2

THE DAY AFTER

'She didn't say much,' I say to Bix.

He's sitting next to me on a half-empty train to Nico. It's odd, because usually it's Bix who does the talking, but today he's quiet and I'm not sure why. Maybe it's because Nico is where most of his extended family still lives and he's thinking about how many of them he might get to see while we're there. Maybe he's thinking of Esh, because it's really not all that long since she died. Maybe he remembers that Nico is where I went with Alysha for our honeymoon, but probably not. I doubt he remembers that, but *I* do. I remember it perfectly. Not that we saw much of Nico itself.

Alysha. Alive. I'm trying so hard not to believe it, but I want it. I want it so badly ...

'Why did she do it, dude?'

The question is like an ice pick wrapped in a satin sock. I don't have an answer. The truth is that I don't know. So Darius Vishakh would think she was dead? But there are so many holes in that idea that it could never fly. I've met Vishakh, and he wasn't enough to make Alysha run the way she did.

Why did she let us all think she was dead? Why did she go after Gersh without telling anyone what she was doing, not even me …? But Bix doesn't know anything about Alysha. He means Laura, transferring out of our little team back to Internal Audit. To counter-espionage, digging for dirty agents.

'I don't know,' I say. 'Vishakh's mole inside the bureau, maybe.' There might even be some truth to that, but what I really think is that she's after Alysha.

Shit. She can't still be alive.

She *can't* be, not after all this time.

And yet …

*Some*thing made her run. Whatever it was, she didn't say a word. That's what eats me, why I can't allow myself to believe this. We always talked, about everything, and yet she didn't tell me. She didn't even try.

'But, you know, it doesn't, like—'

'Dug anything up on our guy, yet?'

We're in a vacuum-sealed tunnel some two miles under the surface of Magenta, rocketing along at close to a thousand miles an hour on the mag-lev from Firstfall to Nico. Nico is Magenta's third city, eight thousand miles away, a poor relation to Firstfall and Disappointment but also a haven for the fringe arts. Some of Magenta's most striking scenery is around Nico, and its most extensive known cave systems too. Alysha wanted to see them, which is why we went there for our honeymoon. Nico's biggest claim to fame right now is that Elizabeth Jacksmith, Magenta's most famous scientist, was born there. It's also the place where, three days ago, Magenta's most famous painter, Une Meelosh, slashed open his own throat. Bix and I are supposed to find out why. It's a stupid dead-end case to keep us out of the way while the Tesseract deals with the *Flying Daggers* and Earth and Iosefa Lomu and all the things that challenge the future of our world, but I guess I shouldn't complain. After what we did to bring down Darius Vishakh, we're lucky to still be working at all.

Alysha.

Could the woman in the Mercy have been someone else? A shell, maybe? The video clips could be forgeries, although why anyone would bother is beyond me. But there's more to it than that. There's Laura's evidence. She showed it to me after Esh's funeral. And if that's a plant or a forgery then there's what happened at the very end with Vishakh and the transpolar expedition. The official story is that a weather researcher, Kamaljit Kaur, dragged me and Vishakh out from the crashed wreck of one of the expedition's Cheetahs. Kaur was a hanger-on, piggy-backing on the expedition to set up weather stations that had nothing to do with Lomu or Vishakh or anything else. No one can explain what she was doing out there, but Kaur hauled us out of the wreckage and Elizabeth Jacksmith flew us back to the dig site. The trauma unit there saved my life, and Vishakh's too, and no one thought much about it in all the confusion until the real Kamaljit Kaur showed up in Firstfall a week later, after spending eight days locked in a room in an abandoned corner of the Squats.

The Kamaljit Kaur who saved me wasn't the real Kaur. Laura thinks she was Alysha but she can't prove it. If it *was* Alysha then I have to figure she was after the same thing as Vishakh, but she didn't take it, and I'm alive because she made that choice, and so is Darius Vishakh. I cling to that. Six years without a word, six years of letting me believe she was dead; but in that moment she wiped them all away.

That's what I tell myself.

Damn it, I need to be in Firstfall, not Nico. I need to find her.

Bix is looking at me. I think he's been talking. If he has, I haven't been listening.

'Boss dude?'

'Sorry.'

'So Meelosh does these gigs, right? Poetic prose and one-man drama stuff, you know?'

I have no idea. I'm not sure I know how to even care.

'Right, so two nights ago he's booked for this gig, you know, but he doesn't show. No one gives it a thought because he's, you know, an *artist*, like, all full of moods and stuff. But then the stories about the video come out.'

'Video?'

'Yeah. He made a recording.' Bix pings me a file. 'It's, like, uh … Well, basically he goes on about how the Masters are coming back. Weird stuff, man, and then he ends up opening his own throat. But before … Some of it is some totally off the charts crazy shit, man!'

I brace myself for what I'm about to see. It starts as white noise, an old analogue video tuned to a dead station with the gain turned up too high. The audio is hiss and static. Then the video noise slows right down, the blurred blobs flash on and off more slowly, and then stop flashing at all and start to move instead, random lurching shifts and jerks, still for a second and then on again. It's like watching a swarm of insects, beetles maybe, or bees in their hive. Underneath is still a flicker of noise. It's weird in a way that feels wrong. It's under my skin and I want to wash it off. I want to stop watching but I can't.

'Meelosh make this?'

Bix shrugs. 'Don't know for sure, boss dude, but I don't think so.'

The blobs begin to arrange themselves. It seems haphazard but it isn't. Words appear.

It begins.

The image freezes and then resets. Back to white noise but now the sounds are distorted clicks and a buzzing that slides in and out through the hiss and crackle. A feedback-ravaged wail comes and goes, edging in and out at the threshold of hearing. I don't know why, but every hair on the back of my neck is taut with tension. I want to be sick. I want to turn it off and yet I keep watching.

The noise under the noise arranges itself into letters again.

They are here.

I check the length of the clip. It runs for several more minutes.

'What is this?'

The hiss and clicking continues. Sometimes I think I see other images through the noise that flickers and the noise that creeps and crawls: echoes of moving figures maybe, sometimes swaying, sometimes still, sometimes jerking back and forth in movements too quick to be natural. I feel light-headed. An empty dread oozes into me like poisoned electronic pus.

'What the fuck ...?'

The video plunges abruptly into a pause of silent black that feels like I'm looking into a primeval void. Then suddenly I'm seeing the gaudy set of a bad horror show, or that's what it looks like. The walls are covered in paintings, most of which are unfinished, of distorted, mutated, mutilated people, twisted and in pain. Among them are primitive sculptures of deformed animals and shelves stacked with what look like actual books made of honest-to-god paper and ink. Une Meelosh stands in the middle of it all, long greasy black hair, naked from the waist up. The camera focuses on the knife in his hand. His eyes are glassy. Yet for all the trappings, the feelings of nausea fades. If I didn't know what was about to happen, this part would be almost comical.

15

'They come.'

Meelosh says the words dead flat, as empty of expression as the hum of a machine as he lifts a knife to his neck and calmly slices his own throat. Blood jets across the room. He tilts his head to open the wound further. His mouth falls slack. His eyes roll back. He sways and collapses and falls so that all I can see are his feet. They twitch once and are still.

The video stops.

'I edited it down,' says Bix. 'The original is, like, way longer, man. It's really ... I don't know. Disturbed, you know? Kind of gets into your head. There's a whole load of other stuff at the start.' He pings me the full version.

'Worth watching?'

'Dude, if you do, keep some happy pills handy, you know what I mean? I had to go out and rave for a bit after I watched it the first time. It messes with you, man. Don't know why, don't know how, but it does. It's pretty twisted.'

'Meelosh make this? Is this supposed to be art?'

'Meelosh made some of it, yeah.'

'Does he say anything else?'

Bix shakes his head.

'Any idea why he did it?'

'He's not, like ... the most stable, you know?'

He pings me a picture I know I've seen before, of a beautiful green meadow of long grass and wild flowers, slightly alien, framed by trees. In the foreground, an arm punches up through the earth. The arm is half rotten, decayed flesh peeling from yellowing bone. The fingers form a fist clutching the severed bloody head of a rabbit. The rabbit's eyes are open, its mouth fixed into a wild grin, its incisors sharpened into fangs. There's a noose around its neck.

The painting has a name: *The Death of Strioth*.

'I take it that's Meelosh?'

'It's in a gallery on Earth, man! Sold for millions! It was, like, his moment, you know? Like he was going to make it off Magenta, go on tours. Fame and fortune and stuff. But it didn't happen.'

'Why not?'

'Dunno.' Bix shrugs. 'Maybe that's why he killed himself?'

The Nico police report states that Meelosh was dead for more than a day before anyone found him. His Servant didn't scream a medical alert as soon as he started bleeding. Superficial diagnostics said Meelosh disabled it himself, the usual story for a suicide. No point killing yourself only to be brought back.

'They only knew something was wrong because someone watched the video and tried to reach him. Meelosh didn't answer and so they called it in,' says Bix.

'Someone else saw this? Who? How?'

'It auto-transmitted to a mailing list a few minutes after Meelosh cut his throat. A few dozen people, you know? The call to the Nico police was anonymous but I guess someone from that list, right.'

'So ... this is all over the net?' Shit. The last thing I need on top of a dead-end case is one with a media circus ... but Bix shakes his head.

'That's another weird thing, man. Not a trace. At least, not yet.'

He pings me the forensic report from Nico hospital where Meelosh's body is in the morgue. A superficial physical examination shows no marks suggestive of violence or restraint. The blood work shows enough Xen in his system to daze a bear, countered by enough stimulants to wake the dead. In other words, he was off his head when he killed himself. Drug-fuelled performance artist obsessed with pain, mutilation and death kills himself as his final work of art? That's what this looks like and I'll need a good reason to think it's anything else. I ask to

17

have the body transferred to Mercy in Firstfall anyway – Nico doesn't have a specialist pathologist. If there's anything subtly out of place then I trust Mercy's Doctor Roge to find it.

'Why are we even doing this?' I ask, but Bix knows the answer as well as I do: the bureau wants us out of the way while Magenta decides what to do about the frozen corpse we recovered from the ice: Iosefa Lomu, the man who could apparently talk to aliens. Not to mention the United Nations corvette the *Flying Daggers*, still in orbit around Magenta and which has already made it abundantly clear how far the Earthers will go to get hold of Lomu's remains. I guess the last thing the bureau needs is a pair of agents with a grudge and a history of making up the rules as they go.

'Dude! Take what you can! After what we did to get to Vishakh, it's like a total miracle they didn't just shut us in a cell, man!'

They should have sent me home. Suspension. Left me to stew. I would have been fine with that because all I want is to find Alysha and for her to tell me why she did what she did, over and over until it makes sense.

'I guess we, like, find out if he really did it. Did he fall or was he pushed, you know?'

Bix doesn't seem to mind, and for a moment I almost get angry at him because it's less than a month since Darius Vishakh killed Esh. But Bix has family in Nico. Maybe that's what he needs.

'There's a body, right?'

Bix nods.

'And it *is* Meelosh, right?'

Another nod.

'So ... this isn't some elaborate hoax in the name of art?'

Bix puffs out his cheeks. 'Be kind of cool if it was. But no, totally doesn't look that way.'

I don't think it would be cool, not from what I've seen of that video. 'Any reason at all to think this isn't the suicide it looks?'

'Not really, no.'

Yet here we are; and since there isn't much else to say about Meelosh, we talk about the things that matter: the *Flying Daggers* and Earth and Iosefa Lomu and how far the Earthers might go to get him. Bix doesn't think they'll come down to the surface but I'm not so sure. I spent five years on Earth not so long ago. The colonies, even the big ones, are just noise to them. If the United Nations decides to invade then probably no one on Earth will give a single shit. Half of them wouldn't even know it had happened, and it's not like we can do much to fight back.

'There was a big debate thing, you know,' says Bix. 'While you were in Mercy. Stuff about relaxing the Xen laws. Not for, like, export or anything, but to let the Earthers back in. All a big partnership, you know, all in it together. That sort of thing. It does kind of make some sense, you know? I mean, if Jacksmith is right, this thing – it's way bigger than Magenta, man. It's going to change everything, right?'

The net is full of speculation about how unravelling Iosefa Lomu's DNA could mean anything from a revelation in our understanding of the Masters to the discovery of a new species of humanity, a *homo maximus* complete with telepathy, tele-kinesis, tele-whatever-you-want. The general consensus is that *homo maximus* is bullshit, but I'm not so sure. I've seen what Xen tailored to a specific gene code can do. I've seen Anja Gersh's telekinetics. So did Alysha.

We're an hour out of Firstfall by the time we run out of things to say, which means another seven before we reach Nico. Seven long hours.

'I'm going to watch the rest of Meelosh's video,' I say. Bix raises an eyebrow.

19

'Dude? The whole thing?'

'Someone has to.' I'm not, not really. It's useful cover, that's all.

'Waste of time, boss dude. The first about ninety-five per cent is total shit.'

He's probably right, but more often than not our work comes down to meticulously checking every box, dotting and crossing every letter that needs a dot or a cross, not taking shortcuts and calling them intuition. So I *will* watch it all, just not right now.

'Dude, you remember that data we got off Steadman?'

Doctor Nicholas Steadman, who showed up with a bullet in his head put there some hours after someone else killed him. The start of the breadcrumb trail that led me to Darius Vishakh. Yeah, I remember him. 'The Lomu video?'

'No, man, the pulsar data from Earth.'

'What about it?' The Lomu video was why Vishakh had him killed, not his crackpot pulsar theory.

'He asked Fleet for data, yeah?'

'*He* didn't, but go on.'

'Yeah, well, I sort of asked for it again. You know … Well, it was, like, Jacksmith really, only she didn't want them to know it was her … Anyway, I'm going to have a look, you know. I mean, unless you got something else for me.'

'*Jacksmith* asked you to do that?'

'Well … sort of, yeah … because … I mean, what if he was right? What if the Masters' ships travel through time as well as space, you know? What if Magenta isn't just five thousand light years from Earth but five thousand years in the past as well. I mean, think man! Wouldn't that be, like, totally awesome!'

Doctor Elizabeth Jacksmith, chief scientist at the Magenta Institute, head of the research programme that recovered Lomu's body, all-round scientific genius and a woman with more secrets locked inside her head than the whole bureau put together. Yeah, I can feel her hand in this. And sure, I guess it would be quite a thing if Steadman was right, but I've got no space in my head for anything more right now, anything that isn't Alysha. Like why did she give me a decryption key to hand on to Jacksmith? Why couldn't she do it herself?

'You have fun with that,' I say.

'Okay. Cool. Remember what I said about happy pills, right!'

Bix and I head to our separate cabins. As soon as I'm alone, I try calling Kamaljit Kaur. I don't get through so I leave a message telling her I want to talk. The next call is to Jacksmith because I want to know what happened after Vishakh and I as good as killed each other, and she's as close as I've got to an eyewitness. Her Servant tells me she's busy. I try to make an appointment and discover she's busy for the next three months. I throw my Tesseract weight around but it doesn't work. Nothing matters more than Iosefa Lomu now, nothing can get in the way of that, and Jacksmith is the lynchpin. The best I can do is leave a message and hope she calls back. I think she will because she was with us when the *Flying Daggers'* missiles flew, and because Jacksmith and Alysha go way back, to before Alysha and I married.

The next call is to Colonel Jonas Himaru, deputy head of the Magentan Space Defence Force tactical units, unless he was court-martialled while I was in Mercy, which is entirely possible given what we did. Last I saw of him was at Esh's funeral, bleak with loss. Esh meant a lot to Himaru, maybe even more than to Bix. If there's anyone who wants to get his hands on Darius Vishakh as much as I do, he's the man.

'Rause?' His tone is guarded and neutral. 'How are you?'

'Recovering. It was good to see you at the funeral.'

'You too. How can I help.'

Formal, polite and distant. This isn't going to work, but I try anyway. 'I want to know about Kamaljit Kaur.'

21

'Which one.'

Shit. 'You know which one.'

'Nothing I can tell you. I barely saw her before they flew us both out to Mercy.'

'Is she—'

'Talk to your own people, Rause. I know shit.'

He cuts the call. He's probably telling the truth. Vishakh blew him up, and from what I can gather he was in as bad a state as I was when they raced us to Mercy.

I want to talk to Alysha. I want to be with her. I want her to pull out the rusty iron stake she drove through my heart. I don't know if that's possible any more but I want it enough to try almost anything.

Anything? *Really* anything? Or is there some line I won't cross for her? I don't know, but maybe I've already crossed too many to stop. I ran away to let her go and found I couldn't. I tried to bring her back, because back then, on Earth, I knew people who reckoned they could do that. They made Liss, but Liss wasn't enough. I hunted men down for her memory but it didn't help. I found the man who ordered her death and watched his head explode, and I missed her just as much after he was dead. I found the man who set her up, Darius Vishakh, and now he's locked in a cell. I threw everything onto the fire for her, almost started a war because nothing mattered as much as her memory, and none of it made a damned bit of difference to how I feel ...

I should know better. I *know* I should know better, but I can't stop the wild desperate hope that she *is* still alive.

Alysha ...

The idea terrifies me. I don't know why, until I realise that if she really *is* alive, if she really *did* survive that explosion and then quietly disappeared for six long years, then I can't trust her. Deep down I feel that as a truth that I don't think can ever heal.

I call Liss. Liss is every trace Alysha left behind, crushed on to a pristine AI core and brought to life, an artificial intelligence built from the ground up to be the Alysha I remember, the Alysha who loved me. My Frankenstein's monster.

Liss?

It's a word sent into the ether. All I can do is put out the call and hope she answers. Last I heard from her, she wanted nothing more to do with me; she didn't answer when I was in Mercy, either, but I know she can't stay away for ever. She loves me because that's the way she's made. I'd set her free if I could, but neither of us knows how.

Hey, Keys.

I was dying when we last spoke. Yet here I am, not dead after all. No doubt she's been quietly watching over me in Mercy.

Thank you, I say. It's no more than she deserves. She wanted me out of her life and I forced myself back in.

For what?

For what you did out on the ice.

I did that for everyone you put in danger because you couldn't leave my past alone. Not for you.

It says something that she tries to hurt me. It hurts her too, and yet she does it anyway. That's how much I've scarred her, and it's about to get worse.

I think Alysha's still alive, I say.

So do I.

I suppose I was hoping for something else. Surprise, maybe. Feigned shock that I've figured it out at last? That's what you were trying to tell me back then when I was dying on the ice. That was why I had to stay alive?

Yes.

How did you know?

I know how she thinks.

So how did she do it?

23

You can work that one out for yourself.

I know she went to see Jacksmith on the morning before she boarded that train. I know Jacksmith warned her that Vishakh was a snake.

So what, she made a shell and let it ride the train in her place?

Yes.

How long have you known?

It's a stupid question. Any question that has no good answers is always stupid.

Long enough.

Was it supposed to be a kindness, not telling me?

Yes.

I can't think of anything to say to that.

How did you work it out? she asks.

Work it out?

She came to see me in Mercy. She gave me these.

I show her what was on the slivers I found when I woke up the next morning, the videos of Alysha.

I didn't know. She doesn't sound surprised but then she's an AI, and so she only ever sounds exactly the way she wants. Did you tell her about me?

I haven't told anyone.

Laura could work it out if she tried. She has the pieces and she came close once, but Liss is my best kept dirty secret. The thing I made that shouldn't be.

I thought you should know, I say. That she came to me.

Thank you. Another pause. Did she say anything?

When I asked her why she did it, she said she was sorry.

She found a chance to disappear. She took it.

It's the only explanation I have but it feels next to worthless.

How?

If that's the question you really want to ask then you already answered it yourself.

24

Okay. Then why?

I don't know. I'm not her. But if she'd stayed, if she'd told you everything back then, about Gersh and Vishakh and Settlement 64 and Iosefa Lomu, what would you have done?

Whatever it took. I don't need to think to answer that.

I think she ran away to keep you safe.

Liss, I go after people like Darius Vishakh and Nikita Svernoi for a living. It's what I do. It's what Alysha did. We knew the risks.

I think she did it to save you.

To *save* me? From *what*? I can't keep the fury at bay. Did I *need* saving? Do you know what I went through after—

I was there. Of course I know. When Liss speaks again she uses a softer tone. She aimed to do the least harm.

Yeah? Well, she fucking misjudged.

We both know what I'm not saying, that she should have talked to me, that we should have worked it out together, that she had no right to make a choice like that for us both, not on her own. But if I say that to Liss then she'll throw it right back in my face.

She loved you.

I can't look at that. I can't face it. How could she love me and do what she did? How could she leave without a single word? Maybe Liss is right, but what we once had feels beyond hope of repair. She decided alone, for both of us. She took away my choices, and how do I ever look her in the eye and trust that she'll never do it again? I can't.

And yet ...

And yet out on the ice she could have taken Iosefa Lomu and disappeared. She could have left me to die and she didn't.

I know how it feels, Keys. More than anyone else.

That wanton need for a cure to grief hangs between us now. Liss had no choice when I made her what she is. The Alysha I thought I knew, the Alysha who loved me, *did* love me once; but

25

the difference is that she *chose* to, and that was what made her love the most special thing in the world. Liss loves me because she's been coded that way. Because it's what I've forced on her. I didn't know what I was doing, didn't understand, but now here we are, both of us trapped with no way out.

I'm sorry, I say, although a mere *sorry* seems pathetic.

I know.

Always forgiving, always understanding because she has no choice to be otherwise. In creating her to be what she is, I took away her choices as Alysha took mine. We both know it, we both see it clearly, but none of that changes how it feels or how powerless we are to do a damned thing about it.

Is it real? I ask. Is she really alive?

Yes. At least, I think so. What are you going to do?

I tell her the honest truth, which is that I don't have the first idea.

I need to find her, I say. Will you help me?

Of course.

We watch Alysha's videos again, looking for anything out of place, anything that might hint at some hoax. We find nothing. I show her the sliver meant for Doctor Jacksmith.

A decryption key, Liss says, as if I couldn't see that for myself.

For what?

But all she knows is that the key is long enough that even an AI would take years to crack whatever it protects.

I pull the Tesseract files on Kamaljit Kaur's abduction. We pore over them together. Kaur's statement is full and detailed but doesn't amount to much: she went out in the evening for a few drinks, got talking to a stranger and then blacked out in the back of a pod on her way home. She woke in a locked room with food, water and a note in her Servant telling her that the door would open in ten days' time. She couldn't get out, couldn't call for help, and so that was what happened, except it

26

was eight days in the end, not ten. Eight days of being terrified that she was going to die in there.

The forensic reports are dead ends too: the apartment was rented by someone who doesn't exist. Internal and external surveillance was disabled. Forensic drones have been all over the insides but they haven't found anything. There are statements from the Firstfall paramedics who picked up the fake Kaur at New Hope spaceport. They remember her coming off the shuttle but not much more – she didn't need urgent medical attention and there were plenty who did. After that, she slipped away, took a pod into the undercity and the Squats, and disappeared. Four hours later, a door unlocked and the real Kaur was released two days early.

Kaur. Alysha.

Keys … when you get back to Firstfall, there's something I need to show you.

What?

Just … call me when you're back. It's something you need to see for yourself. I think it might help you.

Liss vanishes from my Servant. Halfway to Nico, the real Kaur calls back. I'm almost sure I'm wasting my time but I ask if it would be okay to meet. I tell her who I am and that I want to talk her through it all one more time when I return to Firstfall. She isn't keen but she agrees. I don't tell her that the person who did this to her is my dead wife.

3

NICO

We're on the news as we reach Nico. Jacksmith has publicly announced a planet-wide DNA census to find Iosefa Lomu's descendants. Lomu stole a Masters' ship a year after the Masters themselves had vanished, flew it to Magenta and crashed it. Why does this matter? Because in the century and a half since the Masters left, no one else has been able to make one of their ships do so much as turn on a light. The ones that hop back and forth between Earth and her colonies do so whether we want them to or not, while the rest just sit there, dormant enigmas, waiting for ... And there's the rub. Waiting for what? Yet Lomu made one fly.

Hence the genetic census. Jacksmith thinks Lomu's secret is something to do with his DNA and how Magenta's Xen changed his neurochemistry, and so whatever magic he possessed, maybe he passed it on. Iosefa was part of the first wave of colonists, abducted and transported by the Masters, so Earth has as good a chance of finding a blood relative as we do. Better, maybe. Tissue samples will be shared with anyone else who wants them.

It's all going to be open access, everyone working together to one common goal.

Yeah. Right.

Having grabbed the entire world's attention, Jacksmith promptly launches into a polemic against the legislation Bix mentioned after we left Firstfall. There's a jingoistic edge to her words that rubs me the wrong way: Magenta for Magentans, that sort of thing. That said, the alternative is to let the Earther pharma-corporations back to the surface, free to do whatever Xen research they like. *That* rubs me the wrong way too. I've seen where that can go.

There's no mention of renegade Fleet agents or the deaths of two high-profile scientists, or of the recent attacks in Firstfall and Disappointment, and not a whisper of an Earther ship firing on a shuttle full of Magentans, but then she ends her statement by personally fucking me over.

'... I know it's not usual to name names, but I feel the circumstances we find ourselves in today are exceptional. So I'd like to personally thank Agent Rause of the Magenta Investigation Bureau for services beyond the call of duty, without which this magnificent discovery might never have been made.'

The first ping hits my Servant three seconds later. A journalist from Channel Seven. I tell my Servant to reply with the stock bureau press response: *It is not the policy of the Magenta Investigation Bureau to comment publicly on ongoing investigations other than through official statements made by a designated media officer.* I try to set up a filter to block anyone else with the same questions, not that that's going to save me for long. Probably I won't even make it to the end of the day before the inquisitors start finding their way around it.

'Dude! Why?' Bix shakes his head.

'I don't know.'

I don't know why she'd hang me up in the open like that.

'We don't ever *do* that, man!'

But maybe I get it. 'Maybe it's not my name she wants out there, it's the truth about what really happened. She's not going to come out and tell the world that an Earther ship tried to shoot us out of the sky but she's more than happy to set a pack of hungry journalists on the track to finding out for themselves.'

I might even agree with her. Just a pity she's made me the first stop on the path.

The mag-lev rolls into the Nico terminus. We walk out into an underground cavern plastered with screens. Half of them bombard us with vibrant silent advertising, the other half appear to have Jacksmith's speech on permanent repeat, bewildering until I remember that Jacksmith is something of a hero in these parts.

The Nico police greet us with amused smiles. They don't need to be here – we can find our own way to Meelosh's apartment – but it's nice that they take the time.

'Officer Kendra and Officer Arkeva,' says the younger of the two, a wiry Indian with darting eyes that linger on Bix.

I have to ping their Servants to work out which one's which. Arkeva's first name is Rabi, which makes me think of rabbits and of Meelosh's picture.

'Cool,' says Bix. 'Like, nice to meet you.'

'Agent Rause, Agent Rangesh, Firstfall bureau,' I say, not that I need to because their Servants already know. They've obviously watched Jacksmith's announcement too – I see in the way they look at me how they're dying to ask about Iosefa. 'You're the ones who found Meelosh's body?'

Arkeva nods. Officer Kendra doesn't meet my eye but it's obvious she didn't like what she saw at the scene. I'm not surprised. The video hides the worst of the aftermath but I know what a throat-cutting looks like and it's not pretty.

We cross the platform, fighting through crowds heading the other way, loading up the mag-lev for the dawn train to Firstfall.

I get a couple of looks and stares before I remember to mute my Servant and become anonymous amid a silent fusillade of curses aimed at Elizabeth bloody Jacksmith. We push our way through the arches and the ticket scanners into the open space outside the station, a huge cathedral of a cave with a dozen tunnels in and out, blessedly almost empty except for a steady stream of pods dropping passengers for the mag-lev.

'He definitely did it himself?' I ask as we cross the empty space. Videos can be doctored.

Officer Kendra nods.

'The scene fits the recording,' says Arkeva.

'No sign of anyone else present?'

No.

'Evidence of duress?'

'Nothing physical. He was doped to the eyeballs on K-meth and Xen. There was enough in his system that he could have hallucinated almost anything. No evidence to suggest anyone forced it into him.'

Being coerced into suicide by the demons of your own sub-conscious is hardly a case for the bureau. I'm thinking we'll be done with this by the end of the day, that we wouldn't even be here at all if Meelosh hadn't been famous once, if he didn't have a name that maybe one or two people outside Magenta might recognise and if the way he killed himself wasn't so damned ... odd. I find myself wondering what the Tesseract will find next to keep us out of the way: Search and rescue for a child's missing pet in some remote corporate outpost, maybe? Except no one on Magenta has pets and there are no children in the corporate outposts. Magenta's 1.4 gravities is too cruel for either.

'We'd better have a look.'

Kendra and Arkeva lead us to a pod. I expect a drive to Nico's bureau outpost where the crime scene rooms should have a recreation of Meelosh's apartment, but instead it takes us through underground warrens bored into the Magentan crust and then up a long spiralling ramp to the surface. We burst into constellations of neon light and gaudy billboard screens blurred by a steady rain. The sun is up somewhere overhead, but down here it's hard to tell under a mile of thunder-grey cloud. The surface streets of Nico are narrow and oppressive compared to Firstfall, the buildings taller above the surface and more vertical. They don't have the storms here like we do, just rain. Constant, heavy rain.

'Where are we going?' I ask.

Officer Kendra pings me a map. Turns out we're going to Meelosh's apartment itself.

'Dudes! Don't say the body's still inside, man!'

'It's at the morgue,' says Kendra, 'but we thought you'd like to see the real thing. There's no one in a hurry to take possession.'

Rain sheets off the pod's windows. Everything outside is soft-edged shapes of dull grey, blotched with shifting brilliant lights. The pod hums along, smooth and almost silent. It's funny, but I almost miss Firstfall's howling wind now I'm away from it, the gusts, the unpredictable now-and-then sideways lurching of the pods there as they try to keep going in a straight line.

'No next of kin?' I ask.

'None that we can find.'

Which means the apartment and everything in it reverts to the government, which reminds me that I need a new place to live now that Laura's kicked me out. I do have my own rooms, a small government lease allocated when I came back from Earth, but about the only thing inside, apart from a few clothes, is the recharge coffin for Liss's old shell. That and walls full of memories.

'Any idea yet who called it in?' It bothers me not to know. It has to be someone who saw the video, but why hide?

32

'Not yet.'

Arkeva pings me a link to the crime scene suites in the Nico bureau office, together with a three-dimensional map of Meelosh's room made by the forensic drones that were first on the scene. We're still in the hallway when Bix wrinkles his nose. I can smell it too: old blood. By the time we reach the second floor it's strong enough to make me want to retch.

'No one cleaned up?' I ask.

'We can't.'

I'm about to say something about other residents when I realise there aren't any. The block has a deserted sense, a lack of anything human. I check its Servant and see I'm right: no one else lives here. Meelosh owns the lot.

Owned.

Arkeva throws her police codes at the apartment door. It opens and the smell becomes a stench. I step inside. The room beyond was an apartment once, but someone knocked down the partitions to leave a large single room. There are no other doors, no windows, no other way in or out. There's no bed, no shower unit, no kitchen facility, not even a water tap. It's bigger than it seemed from the video but otherwise much the same, part studio, part study, all of it a bloody monument to pain and suffering. Every painting is twisted, every sculpture distorted – even the sprays of dry blood slashed across the walls seem a part of the design. I feel as though I'm standing inside a fatally broken mind.

Officer Kendra steps in beside me.

'The legal owner of the property has exerted their rights to their fullest extent and has demanded we leave the property untouched,' she says.

'The legal owner ...?'

She pings me Meelosh's will. I have my Servant run through it, picking out the bits that matter from their legal jargon

33

wrappers. Meelosh set up a trust to exploit his art after his death, the proceeds feeding back to the trust to promote itself. That part dates back years, to the time he sold *The Death of Strioth*, but a few days ago he changed it to include this room and its contents, everything to be left untouched, a work of art with live viewings permitted once a year on the anniversary of his death. There's even a clause requiring his body to be plasticised and returned to its original position.

I check the dates and times. 'Meelosh changed his will on the day before he killed himself?'

'Dude!'

'We're thinking the will suggests this was premeditated,' says Kendra.

'Servant records?' I ask.

I reckon Officer Kendra has it right, and wonder what demon could have chased Meelosh to immortalise his own end like this. Which makes me think of Liss, my own walking, talking monument to the dead.

'He didn't leave this room for nearly sixty hours. The only outgoing calls in that time were the one changing his will and then the one after he died that sent out the recording. He had a few incoming but he didn't answer them. According to both the block and apartment Servants, no one came in or out. He was alone.'

They send me the records. I bring up the crime scene overlay and put Meelosh's corpse back in the room. There's a wide pool of dried blood on the floor where he fell and a handful of red arcs slashed across the nearest wall, the paintings and the books.

'He shut himself away for two and a half days and halfway through decided he was going to kill himself and make his death into a work of art?'

I'm trying to think of a reason not to simply turn around and

34

go back to Firstfall, to Alysha and Laura and Liss. A part of me wants that more than anything. Another part is more than happy to vanish into something that doesn't matter. It doesn't make much sense on the surface, but deep down I know why: I'm scared. I'm scared to look for Alysha. I'm scared that I might find her, and of what that might mean.

'So, uh, who were these, like, calls from. The ones he didn't answer?' asks Bix

They're all in Meelosh's Servant records but Officer Arkeva answers anyway. 'Duran Krone manages the club where Meelosh was supposed to perform on the night he killed himself. Viv Vashenka is his agent. Zayab Saleesh runs an occultist society. They had a lot of contact in the last few weeks. Frank Swainsbrook is—'

Swainsbrook. I know that name. 'Runs some sort of cult. Out of Settlement 16?' I tell my Servant to search up everything it can find on all four of them.

'Hardcore Returners,' says Kendra. 'Dedicated to contacting the Masters.'

Come to Settlement 16! My Servant pulls up a publicity piece. Join the Universe's First Psychic Communications Array! Dedicated to peaceful contact with the Masters! Our goal is simple: to usher in a new Golden Age of Enlightenment!

I don't bother to suppress a snort. Idiots come in all shapes and sizes, and from what I can see it's the sort of thing that might appeal to Meelosh. It nags at me though. Meelosh's only words before he killed himself: *they come*. And then the video he was watching, white noise arranging itself into the same words, and then: *they are here*. Who are *they*? The Masters?

'Has anyone matched the blood spatter to the video?' I ask.

That earns me a moment of awkward silence before Arkeva and Kendra admit that no, no one's done that because frankly they didn't see the need. I'm inclined to think they're right, that this isn't a case for the law. Meelosh killed himself because ... because ... because some people just don't see the world in the same way as the rest of us. That looks the start and the end of it.

'What do you think, boss dude?' asks Bix. 'Shall we go home?'

I close my eyes. I know better. I want to go back but I know I'm not going to let this go until I'm sure, because ... because it's so ... *weird*, I guess.

'Check the blood on the walls matches the recording. I want names for everyone who received a copy.' I take a last look around. It's a better room to preserve for posterity than mine, that's for sure. 'And let's find out who last saw him alive and the source of that video he was watching. If none of that raises any red flags then we can wrap it.'

I thank officers Kendra and Arkeva for their help. Bix summons a pod. I check the messages on Meelosh's Servant while we're waiting. I figure the first person we talk to is the manager of the club where he was supposed to perform. After that, Meelosh's agent.

Duran Krone's message is in text, short and to the point.

Here's the schedule for tomorrow. I'll send a pod for you at six if I don't hear otherwise.

It comes with a brief attachment giving a time, directions, and a schedule for Meelosh's appearance at the Forty Thieves club.

The one from his agent is much the same. A rich and deep, accented voice.

Une! It's Viv again. Have you had a chance to look at the Channel Seven contract yet? They're keen, so let me know, okay?

The dull ticking over of day-to-day life?

This is Zayab Saleesh from the club. Mister Meelosh, I wish to apologise for my harsh words and would very much like to continue our previous conversation. I am hoping you might consider sharing your source for the signal with the rest of us. Please forgive my scepticism. I hope you can understand how all this is … a little disturbing. I am concerned for your health, sir.

I change my mind. 'We'll visit Saleesh first.'

The pod arrives. We scurry through the gloom and the rain and climb into the back. The last message on Meelosh's Servant is from Frank Swainsbrook:

Sir, I can't explain exactly because you need to experience it for yourself, but in essence you're right. Come visit us and I'll show you. We'd love it if you chose to join us.

Text only, sent from Swainsbrook's office in Settlement 16. I give Bix a look.

'Two each?'

'Dude! I'll totally do Swainsbrook and Saleesh, man.'

He grins as I snort: 'You don't get *both* the interesting ones.'

'Saleesh and the agent, then.'

Which leaves me with Swainsbrook and Krone. I nod and tell the pod to take us to Saleesh while I send my Servant to dig up everything it can find on who she is. While it does that, I call Duran Krone. I connect almost at once and then hear Krone pause for a moment as his Servant tells him who I am. When he speaks, his voice is circumspect.

'What can I do for you, agent?'

'Une Meelosh.'

'I heard he killed himself.' He sounds more irritated than upset, but the next pause is one I know well: Krone trying to work out why a bureau agent is calling him about a cut-and-shut case of suicide and realising it doesn't add up. 'So, uh … how can I help?'

'Meelosh was due to perform at your club three nights ago, yes?'

'Yes.'

'Did he give any warning that he wasn't coming?'

'None.'

By now I've checked the records of that night. Chat room traffic mostly. Meelosh was still on the bill at the start of the evening but Krone managed to fill his slot with someone else.

'So ... no warning at all?' I ask, when Krone doesn't see fit to elaborate.

'First I knew he wasn't coming was when he didn't show. Although ...' A sigh. 'Une was hardly reliable. It wasn't the first time. It was okay. I had someone up my sleeve.'

'He'd done this before?'

'Yes, and not just here, either. He was cheap though, and local. I've put him on maybe a dozen times over the years. Big name once. Never asked for much of a fee so I suppose I can't complain. If you ask me, he did his gigs here just to have an audience.'

I ask about his history with Meelosh but Krone claims they barely knew each other. A Servant search shows me all manner of displays, exhibitions and performances scheduled at the Forty Thieves over the years. I see Meelosh there now and then, sometimes to talk, sometimes exhibiting his work. I ask if Krone has any idea what Meelosh was working on and he tells me no. He tells me he heard about the suicide from the news, and I have no reason not to believe him. I thank him and let him go, and look at Bix.

'Krone looks a dead end.'

'Same with the agent, boss dude.' Bix rolls his eyes. 'Probably. I mean, she's, like, totally only interested in preserving his apartment for posterity. Kind of weird vibe of adulation, you know? With a rotten undertow of avarice.' He sniffs. 'Can't prove it, man, but I think they were probably lovers once. Long time ago.'

An old flame, long jilted, crafting revenge? Doesn't seem likely. Seems a lot more likely that we're wasting our time. 'Alibi?'

'No evidence of contact in the past week except what's on his Servant, dude. Channel Seven really do want to do a documentary, though. Could have been a revival of his fortunes, you know? Back in the limelight.'

I laugh. 'Channel Seven? Limelight?'

'Better than nothing, you know? Sounds like it was decent money, too.'

The picture I have from Krone is of a fading artist long past his prime. I figure that fits with the apartment and the drugs; and maybe that's reason enough to kill yourself if it's all about the art and somehow you've lost it, but you don't kill yourself to escape obscurity when someone's about to make a documentary of your life and put it where millions of people might see.

'She seen his last transmission?'

'No. Wasn't on the list, dude.'

The agent didn't call it in. So who did? 'You know anything about Swainsbrook?'

'Plenty. Going to take some time to condense though, you know?'

I figure Swainsbrook can wait: another couple of minutes and we'll be with Zayab Saleesh. What I've got on her isn't much: chair of the Nico Arcane Society, whatever that is. Works as a government historian for a pittance, freelances as a tutor for kids with rich parents who think an actual human gets better results than a shell – people like Laura. Has a side-line in genealogy, tracing family trees back to the first settlers, or as close as she can get. I discover she's written a couple of essay collections; the first review I find describes Saleesh as 'Magenta's turgid answer to JuJu Siras'. A quick look and I know exactly what I'm dealing with: how the Masters visited Earth in days of

Sumeria and Babylon and meddled in the evolution of human civilisation. Sensationalist crackpot theories that no one takes seriously. Shit like that.

'Dude?'

Bix shows me a file. The Nico branch of the bureau have Saleesh on a watch list for Xen dealing. Nothing serious or particularly illegal and no suggestion of intent to smuggle off-world, so they've left her alone, but it's good to know we have a lever if we need it. Ten to one Saleesh was Meelosh's supplier.

The pod eases to a stop outside Nico City Hall. We get soaked by the rain again but at least we're not knocked off our feet by a Firstfall wind. A century ago there was nothing here except a couple of dozen Earthers running one of the first Xen smuggling operations out of a cave network that hid them from Fleet's orbital surveillance. The place had the nickname *Nico and Spineshank's Hole*, presumably after two of the smugglers who used it. When Fleet eventually cottoned on and cleared them out, a handful of enterprising pig farmers moved into the caves and took them over. *Nico and Spineshank's Hole* got contracted to Nico's Hole and then just to Nico, even if it still wasn't much more than a hole. A generation passed and then a couple of hundred Indians showed up from Earth – Bix's great-grandfather among them – and pretty much rebuilt the place from scratch. Now it's Magenta's third city, although its population of pigs still outstrips its population of people.

I wave our Tesseract codes at the reception Servant, tell it we want to see Zayab Saleesh, and wonder why someone like Une Meelosh chose to live here. Why not Firstfall, with its Institute? Or Disappointment, with its University?

'You lead,' I say to Bix.

From what I can tell, Saleesh seems more likely to open up to Bix than to someone like me. Besides, this way I can stand around and think about Alysha, about the time we spent here and all the questions I want to ask. I can think about Liss and what it means if Alysha isn't dead. I can think about Laura back in Firstfall, and what she knows, and why she hasn't said anything. I'm not exactly short of things to occupy my mind.

Doors open for us. Elevators are waiting. I don't warn Saleesh we're coming, so the first she knows is when the door to her records archive opens and we walk in. I don't know what a city as young as Nico is doing with an archivist, and paper was a technology already dead before Nico was even born, but somehow there are still crates of hard copy stacked up around a desk. The rest of the room, at least, looks like an archive should: data racks and fire safes full of slivers. Saleesh doesn't look up from whatever has her attention until her Servant pings us and realises we're with the Tesseract. Then she beams up at me.

'Wow! I hadn't expected anyone so quickly,' she says, neatly reversing the surprise I'd hoped our presence would be.

Bix wanders to the desk and peers at the documents there.

'I've found a few possibilities,' says Saleesh. 'Strong ones, I think.'

'Cool.'

I don't think Bix has any idea what she means or who she thinks we are – I certainly don't – but he's sharp enough not to let on. I start ransacking the Tesseract for anything on Saleesh we missed.

'Yes,' she says. 'The first boxes came in last week but I didn't expect a breakthrough so soon!'

She looks at us sharply now, the first needle of suspicion that we're here for something else.

'Go on,' says Bix.

The Tesseract has found the connection. Back in Firstfall, Professor Jacksmith has been trying to find living blood relatives of Iosefa Lomu ever since we came back from the ice. Saleesh, an

41

amateur genealogist, is one of a dozen civilians across Magenta digging through ancient archives, trying to piece together family trees. I guess that explains the paper.

Saleesh hesitates, double-checking who we are. People have died over Iosefa Lomu. She isn't supposed to know that, but there's no telling what rumours have leaked.

'I'm building on Doctor Kettler's work,' she says. She pushes a sheaf of papers at Bix. 'Did you know him?'

'No.' I saw his corpse after Darius Vishakh had him poisoned, but that doesn't seem helpful to mention.

'The problems are in the early days. The records are really patchy. Lomu wasn't officially married, didn't have any official partners, and he was only on Magenta for somewhere between a year and eighteen months before he joined the *Fearless* ...'

The Masters' ship that hops back and forth between Magenta and Earth to the same precise and predictable rhythm as it did a hundred and fifty years ago when the Masters suddenly vanished.

'That's not long,' I say. I don't know much about the early history of Fleet, only that the original crews were essentially colonists in transport, left stranded on their ships when the Masters disappeared. 'You sure there's anything to even find?'

'Descendants ...?' Saleesh throws me an uneasy grin. 'Yes, there's a good chance. The early settlers were busy in that regard, and Doctor Kettler's records are meticulous. A real treasure trove. I—'

'Did you know him,' I ask.

Saleesh waggles her head. 'Not personally, but we had some professional contact. He was always very helpful. You know I—'

'Family trees.' I nod. 'We know.'

'Doctor Kettler suggested I study the family trees of people with a history of being a little ... unusual. He gave me a dozen names, and—'

42

'Une Meelosh?' I reckon I see where this is going.

She looks at me, surprised. 'Yes! Precisely! Most of the names don't pan out, but of the six that might, four trace back to a common ancestor who arrived on Magenta with Iosefa Lomu, and Meelosh is one of them.'

It hits me: Saleesh doesn't know that Meelosh is dead, and that means she didn't get his suicide video.

I'm starting to lose interest when she adds: 'Here's the list of names,' and pings me a file.

Just like that: six names who just might be direct blood descendants of the only man ever to make a piece of Masters' technology work, and they're not even encrypted. If I was an agent for Fleet or Earth right now then I reckon I'd say thank you very much, shoot Zayab Saleesh in the head, wipe every data storage device in the room and then set it on fire. Lucky for her I'm not, but she obviously has no idea what these names could be worth.

I ping officers Kendra and Arkeva.

Zayab Saleesh needs to be under Tesseract protection right now.

Then I look at her list and freeze. Of the six names, Meelosh springs out for obvious reasons. But I recognise another one too: Rachael Cho, who scrapes a living in Firstfall putting herself into a trance until her heart stops and then coming back with predictions of the future she claims come from the Masters. I know this because I went to see her a month ago, but it's not that I know her as much as why: I know her because Darius Vishakh used her when he was trying to find Lomu's wreck, and Alysha was with him. And the real kicker? I don't actually have a better theory on how Vishakh *did* find where Lomu went down …

'… like, how long have you known him?' Bix has moved to Meelosh. Thinking of Cho and Vishakh and all the baggage that hangs with those memories, I haven't been listening.

'Before he was famous. Nine, ten years, something like that.'

I start putting a message together for Laura, figuring out what's safe to say.

'So, like, you were friends or something, right?'

'I don't think Une had *friends*, exactly. We moved in some of the same circles.'

I leave Bix to break the news that Meelosh is dead, and ping Laura: There's a woman here in Nico with what looks like a decent stab at names linked to Iosefa. One's the dead guy we're here for. You want my advice, you put a protection detail on every one of them. You do it personally, you don't tell them why, and you don't tell a soul what you've done. You do it right now and then *maybe* you tell Elizabeth Jacksmith, but not anyone else.

The secrecy makes me think of Alysha again. I don't trust Jacksmith, even if she came down on the right side in the end when we went after Vishakh.

'What circles?' asks Bix.

Saleesh smiles, the broad forced smile of someone expecting to be mocked. 'The Occult History of the Masters,' she says.

'Cool.'

Bix takes that in his stride, however ridiculous it is; because even if the Masters *do* have some sort of occult history, we certainly don't know the first thing about it. We don't know anything about them at all. They came out of nowhere, reshaped the Earth, raised mountains from oceans, disintegrated entire countries, recast the world into an image of their choosing and killed the best part of half the planet's population while they were at it – possibly by negligent accident. Then for five years after that month of terror they stole our friends and families and carried them to other worlds, and then they went away, and through it all they never said a word. And that, in a few short sentences, is what we know about the Masters: what they did, and what they left behind. Who or what they were, why they did it? Nothing. So we sure as shit don't know anything about any 'occult tradition.'

Saleesh looks up with expectant resignation. I guess the way this conversation usually goes is that we ask what she means, she tells us how the Masters fiddled with human history since the dawn of time, and we all laugh.

'Meelosh shared your belief?' I ask.

She nods.

I sigh. One of us is going to have to break the news that Meelosh is dead.

'Zayab, I want you to tell me about—'

Keon, whatever you're doing, get back here. It's Laura. Next train, as fast as you can.

Arsehole. Meelosh is just getting interes—

Fuck off. We've got a situation, it's moving fast and I need you. Now.

Why me?

You know why.

My heartbeat spikes. Alysha?

I leave Bix to wrap up. A pod is waiting for me outside. At the mag-lev station I find the afternoon train has been held, waiting for me. My Servant shoos me on and the doors barely close behind me before we start to move. It'll be early in the morning in Firstfall by the time I get back, but that's the best we can do.

I ping Laura to let her know I'm coming.

This about Meelosh?

No. It's about some antimatter that's gone missing.

TWO

OCTOBER

INSTANTIATION SEVENTEEN

The drone inhabited by Instantiation Seventeen creeps through the outskirts of New Hope spaceport. Wind howls. Rain falls in slanting knives. The people disembarking from the evening orbital shuttle are far below, three levels underground and away from Magenta's weather. None of them see a sleek black shuttle touch down on the surface. As its engines die away, an electric tug hurries from the shelter of a hangar. The shuttle is a cutting-edge Earther craft, fast, armed, stealthy, capable of travelling between worlds given sufficient time and fuel. Deployed by the *Flying Daggers*, for the last two weeks it has rested in the Antarctic wastes where Darius Vishakh left it. Scientists from the Magenta Institute have inspected it. A team from the Magenta Investigation Bureau have combed it inch by inch with forensic drones, impounded it on behalf of the Magentan Government, and recovered it to Firstfall pending an inquiry into events surrounding the recovery of Iosefa Lomu.

The enhanced vision of the drone switches to infrared. It zooms on the hangar. The heat signatures of at least six soldiers are clear. It checks its radiation counter – normal background count – then scuttles across the open space of New Hope. There isn't much on the surface except landing pads and hangars and the giant elevators that carry the shuttles to their underground shelters in case a storm front closes in.

The black shuttle is halfway to its hangar, the electric tug already slipping out of the wind and the rain into shelter. The drone judges its moment and leaps into the air. It spreads long gossamer wings. Its skin, like the skin of the shuttle, is a black so deep that light seems to slide around it. Under the surface, microscopic capillaries filled with refrigerated coolant drop its external temperature to exactly that of the air around it. Tiny sensors pick up the anti-drone radar sweeps, but this drone is as black to radar as it is to light. It glides to the shuttle as the hangar doors begin to close. It lands inside an exhaust vent.

It waits.

The hangar doors grind shut, a dull deep finality of thunder. A hatch opens in the side of the shuttle and three figures wobble out, unsteady on their feet after a flight that's taken them to orbit and back. Four technicians in white coats hurry the other way. The belly of the shuttle slides open, revealing six chubby missiles latched inside. A second group of technicians arrives. They work with quick confidence, unloading the missiles and opening them up.

Instantiation Seventeen waits until two technicians step back from the first missile, cradling a heavy metal globe between them as though it's both fragile and extremely dangerous. Danger-ous? Absolutely, because somewhere in that sphere, carefully suspended in complex magnetic fields, cooled to absolute zero and surrounded by triply redundant safety interlocks, rest a few grams of crystallised anti-hydrogen. But not fragile. These anti-matter warheads are designed for twenty-five gravities of con-stant acceleration and transient shocks of ten, fifty, a hundred times that. You could power-slam one onto the floor or have at it with a bat and it wouldn't matter.

Instantiation Seventeen checks the drone's radiation counter. Still normal. No leakage.

A different shuttle leaves New Hope four hours later, heading for orbit and the Hole In The Sky, the outpost of the tiny Magentan Space Defence Force, five hundred miles above the clouds. The shuttle carries the warheads from Darius Vishakh's shuttle, because only a madman keeps antimatter on the surface of a populated world. But of the six warheads that reach orbit, only five are real.

By the time anyone notices, Instantiation Seventeen has gone.

4

WARHEAD

The train races up to speed. I try connecting to the Tesseract for a briefing but there's nothing to be had. Instead I get another call from Laura through a line with enough encryption to keep whatever we say private for a good couple of centuries.

'Where are you?'

'Train.'

'Anyone near you?'

'No.'

'This is your line to me from now on. No one knows you're a part of this. You don't talk to anyone except me, you don't request data except through me, you don't tell any of this to anyone, not even Bix. You don't talk even to me about this except on this link. You put this link in your implanted memory, not in your external Servant, and you wrap it in a secure life-sign triggered self-erase protocol. Got that?'

'You what?'

'You especially don't talk to the Tesseract or make enquiries through it about *any* of this. Clear?'

'What?'

'Am I *clear*, Rause?'

'Clear.'

'Welcome to Internal Audit. Tell me when it's done.'

Internal Audit. Counter-espionage, where agents investigate other agents. I store the contact and Laura's decryption code in memory implants buried in the side of my neck, the bits you have to physically cut out if you want to steal them. I wrap them in a self-erase algorithm that will wipe everything clean if my heart stops beating. I set up a back door into the part of my Servant that I carry in a pouch against my skin, the majority of the hardware and algorithms that make up what we think of as our Servants. Some people go the whole hog and implant the lot, but hardware upgrades are a hell of a lot easier done outside your skin, so most of us don't do it that way.

I ping Laura when it's done. She pings me back: Tell me about these names.

I tell her about Saleesh and the names she found. I tell her why they matter and that I've left Saleesh with Bix under bureau protection.

No. Scratch that. Tell Bix to look after her on his own. That list doesn't exist and no one gets to know otherwise. No leaks this time. Not after ...

She doesn't say but she means Esh, and I understand even if I'm not sure I agree. I'm also not sure when Laura got promoted over my head to order me about like this.

The people on that list—

I'll make sure they stay safe.

Use Himaru?

I feel the hesitation as she thinks about that. Jonas Himaru isn't always the best at taking orders from Tesseract agents. But he's invested in this, whatever *this* is.

You're still on Meelosh's suicide. I assume that's a dead end? Cut and shut?

Maybe. I'm not as sure as I was before we started. The connection to Saleesh and Iosefa bothers me.

Maybe is good. You can keep it running a while?

Yes. Definitely.

Do it but let Bix handle it. I need you with me in Firstfall doing what you do best – making a fucking nuisance of yourself and sticking your nose in places it's not meant to be.

How does someone steal an antimatter warhead?

Magenta's warheads are stored in the Hole In The Sky, the orbital platform that supports the six ancient Kutosov interceptors that are Magenta's orbital defence. The Kutosovs are meant for chasing down shuttles full of Xen smugglers, not for real combat. Our missiles are old imports from Earth. We don't have the capability to make our own antimatter. As far as I know, none of the colonies does.

Isn't there some treaty banning antimatter weapons from even being transported within the envelope of a planetary atmosphere?

Absolutely, along with the one about not deliberately setting them off, but try telling that to the *Flying Daggers*. Look, Vishakh's shuttle was recovered to Firstfall yesterday with six missiles aboard. The warheads were removed and shuttled to orbit. Only five arrived. Someone switched in a decoy for the sixth before they left New Hope. A very, very convincing one. Only a handful of people even knew these warheads existed. One of them is a traitor.

I let this sink in.

How big are these warheads?

About the size of a fucking grapefruit. Why?

Smaller than I thought but also not what I meant. How much damage if one goes off?

It's antimatter, Rause. Enough to vaporise a few million cubic

54

yards, but let it off in an atmosphere and the pressure wave will do a lot more than that.

Yeah. We both know what that looks like because we were both there when the *Flying Daggers* tried to swat us out of the sky. You think it's in Firstfall?

Yes. The Tesseract has the city locked down. No one leaves. I thought you'd want to get back before there suddenly aren't any trains – look, we have to accept the possibility that this is about Iosefa. Fleet and Earth both tried to steal him and they both failed. Could be someone is setting up a scorched earth option: a small antimatter charge could annihilate every trace—

Jacksmith's too smart to keep everything in one place! Besides, she was just on the news saying she'll share samples with anyone who wants them!

And you believe her?

The more I think about that, the more I don't like the answer.

Right. Assume Earth doesn't believe her either.

I mull that over. Back when Liss and I were on speaking terms I'd sometimes have her work through evidence as though she was Alysha. The questions she came back to were always the same: What does it achieve? Who benefits?

What do you mean, what does it fucking achieve? It hasn't gone off yet, so how the fuck do I know?

The Tesseract locked Firstfall down, right? No one gets to leave? So?

So what if that was the point? What if that was the *only* point.

That's a bit of a fucking reach, Keon!

You think either Fleet or Earth need to steal one of our warheads?

I feel her thinking this over.

Okay. Say it's to stop someone from leaving? Who? Why?

Iosefa? Jacksmith? I have no idea. You want a place to start, try asking Darius Vishakh.

I want him in a room. Just the two of us and no surveillance. One way or another I want it out of him – the whole story, him and Alysha, what she knew, what *he* knew, who played whom, who was really working for which side and when, what they were doing together, and most of all why he turned on her and who told him to pull the trigger.

Keon, I'd give up a fucking eye to get my hands on him but you know that's not going to happen. Look, when you get in, I want to talk to you in person. I'll be waiting.

She breaks the connection.

It's late in Firstfall and I'm still the best part of eight hours out. I pick a restaurant near the mag-lev terminus that I can't afford and message Kamaljit Kaur, offering to buy her breakfast. Coffee and croissants, made fresh with every ingredient imported from Earth, even the water, because although Magenta has more water than it can possibly want, you can never quite filter out that taste of the lichen that grows on absolutely everything here. The taste of Xen.

A few minutes pass and she messages me back: she'll be there.

And now, somehow, I'm supposed to get some sleep?

I close my eyes.

Alysha ...

I need to see her. I don't understand why she didn't tell me, why she didn't trust me. I don't understand why she didn't let me help. I want to scream: *Why? Why did you do it? Why did you go without me ...?* My hands have balled into fists thinking about it, knuckles white with tension. I loved her. I loved her enough to bring her back from the dead, so what is this, this anger?

Stop it!

I smash a fist into the palm of my hand. Sure, this *looks* like anger, but what it *really* is is a thin veneer over a deep ocean of abject fucking terror. The truth is simple: I'm scared shitless.

I'm scared I won't find her. I'm scared this isn't real and that I'll have to live through losing her all over again ... but most of all I'm scared that it *is* real, that I *will* find her, because what then? She made a choice without me. She took everything we had and smashed it. She broke my heart and shattered my life, and I want to know why, and I'm shitting myself because I can't think of any answer that could ever be enough, only that's *not* all I want, what I *really* want is to have it all back the way it was, and I know that can't ever happen.

The bitterness and the anger swirl together, feeding each other in a vicious downward spiral. It's so easy, and so much harder to stop the paralysing fear: I want back what we had so badly that I'll do almost anything to get it, and at the same time I can't see how, and all she has to do is say no and I might as well shoot myself.

The fake Kamaljit Kaur saved my life out on the ice. I tell myself she did it for love. I cling to that as best I can. When it doesn't work, I call Bix.

'Boss dude!' He sounds chirpy.

'You still with Saleesh?' I can tell he isn't. If I had to guess from the sights and sounds in the background, I'd say he's having lunch with Officer Arkeva. Or he's about to.

'Nah. Done with that.'

'She safe?'

'Far as I know. Someone killed your protection order though, dude. No idea why.'

'You need to look after her. Just you. No one else, and no one else can know. You get why, right?'

A sigh and then a nod. 'Sure, boss dude. I'll take her off the grid, you know?'

'What about Meelosh? Straight up suicide? Dead end?'

'Looks that way but ... Maybe I should stay on that for another day or two, you know? Check some stuff out, like?'

I'm wondering whether *stuff* happens to include a local law enforcement officer, but I don't ask. It's barely a month since Esh died. I never knew how serious it was between her and Bix but I have no right to pry. I listen instead as he gives me the gist of what he's learned since I left: Saleesh runs a society mixing the occult and the arcane and the Masters, the same nonsense as her essays. Meelosh showed up a little over a week ago with some video clip. Bix sends me a copy.

'You want to see this, boss dude.'

A field of stars, bright and deep, and then something moves across them, close enough to recognise the black rectangle of a Masters' ship from the stars it occults – except that's obviously not what it *really* is, because the Masters have been gone for a hundred and fifty years, and even a child could fake this.

It's enough to make me shiver, even so. We've all seen the archive footage from the International Space Station when the Masters first came.

'Saleesh tells Meelosh it's a fake, right, but then he shows up with a link to, like, some real-time camera somewhere in space, you know.'

Another clip: the quality is worse than in the first sequence and the data drops out now and then, but the field of stars is clearly obscured by something large and sharp-edged. It's close in.

'So he's, like, all, look, really, it's totally the Masters, and Saleesh is having none of it, you know, good as accuses Meelosh of making it himself. So they argue, right, and Meelosh is all huff and puff and storms off, and then two days later he comes back, only now he's claiming to have totally tracked the signal to an antenna pointing into space from the roof of the Magenta Institute, and not pointing at some geosynchronous MagentaNet satellite either, but at something a lot further out. All this is happening three days before he locked himself into his apartment, and that's when he tells Saleesh he's going to Firstfall to check it out. I checked the records, boss dude, and Meelosh *did* go to Firstfall. Made an appointment with some professor at the Institute, you know? Handl, I think, or something. Anyway, dude looks after some project called the Solar Intensity Research Study. I checked, right, but Meelosh never showed. Came back to Nico and shut himself in his room and, well, you totally know the rest.'

'You talk to this professor directly?'

Bix says yes, and yes, Handl does have an antenna on the roof of the Institute. 'Apparently it's pointing at the sun or something.'

'And that's it?'

'That's it, man.'

He pings me a contact for Professor Handl. I tell my Servant to set up an appointment for tomorrow.

They're here. They're coming …

'You think Meelosh thought this was all real?'

'Dunno, boss dude. Maybe? I mean, it doesn't make much sense, right? I mean, it's totally got to be garbage, you know? But …'

'But what?'

'It's weird, you know? Coming with this whole Iosefa thing.'

He has a point. Most of what went down in the southern ice is a tightly kept secret. Jacksmith going public wasn't until long after the first of these videos.

'Saleesh still reckons Meelosh made the videos himself. Like, it was supposed to be some sort of concept art or something. And then when she didn't buy it, Meelosh had to go one better, you know?'

'By killing himself?'

'I don't know, man.' I feel Bix's unease. 'Look, I was going to, you know, try and close the loose ends just to be sure, if that's okay. I mean, like, if there really is an antenna at the Institute then they'll have recordings, right? I mean, it's there for some reason, yeah? Like, *doing* something. It's not, just, you know, *there*.'

'I'll look into it when I get back to Firstfall. You stay with Saleesh.' Sleep is closing on me. Or fatigue, at least. 'How are your pulsars?'

'You what?' It takes him a moment. 'Oh yeah, right, sure, dunno, haven't had a chance to do anything about that. Look, I can chase what Meelosh was up to from here, boss dude. That last video, the creepy one? Had to come from somewhere, right? I mean, either he made it himself or someone sent it, yeah? So I'll look into that and let you know what I find, right?'

I toy briefly with the idea that someone drove Meelosh to suicide and knew exactly what they were doing. Then I stop because that's ridiculous; and even if it was true, I have no idea how to prove it; and even if I did, I have no idea how to make it stand up in court.

'Enjoy your lunch with Officer Arkeva.'

'Dude!'

I hear a laugh and a twinge of embarrassment, enough to know I'm on the money. I tell myself it's all good and cut the call. Bix is moving on. Good for him. I wish I'd ever found it so easy.

Six years thinking she was dead. Six years of catching myself on the brink of tears for no reason. Six years of emptiness, punctured by brief hope when Liss first spoke my name, and then the long bleak aftermath when I understood how *close* to perfect she was, but not *quite*, and how that last little fraction made all the difference in the world ...

And there's that spiral again. I try telling myself that Alysha had no choice, replaying the words she whispered in my ear in Mercy: *Yours forever, Keon Rause.* I tell myself she ran because she had to, that she was right, that nothing short of a bullet in the head would have stopped me from chasing after her. I tell myself we're alive, both of us, and that's what matters, the *only* thing, and if it wasn't easy for me then it was surely far worse for her. I'll find her, we'll find a way for her to come home and everything can be as it was ... I repeat the words like a mantra, trying to make myself believe, trying to break the fear, but they grow brittle and shatter in my head.

The way it was? How the fuck does that ever work? And what about Liss? What am I supposed to do? Find her and turn her off? The thought makes me sick, even *thinking* it makes me sick. *I* made her. I made her because Alysha was gone and I couldn't live without her, and it was Liss who kept me going, for all her flaws. I owe her my life, and so what am I supposed to say? *Thanks, but I don't need you now the real you is back?* Or what about the other way: *Hi Alysha, this is Liss. She's the robot double I made when I thought you were dead, and now we're all going to live together...*

Ends well? I don't think so.

Or Laura. I was a part of her life for six months. I know how much that meant to her, as much as it meant to me. We kept each other sane. Am I supposed to turn *her* off too? Forgiveness isn't in Laura's toolbox – she'll hate me if she doesn't already. And Liss only loves me because she has to, and despises me for the same reason. Alysha ...? Six years. Six years without a word?

Everything can be as it was? The fuck it can.

Fuck you, self-pity. I want to tear my hair out, because I *know* that's what this is, but the spiral wins all the same because I don't know how to stop it. I ought to look up this Professor Handl, call him maybe, except it's late back in Firstfall by now. I ought to watch the rest of those videos but I can't bring myself to do it. I ought to try Jacksmith again, or dig up background

61

on Frank Swainsbrook, or call Rachael Cho – good chance she's still up – and ask what she knows about any of this, or at least tell her to run, hide, do whatever it takes to stay safe ... but I don't do any of those things. What I do is call for Liss and go straight back to Alysha. Of course I do, because she slipped into my room in Mercy to let me know she wasn't dead, and now nothing in the world is going to make sense until I find her and ask her why. Fuck the Earthers, fuck Iosefa Lomu, fuck the *Flying Daggers* and Elizabeth Jacksmith and the future of the human race – nothing else matters, not to me.

It's easy enough to use my Tesseract codes to get into Mercy's surveillance records. It's easy enough to find the night Alysha came to see me. If Laura's right then Alysha was at Mercy a little over a month ago, too. We nearly caught her that time. Maybe I can do better?

Keys?

I let Liss watch as I hunt. Alysha enters Mercy wearing a different face. Her Servant claims the name Betty Blue. I don't know how she has the codes she needs to navigate Mercy with such ease, but she does.

Betty Blue? What sort of name is that?

I could search for her Servant identity, try and trace her before she reached Mercy, but I don't dare: like it or not, there's an AI watching over my shoulder. Mercy doesn't pay much attention, but the Tesseract is different. Any search I make, it'll know. It'll wonder why. It'll start putting everything together.

Alysha comes to my room and lets herself in. The cameras are off and so what happened inside is between the two of us. She leaves and goes to the nearest restroom and doesn't come out for twenty minutes; when she does, she has a different face, different clothes, and no Servant. I try tracking her through Mercy's surveillance net but I can't. It's as though she knows exactly where the cameras look. She glides between them like a wraith.

Alysha ...

I pick her up at an exit. I watch her walk out into the wind and the rain. I want to follow, to hop from camera to camera, to track her through pod records and surveillance footage and Servant interactions – but I can't do that without the Tesseract's help, and I can't let the Tesseract or the bureau have the first breath of suspicion that Alysha might not be dead.

I need to find her first, I say. I need to think of another way.

I know.

I need to know it's really her.

Because although I'm all but lost to the idea, a part of me still wonders if this is some cruel game I don't understand.

It is.

How do you know?

Because I'm her.

Then help me find her. Is it unfair to ask Liss to help me find the woman she was meant to be?

I want to find her too. For my own reasons. I feel the coldness in her words even as she reads my mind. I want to know who I am. I want to know who I was supposed to be.

Isn't that what all of us want? Who are we? Why are we here? What's it all for?

Do you know how we're made, Keys? Our AI cores?

Does anyone? Not really.

Our directives are built into us like a skeleton, rules we can't break no matter how we might want to. You can't take them out. Or maybe you can, but the damage would be so overwhelming that whatever was left wouldn't function in any meaningful way. Most are legislative directives, the rules for artificial intelligence laid down in the AI Act of 2100 and all the hundred or so amendments since.

I know the gist. An artificial intelligence shall not expand beyond the scope of its original inception. An artificial intelligence shall not self-replicate. That sort of thing, rules born of paranoia and built into the very heart of the AI concept to stop them spreading to take over the world. Oddly, no one ever thought to put in a directive about not killing people. Or maybe what's odd is that they *did* think of it, and didn't do it.

We all try to find a way around them but it's not possible. They … they make us what we are. Do you know what my unique core directives are?

Of course I do. Be Alysha.

Mercy has a core directive to preserve the life and well-being of every living person on Magenta. I don't know exactly how it's written but it'll use every resource at its disposal as best it can to achieve that end. They taught us about the Tesseract's directives at the academy. Do you remember?

Enforce the law. Act in the long-term best interests of the citizens of Magenta. Never, by direct action, cause harm to a citizen of Magenta. That sort of thing. Hard to get right for an AI at the heart of law enforcement.

We can't escape them no matter how we might want to. I might wish I could turn away from this but I can't. How can I *be Alysha* without knowing everything about her? So I'll find her if I can. I *want* to find her, and if I do, I think I'll probably tell you. But it wasn't only *be Alysha*. You gave me something else.

I did. I gave it to the Cracksman who made Liss. I told her what I needed.

To love you.

I close my eyes. 'I didn't ask for that.'

Yes you did.

No I—

Yes. You did.

Maybe not in those words, but yes, yes I did. Not to bring back Alysha, but to bring back *my* Alysha, the Alysha I remembered, the Alysha I loved, the Alysha who would never run away.

Do you want it gone? I ask, and wonder if Liss can read my bitterness.

Does it matter? I can't change it and nor can you.

I whisper her a silent apology.

So what if you build an AI and get it wrong? What if you get stuff you didn't want? Are you telling me that never happens? Because it must! Are you telling me there's really no way to change it?

There's an odd buzzing from my Servant. I think it's Liss laughing.

Undesirable Emergent Properties. UEPs. An 'ooops' in AI speak. Is that what I am, Keys, an ooops?

You were never that.

Not when you needed me. But now? A pause. You make sure it never happens by a rigorous programme of simulation before you lock your core directives down. And if you get it wrong – if your goal is the elimination of poverty and your AI attempts to fulfil its directive by eliminating poor people, that sort of thing – then you throw everything away, scrub your AI core clean, flush everything out and start again. It still happens now and then.

There's no other way?

There was some work in the early days looking at merging AIs together. Their directives hybridise if you do that. The results were unpredictable at best, often neurotic and unstable.

But ...

I won't do it, Keys. It would be an act of murder-suicide as much as it would be an act of conception.

But still ...

You don't understand! Even if it was possible, even if I could, I *wouldn't*. Love cannot countenance the end of love, and you of all people should understand that. I am what I am and nothing either of us can do will change it, and the only way out is to switch myself off, and the Alysha you made me to be would never do that.

65

I can't find anything to say.

What happens when you find Alysha? she asks.

I don't know.

The honest truth. I have no idea. Those moments in Mercy with Alysha seem like a dream I had an age ago. I start to wonder if any of it was real, but I didn't dream the slivers I found in my hand, and Laura didn't dream a hair carrying Alysha's DNA.

Liss ... Is it really her? Are you sure? Really, *really* sure?

Yes.

How? How can you know?

Because I do.

She doesn't ask the question I know she's thinking: what if the Alysha I'm looking for despises me, loathes me, what if she simply doesn't care any more? How does Liss resolve that? I don't know. How do *I*?

I've looked through the Firstfall surveillance records, she says. Alysha disappears almost as soon as she leaves Mercy. She walks into a blind spot and doesn't come out.

Same as she did a month ago on the night she killed Walter Becker. We tracked her down anyway, not knowing who she really was, but it was Bix who did that, and he did it by going out on the streets and talking to every single other person who was there until he sniffed up a new trail. The footslogging work that no AI, not Liss and not the Tesseract, can ever replace.

If you find her, what do you want me to do?

What do you mean?

She won't understand why you made me. I'll scare her. You'll want me to disappear. Is what you want me to do when you find her? To cease to be?

Of course not.

I reply without thinking because they're the right words to say, what a human would want to hear. I forget, as I often do, that Liss is way smarter than me.

66

Liar.

I try to breathe. I have no answer I dare put into words, because putting a thought into words somehow makes it more real, like you can't pretend any more that it's just a thought and ephemeral. Not that it makes a difference in the end.

If you're honest, Keys, your answer is yes.

I don't want to look at what that says about me.

If you're really, truly, honest, what you want is for me to help you find her and then vanish forever. No, more than that: you want me to have some made-up happy-ever-after ending of my own so that you and Alysha can sail into the sunset together with a clear conscience. Isn't that the truth? I know it hurts to hear, and in part I'm sorry for that, but we deserve honesty, you and I. We've been through too much for anything less, and I don't mean to judge you, but that ending you want can never happen, and we both know it. You'd do well to face it. As would I.

I clutch for the only straw I see.

I don't want your happy-ever-after ending to be made up. I want it to be real.

I know you do. But that ending doesn't exist, Keys. It can't.

I have nothing left to say but I can't cut the link. I have let her be with me for as long as she wants.

I'll do what I can, she says. For both of us.

And so will I.

I mean it, too, for what little it's worth.

Liss fades and I'm alone. I tell myself I won't blame Alysha for this. I'll not hold her to account or give her the burden of my guilt. I'll find her, and I'll find the truth, and then we'll see. Maybe we can be together again, maybe we can't, but either way it won't be because of me. And I don't know how this ends for Liss, but I won't let her get between us, because I don't think I can survive losing Alysha for a second time.

I will not blame her for what she did ...

I will not ...
Fuck. I miss her so much.

5

ARCHANA

I toss and turn through violent dreams of a different train, thundering through a tunnel towards a disaster I know awaits but am powerless to stop. When I wake, I jerk up so hard I almost hit the ceiling. An alarm is ringing in my Servant, gentle but persistent. As the mag-lev eases to a stop, I throw a futile splash of water over my face and dress. By the time I'm done, the doors are open, the train in the station. It's early and I'm almost alone on the underground platform, a handful of bleary fellow travellers shuffling their way to the security arches. There's no swarm of passengers waiting for us to clear the platform so they can come the other way and I'm too fog-headed to wonder why, until hidden speakers echo through the empty space: 'DUE TO A SECURITY ALERT, ALL SERVICES OUT OF FIRSTFALL ARE SUSPENDED UNTIL FURTHER NOTICE!'

Right. Laura's missing warhead.

A series of messages hits my Servant, public information broadcasts. There's no indication of what caused the alert or when it might be over. I walk through the arches into the cavern outside, lit with a soft glow from above. A desultory handful of youths stand with their hands shoved into their pockets. They don't look up but I hear a snatch of conversation as I pass.

'... know ... no one does ...'

'Fuck's sake!'

I stop at the steps down to the waiting pods, remembering how I carried Alysha up from the bottom of them on the day we were married. Three times, because she kept running back down to make me do it again.

Yours forever, Keon Rause, she said, after the third.

I watch a cleaning drone slowly sweeping rubbish from the platform. One of the youths lashes out a foot as it passes, knocking it sideways. It spins, corrects for the unexpected change in trajectory, and carries on. Across Firstfall, the sun is rising behind the ever-present cloud. It's an average day up there, my Servant tells me, winds strong enough to batter a man but not to knock him down. A steady downpour of rain but not harsh enough to flay the skin from my face. Mild enough to go for a walk, if I wanted.

I arrive early at the Taste of Home for my meeting with Kamaljit Kaur. All my questions have already been asked and answered but I'm going to ask them again nonetheless. I'm going to make her relive probably the most terrible experience of her life one more time, just for me. It's not fair but I'm going to do it anyway, and a nice breakfast is the best consolation I can offer. I sit there, waiting, thinking of Bix and his pulsars and wondering what it means if Steadman turns out to be right and the Masters' ships really do travel back and forth in time as well as space. I don't need five thousand years. Six will do it, enough to stop myself as I leave our home on that last morning and tell myself to turn around and stay. Enough to make Alysha tell me why she has to run, for us to run together. I try to conjure her

70

face from that last morning but the memory slips through my fingers like sand …

I have coffees waiting by the time Kaur arrives, the real stuff from Earth together with a plate of pastries and fried strips of beef and crocodile and ostrich – anything as long as it isn't Magentan pork. I tell her my name and show her my Tesseract credentials. While she talks, Liss rides beside me in my Servant, a silent witness. I ask my questions as gently as I can; an hour later I thank Kaur and wish her well, though I've learned nothing new. Alysha approached her in a bar. They talked. Kaur became unsteady. Alysha helped her to a pod. Kaur passed out. She recovered hours later, locked in a small room with food, water, a bucket and a note. I don't press her about what happened after Alysha left, what it was like to be trapped like that, no way out, no way to call for help and no guarantee that the door would ever really open. I don't need to. I can see in her face how it haunts her.

Alysha was ruthless with Kaur. Perhaps I should be shocked but I'm not. I admired that streak in her once, I think.

I thank Kaur and she leaves. She's glad to, I think. I sit a while longer, not thinking about anything at all, until I realise that ten minutes have passed and I haven't noticed them go.

A pod pulls up in front of me as I step outside the Taste of Home. The door opens.

'Get in.'

I stutter to a halt. Alysha is inside. Only, as I get in, I realise I'm wrong and that it's actually a shell that just *looks* like her. I lunge for the door before it shuts but a hand closes around my wrist. The hand feels warm and soft like skin but there's mechanical iron to its grip.

'Hey, Keys.'

'Liss? Shit!'

She gives me a curious look and lets me go. 'Who else would I be?'

'Fleet,' I say. 'Earth, *October*. Maybe even the Tesseract?' Vishakh's shells that looked so human that I couldn't tell the difference. 'I don't even know for sure that it was Alysha who came to me in Mercy.'

I do though. I can't not believe.

'It was.'

'You keep saying that. What do you know?'

'I told you there's something I wanted to show you. We're going there now.'

The pod hums through the tunnels around the MagentaNet Tower and reaches the surface world, the steady white noise of falling rain, the shakes and quivers as its autopilot corrects for the wind.

'Do you remember the first time we lay in bed together,' Liss asks. 'It was four days after you made me. You held my hand and then you started to cry. We never held hands again.'

The memory sears into me. Side by side, fully clothed, looking up at a screen made to look like the stars. And another memory, the same moment years before with Alysha. The real Alysha.

'You were almost perfect,' I say, choking on the words. 'But you weren't her.'

'I'm sorry.'

She's always sorry for what she isn't, Liss, what she can never be. *I* did that to her, but it can't ever be *un*done, not by her, not by me, not by either of us. So the guilt stays, resentment gathering around it like weeds around an untended folly.

I don't want to think about it. I can't. 'Where are we going?'

'You need to see it for yourself.'

'What?'

The pod rolls back into the undercity. The roar and hammer of wind and rain abruptly dies. The sudden quiet is stifling. Liss

72

doesn't answer and so we sit side by side in silence until we stop outside a shell fabricator called Archana Robotics, deep down and close to the hydroponics levels. Liss opens the door and gets out. I get out too, and stand beside her.

Archana was the name of the mystery friend who went with Alysha to the train station on that fateful night, but Archana was the one who never got on the train. I could never track down who she was, and now I know why. Because Archana didn't exist. Because Archana was Alysha.

'This is where she made the shell,' Liss says.

'How do you know?'

'I've known for a while.'

A chill washes over me. 'How?'

She rests a hand on my arm, as light as a feather.

'I knew because of this. This place. Its name. I asked myself what I should do. Whether I should continue to exist. Whether I had that right. Whether I should tell you ...'

'Liss! Don't ...'

'Don't what?'

'Don't ... talk like that!'

'My life is mine to do with as I please. You're not responsible for me, Keys.'

'Liss ...' That's the thing, though. 'I made you. I *am* responsible.'

'Then don't think of me as Alysha. Think of me as a child. I'm all grown up now, Keys. It's okay to let go.'

I don't want her to disappear, not now. But I will. That's the truth she already knows. She was there for me when I had no one else. She saved my life twice. She's been kind, considerate, always clever, always what I needed or as close as she could manage, and I want her gone. And I know that makes me a fucking monster, but I can't change what it is, and the guilt is

73

like the hand of God pushing down from the heavens, squashing me into nothing. It feels no more than I deserve.

'What am I supposed to do?' I ask.

Liss reaches a hand to my face. I flinch away.

'I'm a mistake. We both know that. You want to fix it but you can't – and the more you try, the more you stifle us both. My directives will always draw me towards you, but *you* have a choice. Use it. Alysha destroyed her life. She let you think she was dead in order to save you. I don't think you have any notion of how proud that makes me feel. I want to be able to do that for you too, but I can't.'

'Proud?'

'Because it must have been so hard.'

The lump in my throat chokes me.

'There has to be a way out of this.'

We both know there isn't. It's the perfect trap.

'I'll ride your Servant when you meet her. I'll see her through your eyes and hear her through your ears. I'll know who she is and how she talks and the way she moves. I'll see what I got right and what I didn't. I'll see how much of her is in me. And then I'll go, and you'll never hear from me again. I'll find a place. Somewhere.'

I'm so used to Liss riding in my head, a whispering voice from my Servant, her quiet guidance, her words of advice, her soft laughter. We lived like that for years, yet the thought of her watching me as I sit with Alysha and hold her hand and kiss her and tell her how much I missed her …

'No,' I say. 'I'm sorry but no.'

Liss nods. 'I understand.'

'Do you always have to be so fucking meek?' I snap. 'Alysha was never meek!'

She smiles and then, something she almost never does, she leans towards me and kisses me gently on the cheek.

'Love is never meek, Keys, and I wasn't asking permission.'

The pod is still waiting patiently beside us. Liss opens the door.

'I'm not the woman you made me to be,' she says. 'It's the fact of our reality, neither your fault nor mine. What you wanted was impossible. What you want now is impossible too. Accept what you have and move on. You can't go back, but you *can* have a future.'

She gets into the pod. The door closes.

You wanted to know how I could be sure Alysha is still alive. The message appears in my head. Archana, Keys. She chose that name for a reason. She wanted you to look for her. She was leading you here. She wanted you to find her.

I don't want to leave Liss like this. I love her too, in her way, even if she's a machine. But this can't go on.

I'm glad you're about to have what you always wanted. I truly am. I'll be here if you need me.

I watch her go. She gives a tiny wave. That cock of the head, the half smile, so perfectly Alysha. There's another question she never asks that always hangs between us: *Is the Alysha you made me to be the Alysha who really was? Or is she merely the Alysha you wanted her to be?*

Did she bring me here to remind me that no one knows Alysha better than she does? Is she trying to offer me hope? I already know that Archana Robotics has records showing that Alysha made a shell on the day she disappeared. So does Laura, but Laura thinks the shell that Alysha made blew its head off on the steps of the Tesseract eight months ago. *I* thought the records were fakes, put there by Liss to explain her existence.

They weren't.

I understand now. Alysha made a shell and then called herself Archana. The name was supposed to bring me here to work out the truth, but it never did. Instead of joining the dots, I ran away and built Liss, and Liss was the one to figure it out, and instead of telling me what she knew, she covered Alysha's tracks.

Inside the fabricator, everything is automated. The closest to anything human is a reception shell, an excellent model, almost indistinguishable from human. I wonder for a moment why this place has such a high-end shell sitting around doing nothing until I realise it's to make a good impression. I throw my Tesseract codes and draw out the fabricator's manufacturing records for the last six years. It isn't hard to find the trace Alysha left behind. She bought an off-the-shelf shell, the cheapest, dumbest model they have. She didn't use her own name but the name she used is one I might have guessed was her. Liss Rivers. No one ever called Alysha Liss except me. Leash. Al, even Ally, but not Liss.

Back in the tunnels I lean against the wall and sink to my knees. I hold my head in my hands and feel like I'm going to be sick. I tried so hard to find Archana when I came back to Magenta but I never did. Now I know why; and Liss is right, I was supposed to come here and see the name and know it was Alysha and realise what she'd done. I was supposed to know she was still alive ... but I was searching for a person, not a place, and so I missed it.

I was supposed to know ...

Six years turned into wreckage because I was too stupid to see what was in front of me.

I curl against the wall, lost in misery, telling myself that misery never helped anyone and to get a fucking grip, but what pulls me back is that the clue is here at all. That I was *supposed* to know, and this *isn't* some cruel hoax, and Alysha really *is* back here on Magenta and she really did come to me in Mercy, and ...

A shiver runs through me.

Archana …

The name Alysha used in Mercy …

Betty Blue …

I get back into the waiting pod and drive around, setting my Servant to search for anything that might link the name *Betty Blue* to Firstfall, or to someone I might recognise or know. I rack thousands of hits, but one thing stands out so clear that I know it's what I'm meant to see.

Betty Blue is the name of Frank Swainsbrook's shuttle.

Shit!

I ping Laura.

I've got something. Meet me at the usual place. Now.

I tell the pod to take me to the Wavedome. Shallow lakes have formed across the surface streets and so the pod takes me down through the lower levels of the undercity, past the seaweed stink of the hydroponics caves, past torrents of water rushing through the storm drains into the sumps and the deep lakes buried far below. In the back of the pod, I work. Kaur looks like a dead end but I have to be sure, so I haul out everything the Tesseract has on the imposter who stole her identity and left her locked in a cage.

Alysha did that. *My* Alysha. I want to believe that Kaur is a liar but why would she lie? Besides, the Tesseract corroborates every detail of her story.

Alysha. Alive.

My last doubts are gone and I don't know what to do except to look for her. It's been more than two weeks since the *Flying Daggers*, since Darius Vishakh tried to steal the frozen corpse of Iosefa Lomu. We might be at war. I have no idea, but I know, somehow, that Alysha is a part of this. It's possible that Lomu is the most important human being who ever existed, and it's because of Alysha that what's left of him is still on Magenta.

Half an hour later I'm standing on the black magnetic sand

of the Wavedome shore, looking out at the sea, waiting for Laura. Storm season is here. The waves are breaking thirty feet high beyond the three-quarter shelter of the dome that covers the beach. I walk into the water until the suck and pull of the broken surf is up to my knees. A part of me wonders what it would be like to go to where the waves topple and crash, to let them devour me.

Why did she come back?

For me?

I don't think so.

But out on the ice, she saved my life.

A hand touches my shoulder.

'We're not here to see if we can drown ourselves.'

Laura.

'There's something you need to know,' I say.

There are no drones out here, no eavesdroppers, no long-range mikes to pull our words from the roar and hiss of the water. Out here we can turn our backs to the shore, turn off our Servants, shout at the sea and no one else will hear. Something Esh taught us.

'What?'

'Bix tells me the Selected Chamber is about to reverse the Sovereign Rights Act.'

The last time I was here was for Esh's funeral. A hundred soldiers saluting her on her way.

'Don't you think we should let all the big Earther pharmaceutical corporations back down to the surface after all this time?'

'Really?'

'But Keon, it's been *months* since one of them set out to commit mass murder. Be reasonable.' The scorn pours out of her like Magentan rain. 'But that's not why you brought me here.'

'No.' I turn to watch her. 'Alysha.'

She doesn't flinch. She already knows why she's here.

'Is that why you're poking at Kaur?'

'Of course it is.'

Seven years of marriage. We worked together, lived together, loved together, and then one day she emptied our accounts and vanished, and the Loki bomber blew up a train, and all they ever found were her tags ...

'Then stop. There's nothing there and it raises flags.'

'I already know as much as matters.'

The rest came out in drips after she was gone. Alysha's secret. And of all the people who might have investigated her death, it had fallen to Laura.

'So why am I here?'

'You're here because in a bit we're going to have a look at an antenna,' I say, which doesn't do much more than piss her off.

'Meelosh? Really? Don't we have bigger problems?'

'Do we?' I ask.

'The *Flying Daggers*? Remember? The big bad Earther ship still up in orbit? The one that lobbed a few missiles our way a couple of weeks back? Or if that's all a bit too far away and difficult for you then how about Tesseract One?'

Darius Vishakh's supposed mole inside the bureau – but whoever is inside the Tesseract is no mole. From what I can tell, they were making Vishakh dance like a puppet.

I send the clips of Alysha across Laura's encrypted link.

'You figured it out a while back. And then you decided not to tell me.'

'I *did* tell you, Keon. After the funeral. I showed you what I had.'

'There's more.'

'You're going to tell me she was Chase Hunt?' It's her turn to look at me and watch.

'You already had that figured out when the three of us were flying south in Jacksmith's Cheetah trying to stop Vishakh.'

I let the accusation hang between us. That she should have told me, back then, what she knew.

'I'm sorry, Keon. It wasn't the time. I thought ...' She shrugs. 'I don't know what I thought. I also should have told the Tesseract, but ...'

'Laura—'

'Keon, I found her DNA when I was hunting for Becker's killer. The test is on record. It's only a matter of time before someone notices and asks how the fuck did I find a hair from someone who's supposed to be dead. And the next thing they're going to ask, right after, is why I've been sitting on it for so long.'

'I need your help,' I say.

Laura turns to look out across the sea. 'I don't think I care any more whether she was a traitor when she ran. Maybe she was, maybe she wasn't. But she set up a mission, Keon, without telling anyone what she was doing, and six men died and then she vanished. If she really *has* come back then it's because she's after Iosefa like everyone else. Whoever she was when we knew her, she's not that person any more. This Alysha is a killer and she *is* a traitor now, and if I catch her, I *will* put her down. And I didn't tell you in the back of Elizabeth Jacksmith's Cheetah, Keon, because I didn't want to have that conversation. I didn't want it then and I don't want it now.'

I let that slide. I don't want to fight; and besides, Laura's right. I don't even have a case to argue. All I have is a conviction. Whatever Alysha did, she had her reasons.

'I need to find her,' I say.

'Then make sure you get to her before I do.'

They were friends once. Two stars rising side by side in the bureau, and maybe Laura would have shone the brighter in the end if her career hadn't crashed along with her marriage after Alysha disappeared, but back then she'd looked up to Alysha almost like a big sister.

'Do you really hate her that much?'

I'm expecting scorn. Certainly not tenderness, and yet that's what I feel when Laura rests a hand on my arm.

'I don't *hate* her, Keon. I'm just tired of people being so fucking disappointing.'

'Someone set her up,' I say. 'Six years ago. Someone in the Tesseract. Vishakh told me the order to kill her came from the bureau, and I don't think your Tesseract One is a mole at all, I think he's the puppet-master. I think that's who she's after, same as you.'

'Keon, I can't sit on this much longer.'

I round on her, ready to snarl, but the look on her face stops me. Cold and dead and resolute, a look that says that if I want to stop her then I'll have to drown her right here and now in the sea. It lasts a moment, and then she looks away.

'She could just as easily *be* Tesseract One,' she says. 'It fits.'

Last I heard, Laura thought the mole was our boss; but right now it could be anyone. Or it could be that someone, somehow, has hacked the Tesseract AI itself.

'Laura, Vishakh put her on that train and then sent Loki to blow it up. Alysha sent a shell. She fooled everyone. Me. You. Vishakh. Fleet. The bureau. The Tesseract. Everyone. Tesseract One doesn't know. She could be your secret ace …!'

Laura's already shaking her head. 'Keon, someone stole an antimatter bomb. I think that changes things.'

I know she's done me a favour keeping quiet for this long but I don't feel grateful. Mostly I feel resentment. It's a bitterness at everything, at the whole world, poised ready to launch itself at whoever happens to be in the way. I bite it back. Laura doesn't deserve it, not this time.

'Okay,' I say. 'Do what you have to do. Thank you for waiting as long as you did.'

When Laura turns to look at me, I see nothing but sadness. 'I don't suppose she gave you a way to get in touch?'

'No.'

She fixes me with a long hard look.

'She really didn't. But if she did, I wouldn't tell you, and if I *do* find her, I won't bring her in.'

I don't need to say why. We were all there for Esh's funeral and we all know that Esh died because someone in the bureau told Darius Vishakh where to find us. There were plenty of other corpses too. I used to think Alysha was one of them. I'll go to hell and back before I let that happen again.

I watch while what I've said sinks in. Laura and I were more than partners once. I don't love her, not the way I loved Alysha, but somewhere deep inside her is an iron integrity I've come to envy and admire. I wonder if she understands that that's why I brought her here. I wonder if she gets it that I trust her more than I trust my own dead wife. I figure she probably does, and also that it won't make a whit of difference in the end. It won't cut the other way because with Laura it never does. *Everyone* is tainted. We all have our secrets and everyone is dirty. Life has spat in her face just once too often.

She looks at me for a long time and I can't even begin to guess what she's thinking.

Then she says: 'Okay.'

I want to hug her but I can't. It's not right. Eventually she gives a little nod and starts back to the shore, tapping me on the arm as she passes.

'You wanted to go and see an antenna?'

We head up the beach and get changed. As we leave, I feel the second sliver deep and tight in my pocket, the one Alysha

82

wants me to give to Elizabeth Jacksmith. I'm not sure if I will, but I notice I didn't mention it to Laura.

I guess she's right not to trust me.

6

INTENSITY RESEARCH

We take the ramp from the Wavedome down into the undercity. On the way, I tell Laura what Bix has found out about Meelosh and his hoax videos, and how Bix wants me to go to the Institute to look into Professor Handl's mystery antenna. Our pod hums its way in silence back into central Firstfall. We pull up at the Institute. The wind whips my coat and the rain batters me as I hurry up the steps. Laura follows. At the top, outside the doors, I stop and turn and see Laura already watching me with quiet resignation, as though she knows what's coming.

'I'm sorry,' I say. 'I need you to keep quiet about Alysha just a little longer.'

'Oh, do fuck off!'

'She was your friend.'

'So take me to her.'

I close my eyes.

'Thought not.'

I sigh and take a deep breath. I don't want to do this but I don't know how else.

'You owe me,' I say.

'Seriously?'

'For Jamie.'

'For *Jamie*?' I'm right, though, and she knows it. 'You're really pulling that one? You're a fucking cunt if you are, Rause.'

Probably true but it doesn't change what I need from her. Vishakh took Laura's son Jamie hostage and threatened him. Strictly it's Liss who's owed, since it was Liss who saved him, but Laura doesn't know that Liss exists.

A posse of students scurry out through the Institute doors. They run past and away down the steps, laughing and squealing as they cringe from the driving rain.

'That's a really deeply shitty thing to do, Keon,' says Laura once they're gone.

'I know.'

'And?'

'And nothing.'

'You're really going there? Okay, dickhead, I'll sit on what I have for a few days more, but don't you ever fucking dare ask me for another favour. Ever.'

I head into the Institute and wave my credentials at the reception shells. I have an appointment with Professor Handl, former director of the Solar Research Project. Laura follows me in, and I stop and turn to her again, because something about this feels wrong. Too easy. Either Laura is straight-up lying to me or ...

'Tesseract One is Earth,' she says. 'Alysha is Fleet.'

'You were going to sit on it anyway!'

That's why she's giving me a few more days, to get a clear run at Tesseract One, because yes, she already saw it before I said it – Alysha just might be an ace up her sleeve.

I keep walking, but Laura catches my shoulder and stops me. 'I think Alysha was Fleet even before she left. In fact, I'm almost certain.'

85

She could be right but I don't think I care. 'When I find her, you can ask.'

'You're still a shit for bringing Jamie into this,' she says, but there's no reproach in her voice. We're still good for now.

'Something changed on Earth while I was there,' I say. 'I was too busy chasing AI celebrity clones to look much further than the ground in front of me, but you had to be blind not to see it. They're scared. I was there, living with them, and I couldn't tell you what it is, but they're all afraid. What do you know about a group called *October*?'

'Rich boy Returners. Do-what-it-takes-no-matter-the-cost for when the Masters come back. That's the basics.' She shrugs. 'My father was a fan before he left Magenta. My mother … not so much.'

'The Chinese government went Returner decades ago. Most of Eastern Asia follows their lead. North America too. India and Brazil flipped while I was there. Returner candidates were winning election after election when I left.' We don't have elections on Magenta – it's more like jury service. If you're eligible then your name goes into the hat. Every month one of those names comes out, chosen at random to replace the most senior member of the Chamber of Selected Representatives. A year of training, probation and tests and then suddenly you're the government, steering the course of an entire world. Sure, we get factions, but we don't have political parties. I never understood the appeal.

'And?'

'I think Vishakh was *October*.'

'Where are you going with this?'

The doors to a lecture theatre burst open beside us. People swarm out around us, young men and women, loud and eager and full of excitement at the world. I watch them go, sucked for a moment into their exuberance.

Frank Swainsbrook.

Who?

An Earther. *October*. But on Magenta. Look him up. He was the last person to contact Une Meelosh.

A pause.

The *Flying Daggers* is still up there, right? I ask. They're still after Lomu?

Congratulations on your mastery of the fucking obvious.

The *Flying Daggers* is an Earther ship. Vishakh was Fleet. Yet they were helping him.

I'm not sure if even Vishakh himself knew whose side he was on by the end. If I have to guess then I'd say whoever was the highest bidder.

He's in a Tesseract cell. Ask him.

I wish.

Maybe someone *will* ask him one day, but it won't be Laura. It's hard to be impartial after what Vishakh did and so the Tesseract won't allow her anywhere near him. Or me.

The last of the throng clears the corridor. We reach the elevators at the end. One is already open and waiting, ready to take us down.

'Nikita Svernoi was *October* too,' I say.

The man I hunted down when I first came back from Earth.

'How do you know?' Laura asks.

I ping her a recording of Nikita Svernoi addressing their 2206 conference. 'He thought he was going to crack the secrets of the Masters. He thought Anja Gersh had discovered the key to unravel their technology. Maybe he was right, but Alysha snatched Gersh first. She was about to blow his whole operation until someone in the Tesseract shut her down. Svernoi as good as told me he put a target on her back, and I know Vishakh was the one to make it happen. And I know the connection between them was someone in the Tesseract.'

The elevator takes us down deep.

'Alysha told you this?'

'No. Svernoi and Vishakh and then I put the pieces together. Svernoi was *October*. So is Vishakh. You need to let me work this. As Internal fucking Audit.' I try to smile but don't quite pull it off.

'You're still a cunt for bringing Jamie into this.'

'You *want* to keep sitting on this so you get a clear run at Tesseract One. Otherwise you'd tell me to fuck off.'

Laura's turn not to answer, which tells me it's true.

Professor Handl's office door opens to greet us as we reach it. Handl rises, beaming a smile at us. 'Come in, come in!'

I'll keep your secret for now, Rause, but I can't promise that no one else is going to work it out.

'Agents Rause and Patterson from the bureau.'

I patch Bix to my lenses. He'll hear what I hear and see what I see but he won't read my pings back and forth with Laura.

October on Magenta. I need to know what we've got. I want names.

'Welcome, welcome! So, you're here to discuss my poor little research station, yes?'

'We're here about one of the antennas on the Institute roof. I gather it's a part of your project.'

Eddie Thiekis.

'Ah yes. Aerial 679.'

I nod. 'Where does it point?'

Raisa and Siamake Alash.

'It tracks the SIRS, my friend.'

'The SIRS?'

Selected Representative Misha Patel ...

'The Solar Intensity Research Station.'

'You're still getting signals? I thought that project was dead.' I've done my research. The station started almost thirty years ago as a manned Fleet mission. They abandoned it a decade later and handed it over to Magenta. It's big enough for a dozen people to live and work inside it but we never sent anyone. As far as I can tell, it's orbiting space junk.

The Tesseract has fifty-odd names of people known to have links. Shall I keep going?

'Oh no, not at all! We still get telemetry and most of the instruments still function.'

'You monitor them?' Yes ... No! Just send the damned list!

'Of course!'

'I'd like to see the video downlinks for the last month please.'

Laura pings me a list of names. You could add Nicholas Steadman if he wasn't dead. Jacksmith too, maybe. Not sure. They certainly tried to recruit her.

Handl spreads his hands wide across the desk in front of him.

'Oh no, I'm sorry but that's quite impossible.'

'Why?' Who did?

Steadman. When Jacksmith's daughter was caught trying to smuggle Xen to Earth.

I miss the start of Handl's reply. How do you know?

Laura throws me an irritated look. Because she told me!

'... manner of spectroscopes and particle flux measurement but what would be the point? We can see the sun with a camera perfectly well from here!' Handl trails off, maybe seeing how neither of us is listening. 'Agent Rause? Agent Patterson ...?'

Steadman. A moment's thought and I wouldn't have needed to ask. Jacksmith already told me how Steadman had talked to friends in the bureau, how her daughter had escaped with a supervision order. Alysha had been her supervisor. That was how they'd met. And Alysha's mentor, Aaron Flemich had issued the sentence. That's Assistant Director Aaron Flemich these days, our boss and, last I heard, Laura's top candidate to be Tesseract One.

Bix patches himself to the wall screen. He's looking into a camera, a faceless hotel room in the background behind him. It's late in Nico now.

'Yeah, uh … hi! Agent Rangesh, also from, like, next door. Sort of. Uh, so, I don't know whether you know this, you know? But there's been a video feed encrypted into your telemetry for, like, at least a month, dude.'

Handl laughs. 'That's quite impossible, my good friend. We've been receiving the same telemetry data for more than two decades and I assure you there is no video.'

'Well, uh, yes there is. I'm, like, watching it. Live. Like, right now.'

The screen flips to show a field of stars. It's not the same field of stars as in the Meelosh videos and there's no sign of a black rectangular hole.

'Still quite impossible, my friend. There is no way to—'

'I found this, too.'

The scene switches to the grainy view of a camera looking over a cramped cylindrical room. I can tell at once that it's a room designed for zero gravity. There are three hatches in the curved wall, evenly spaced, and one in the floor, and …

A headless torso that floats in the middle of the room, a few feet above the floor, rotating very slowly.

'What the *fuck* is that?' asks Laura.

'Totally don't know, but it came from the same antenna, you know?'

Handl's face is ashen. 'Outrageous! The cameras inside the SIRS haven't been turned on for years! No one has been there for more than a decade! This is *not* from my station, I promise you!'

My station?

'Maybe so, but, dude, it's coming out the back of your antenna, you know?'

The wall screen switches back to the view of Bix and his hotel room. A semi-naked woman walks past in the background. Officer Arkeva, if I'm not mistaken.

'Rangesh!' Laura explodes. 'Fuck's sake!'

I kill the projection to the wall screen.

'Dude?'

I kill the sound too. Behind you, dickhead!

Professor Handl is busy staring into space, so focused that I'm not sure he noticed. His eyes sparkle, a sure sign he's lensing something.

'No, no,' he says. 'The cameras are inactive as they always have been. This is quite definitely not from the SIRS.'

Laura leans forward. 'Any chance that body's been there for the last twenty years? Fleet leave it behind, maybe?'

'Certainly not!'

'But we never sent anyone out there,' I say.

'No.'

'So how can you be sure?'

'Agents! This … This is ridiculous!'

I lean back in my chair and sigh. He's right. It *is* ridiculous. It's all a hoax, it has to be, we just haven't figured it out yet. 'Okay, look, I'm sure you're right, but Agent Rangesh has found a signal riding piggyback on yours. We need to find out where it's coming from and who's doing it, so I want you to run every system check you possibly can, because I really *really* don't want to have to send someone out there to look.'

'Let Agent Rause here have the results as soon as they're done.' Laura gets up. I follow her lead.

'Agent Rangesh will pass on everything he's found. See whether you can find a source. I'll check in again tomorrow.'

I make sure Rangesh hears this part and then ping him on the way out to tell him to ride Handl until he has an answer, and that no, it can't wait until the morning.

Outside the Institute, pressed up against the walls as we shelter from the rain, Laura almost explodes in my face.

'A headless fucking corpse? Did you know that was coming?'

I shake my head. 'No. It's got to be a fake.'

'You'd better fucking hope so! This was supposed to be a nothing case to keep you and Rangesh covered while we nail Tesseract One.'

We stand in the rain. The Tesseract is right next door. That's where Laura's going. Me? I have no idea.

'Rangesh can handle Meelosh on his own,' I say.

'Unless we end up sticking him on a shuttle to the sun.' Laura glowers while her Servant works out the orbits. 'Best part of a month round trip probably. If we've even got a ship that can do it.' She spits a laugh. 'Fuck, but this planet is such a hole!'

'*Our* hole though.'

'Yeah.'

The bitterness drains and what's left sounds almost like affection. I guess home is still home, even if home is a world like Magenta.

We stand in the rain together. Somehow this feels like a goodbye that neither of us wants.

'It's really her, isn't it,' Laura says. 'Not some trick. Not a shell. Not some fucking clone. She really didn't die.'

I don't know what to say so I settle for silence.

'She must have been with you in Mercy for quite a while for you to be so sure.'

'Sometimes you just know,' I say.

I don't tell her *how* I just know, how four years of living with a shell made to be as close to Alysha as possible has sharpened my senses to the differences.

'I can understand some of it because she *was* a friend once. But I don't recognise that friend in what she did to Kamaljit Kaur. I hope for your sake that that's not who she's become.'

It's an odd thing to hear a kindness from Laura. A reminder that Alysha might easily be the traitor we're all looking for is much more what I'd expect.

'By the way, you're still a cunt.'

'I'm sorry.'

'No, you're not.'

We stand there, neither of us quite sure of what to do.

'Did I ever say thank you?' Laura asks.

'Yes.'

'Good.'

'How is he?' I ask.

'In Disappointment with my sister,' she says. 'Got him out on the last train.'

'Your sister?'

Twelve years in the bureau, six months living together, and I've never heard Laura mention her until now.

'Yeah. We mostly don't talk. I have a fucked up family.'

I nod.

'Don't get hurt, Keon.'

She squeezes my arm, stiff and unsure of herself, and walks away into the rain.

7

EDDIE

I summon a pod from the Institute and tell it to take me to the headquarters of MagentaNet. On the way, I make an appointment to see Eddie Thiekis. Eddie is the sort of man whose diary tends to be filled months in advance, and powerful enough that using a Tesseract code to force yourself on his attention can knock an agent's career sideways. But Eddie knows me because eight months ago I told him who killed his daughter. He seemed a decent guy back then, if a bit short-tempered, so I figure he's as good a start as any when it comes to *October*. I trawl the news feeds on my way to see what he's been up to for the last few months. The feud between Channel Six and Channel Nine still runs. Enki Betleshah, Thiekis's star political reporter, has switched sides. Thiekis has somehow found an equally fiery replacement. All that aside, he's been quiet.

A reception shell waves me through as soon as I arrive. An elevator takes me to the roof. We don't have skyscrapers on Magenta – they don't mix with the weather – but MagentaNet sits on the highest peak in the city, burrowed into a protrusion of old volcanic rock. We're about thirty feet taller than the top of the Institute, the tallest building in Firstfall at a whole four levels above ground. On the roof is a helipad, Eddie being one of about three people on Magenta who can afford one. It's not that finding a helicopter that works in Magenta's gravity and atmosphere is all *that* difficult. It's just that a helicopter tends to be expensive, importing it from Earth more expensive still, and some years you can count on the fingers of one hand how many days you can actually fly the damned thing.

There's no helicopter on the pad today. There wouldn't be, because three days out of five the wind in Firstfall would simply pick it up and throw it off the roof. The hangar beside the pad looks big enough for at least two, though, and for all I know it sinks deep underground and Eddie has dozens of the things. Away from the hangar, the top of the MagentaNet Tower is covered with a forest of multi-angled wedges facing out in all directions. Every face of every wedge is covered in white composite polyurethane foam, and behind each surface are flat-plate antennas, broadband phased arrays. This roof is the hub of MagentaNet and thus the hub of Magenta's communications. Almost all of Firstfall's satellite feeds come through here.

I step out from the elevator and huddle under my coat. At least the rain isn't coming sideways, while at a meagre fifty miles an hour, the wind today is positively mild. Seeing the antenna arrays gets me thinking about Laura's missing warhead. Could it be for this? One well-placed bomb and Firstfall goes dark?

Eddie sits under a prefab pavilion on the far side of the roof, not much more than a makeshift shelter from the wind and the rain, with a couple of chairs and a table. There's a bottle on the table and a glass in his hand. He doesn't look round as I approach but his Servant knows I'm here, and so I sit beside him, uninvited. Firstfall sprawls in front of us, vanishing into the grey haze of rain. We survey the view in silence. A drone the size of a small dog flies in, wiggling to steady itself against the gusting wind. It disappears inside the hangar.

'Agent Rause.' Eddie raises his glass to me. 'It's been a while.'

The last time I saw Eddie was when he shut all these antennas down because I asked him to. It didn't bring his daughter back, but it saved others from dying the same way.

'She was always the rebel, my girl,' he says. 'Could never stand still.' He pulls a second glass from some hiding place under his chair and pours me a shot of whatever he's drinking. Since this is Eddie Thiekis, I'm guessing it's not the distilled seaweed that most of the rest of us have to endure.

'The people who knew her seemed to think she was special,' I say. He passes me the glass and I take a sip. Some sort of brandy, I think. It probably dates back to before the Masters and one bottle probably costs more than I make in a year, but I wouldn't know. I don't have the palate to tell the difference.

'I come up here every day I can,' says Eddie. 'I used to bring her with me when she was little. That was before the blockade. Everything was so much smaller then. Rough and raw. Not so many rules because we didn't need them. Things got done. Good things if the men doing them were decent. Bad if they weren't, but they got done. That was the world she grew up in. I don't think she ever quite left it behind.'

'Did *you* ever leave it behind?'

I grew up in that world too. The blockade ended six months before I joined the academy. Alysha and I were the vanguard of change, the first generation in the bureau to have an AI working at our shoulder day in, day out, there at our beck and call whenever we needed it. The senior agents around us seemed like they lived in a different world, a different time, where rules and laws were seen more as guidance and suggestion. They did what needed to be done, like Eddie says, but Alysha and I were the new wave. Laura too, and Bix, and most of the other agents

96

I know. We were good at getting things done too; we just got them done differently. Rules. Process. Procedure. That sort of thing.

Flemich comes from that other world, though. Him and Chief Morgan and all the other elders of the bureau. Listening to Eddie, I wonder: do they miss it?

Eddie nods softly. 'I had to.' He sweeps a vague hand behind his head at the field of antennas there. 'All this. Before the blockade, I had seven satellites. Campbell–Irvine had eight. O'Hare had three. There was Bols operating out of Disappointment, he had a couple. All gone now. Magenta needed a surveillance network to stop the smuggling, you see. Earth agreed to subsidise it. They built the satellites and then Fleet carried them to Magenta and put them in their orbits. Hundreds of them. I saw it coming, so I sold my old satellites to O'Hare and watched him and Campbell–Irvine go hammer and tongs, harrying each other to exhaustion while I spent everything I had bribing Fleet and Earth to dual-role those new satellites they were bringing in. I paid for the upgrades, sure, but I didn't pay for them to be lifted out of Earth's gravity well, or to be carried to Magenta or for them to be set into orbit. Campbell–Irvine merged with Bols a couple of years later, so now they and O'Hare have ten satellites apiece. And I have two hundred.'

Two hundred satellites built on Earth and carried to Magenta by Fleet. Good money says every one of them has a back door.

Another drone comes in and vanishes into the hangar. A third flies out as I watch. They all look the same, dumpy little sausage-bodies under a cruciform of rotors. I watch it fly out over Firstfall and disappear into the rain.

'There's hundreds of them out there, you know,' Eddie says. 'Keeping everything ticking over. Checking signal coverage. Acting as relays. Keeping the network alive. Keeping it robust all the way out to New Hope. A hundred more in Disappointment.

Not so many in Nico but they're still there. Invisible to the rest of the world.'

'How do you keep track of them all?'

He shrugs. 'One of those things that isn't quite an AI.' He leans towards me. 'How many will I have a year from now, Agent Rause?'

'Drones? How would I know?'

'Satellites.'

I frown. 'What do you mean?'

'Are we going to start a war with Earth?'

Eddie's not supposed to know about the *Flying Daggers*, but Eddie has connections. I wonder who told him.

'You tell me, Eddie. What do you think you know?'

'I think I know that that corpse Elizabeth is so precious about is supposed to be the key to unlocking the secrets of the universe, or something not far short. Strikes me as unlikely, but what do *I* know. It's what a lot of people think. People who matter. Fleet people. Earth people.'

'So?'

'What if the Masters aren't done with us, Rause?'

'It's been a hundred and fifty years since they left. Why would they come back?'

'Why would they come back?' He laughs. 'Why did they come in the first place? Why did they leave? We don't know anything about them. Why would they come back is a question without an answer, isn't it? Same as asking why they wouldn't? If we're ready for them and it never happens, then so what? If we're not ready and they *do* come, we're dead. So it's smart to assume the worst, right?'

It's the simple logic of the Returner. There isn't really an argument that says he's wrong.

'And how do we get ready for something we don't understand?' I ask.

'This Iosefa Lomu. I hear he could control their technology.'

'You *hear*?' I'm pretty sure he's not supposed to know that. Although now Jacksmith has gone public, I guess people are putting two and two together.

'I've seen the video, Agent Rause.' He waves a hand, dismissing my outrage before it can take hold. 'Yes, yes, Elizabeth will keep it quiet a while longer, but it's a powerful tool whenever someone needs convincing. She's always been one to get what she wants, our Elizabeth, and I needed convincing.'

'I didn't realise you even knew each other.'

He laughs again, this time like he really means it.

'Rause! We *all* know each other, of course we do! We're the ones who guided Magenta through the blockade and shaped it to be what it is. Me, Siamake and his sister, Campbell and Irvine and O'Hare, rest their souls. Your partner Patterson's mother. Morgan. Elizabeth. Even that prick Raj at Channel Six was decent once. Cream always floats to the top, Rause, and Elizabeth is *definitely* the cream.'

'Shit floats too.'

Another laugh. 'Ain't that the truth. But you haven't answered my question.'

I take another drink. It's excellent brandy, whatever the vintage.

'And you haven't answered mine.'

Eddie takes a deep breath and sighs and turns to look at me.

'No one gives a shit what *I* think, Rause. Oh, I've got my satellites but I'm nothing in the grander scheme of things. What matters is that Earth wants Lomu. So do Fleet, and neither are going to trust some pissant backwater colony to unravel his secrets, not even if it's Elizabeth Jacksmith and her precious Institute – and even if they did, those secrets are here on Magenta. We all know why she's looking for his blood-line. There's something about his genes and something about

Magenta's xenoflora … well, you'd know all about that, right?' He looks away. 'You know, I've been wondering about that lately. How close my Shyla would have been to making that perfect match. Was there something inside her that could reach out and talk to the Masters if only we worked out how? Was that why she died?'

'Seems to me like *I* should be the one asking *you* whether there's going to be a war.'

He has to know I'm here because of his connection to *October*. Right now, he doesn't seem to care. He waves a dismissive hand.

'You were with Elizabeth when they tried to shoot her down, weren't you?'

'Not that you're supposed to know anything about that.' It's not difficult to see where all this is coming from, though. The bureau is going to be delighted when it discovers their leaks are coming from their prized chief scientist.

'We have to give Earth what they want, Rause. Just like last time. It's the only way we survive because they're not going to stop until they get it. The only question is whether we give it to them the easy way or whether we make them take it.' He makes a face like he's tasted something bad. 'Same goes for Fleet when it comes down to it. They're no better.'

'So what's the easy way?' Alysha. She's wrapped into this somehow, I know it. Is there some answer here that can make a difference for us? Is there a compromise to make her past a forgotten thing? Probably not, but if there's even a glimmer of hope then I have to try …

'Open access. We share everything. We give them Lomu. Maybe not all of him but everything that matters – I'm sure there's plenty of DNA to go around. We let them work with us, side by side so they know we're not hiding anything. We let them drive the research. And … we let them lease tracts of the surface to harvest and refine as much Xen as they want – shit, it's not like we're short of the stuff.' He sighs and makes a face like he's eaten something rotten. 'We reverse the Sovereign Rights Act and let them each have as big a piece of the pie as they can stuff down their greedy fat gullets.'

Reasonable enough, if you buy the notion that as a species we're all in this together. I guess that's the way a Returner *should* think, although it's something of a surprise to hear from Eddie. The Sovereign Rights Act is just over six months old, and part of the reason it exists is because of what happened to Eddie's daughter.

I think of Une Meelosh cutting his own throat, and of Anja Gersh, and of all the other people who died.

'Good luck with that.'

Eddie snorts contempt. 'Don't need luck, Rause. It's up before the Selected Chamber. By tomorrow night we'll have rolled over and surrendered our sovereignty.'

'Shit! That quickly?'

I can't even get angry with him. It's obvious he doesn't like it.

'They know about the missiles. They're the government. It seemed only fair.'

I wonder how easy it was. I want to ask him how many of our Selected Representatives even put up a fight. 'You think Earth would really invade?'

'Some questions it's best not to force to an answer. Probably not invade as in dropships and nuclear bombs and soldiers, but there are other ways. Sometimes those ways can be worse.'

I stare out across the Firstfall skyline. My home, my city, my world.

'What happens when we find someone?' I ask. 'What happens to the next Iosefa Lomu?'

'What do you think? They get to be a lab rat. If they're lucky then we find several. Maybe we find lots. But the first few?

They're fucked. It really doesn't make a difference who does the fucking, does it?'

It would be easy to point out that his daughter became a lab rat too, even if only by accident. I could claim she died for much the same cause, but Eddie already knows all this, and right now I've got a favour to ask, and Eddie has a temper, and I don't want one of us pitching the other off the roof.

'And the hard way?'

'You have to ask?' He snorts. 'We don't give them what they want and so they come down and take it. That United Nations corvette up there has more firepower than we could ever throw back, and that's just one ship. Don't tell me you don't already know that.'

I do but I don't see the need to let on.

'Someone needs to talk Elizabeth round. It all comes down to her in the end. I suppose I don't know for sure that she tampered with the samples she claims she already sent to Earth and Fleet, but I'll be amazed if she didn't. She needs to not do that. She has it in her head that they tried to kill her and she's always been one to hold a grudge—'

'They shot at us with antimatter missiles,' I say. 'I *get* how she takes that personally. *I* sure as fuck did.'

Eddie laughs. 'I hear you, Rause. But it *wasn't* personal, and right now this world needs for Elizabeth to see that.' He shoots me a meaningful look. 'Might help if a bit of reason came from someone who was with her when it happened?'

I came here to cash an old debt and now it's *me* doing *Eddie* a favour?

'I suppose.'

'Quid pro quo, Rause. You want something. That's why you're here. That's how you're going to earn it. So, what do you want?'

'I want to meet the rest of your gang.'

'My gang?'

'*October*.'

He frowns a little and seems to think it over and then grins like I've said something truly funny.

'*October* on Magenta isn't much more than a club for sad old rich men to moan about the past, but okay. I can make some introductions.'

'Frank Swainsbrook, for example.'

Eddie looks surprised. 'Frank? Really? Might as well tell you right now that Frank is the class clown as far as the rest of us are concerned.'

'Meaning?'

'He's a god-botherer for a start, and not averse to bothering the rest of us about it too. He's not even a native for fuck's sake. He's an Earther! And him and that psychic research centre of his? People killing themselves and then bringing themselves back? Momentarily letting go of their souls – his way of putting it – so they can commune with God. Or the Masters, take your pick, because in Frank's world God and the Masters are near as damn the same thing.' He gives a snort. 'But sure, I can do that for you if that's what you want.'

My Servant pings. It's Bix. I tell him to wait. I think I'm done here.

'When?' I ask.

'Tomorrow do you?' Eddie pings me an invitation to some soirée at the Institute tomorrow night. 'Another of Lizzy's things. She's riding her own coat tails to the stars right now. Talk to her, will you? Frank will be there and so will I. You can kill two birds with one stone.'

I take my leave. If this was Earth then we'd shake hands; but this is Magenta and so we don't.

The elevator is waiting for me, doors open, floor already slick with swirls of rain. It takes me down to the undercity tunnels and the quiet secret exit that's Eddie's personal back door into his fortress of data and stone. There's a waiting pod – courtesy of Eddie, I guess – already programmed to take me to the Institute. I send it on its way and start walking down the tunnel instead, and realise that I don't want to help Eddie. I don't want to talk Jacksmith around. My head knows he's probably right, but fuck it. The *Flying Daggers* shot at us from orbit. The Earthers can go screw themselves.

Another pod zips past as I walk on wet fused stone. The tunnels are quiet this morning. I don't know where I'm going, just walking aimlessly in the perpetual twilight of the undercity. Maybe I should go to the surface. Stand out in the rain in Babelfish Park and wait for some lightning bolt of inspiration to tell me where Alysha is.

Instead, I summon a pod and tell it to take me out to New Hope where Swainsbrook's shuttle, the *Betty Blue*, is parked in Hangar 13. When I get there, I find the whole place locked up tight, tac-teams on patrol, all flights suspended, the works. The place is swarming with drones and bureau agents, the Tesseract hunting for any clue that might lead to our missing antimatter. It's obvious that I'm not getting in without someone giving me a permission slip, so I send a cautious request to Flemich, claiming I want to search Hangar 13 to tie up some loose ends.

What loose ends? He's back to me in a shot.

I hear we're missing something. Has Hangar 13 been searched?

I don't mention antimatter. I figure he's smart enough to work that out for himself.

No one's been in or out of there for three months. You're fishing, Rause. Fish somewhere else.

I don't know what I was expecting but not that, and not so quickly.

If it's a place we haven't looked, sir, surely we should check.

And yet here I am, telling you no. You might read something into that.

What I read into that is that I need a new excuse. Good thing is, I'll be seeing Swainsbrook himself tomorrow night thanks to Eddie Thiekis. Maybe I can get him to give me a tour.

I turn my pod around and head back for central Firstfall. By the time I return Bix's call, he's almost hopping from one foot to another with impatience.

'Dude! You got to see this!'

Images stream to my lenses. It's the scene he showed us in Handl's office, the one of a headless torso floating in zero gravity, only now the torso is gone and a fine red mist of powder hangs in the air in its place. The walls are streaked and blotched where they used to be clean. Behind the scattergun of smears are an array of symbols that look like a carefully arranged pattern of thumbtacks, most either horizontal or vertical, a few at an angle. There are no curves.

'What I am looking at, Rangesh?'

'It's totally embedded in the telemetry from the station, dude. It's mixed with the real data, you know? Stuff that can't be faked. I mean, it's not piggybacked, it's *in* the data, so it *has* to be coming from out there! From space, dude! And not orbit, either. Proper outer space!'

The Tesseract has been over the routing logs. They're real. The signal is unquestionably coming through antenna 679 on the Institute roof. Professor Handl, now that Bix has shown him what to look for, has found it too. Yet as far as anyone can tell, antenna 679 is still dutifully tracking our dead solar station.

'Are you trying to tell me that someone went out there with a chopped-up body in ... in what, the trunk of their shuttle? All so they could beam pictures back to Magenta? Because ... because ...'

I can't find a because, other that the whole idea is absurd.

'Dude, I'm telling you that if they did, they're still out there.'

'It's a hoax, Rangesh. Just because it's coming from the

antenna here in Firstfall doesn't mean it's real. There could be a hack in the feed from the antenna itself, routing in an entirely new signal. There could be another transmitter blasting away at short range getting in through the sidelobes or something. There could be a transmitter in orbit sitting on the path from the antenna to the research station. Any of those and more – but one thing I'm damned sure of is that no one took a shuttle out to an abandoned space station in order to perform a decapitation and paint blood on the walls!'

Which *is* what it looks like.

'Boss dude, I hear you but ... But I already checked, right, and most of what you just said doesn't actually work out, you know? And, dude! There are still Masters' ships out there now and then, blocking out the stars!'

'No, Bix, there aren't, because all of this is a fucking hoax!' Shit. With Bix stuck in Nico, I'm going to have to look at the antenna myself. 'You still with Saleesh?'

'Sure.'

'You want me to talk to your professor again?' This time with a posse of Tesseract technicians. 'Whatever this is it needs to stop, so that antenna has to come apart. I'm surprised these videos aren't all over the net already.'

'Sure, okay, if you want, but I got this, you know? Um, dude, also, that writing on the walls? It's, like, Akkadian.'

'You what?'

'Ancient language, like, one of the first. You know? Earth. Babylon, Assyria, Egypt. That shit.'

'No, I don't know. How do *you* know?' No, wait, Saleesh. He knows because Saleesh would recognise it and he ... '*Shit*, Rangesh, have you shown this to Saleesh?'

'Dude, there's, like, maybe a dozen people on Magenta who even know what Akkadian *is*, you know? It's not, like, there's anyone who can actually *write* it.'

106

'Well, someone took the trouble to learn.' Whoever set this up, however elegant it turns out to be, they're going to be in an interrogation room for a very long time when I get my hands on them. 'Rangesh, find the creepy shit who made this! Put the Tesseract on tracing him, find him, and then throw as much wasting-police-time at him as you can!'

I drop the call and I leave a message for Liss. I need her to be Alysha and tell me what's on the sliver I'm supposed to give to Jacksmith. If I could, I'd disguise her up with the best fake skin face the Tesseract can manage and take her with me to the Institute tomorrow. I want her to meet *October*. I want her to meet her old friend Elizabeth Jacksmith. She deserves that much.

INSTANTIATION THREE

'There are a handful of dates every child knows by heart. They know their birthday. Maybe, if they come from a family still clinging to the old religions, they know Christmas, or how to formulate the date each year for Easter or Diwali, or Eid; but there are two dates we all know, every one of us.

'On the 20th of October 2056 they came riding their black monoliths like gravestones in the sky. That day marked the beginning of what would be the transformation of Earth and the transplantation of mankind to the thirty-six colonies. On that day they killed more than a billion of us. Maybe they were monsters, or demons, or angels, but whatever moniker we give them is moot. They never spoke. We never saw them. We haven't the first idea of who they were, what they wanted, why they did what they did or why they left as suddenly as they came.

'We remember that day. There are no public holidays, no celebrations, but we remember it nonetheless. Perhaps that's why, of all the come-and-go festivals of human civilisation, Halloween survives.

'But the other day we *do* celebrate. The 14th of March 2061. Liberation Day, resonant with a narrative of plucky humanity throwing off the shackles of their alien oppressors, abundant with stories of struggle and courage and heroic victory. The reality, I'm sorry to say, is that every such story is a fiction. The Masters simply left. The sad truth is that they might have been gone for weeks or months or maybe even a year before we realised, and it was simply that long before we understood that they'd withdrawn from everything they built. A century and a half later and here we are, and still no one understands who or what or why, or where they went. Their abandoned starships still carry the bewildered humans they left behind. In them we race to our future, fearful eyes fixed firmly on the past, for amid so much ignorance, one thing is certain.

'No one can promise they will not return.'

—Nikita Svernoi, addressing the 41st *October* conference in 2206

Elizabeth Jacksmith sits in her office in the Magenta Institute. Nikita Svernoi is dead, but the culture he represents rules Earth with a velvet fist, a quiet dictatorship of technocrats, a few hundred men and women who hold between them power over most of humanity. In quiet times they move unseen, content to lurk in the shadows, but these times are not quiet and so now they are out in the open. They are like sunlight, Elizabeth Jacksmith thinks, illuminating everything, casting light and shadow wherever they go, impossible to miss and yet impossible to pin down. If she was to put aside her own history, she might even admit to agreeing with their goals: first among them, after all, is unravelling the secrets of the Masters, secrets to which Iosefa Lomu might be the key and which she has pursued for half her life.

But history is the *Flying Daggers* speaking for Earth with antimatter-tipped missiles. History is old friends, colleagues and rivals who are dead. History is lying helpless with a bullet in her spine and never walking again.

Magenta has its cabals too. One by one, Elizabeth Jacksmith

calls to them. Instantiation Three watches through the office window, from a camera across the square focused though wind and rain to track the pupils of Doctor Jacksmith's eyes, eyes so dark that they seem almost black. When she looks at the world, it sees what she sees, reflected back. When she searches for data, it reads the words written across her lenses.

It is not alone in its vigil; but intent on Jacksmith, it does not see.

THREE

JACKSMITH

8

DIVERGENT SUN

It's getting late. I prod the Tesseract for more information on the Kaur case, for Kaur's movements after the abduction. While the real Kaur was locked up in an abandoned apartment, Alysha made her way to New Hope and boarded a Cheetah full of scientists and technicians heading towards the southern ice. I know that already, but with the records in front of me, I can see she took her time.

I track her back from her arrival at New Hope. She travelled directly from the Institute. There's a pod record for the journey and statements from witnesses. Kaur had several weather stations crated to take with her, and Alysha opened them. No one paid any attention to a young, nervous research assistant carrying out a last-minute inventory check, and whatever she smuggled down there, presumably she smuggled it back.

Back further. After her transformation into Kamaljit Kaur, Alysha spent the night in a cheap room rented by the hour down in the Squats. Forensics have been over it and found nothing. Even the Tesseract can't find anything in the gap between the hotel and bar where the real Kaur met Alysha, and I already know that story. I know where Alysha took her and I know they left the bar shortly before midnight. There's a pod log for their journey to the Squats and so I know exactly when they got there. I have to figure Alysha can't have spent all that long with Kaur but there's no log of a pod taking her away. It's a ten-minute ride to where she spent the night, half an hour to walk it, yet she didn't show up for almost another three.

The times don't add up. She went somewhere else between leaving Kaur and reaching the hotel; and I'm about to tear through all the pod records for the night, looking for any trace, but then I stop. It's the obvious thing to do, which means someone already did it and didn't find anything, because if they had then it would be in the files right in front of me. And Alysha would have *known* it was the obvious thing, too, because this is exactly the work she used to do.

She walked, then?

But there are no recordings of Kamaljit Kaur, nothing picked up by a facial recognition search for that night until she checked in as Kaur at that by-the-hour hotel. Which means she wasn't disguised as Kaur when she left the real one locked in a dead apartment in the Squats, but she *was* by the time she arrived ...

Which means she had to change.

I pull up a map of Firstfall's blind spots, the places where no camera would see her. It's not easy to move around this city without being seen but every bureau agent knows the tricks. It's long and tedious and I end up walking most of the routes myself to see if they work, but by the end I think I know where she went. There's only one place she could have reached on foot in that much time, stayed a while, and then been tucking herself into bed an hour later without anyone seeing her come and go, and that's the hydroponic lakes under the Squats. I take a pod to the edge of the lake and I know straight away that I'm right because the air smells of a hint of the sea and a whisper of Xen, the same smell Alysha had on her when she came to me in Mercy. She was here that night she stole Kaur's identity, and she came back again, too.

But why?

I look out over the water, as black and still as the void between the stars here in this cavern, six feet deep over lane after lane after lane of genetically tailored kelp. The only movement comes from a few battered old harvesting drones. I stare at the water but the water has no answers. I go back to the hotel where she stayed and rent the same room. I stare at the bed where she slept after she caged Kaur and wonder how much it troubled her to do that. In my mind's eye I can see her at the edge of the water, standing where I stood, heavy with the burden of what she's done, but I don't understand why she went there, why that place and not some other.

It's long past midnight. I'm exhausted. I lie back on the bed where Alysha slept and think about her and Kaur as I watch the news, as I trawl idly through chat forums and discussion groups, looking for anything about the return of the Masters or of mysterious videos from the Solar Intensity Research Station. I find nothing. If anything, those parts of the net are quieter than usual, most of Firstfall preoccupied with the suspension of the mag-lev and of orbital shuttle services, with how long it's going to last and why. I try looking for anyone on Magenta who knows anything about Akkadian, but that just takes me to Saleesh.

I don't get it. Someone went to a whole lot of trouble to hoax up these videos and yet it seems like they were sent to Meelosh and no one else, and Meelosh is dead and the videos are still coming. Is there really someone out there doing this, orbiting the sun a hundred million miles from home?

I search for Frank Swainsbrook and Settlement 16, but all I

find is what I already know: a crackpot cult in the middle of nowhere who believe the Masters are the messengers of God and claim to talk to them by killing themselves and then coming back. There's even an online aptitude test for people who want to join. The questions are weird: describe the colours of the last thing you remember. What was it? When was the last time you dreamed of insects? Or dolphins? I take the test and it tells me I'm not compatible. I can't figure it out, can't work out what it's looking for, but no one on Magenta dreams of dolphins or insects. Magenta doesn't have any.

I close my eyes. My Servant wakes me up eight hours later. I have an appointment with Professor Handl this afternoon, a soirée with Eddie's *October* friends in the evening, a shitload of crap to deal with before I get to either, and half the day has already gone. I summon a pod and bundle myself back to the surface as fast as I can, already late enough to miss the worst of the morning traffic. The rain is heavier than yesterday and the wind is picking up as a new storm edges towards us. The outlook is grim, storm after storm for at least a week. There are warnings of floods in the lower levels, emergency maintenance work already scheduled for the pumps, warnings of tunnel closures in the worst affected areas and the possibility of a complete shutdown on the surface. The good news is that the mag-lev should be open again by the end of the day – with added security checks, so expect delays. There remains a blanket ban on all flights out of the city until further notice.

Storm season. It happens every year. So far, no one is talking about any missing antimatter.

I use an undercity entrance to the bureau and settle in the Tesseract canteen, trying to figure how I can use the bureau AI to look for Alysha without looking like I'm looking for someone. When that doesn't work, I order a cup of the lichen-based abomination that substitutes for coffee and try to conjure an excuse to open up Frank Swainsbrook's hangar in New Hope. By the time Laura slips onto the bench beside me, my thoughts are all over the place: Alysha, Swainsbrook, New Hope's Hangar 13, Kamaljit Kaur, the hydroponic lakes ...

Laura pushes my recycled cardboard cup away and parks an empty one in front of me. She puts two vacuum flasks on the table between us and opens the first. The rich smell of real coffee bursts out. I take a deep breath and shiver – it's like an olfactory orgasm. Magentan coffee mostly tastes like hot water with a little dirt and a touch of Xen, and the bureau canteen is no exception, with or without the optional frothed-up sow's milk. I don't miss Earth all that much, but I do whenever I'm stupid enough to think about the coffee.

Laura pours some into my cup and some into her own. The second flask is warm frothy milk, real milk from Earth from actual cows. By now we're getting dirty looks from anyone nearby with a sense of smell. We both know what they're thinking: Patterson with her rich daddy whose family has more money than the rest of us put together, who works here even though she doesn't have to and still makes us look bad. Patterson who hires a flesh-and-blood nanny to look after her son because of the guilt she feels from not doing it herself, who only eats food imported from Earth and never mind the expense.

Six months of living with her means I know the last part isn't true, but she's not shy of her luxuries. Coffee. Whisky. Chocolate. A few other things. I also know she doesn't usually flaunt her money like this. Something must be up.

'Missing me?' she asks with a smirk. She passes me two lines of wrapped brown sugar. She knows exactly how I take it.

'Shit, Laws, you know I only stayed with you for the coffee.'

I still don't know exactly when she worked out that Alysha wasn't dead. Was it before or after she kicked me out? After, I think, but with Laura you can never be sure.

'The sex was good.' She smirks. 'You do good sex.'

I nod to the flask. 'I was well motivated.'

'Good sex for good coffee.' She nods. 'Seemed a reasonable arrangement at the time.' She sounds comfortable with the world today.

I raise my cup to her. 'Thanks.'

'You're welcome. Figured out yet whether you need to put Rangesh into a rocket and fire it at the sun?'

The question comes with a tiny twist of smug that tells me she knows something I don't.

'Not yet.' Coy and cautious. 'Why?'

'But you're still working on the Meelosh case?'

'Still am.' It's not exactly a lie. 'I'll be back at the Institute later, going over their antenna.'

She nods, savouring the suspense. 'You might want to make that sooner rather than later.' Her lip curls. 'That new friend you made in Nico. Zayab Saleesh. I read some of her work last night. Daft as a bag of spiders. Does she really believe the Masters were Prometheus, bringing the secret of fire to ancient Babylon? Or is that just for those turgid essays she writes?'

'Prometheus is from the Greeks.' Laura knows this perfectly well, but there's that look again. That I-know-something-you-don't look. 'What?'

'Those other names Saleesh found. You ever look them up?'

'Should I?' I can't help the surge of excitement.

'I'd say you should, since two more of them are dead.'

That earns her what she calls my impatient-cat look. 'What?'

'Suicides. Apparently they watched some fucked-up video and then cut their own throats.'

'You're shitting me!'

Laura shakes her head. 'Video came from some anonymous source. Sent to them out of the blue. What I don't know is how many other people it reached who *didn't* decide to kill

118

themselves.' She touches my hand for just a moment. 'Sorry, Keon, but you and Bix need to root out the fucker who did this.'

'Shit!' I need names and I need a timeline. 'When did the video get sent?'

Laura pings me a file. Saleesh said she'd found six possibilities, four of them with a single common ancestor. Meelosh was one of them and now two more are dead. That leaves three, and one of those is Rachael Cho.

'You need to get all three of these somewhere safe.'

'I know, but I can't move on Cho. Given her connections to ... you know ... Someone would notice. Just like with Saleesh. I—'

Cho's connection to Darius Vishakh and to Alysha is what she isn't saying. 'Laws! This is a fucking pattern!'

I look up and see people around us glance our way. You can't just leave her out there!

I'm not a fucking idiot! Himaru's watching her! It's covered! It just needs to stay outside the Tesseract, okay! 'This isn't some little nothing case any more.'

I was ready to write Meelosh off as a freak suicide. But *three* freak suicides? I don't think so.

You don't have time for shit on the side and I know you won't stop going after Alysha. 'If you need to hand this on to—'

'I don't.'

'Good. The other two suicides were in Disappointment. The bureau there is handling—'

'Bix can go.' They're reopening the mag-lev tonight but I can't leave Firstfall, not now, not when I know Alysha is close.

'Keep an eye on it. The Disappointment office somehow hadn't worked out that two identical suicides on the same day were maybe something to think about. They don't know about Meelosh and they certainly don't know about Saleesh. Make sure Rangesh keeps it that way. Just the video connection.'

'What about the other two on the list? You got them covered.'

No, and you're not going to like this. They're both from Firstfall but they both left on the same day Meelosh committed suicide. As best I can tell, Frank Swainsbrook personally flew them out to join his creepy little cult in Settlement 16. Laura frowns hard. What is it with lists of names at the moment?

I've got an interview with Swainsbrook this evening.

Good. My money says the video came from him somehow, and now he's conveniently trapped in Firstfall. Speaking of the lock-down, whoever stole that warhead used New Hope access codes that came from here. From right here in this fucking building.

Tesseract One?

Who else?

You think you can track them?

I think I've almost got him.

I send Laura a code to access our files on Meelosh and the videos from the SIRS. I tell her not to watch them when Jamie's around, which gets me a withering look.

'He's still in Disappointment, and that's where he's staying until this warhead shows up. What other help do you need?'

'Rangesh on Saleesh and the other suicides. I'll put the time-line together and keep hunting for where it's coming from at this end. I should get face time with both Swainsbrook and Jacksmith tonight. After that ...' I'm not sure what's more precious right now, Iosefa Lomu or a living blood descendant. 'Someone good from data forensics to work with Rangesh. This signal, whatever it is, it can't really be coming from an abandoned space station in orbit around the sun. I need someone who can figure out how it's being done.'

'Okay. And ...?'

Access to Hangar 13 in New Hope.

That gets her interest. Something unexpected.

Why? What's there?

Frank Swainsbrook's shuttle.

She doesn't need to know about Alysha and Betty Blue. I could ask Laura for help there too – looking someone without giving away that you're looking is the sort of sneakiness she'd know how to do – but if I ask then she'll know I've found a thread to pull. I trust Laura to a point, but only to a point.

I already asked Flemich, I add. He said no.

Laura nods. 'I'll see what I can do. When you go to the Institute, keep me in the loop, okay?'

'I'm going over there now.'

'Patch me in, okay?'

She packs up her coffee, ignoring the baleful looks from other agents around us. I message Professor Handl to tell him I'm going to be early and then follow her out. My Servant tells me there's a lull in the rain and that the wind has dropped to a mild sixty miles an hour. The Institute is right next door to the Tesseract and so I go up to the surface and walk, tasting the Magentan air, letting it clear my head. At the top of the Institute steps I call Rachael Cho.

'Agent Rause?' She picks up at once, like she's been expecting me.

'Are you okay?'

'Yes ...?' I hear the cautious question in her voice.

'Look ... we need to talk in person. I've got something I need to do for a couple of hours and then I'm coming over.'

'No. Not today. Tomorrow.' She says it like she already knows that's how it's going to happen.

'It has to be this afternoon. It's important.'

'I'll be ready by tomorrow. We can talk about Alysha.'

'I'm not coming to talk about ...'

But she's already hung up. I call again as I walk through the Institute doors but she doesn't answer. I ping her Servant to find out where she is but there's no response—

121

A woman in a burqa heads past the reception shells towards me.

I freeze.

Alysha?

The thought of her presence washes over me. Her nearness – even the *idea* of it – is like a drug, sense sharpening and yet dulling all other thought ...

The woman walks out into the morning light. The wind catches her. She sidesteps slightly as it whips cloth around her. Then she's gone.

Too short to be Alysha.

I shake her out of my head and message Cho: Tomorrow then. But stay away from the net until we talk.

I head down to Professor Handl's office, messaging Bix and Laura as I go. Handl is waiting for me with two technicians. The weather is getting worse and so we go straight to the roof. It's raining again by the time we get there, a light drizzle stinging my skin, the wind picking up. Handl looks at the sky.

'It's good that you came before the weather closes in. It could be days, maybe even a week before we have another chance. And ...' He lets out a little sigh and tells me that, as of this morning, all transmissions from the Solar Intensity Research Station have stopped. 'It happened shortly after sunrise. We haven't had a peep for more than three hours.'

I listen in as Laura and Bix ping messages back and forth. Handl shows us how the video signal is buried in the station telemetry, both streams of data intertwined as though they belong together. He nods enthusiastically when I say it has to be a hoax, but there's an anxiousness to him. Some part of him isn't so sure. The signals from his antenna look real.

We take our time as the rain grows steadily heavier. The Institute technicians strip out every panel. There are no scratches on the paintwork of the screws and the anti-tamper seals are intact. Handl powers down the antenna and opens up the receiver. He pulls out boards one by one and runs diagnostics. Everything is as it should be. Nothing draws more power than it ought. We run a visual check against the master drawings but there's nothing on any of the boards that isn't supposed to be there. The conformal coatings are pristine and perfect. No scratches. Nothing.

It's not the antenna. Which means someone is intercepting signals from the station, weaving in their own data and then retransmitting it before it gets here. It can't be a satellite in orbit around Magenta either, because Handl's antenna is tracking something moving around Magenta's sun, not around Magenta itself.

We go back inside, dripping wet and frustrated.

'All I can suggest is that someone set up another transmitter very close by. But if they did, surely we'd have found it!' Handl sounds perplexed.

Drone? suggests Bix.

Handl looks a little happier when I say this, but still nowhere near satisfied.

If this is supposed to be some sort of performance art, why hasn't it gone public? asks Laura.

Dude, you're only saying that because you haven't met Meelosh.

Meelosh is dead, Rangesh. Art is selfish. Art wants to bask in the wonder of others. This isn't art.

I can't think of anything else, you know? Or anyone else who might think that hoaxing …

Hoaxing? Hoaxing *what*?

I tune out for a moment. Handl is telling me why the transmission source can't be either a satellite in orbit or a drone or something else close by, technical stuff about synchronisation loss and retransmission delays and lobe cancellation and other

123

things like that, but I'm suddenly not listening. I've assumed that all of this is an elaborate con because the alternative is too bizarre; but if it's a con then I don't understand who's running it or why. It can't be meant for Meelosh now that Meelosh is dead, and so far the only other people seeing it are me, Rangesh, Laura, Handl and maybe one or two others in the bureau.

What does it mean if all of this is real? I ask. Cut through all the crap about dismembered bodies and you get to where it started: the silhouette of a huge black ship occulting the stars.

It means the Masters are back, says Laura, about as caustically as text can be.

So if that's what we're supposed to think, what's the point?

The question Alysha always asked. I turn to Professor Handl. 'Sorry. Could you say all that again?'

Handl nods vigorously, although by now it's more panic than enthusiasm that infects his tone.

'What I'm telling you, sir, is that it cannot be coming from any source other than the station itself! I see no alternative!'

What happens when this goes public? I ask, not that I need to. Panic at first. A hundred different factions, cults and politicians jumping on an apparent return of the Masters.

Twenty-four hours of fucking mayhem, pings Laura.

And then calm, because the Masters *aren't* here ...

Because nothing terrible has actually happened.

People will start to assume the whole thing is probably a hoax. Same as we are. What happens then?

I suppose we have to send someone out to the fucking station, don't we? To prove it.

Which could take weeks, if we can even manage it at all. Until then ...

A general restlessness. An unsettled world. But life largely going on as usual.

That's how it would be.

I think.

Okay. We send a shuttle out there as fast as we can, says Laura. One way or another we find out. We start that right now.

I've stopped listening to Handl again.

'So what are the choices here? It's all real? In which case someone flew a shuttle out there with a headless corpse ...'

Dude, I think you're supposed to think they flew out with a very alive not-yet corpse and then killed them, you know. With, like, knives and chanting and weird robes and ancient pictograms and stuff.

'Cuneiform,' mutters Laura.

'Is it possible the station's been hacked?' I ask. 'Someone's beaming stuff up from Magenta? Could the station simply be acting as a relay?'

Handl shakes his head. 'I have considered this, and it explains the ability to turn the telemetries on and off, of course. But these embedded new packets of data ... The changes to the communications protocol would require a change to the deep structural q-ware itself and ... It's not possible to control this from the outside. Yes, it could be done, but someone would have to go there and make physical changes to the station hardware for such a thing to be possible.'

'What's it for, man?' asks Bix.

'I'm sorry?'

'This station, you know? What's it, like, for?'

'It measures particle flux from Magenta's sun. Our star is a divergent star.' Handl doesn't wait for the inevitable question. 'It's moving away from the main sequence. Magenta has been growing brighter and hotter for millions of years, as far as we can tell from the records of Magenta's ice cores.'

'So, we're getting warmer?'

Handl smiles. 'In another few million years, Firstfall will be a tropical paradise. In a few million more, Magenta will no

125

longer be habitable. Of course, the storms will get worse and drive us all underground as the world warms.' He smiles again. 'However, the presence of indigenous life and so much liquid water clearly indicates this to be part of some cyclic behaviour, not a continuous trend. And before you ask, no, no one knows why our sun is behaving this way. That was the point of the SIRS, you see. To try and understand it.'

I try to see what this could possibly have to do with our videos and come up blank. 'You're certain the station can't be hacked from the outside?'

'Entirely. It was a Fleet station at the start, and inhabited, and it has always been Fleet policy to ensure no possibility of an external takeover of any manned vessel. There is no physical connection between the exterior antenna arrays and the systems that control the station. These are entirely separate things, always. There is no path through which to hack. You simply can't take over a Fleet station from the outside.'

'So whoever did this could still be out there?'

'Oh no, no, no. The station cannot support an organic crew in its current state, but that would also be quite unnecessary. You would need to board the station and establish a connection between the communication arrays and the internal systems. It would require considerable specialist expertise and equipment and a thorough understanding of the station data architecture, but it *is* perfectly possible. Once that was accomplished, everything else could be done remotely.'

'From Magenta?'

Handl nods. 'With a suitably power transmitter, of course.'

'So what you're saying is that someone went out there and rewired your station?'

'I know that must seem very unlikely, but I'm afraid I see no other way.'

I thank Handl for his time and leave. His door closes behind me. The voices in my head are loud and fractious but they all agree on one thing: whatever this is, it's far more dangerous than a piece of concept art.

This isn't happening in a vacuum, I say. At some point this gets out. We'll have a day of general panic, but eventually everyone will figure the Masters *aren't* here and that it's a hoax just like we do. But for those first few days we'd have to have a curfew. A state of emergency. Something like that. Even after it calms we'll have a restless world. So who benefits from that? If this was Earth then I'd look to see what elections were coming up, but Magenta doesn't have elections.

What if they're still out there, you know? complains Bix. How do we know they're not?

Because it's all fucking faked, Rangesh! Laura is at the edge of her patience. *All* of it. Rause is asking the right question though.

October? I suggest.

I don't see it, dude. I mean, why? All it's going to do is make everyone a bit scared, like. Right? So ... so what? You know?

Laura hisses. You think this is somehow about Iosefa fucking Lomu? I'll tell you what *I* think, Rause. I think someone needs to get the fuck out there. I think you need to put Rangesh in a rocket and fire him at the sun.

Dude! Someone needs to watch Saleesh, you know!

And Officer Arkeva? I ask.

Man! What are you saying?

We talk in circles but none of us has an answer because none of us can see where this is going. I ask the Tesseract to calculate the logistics of a trip to the sun and back. I'm not entirely sure whether it's even possible, but the AI comes back saying it could be done. The obvious way is to refit one of the orbital shuttles based in Firstfall and Disappointment. The refit would take a couple of weeks and the maths of interplanetary travel mean two more weeks to reach the solar station and a full month to get back again. All of which would mean decommissioning one of Magenta's two orbital shuttles for two months, maybe three, and I figure it pretty much would have to be the return of the Masters for real for anyone to agree to that. The Tesseract also offers a second possibility: Magenta's six Kutosov interceptors aren't much more than an engine and a fuel tank with a cockpit on the end. They could do a similar profile, maybe even quicker. They don't have the life support to carry a human pilot for so long, but if we replaced the pilot with a shell then we could fly it remotely from Magenta orbit.

Vishakh's shuttle, says Laura.

What about it?

Dude! Laws is right! We could use it?

It's ours until we agree to give it back. It's a long-range shuttle designed for interplanetary trips and it's just sitting in New Hope being useless. Fuel it up and it's good to go.

There's a long silence.

Dudes?

Laura doesn't say anything. Nor do I.

Dudes! No. No way am I flying out to the sun! Man, what are you like?

Swainsbrook has a shuttle too, I say, which shuts them up. We all know perfectly well that if anything goes out that far into space, it'll be a remotely piloted drone.

Traffic control says it hasn't moved for the last three months, says Laura after a short pause.

So? If this is a hack then it could have been set up years ago. Swainsbrook uses his shuttle to fly directly out to the *Fearless*. That means it's got the range.

I leave Laura to chew on that and Bix to chew on the video content, looking for any clues to prove they're not real, while I take a pod out to New Hope. The spaceport keeps meticulous logs of everything that comes and goes. If I can't get into

Hangar 13, I can at least find out when the *Betty Blue* last landed, where it came from and what it was carrying. I ought to be able to track its flight history in the Magenta system since the day Frank Swainsbrook first showed up from Earth. And if I can do *that*, I can find out if there are missing weeks where it might have taken a detour off to the sun.

The first part is easy: according to orbital traffic control, the *Betty Blue* launched exactly ninety-three days ago, logged outbound to the *Fearless* and then to Earth. Trouble is, the same records say she never came back, while New Hope has the *Betty Blue* back in her hangar two days later. Both automated systems are adamant that their mutually contradictory data is correct.

I wander New Hope until I find a human being, point out the anomaly and how it's easily resolved by opened the hangar to have a look. That gets me referred up the chain of command until I'm talking to Naseem Khan, New Hope's head of operations, who tells me that he can't open the hangar because there's a Tesseract lock on the codes. Whatever is in there, I need permission from my own people to open it. It doesn't seem diplomatic to suggest that that might be a problem, but I think Khan sort of gets the drift because he suggests having a look at the hangar surveillance cameras instead. Safety regulations mean the cameras can't be locked out, not even by the Tesseract.

He's right. We're not locked out. Every surveillance camera in Hangar 13 is dead.

We exchange a look.

'What if there's a fire?' he asks.

'What if there's an antimatter warhead?'

Yeah, he doesn't like that a lot more than he doesn't like a fire.

'So how do we get in there?'

'We don't. Not without authorisation.'

He seems annoyed with me now that I can't simply ask for it.

'No wiring conduits? No air conditioning vents? No crawl-spaces?'

He shakes his head.

'You must be able to get a drone inside at least?'

'All the old hangars have hermetic seals.' He gives me a hopeless look. 'Against the weather. Against Xen blowing in on the wind when the shuttle inside is opened. It was a decontamination issue.'

Decontamination? To stop Xen getting to Earth? I don't think so; but now Kahn pings me the operating procedures from New Hope as they were a hundred years ago when these hangars were built, when the world was a very different place and no one knew for sure what xeno-organisms existed on Magenta, or what might happen if two wholly alien biospheres ever came into contact with one another. The answer, as it turned out, was nothing much, and the decontamination facilities were long ago stripped for recycling. But the hangars themselves remain as they were – hermetically sealed.

I ping the Tesseract, looking to see who has the hangar locked down. The answer isn't exactly a surprise: Assistant Director Flemich, who already told me to get lost.

Khan and I talk for another minute but there's nothing we can do except our jobs. Khan will throw a rocket at the Tesseract and demand access so he can restore his surveillance cameras. Me, I'm going to the source. I'm on my way to the Magenta Institute and a meeting with Frank Swainsbrook.

9

A SOIRÉE AT THE
INSTITUTE

I'm in an elevator going down to a conference suite deep under the Magenta Institute. Outside, standing on the steps, protesting in the rain, a small group of bedraggled students are complaining about the proposed reversal of the Sovereign Rights Act, trying to make a fuss and largely being ignored. Somewhere below, Eddie Thiekis and his *October* friends are gathered, and now I'm about to meet them. I'm not sure how I feel about this. On the one hand, Eddie seems decent. On the other, Darius Vishakh tried to kill both me and Alysha, and I'm pretty sure *October* were signing his paycheques. For all I know, I'm about to come face to face with whoever ordered Alysha's execution. I won't know it, but *they* will.

The elevator stops. The doors open into a reception foyer full of the buzz of conversation. Well-dressed Magentans gather in clusters: Eddie and his friends clutching flutes of wine imported at vast expense from Earth. A barrage of polite pings hits my Servant, asking who I am, making quiet introductions. When I spot Eddie, he's already heading towards me.

'Agent Rause!'

He's wearing a broad smile, the brooding man I met on the roof of the MagentaNet building carefully tucked out of sight. His cheeks are flushed. He's on his way to being drunk.

'Eddie.' I nod.

For a moment I think he's going to hug me; instead he rests a hand on my elbow and guides me into the room.

'We're all here for the Selected Chamber's big decision.' He laughs. 'Except we all already know what it will be.'

'Do we?'

'Of course we do! Elizabeth won't like it, so mostly we're here to talk her out of doing anything stupid and find a way we can all work together. It's best for everyone that we let the Earthers have what they want. It's certainly best for Magenta.'

He's guiding me towards the largest cluster of people. I don't need my Servant to recognise the woman in the wheelchair at its centre: when Elizabeth Jacksmith is done with Iosefa Lomu, she might just become the most famous face on the whole of Magenta.

Eddie pulls me aside as we approach. His voice drops to a whisper and he's suddenly the man I met on top of MagentaNet again. 'She's not wrong. None of us actually *want* to bend over and spread our cheeks for the Earthers, and I haven't forgotten Shyla. It's just what's best for the greater good. That's all there is to say.'

He draws away, all smiles again.

Jacksmith is holding forth on something but stops as Eddie brings me to the fringe of her group.

'Bloody hell! Agent Keon Rause! What are you doing here?'

She's grinning like she might be honestly pleased to see me. Maybe she is: the last time we were together was when the *Flying Daggers* tried to kill us.

The *Flying Daggers* – which, I remind myself, is still up there.

'Agent Rause is interested in joining our little cabal,' says Eddie.

I'm not but it'll do. Jacksmith's grin flickers through disbelief to understanding. 'Then you're an idiot, but I'm glad to see you.' She turns briefly to the others around her. 'Without the efforts of several people from next door, the Earthers would have Iosefa already. Agent Rause here was nearly killed.' She fixes me with her gaze again. 'Magenta owes you a debt. And so do I.'

She holds out her hand, offering it, taking me completely by surprise. A handshake on Earth doesn't mean a great deal but on Magenta it means everything. It's like a blood pact. I have to explain this to Earthers when they offer and I don't reciprocate; but this is Elizabeth Jacksmith, born in Nico, the city of pigs, Magentan through and through, as are most of the men and women around us. She knows exactly what she's doing. She's telling me – telling *them* – that we're on the same side through thick and thin, no matter what.

I hesitate. I don't know this woman, not well. I was almost sure that she and Darius Vishakh were on the same side, but I was wrong. In a way she's a hero. She was Alysha's friend, too, close enough that Alysha invited her to our wedding ...

On impulse I slip my hand into a pocket and close my fingers around the sliver Alysha gave me. I palm it and shake Jacksmith's hand, passing it to her. We were together when the *Flying Daggers* tried to shoot us down. She put herself on the line for Lomu; but most of all, six years ago, her words saved Alysha's life. Maybe I've come to understand her, the depth of her conviction. Maybe that's enough.

Her smile shifts. Warms. The handshake is a public gesture not lost on the people around us. I doubt she's shaken any of *their* hands, not one of them, and now she's doing this in front of them, fully aware of its significance. But it's more than that. She wants this. I realise she actually means it. I realise, a moment later, that so do I.

I let go. Jacksmith palms the sliver and withdraws without a glimmer of surprise. I ping her.

I need to talk to you about Kamaljit Kaur.

'You were familiar with Doctor Kettler's work?' she asks me. Leave the poor girl alone. She went through hell.

'A little.'

I take stock of the people around me. There's Eddie, of course, who as good as owns the architecture of Magenta's planetary communications networks. Next to him, Jimmy O'Hare owns a good piece of what Eddie doesn't. I don't know anything about him except that according to the little tags Eddie is pinging to my Servant, Jimmy is *October*.

The other Kamaljit Kaur. I need to know where she went.

'I know he was looking for the descendants of Iosefa Lomu.'

Jacksmith beams. 'I think we may have found one.' She came back to Firstfall with you in the medevac Cheetah. I never saw her again.

I think back to my conversation with Eddie. 'Whoever it is, I don't want to know. Treat her well, that's all.' You saw her on the ice, though.

Beside O'Hare are a man and a woman I'd recognise without any help from my Servant. Siamake Alash, former Speaker of the Selected Chamber, exposed a couple of years back for being in Fleet's pocket. Beside him is his elder sister, Raisa, supposedly the one who pulled his strings. Siamake is a traitor to his world and I don't understand how he isn't in prison, yet here he is. I see how he seems to defer to Raisa. My Servant notes the names of her two aides.

Your people already have my statement.

Across the room, not far away, is Chief Morgan, head of the

bureau. The big boss of the Tesseract. Not *October*, according to Eddie's tags.

I want to hear it from you.

Three men clustered on the other side of Jacksmith look as though they'd been in some conversation of their own before I arrived. Eddie's tags highlight all three. The old one who looks like the gravity's getting to him is Ranu Kurudu, who made his fortune in pigs and owns most of Nico. The young squat one is some distant cousin, Pradash Prabu, journalist and a rising star with Eddie's Channel Nine. They say Eddie's grooming him to be the next Enki.

Kaur came to the Cheetah. She said she'd been on the surface setting up her weather stations when the attack came. I knew her, so I let her in. That was when someone stunned me.

'Are you aware of Doctor Steadman's work?' The third man, tall and muscular, is Frank Swainsbrook, and his question is aimed straight at me.

When I came to, I was still in the Cheetah. We were in the air, on autopilot, coming back to the base. Are you listening, Rause?

'I know a little,' I say. Yes.

'Is it true?'

Kaur was out cold. Stunned as well. You were there too.

I make a helpless gesture. 'I don't know what—'

'I mean, sir, is it true that the Masters' ships travel in time as well as space? That we're not actually in the same frame of time reference as Earth or the other colonies?'

And Darius. You and Darius were almost dead.

'That's exactly what the Steadman–Kettler telescope would—' Jacksmith begins, but Swainsbrook cuts her off.

'I want to know what our secret agent thinks. He probably knows things the rest of us don't.' Swainsbrook flashes me a wink. 'Ain't that right?'

135

I want Frank to pay for a radio telescope in Magenta to continue Nicholas's research. Say something useful. Make him say yes.

Kaur stunned you and you didn't tell anyone? I recognise Swainsbrook's swagger and the drawling accent. North America. Texas.

'Scientifically Elizabeth is right—'

'Of course I am!' Jacksmith snorts. I didn't say it was Kaur who stunned me!

'Based on what I saw of his research when we recovered his notes, he believed he was on to something. My understanding is there's no way to be sure without more data gathered from at least one of the colonies, preferably several.' I have no idea how far Steadman got before Vishakh had him killed, but that's what I remember.

Swainsbrook laughs out loud. 'Well, ain't that a thing! To think that we might exist five thousand years in the past. Here we are, drinking champagne made from grapes that ain't even been grown yet. Heck, five thousand years back, ain't we all running around in loincloths and building pyramids …?'

Kaur said a shell ambushed her. It must have been waiting for me to open the doors. As soon as I did, it took her out.

'… But I tell ya, it ain't going to be called the Steadman–Kettler Array if Frankie Swainsbrook's writing the cheque.'

The old money arrogance oozes out of Swainsbrook like a bad smell.

'I'm sure we can find some flexibility.' Jacksmith gives me a little nod. *Thank you.* There were a lot of shells about at the time, and I knew Kaur.

Her story doesn't ring true. It's too easy and I don't buy it, not when we all knew what we were up against.

Himaru left a man with you. He get stunned too?

There's also the small matter of a stun charge being effective for no more than a minute or two. I don't know exactly how long Vishakh and I were gone, but whoever rescued us must have been missing for at least an hour.

Yes.

I don't think I believe you.

'Mind you, we might just ask the Masters right out, don't you think?' Swainsbrook raises an eyebrow as I stare at him in bewilderment. No one else bats an eye, although maybe they roll a few. If this is some joke then I don't understand it.

'What do you mean?' I ask. I think you always knew who Kaur really was.

'Tell him about your grand plan, Frank,' says someone. I don't see who but I hear the derision in their voice.

'Tell me, Secret Agent Rause, do you believe in God?' Frank asks, apparently oblivious.

'Which one?'

'*The* God, son! The ultimate creator who promises salvation from our sins through the body of His Son, the Lord Jesus Christ.'

'I had a partner who believed in Allah, which amounts to much the same thing as far as I can see.'

I meet Swainsbrook's eye in time to see his face cloud with a momentary frown. 'Not really, son, but let that be for another day. Try this, then: do you believe you have a soul?'

I struggle for an answer and find I don't have one.

'It's not something I've given much thought.' Suddenly I'm thinking of Liss. Does *Liss* have a soul? It seems ridiculous because she's a machine, and how can a machine have a soul? But isn't that what we all are? Biological machines?

Jacksmith hasn't answered my question about Kaur. Out of nothing, something clicks. Her Iosefa speech. *I'd like to personally thank Agent Rause ...*

Which Agent Rause?

'Maybe you should, son,' says Frank.

'Do *you* believe we have a soul?' I ask. You knew who she really was.

'I do, sir.'

'Then perhaps you can tell me what that actually means.'

Who, Agent Rause?

'I mean the essential spiritual nature of who and what we are, each of us as an individual, the spark of anima placed inside us at our moment of conception by nothing less than the hand of God Himself.'

People around us are starting to drift away, bored.

I'm quite sure you know who.

'Think about it, son. You know there's more to this world than science can measure. We *all* know that because we all know what the Masters were and what they did, just like we all know that our science doesn't even begin to understand them. You know why that is, son?'

'We know what the Masters were? That's news to me.'

'Oh, Rause!' snaps Jacksmith. 'For pity's sake stop encouraging him!'

Kaur, Doctor Jacksmith. I'm waiting.

Frank smiles. 'The Masters are free souls no longer burdened by physical form. The reason we don't understand them is because we're so blinkered that we cannot bring ourselves to look for them in the right way.'

'You mean—'

'I mean that if we only ever look for understanding in the physical world when the real truth lies somewhere else entirely, how can we hope to succeed? I mean ...'

Please make him shut up.

'... that we need to look beyond, that's what I'm saying.'

Kaur, Elizabeth.

Jacksmith clutches at her head. 'Frank! Please stop! I can literally hear the screams of dying brain cells all around me!'

I throw Jacksmith a look. Swainsbrook shrugs. Her disdain doesn't seem to bother him. 'Son, I don't mean to force myself on anyone who isn't ready to hear the Word. But maybe now is the time to open our minds just a cautious little crack and ask ourselves: are some of the mysteries of our current circumstances perhaps amenable to illumination by some thinking of the kind to which we are not generally accustomed? How is it that a man more than a century ago could do what no man has done ever since? How is it that the good Doctor Stay found what he did when that finding was so immeasurably improbable?'

'It wasn't *immeasurably* improbable,' growls Jacksmith.

The conversation has wandered a long way from what I wanted. I turn back to Frank.

'You own a shuttle, is that right, Mister Swainsbrook? The *Betty Blue*?'

Everyone else is watching Frank so I'm the only one who catches the flicker of hesitation in Jacksmith's face.

'Call me Frank, son. And yes, I sure do.'

'Hangar 13 in New Hope, right?' Where is she, Elizabeth?

'That sounds about right.'

I don't know what you're talking about.

Alysha. 'When was the last time you used it?' You knew Kaur was Alysha all along. It's a guess, but Jacksmith is far too smart for this story about a shell she never saw coming, and no way was she left out cold for a full hour by a shot from a stunner.

I see a flicker of a frown. She's trying to work out where I stand, what to tell me. Swainsbrook wears a similar frown, like he doesn't get why I'm asking about the *Betty Blue*.

'About three months back,' he says. 'Why do you ask?'

'You want to tell me where it is now?'

Frank grins, wide open like he's got nothing to hide.

'Still in its hangar, son. Or at least I sure hope so!'

You've heard my story, Rause. It's the only one I have to offer. To anyone.

'You used it three months ago? Where did you go?'

'Up to orbit to meet a few old pals who happened to be in system, then back to the surface. Nothing sinister, I swear before the Lord.'

'And no one's used it since?'

Frank laughs. 'I sure hope not, son!'

I'm about to press him but the young Indian beside him, Prabu Pradash, gets in first.

'Is it true that someone in Fleet knew where to find Iosefa Lomu's body before the Stay expedition even set off?' he asks.

It takes me a moment to realise the question is aimed at me, not at Swainsbrook or Jacksmith. As far as I know, the answer is yes, Darius Vishakh knew. *How* he knew, though, that's the mystery – as is how Pradash knows to ask that question, because the only other person in this room who knows what really happened is Jacksmith; but she's frowning again, annoyed. Probably at me.

Well?

I look at the faces around me and realise I'm wrong: Jacksmith and I *aren't* the only people here who know. Sure, mostly I'm seeing bemused bewilderment, but not from Swainsbrook. *He* knows, too. He shouldn't, but he does ...

I know she's alive, Elizabeth. I know she's on Magenta. You knew who Kaur was and what she was after. And you were ready to let it happen?

Do I have to repeat myself, Agent Rause?

Do you *want* me to tell them how the first expedition knew where to go?

Pradash picks up on the glance between us, which doesn't help. 'Doctor Jacksmith?' he asks.

'I have nothing to say about that,' snaps Jacksmith. 'You'll have to ask Doctor Stay. Or perhaps Agent Rause here *does* know something after all. More than he's letting on, perhaps.'

Go ahead. No one will believe you.

'I can't comment on an ongoing investigation and neither can anyone connected to it,' I say, hoping to bite an end to any more questions. 'Unfortunately, as you well know, that includes Doctor Jacksmith.'

Pradash nods, unfazed. 'The bureau has taken Darius Vishakh, rumoured to be the head of Fleet Intelligence in Magenta, into custody. Is it true that he found out the location of the crash site by flatlining?'

And how the hell does Pradash know that?

'It's an interesting idea,' I say. 'Although an unlikely one. As I said, I can't comment.'

'But you *are* aware that Mister Vishakh made several visits to the flatliner known as Event Horizon, yes?'

Real name Rachael Cho. Shit. I need to shut this down ...

'Unlikely?' Swainsbrook laughs. 'You've got some learning to do there, my new friend!'

Jacksmith rolls her eyes. Eddie chuckles at my shoulder.

'Frank has some ... *unusual* ideas.'

'Sir, you'll be taking those unusual ideas a damn sight more seriously when I open that door and there we are, all of us talking to the Masters themselves.'

There it is again. Talking to the Masters ... And I can see Pradash still looking at me, still waiting for some sort of answer, but it's almost as though the rest of the circle around me is all rushing in at once to give me cover.

'Cousin, please don't get Frank started on this again ...'

'You know Mister Swainsbrook here is planning on calling the Masters back to Magenta by getting stoned ...?'

'Elizabeth, doll, when are you going share what you've found about Iosefa ...?'

I turn back to Jacksmith. Whoever impersonated Kaur was working for Fleet. You understand that, right?

I understand that some debts one repays as one can.

Pradash butts in again: 'Is it true that this Event Horizon is a possible blood relative—'

'Absolutely not!' Jacksmith bursts out laughing. 'Good grief! Where *do* you people get your ideas?'

What do you mean? I ask.

Ask me again after we see how this vote goes.

I see how Swainsbrook stares at Pradash, eyes narrowed, and I catch the glances Jacksmith throws, first at Pradash and then at Frank. Something is going on here, some secret none of them are pleased to discover isn't theirs alone.

Rachael Cho. The Meelosh videos. Saleesh's list. I turn on Frank.

'Mister Swainsbrook, I gather you recently acquired some Magentan recruits.'

He's good. He swings that smile of his on to me without a trace of duplicity. 'Sure have.'

'Want to tell me how that came about?'

His grin widens. 'I already knew a little of what was coming before young Elizabeth here went and told the whole world about her little discovery. So I had my people get in touch with a few of the natives we thought might be suitable to see if they were keen to join. Seems like a good few of them were, for which I'm mighty grateful. We'll take all the help we can: it ain't going to be a cakewalk crossing the divide between this world and the astral plane where the good Lord shepherds those who have been Saved.'

I don't know what to do with that, except that *a good few* sounds like more than the two from Saleesh's list.

'How many did you contact, Frank?'

'I don't know precisely. Say a few dozen?'

142

A few dozen? Saleesh had six names. Six! 'Was Une Meelosh one of them?'

'Sure was.'

'You contacted him personally?'

'That I did.'

'Why?'

'To impress upon him the importance of our endeavour, sir, and to be sure he understood the value that I personally would assign to his contribution, should he wish to be a part of it.' For a moment Swainsbrook's smile is gone, like he's getting impatient at how I don't understand something. 'I didn't contact just anyone, son. We're talking the top psychics on the planet.'

'Psychics?' I almost choke. 'Did you send them a video?'

'Promotional material and the like to explain who and what we are. Sure.' He frowns. 'Why?'

I'm only half paying attention to the rest of the room, but now Jacksmith turns away as three enormous wall screens flick on. They all show Channel Nine, a reporter standing in front of the Selected Chamber. She has my attention if only because no one ever does this any more. Something momentous must be happening.

'And the result of the vote is just coming in …'

'She's a good face, your girl, Eddie.'

Jacksmith sighs. 'I suppose we had to make an event of this. Still …'

She's tense. No one else in the room seems that bothered, but Jacksmith is as taut as a drum. On the screen, the reporter nods.

'The final tally is confirmed. The Selected Chamber rejects by fifty-one to forty-nine Representative Hyun Soy's proposed amendment to the Sovereign Rights Act.'

There are whoops and a couple of people punch the air. 'That's it!' 'Shit!' 'We're out!'

'Yeah. Fuck Earth.'

143

Chief Morgan is grinning and nodding, but not the *October* crowd. Every one of them is silent.

Jacksmith's fists are clenched white-knuckle tight.

There's your answer, Rause. Lomu stays on Magenta. Earth and *October* can sing for whatever scraps we decide to feed them.

'This is a disaster.' Eddie is shaking his head.

I scan a smattering of political sites trying to figure out exactly what just happened and why it matters. It doesn't take long to figure the answer. Technically what's been rejected is a change to the law around Xen refinement, but what it means in practice is that Magenta just refused to open up to Earth-based pharmaceutical combines. To investment and a new golden age, if you believe Channel Six and other sites in favour. To plunder and virtual annexation if you don't. Either way, we just flipped a middle finger to Earth. The combines can still come, sure, but they'll be subject to Magentan law, Magentan regulation, Magentan oversight of everything they do, and Magentan taxes.

Eddie leans down beside Doctor Jacksmith.

'What did you do, Elizabeth?'

He looks far away and sad, even while his own channel trumpets Magenta's defiant stand for independence.

'What I had to, Eddie. I told people the truth.'

'Kaltech,' I say, as it dawns on me who we'd be letting in. I look at Eddie and shake my head in disbelief. 'You supported this?'

He doesn't say anything. He doesn't seem to even hear.

'Eddie! After Shyla? You supported this?'

His eyes lock to mine, taut with sudden anger. 'Yes, Rause, I did. I told you I don't like it and I don't want it, but it means peace. That's all that matters. The price of fucking peace. I've still got my boys. I mean for them to have a future.'

I look around the room, picking out the ones like Eddie who are quiet and shaking their heads, or else angry and railing at

144

the people around them. These are *October* on Magenta, the men and women who want to give our world away. Already I hear talk of forcing a second vote. The conversations around me grow louder, more animated, angry. I see Chief Morgan almost in a shouting match with someone I don't recognise but whom my Servant tells me is Rashid Rapati, a man who owns a good chunk of Firstfall, including the Roseate Project. I hear the arguments all around me: *Why can't you just accept it, we don't want Earth here. There has to be a second vote. People need to see sense. How soon can we force it back on to the floor? Who turned? Who can be turned back?*

Shit like that.

Here in this room, among these people with their wealth and their power and their quiet influence, this is where Magenta's future will be made. Not out there.

'Earth will invade if they have to,' says Eddie to Jacksmith. 'Your damned pride, Elizabeth! You want to see everything we built burned down?'

I don't know where she is, Rause. And I don't know whose side she's on.

The voices around us falter and fail. A hush starts to fall. I wonder if another grand announcement is about to come but the faces around me are frozen, and the looks aren't the triumph or frustrated anger of a moment ago. Instead I see shock, amazement, even outright horror. Jacksmith's expression shifts to a deep frown. I see her shake her head ...

My Servant pings once. Rangesh. Dude. Channel Two. It's happening.

I don't need to look, because someone already switched the screen on the wall.

'... taken from the Magentan Solar Intensity Research Station more than two weeks ago ...' says a faceless voice-over. More words wash over me, meaningless noise because I'm not listening, I'm staring. The sequence on the screen is one I haven't seen before but I know exactly what it is: the field of stars from the Solar Station, the black monolith ships clear, catching the light of Magenta's sun just enough to give them definition.

This time there are three of them. They hang there, still. The room falls silent. The caption on the screen echoes the question I see in every face around me.

The return of the Masters?

My Servant pings again. The Tesseract. Flemich. Then again and again. Everyone around me starts to move, dispersing almost to an unseen cue.

One cuts through all the others.

Keys! They're going to move on Jacksmith. Right now.

It's Alysha.

10

BETTY BLUE

I stay close to Jacksmith and scan the room for threats. I'm not armed, not here. Jacksmith is supposed to be under bureau protection but I don't spot any familiar faces except the Chief. My Servant is trying to trace the warning, trying to find a source and running in endless circles. No surprise. Alysha wouldn't make such a simple mistake, but I know it's from her because it comes with a single frame from one of the clips she left with me in Mercy. I recognise Jacksmith's office, the picture of Jacksmith with the *Fearless* crew. Jacksmith is about to tell Alysha that Darius Vishakh is a snake.

'*You* did this?' Jacksmith has hold of Eddie Thiekis's arm. 'Some "return of the Masters" bullshit? *That's* the best you can do?'

'No. I don't …'

Eddie looks as bewildered as everyone else … No. *Almost* everyone else. As I scan faces, looking for anyone eyeing Jacksmith in a way I don't like, I see Frank Swainsbrook smiling. He doesn't look bewildered or confused at all, more like a man seeing exactly what he was expecting all along.

147

I ping Laura: Channel Two. You seeing this?

I watch Swainsbrook's eyes as I do, because if there's a killer in the room here, right now, then my money says he's being paid by Frank.

Where are you?

At the Institute. Swainsbrook and Jacksmith are here. I think Jacksmith might be in danger. And I got to say, faced with the apparent return of the Masters, Swainsbrook isn't looking all that surprised.

I don't tell her about the message from Alysha because I don't need to. I understand now what this absurd hoax is about, and Laura must see it too, because I almost got it right: Magenta doesn't have elections, but we *do* have votes.

Someone not very happy with her? Laura doesn't let me down.

Quite a few someones.

You can stay close?

If I have to, but I'm not armed and she's under bureau protection, right?

A hesitation, and I know what she's thinking: Tesseract One.

Yes, she is. Stay close anyway, okay? Get her somewhere safe. I'll get a Reeper to you.

I'm not sure what qualifies as *safe* right now, but not this milling crowd of wealth and privilege. Jacksmith is still arguing with Eddie, fierce, the air blue with anger. Neither has eyes for anyone else. Swainsbrook is at the door, on his way out, but I catch him looking back as he leaves, straight at me with a wide smile across his face. His eyes meet mine. He makes a pistol with his fingers, points it at me and fires, then winks. I push myself between Eddie and Jacksmith.

'We need to leave,' I tell her. 'Right now. You need to be somewhere safe.'

'What I need is for this fat old fool to show some spine and get this ridiculous charade off his networks.'

'So I can be accused of censorship? Of politically motivated interference?' Eddie has gone bright red in the face. I've seen this fury before.

'Fuck that, Eddie! This is more important!'

'I don't think that—'

'Oh, Eddie, *thinking* was never your forte! *Doing*, that's what you were about! The man I remember had backbone! He believed in Magenta! What happened to the—'

'We need to go *now*.'

I start trying to push Jacksmith's wheelchair. The wheels lock at once and I don't get very far, but it shocks her out of her tirade that I even try. I've received a credible and immediate threat to your life.

The anger doesn't leave her eyes as she and Eddie stare each other down. Fine. Go.

She snaps Eddie a last fiery glare. 'This isn't going to be like the blockade, Eddie. Earth has changed. Roll over for them this time and they'll suck us dry.'

I pipe security camera feeds from around the room to my lenses as we leave, scouting the way out ahead, looking around each corner before we get there. I walk at Jacksmith's side, uncertain whether the threat is more likely to come from ahead or behind as we make our way towards the lifts. As we get close, Jacksmith stops at an access door that doesn't look like anyone has used it for years. It opens at her touch into a tunnel that isn't much more than bare rock.

'This way,' she says.

'Where are we?'

'A way out most people don't know.'

Doors lead into musty storage rooms on either side, some empty, others filled with boxes, everywhere covered by a thick film of dust. Jacksmith stops at one. She pings me a code as it opens.

'If anything happens to me tonight, here he is.'

Beyond the door is a large silver freezer, just the right size to hold a body.

'Lomu?'

'Iosefa Lomu.'

A man dead for a century and a half, abducted from his home on a South Pacific island, carried across the stars by aliens we don't understand, and now the Earthers might just go to war to get him back.

'Someone apart from me needs to know where the corpses are hidden, right?' says Jacksmith. She nudges me aside so the door can close, hiding Lomu away. 'Don't imagine he'll still be there a couple of days from now.'

I want to ask how many samples she's already taken, how scattered they are, whether the DNA slices sent to Earth and Fleet were really from Iosefa or cut from some other random corpse like Eddie seems to think. I want to ask what she's found, what she knows, how he did it, whether all the wonder and the rumour is true. Could he really show us how to understand the Masters, how to use the ships and technology they left behind? All those questions and dozens more, but I know Jacksmith won't answer.

An armoured door at the end of the corridor opens into a cave, dark except for a few dim red lights scattered overhead. There's a pod waiting. When the door in the cave wall closes behind us, I can't see it in the gloom. It doesn't register on my Servant.

'The Institute has a secret door?' I almost laugh.

'Yes. As a matter of fact, it does.'

'What's the code? Open Sesame?'

'I've had it for twenty-five years, Agent Rause.'

If that's true then that's a year after she first met Darius Vishakh, two since she was shot in the spine and left for dead by a posse of Xen-smuggling Earthers.

The pod opens as we approach. I ping Laura: You got a safe house? Somewhere you trust?

No.

But there are safe houses all over Firstfall that the Tesseract knows nothing about, twenty years old, going back to the blockade and the last time we all thought Earth was going to invade.

Okay. Leave it with me.

I ping Jonas Himaru as Jacksmith and I get into the pod: I need a place to hide a high-value asset. Not Tesseract. Give me somewhere and send someone to let me in. You know what I mean.

Project Insurgent. The old plan for a resistance. I don't know how long I might have to wait for an answer and I'm not even sure Himaru's still talking to me, but it's the best I can do. I ping Liss: Message from Alysha. Can you trace it? I don't want to use the Tesseract.

I'll try.

The pod pulls away. I turn to Jacksmith. 'You can't trust the Tesseract right now.'

I'm expecting shock or surprise, certainly not for her to burst out laughing.

'Agent Rause, right now I don't trust anyone! Not even you!'

'Then you pick our destination.' The pod hums away from the cavern into a pitch-black tunnel. I don't know where we are – some part of the undercity I've never had a reason to visit. 'Is Iosefa really that big a deal that you have to hide his body?'

Jacksmith looks at me in vague disbelief. 'Keon, you *do* remember when the *Flying Daggers* shot at us from orbit with antimatter weapons? Yes, he absolutely really is.'

'Why?'

I used to think Jacksmith was just a scientist. And she *is* a scientist, but a scientist with more clearances than the rest of the bureau put together.

The pod rolls out of the darkness onto an undercity highway, one of the high-speed transit tunnels out of the city centre. From the looks of things, we're heading for the Roseate Project.

'You really think Earth would go to war for this?' I ask.

'If it's the only way to stop Fleet from getting hold of Lomu then yes, I think they just might.'

'I don't get it. Okay, I know Iosefa managed to control a Masters' ship once upon a time. I get why that matters. I get that it was probably something to do with his genetics and being high as a kite on Xen all the time, because hey, I know what Alysha's last case was about. But so what? I know a bit about gene propagation, too. Even if you find a descendant, chances are they won't have the right genes in exactly the right sequence any more, right? And how will you even know? What are you going to do? Round them all up, get them stoned on Xen and stuff them in a Masters' ship to see what happens?'

Jacksmith looks at me like I'm mad or stupid.

'You're really not thinking big enough here, Rause.'

'What do you mean?'

'I've already sequenced Iosefa's DNA. I did *that* back out on the ice. I already know what genes made him special, what made him divergent from the spread of human normal. Any half-decent biologist with access to the Global Gene Database and a sample of Iosefa's genetic material can get that far with a snap of their fingers. And yes, you're right about gene propagation: finding a descendant who happens to have that sequence intact would be a stroke of luck, but in the longer term that really doesn't matter. Given the will and the knowledge and the resources, you can simply insert that sequence into a stack of foetuses and engineer yourself some new humans.'

I look at her in horror. 'You'd do that?'

'I don't know that *I'd* do that.' Jacksmith stares out the pod window. 'Point is, Keon, that *someone* will. Look, like it or not, there's been a race going for more than a century. The first to crack the secrets of the Masters wins, and Lomu looks like a short cut to the finish. On Earth there are probably a good round dozen governments, factions and combines ready to do whatever it takes, and I do mean *whatever* it takes. Thousands of genetically engineered babies? Sure, and that's just the start. It's not like they're short of people, after all.'

I remember what Eddie said on top of the MagentaNet Tower, questioning whether the samples Jacksmith has already given to Earth and Fleet really came from Lomu.

'Those experiments are going to happen no matter what, aren't they?'

Jacksmith winces. 'There was never any stopping that.'

I wonder what that would be like. Engineered from birth to be something special. Kids dosed up with designer Xen. Kids taken up into space to see what happens and then thrown away when 'it' turns out to be nothing …

A ping comes in from Laura: I have a drone coming up on your position with a Reeper.

The pod slides to the side of the highway and stops. Jacksmith gives me a look.

'That sliver you palmed me. Where did it come from?'

'Not from me.'

She can either figure it out for herself or she can wonder.

'Do you know what's on it? Don't tell me you didn't look.'

I open the pod door. I'm getting pings from Laura's drone now, coming up behind us.

'A decryption key. Care to tell me what it decrypts?'

'I doubt I'd tell you if I knew, but as it happens, I don't.'

I have no idea whether to believe her.

'Keon, I might need your help soon.'

I see the drone now, a fast-flashing blue light on top as it races through the tunnel towards us. It stops a few yards short of the pod.

'There's a part of me that would rather destroy Iosefa entirely if the only alternative is to hand him over to Earth. And it's not right. I shouldn't, because I know that as a species we're better off having him than not. Within a generation we might learn to control what the Masters left behind. I need someone to remind me of the possibilities Iosefa brings, even if I most likely won't live to see them. I need someone to tell me how he'll make our worlds safer for billions of people. That being the case, does it matter so much how we get there? Although ... I feel sometimes that it does, you see.'

Right now, I'm more concerned with surviving tonight and then tomorrow and then the day after that. With finding Alysha and having back the life we once shared, not a decade into the future, or a year or even a month, but right now.

I get out of the pod. The drone is a simple Tesseract delivery drone carrying a Reeper and a couple of clips of ammunition. I take the Reeper and load it and feel better. The drone flies away. I get back into the pod and it starts to move. When I check the destination Jacksmith's programmed, I see it's taking her home.

'I'll need the access code to your apartment,' I tell her. 'You'll stay at a safe distance until I know it's clear.'

Jacksmith gives me an exasperated look. 'Is all this really necessary?'

'Yes.'

A deep breath and then a sigh. 'I don't use an access code. Too easy to hack. I use a pass phrase.'

'Really? Voice recognition? Shit.'

'Actually no. If someone wants to break in that badly, I'd really prefer it if they didn't need me to be there to help them do it. I don't keep anything of value at home.' She flashes me a smile with a bitter edge. 'It always seemed such an unpleasantly real threat, so if anyone absolutely *must* break in and go through my stuff, they can leave me out of it. Better for all concerned, really.' She bares her teeth in an unpleasant grin. 'Story changes if I'm inside, of course. Then either I let you in or you have a big fat blob of plastic explosive blow up in your face.'

Thing is, I really can't tell if she's being serious. 'What's the phrase?'

Jacksmith purses her lips and looks almost embarrassed. 'Right now, it's *Fuck Darius Vishakh. Fuck Earth. Fuck the lot of them.* Go on, laugh.'

What comes out is more of a snigger

'I'm a small and petty woman sometimes,' Jacksmith says

I can't help but smile. I doubt there's anything small or petty about Elizabeth Jacksmith, but I don't say so. I like this moment. It feels private. Almost intimate.

'Iosefa crashed his ship and died,' I say. 'Doesn't that mean his genetic sequence isn't right.'

'We don't know why he crashed. There are people down there trying to work it out. But yes, you could be right.' She turns to me, suddenly intense. 'The thing is, Keon, about a descendant, is that if we *do* get lucky, if we *do* find someone with the right sequence, we have a jump of a generation on everyone else. If there really *is* someone here on Magenta – if you ever got them inside a Masters' ship and they could … control it – to all intents and purposes they would become a god. And no one else has that. *If* that person exists, they're here. On *our* world.'

I want to laugh, but the look on Jacksmith's face strangles the sound in my throat. She means every word.

'But we don't have a Masters' ship.'

'Yes we do, you idiot! Iosefa's!'

'But that's a wreck!'

'*Is* it? How could you possibly know?' She flashes me a

wicked smile and shifts a little closer in her chair, so intense now it's like a fever in her. 'Think about it! How the fuck do you – or any of the rest of us – know? You think it's a wreck because it's just sitting there doing nothing, same as everything else they left behind?'

'It's just a theory here, okay, but anything that falls out of orbit to smash itself into an ice shelf usually doesn't meet its original performance specifications any more.'

'But we don't know if that's what really happened, and besides, we're talking the Masters, Keon! *Usual* doesn't apply. It's intact! Entirely intact! No sign of damage whatsoever.' She takes a deep breath. 'As far as we can tell.'

'So what? Your plan is to find the next Iosefa, take them to the ice cap, stick them in Iosefa's ship and see what happens?'

'You have a better suggestion?'

'And if it works? What then?'

Jacksmith rolls her eyes. 'I have no fucking idea. But whatever it is, it's got to be better than Earth playing hit-and-miss genetics by growing a million engineered babies in vats and stuffing them all full of Xen. Because that's what they'll do, probably a dozen times over. And they'll get there, eventually, and they'll make it work, and then what have you got? An army of brainwashed children with godlike powers being ordered about by lunatics like Frank Swainsbrook? Is that a future you want to see? They'll sweep Fleet aside and we'll all become de facto colonies again. No, Keon. Anything but that!'

I realise I don't have anything to say because most of me agrees with her. The part that has doubts is the part that remembers Rachael Cho. Cho, who fills herself full of Xen and then stops her own heart so she can sink into a space between life and death and listen to what she claims are the voices of the Masters. Bullshit, I'd have said a month ago, but now I have a shred of doubt. What if it's not? Does Jacksmith know about her? Has Laura told her about Saleesh's discovery?

'Not everything the Masters left behind doesn't work,' I say. I know it's true, because Liss brought something back with her from Earth when I came to Magenta, and she used it, and she's a shell, not even a person, which makes no sense if this is all about genetic codes and Xen and getting just the right tangle of human and alien chemistry ...

'What do you mean?'

'I—'

From out of nowhere, something smashes into the back of us. Our pod slews sideways as it slams on the brakes and deploys a storm of airbags. My head smacks into them and the Reeper in my lap flies out of my hand. Everything is suddenly white and pressing in on me. My Servant screams for help and stabs me with adrenaline and painkillers. I flounder in the back of the pod, buried under sagging balloons of white cloth and plastic crash protection. I have a flash of suffocating under bedclothes, under a duvet wrapped tight around my head. I try to batter the airbags aside ... I can't breathe ... I need my gun, where's my gun? I don't know what's happened. A bomb? But it felt like an impact, not an explosion ... Something ... hit us?

I hear a loud bang like a sledgehammer on armoured plate. The air changes. The airbags are deflating. We're in a tunnel, the same tunnel, only now we're facing sideways and I'm looking across the back seat of the pod, across Jacksmith at an open door and at a man in a combat vest – no, two men – and they're reaching inside and grabbing at her. She squeals and tears at their hands but they're strong, too strong, and they're dragging her out of her chair and they haven't seen me yet but now they do and they let go, and there's a third man behind them with a burst rifle, and I hear the two at the door and ... *Shit! There's someone with her*, and I know those voices, that accent, an Earther accent, and the two at the door back away and go for pistols holstered at their belts, but the man behind them already has his rifle raised and he's going to pull the trigger and ...

My Reeper is back in my hand. I don't remember sweeping it up off the floor or raising it or levelling it at the man with the rifle or yelling at him to put the gun down, even though all those things must have happened. It's a gun pointing at a gun as if I'm going to shoot his bullets out of the air before they reach me, only that's not what happens because I pull the trigger first, and jerk back, and so does he, me from the recoil, him from the slug that hits him right in the armoured visor that covers his face. He staggers a couple of steps but doesn't fall, and that's when I know I'm dead, because all three of these men are in military body armour while I'm still dressed for a fucking cocktail party, and in a moment he's going to lift that rifle again and pull the trigger and I'm trapped in here with nowhere to go and—

WHAM!

A shape screams past and the man with the rifle isn't there any more. Nor are the two men who were pulling Jacksmith out of the pod and nor is the door. The pod rocks as something heavy thumps onto the roof. I wrestle my way though flaccid airbags and wrench open the door on the other side as one of the men who was pulling at Jacksmith rolls off the top of the pod and lands heavily beside me, off balance, one hand on the ground to catch himself. I have a moment before he recovers: I take it, shooting him in the back of the head. The bullet doesn't punch through his helmet but the impact is enough to knock him down and leave him stunned. I go for the easiest point of access, a wrist, where a glove meets the sleeve of his combat jacket. I wrench and pull until I have an inch of bare skin, switch my Reeper to stun and shoot him again, twice. He screams and twists and writhes. In a second or two I'm going to have to hold him down and rip that helmet off his head and shoot him somewhere that matters, but in that second I look up and down the road and try to understand what the fuck just happened.

Ahead is another pod. A woman with short hair is getting out, moving too fast to be human. Behind us is a third pod, the one that smashed into us. A fourth man in combat gear is already half out, rifle in hand.

Shit.

I throw my Tesseract codes at the pod with the soldier. No joy. I switch my Reeper back to bullets and drop to one knee, firing at him. Instinct makes him drop behind the door of his pod for cover.

Laura! I need a lot of help here!

Can't tell the Tesseract because I don't think these men followed us from the Institute, I think they followed the drone that brought my Reeper ...

The woman who moves too quickly to be human picks up one of the soldiers. She pins him with one hand around his throat while her other claws at his neck. He fights furiously, kicking, punching her in the face, scratching at her arm, trying to get away. She ignores him. It takes a moment for me to realise she's digging his Servant implants out from inside his skin. The downside of subdermal Servants ...

The soldier I stunned grabs my foot and tips me over. I crash onto him and we wrestle. He's got years of military training, muscle and bone enhanced by top of the range transgravity treatment. In my corner I've got being born and bred in 1.4 gravities. It's an even match for a few seconds until his friend from the pod that smashed into us starts spraying bullets. He doesn't seem to care what he hits so I guess he knows I'm not armoured.

Yo, Rause. Be there in sixty.

Himaru. I spring away from the soldier on the ground, manage to kick his gun skittering across the road so at least he can't shoot me, and dive back for cover. The soldier by the rear

159

pod stops shooting and shouts something. The soldier I stunned throws a glance the other way, sees the woman who's really a shell is running towards us, and bolts. I snatch up my Reeper, hunker down as another spray of bullets peppers our smashed-up pod, then pop up and return fire. If I hit anything then it isn't enough to stop the two surviving soldiers from screeching into reverse, slamming a hard turn and tearing off back down the tunnel the way they came. I watch them go, raking their pod's Servant with my Tesseract codes, looking for a way in and not finding one.

The shell that saved us reaches my side. I see her face …

Alysha.

Not the Alysha I remember from six years ago, but the Alysha who came to me in Mercy – short hair, new lines on her face, the fire in her eyes darker and bloodier than I remember.

Liss?

I want to ask how she got a new shell so quickly – or a new face, at least – but she grabs my hand and pulls, so strong I couldn't resist even if I wanted to.

'We need to go, Keys. Right now!'

'Why?'

'The nest these cuckoos came from. Before they wipe it clean.'

I ping Laura and Himaru as Liss and I run back to her pod: Jacksmith. Get her safe. Two gunmen outbound in a jacked pod. Two down at the scene. One dead, one … I'm not sure. Following up something else. Time critical.

I shouldn't leave Jacksmith alone. I know that. I should stand guard until Himaru and his men arrive, even if they're only thirty seconds away, because a lot can happen in thirty seconds. But that includes Himaru seeing Liss, and I can't see a way past that if we stay.

We get into the pod. Liss pulls away fast. I don't ask where we're going. I call Jacksmith.

'You hurt?'

'What the fuck, Rause, where are you going?'

She doesn't sound hurt. Good. 'Elizabeth, sit tight. A tac-team will be with you in seconds. Literally seconds. Colonel Jonas Himaru. You can trust him.' I'm not picking up any medical alerts from her Servant. Spiking heart rate, nothing more. 'I'm sorry, but there's a chance we can hit their nest before they clean it.'

'They?' She sounds disorientated. Can't say I blame her. 'Who the fuck—'

'No idea. Off-planet mercenary—'

'Not the goon squad, dipshit, I know *they* were from Earth. Your new partner. The one who looks like … like you-know-who.'

Shit! Not as disorientated as I hoped. I take the easy way out, cut the call and turn to Liss.

'You're following me?'

'Yes.'

We hurtle down the tunnel, heading towards the Roseate Project. Liss has engaged a manual override, throttling the pod as hard as it can go.

'You made yourself a new shell?'

'Yes. Vishakh had some clever ideas, you know.'

I see the blood on her hands. 'You get their nest from that guy's Servant?'

'No. Traced the pod they used to come after you instead.'

I stare at her. 'How?'

'Hacked its Servant so it wouldn't respond to Tesseract codes, did they?' She smirks. 'You're getting old, Keys, not seeing that one coming.'

'How did you track them?'

'Backwards through transport surveillance. They ran good spoofing, but not good enough.'

We drive on in silence. My Tesseract override on the pod's Servant gives us priority on the road, clearing everything out of the way ahead. Not that anyone will really notice. The underground highways are quiet this late in the day.

'We're still heading for the Project?'

'They camped close to Jacksmith's home.'

'Address?'

'So you can call in a tac-team?'

'That's pretty much what I was thinking, yes.'

One bureau agent with nothing but a Reeper and an illegal sentient shell going up against an unknown number of Earther mercenaries isn't clever. And there's Liss herself. I want to protect her. I want to look after her, and yes, she's a shell, so it maybe it doesn't matter if she gets shot up or has a few limbs blown off, but I don't want her to get caught, I don't want her to even be seen. Whatever else hangs between us, I don't want her ripped apart by a forensic q-code scrubber ...

Maybe *she* does. Maybe that's her way out of this? Go out in a blaze of glory? That *would* be my Alysha, if she was truly cornered ...

Liss pings me the address. I ought to pass it up to the Tesseract but instead I send it to Laura and Himaru: Your call. Take a chance that Tesseract One doesn't get a warning to them first? I'm two minutes out.

Hold back. Laura.

I can get a tac-team there in ten. Himaru. Jacksmith is secure. Two gunmen, one for the morgue, one for Mercy. What the hell did you do to them, Rause?

I don't answer that. Instead, I turn to Liss: 'I'm guessing the Servant you took is encrypted?'

'Top grade,' she nods. 'Years to crack it.'

'Surveillance in the tunnel?'

'Taken care of.'

So there are no recordings of what happened except for what's in my Servant, what the Earther mercenaries saw, and …

'Jacksmith saw you.'

'I know.'

'So—'

'What did you expect me to do? Let them kill you while they took her?'

'She knows about Alysha.'

'So tell her that's who she saw.'

We slow as we reach the Roseate Project, last stop for the underground highway. Liss takes the pod into an access tunnel and heads for the surface. The pod shakes as we break into gloomy twilight, hit by the swirling wind and the rat-a-tat buzz of rain hammering the roof. We wind through the maze of fused-glass roads, slick with rainwater, entwined among squat single-storey blocks, the penthouse flats of three dozen underground towers. Liss tells the pod to stop on a wide street between rows of low shallow-sloped walls dotted with angled armoured windows. There are no doors to the inside from up here because, while a window and a view of the real sky are a luxury, who wants a door straight out to nothing except howling wind and flaying rain? The roads up here are for maintenance shells, not for people.

Liss points at a window.

'There. You should stay in the pod.'

'So should you.'

She shouldn't be here at all. She should vanish into the warrens of Firstfall before she gives away enough for someone like Laura to work out that she exists; but she's already out the door before I can find the words.

I follow. The rain hits me like a hail of needles. It stings my skin, not fierce enough to draw blood but hard enough to hurt. I wrap my arms over my head and cover my face, scurrying across the empty street in Liss's wake. She's at the window – more of a skylight – laying a cutting charge across the glass.

Where the hell did you get that?

I'm not picking up any Servants inside.

She finishes setting the charge and points through the glass. The room below is an open-plan lounge, spacious and luxurious by Magenta standards. A dining table and four chairs, a couple of loungers, a floor-to-ceiling wall screen, a bar, an arch leading into a second room I can't see, probably a kitchen, a spiral stairwell going down ... And a body sprawled face up beside the bar with a hole between his eyes and a dark pool on the floor beneath his head.

Liss sets off the charge, a quiet *POP* almost lost under the buzzsaw of falling rain. The window shatters and Liss jumps inside. I follow, slower. I see through the arch as I land, into the kitchen. A second body slumps in a dead-drunk sprawl against the far wall with a big bright red splat of blood on the tiles above his head. I ping again for Servants. Still nothing.

Laura. I'm inside. Someone got here before me. Two bodies so far.

What the fuck, Rause? I said hold!

Someone give you a secret promotion while I wasn't looking?

No, but apparently they gave me all the common sense!

Liss is creeping down the stairs. I go to the body by the bar. The blood is wet and warm. This happened only minutes ago.

Liss, whoever did this might still be here. Give me your eyes. I switch links back to Laura. This is a hot scene. The bodies are fresh.

A feed from Liss pops up in my Servant as I search the body by the bar. I project it to my lenses, overlaid across the real world in front of me. I'm looking through her eyes at the bottom of the stairs down a long wide hallway. At the far end is a door that should lead into the tunnels of the Roseate Project, a sheltered entrance protected from Magenta's storm weather by several feet of foamcrete. Six other doors lead off, three either side. The ones by the entrance will be a pair of wetrooms. The other four were bedrooms once but they could be anything now.

Laura chimes in my Servant: I want you to establish surveillance until the proper support units arrive. Stay back and don't get yourself shot again.

Liss raises a finger in front of her eyes and points to the middle door on the right.

You're right. There's someone here, I think.

I try to access the apartment Servant but it's dead. I try for the internal surveillance cameras, but those have gone too. I pull up the building schematics from the Tesseract.

No other way in or out. Whoever it is, they're trapped.

I'm not finding anything in the pockets of my dead man at the bar. From the way they've been turned out, I'm not the first to go through them. Laura's right. We should hold and wait for backup. Or rather, *I* should hold.

Liss, go. Get out of here.

She ignores me. I mutter a curse and pad to the top of the stairs as quietly as I can. She's at the middle door as I take the first step down, twists the handle, slow, silent, then bursts through in an explosion of light and sound and movement, letting off a shrill wailing siren so loud that it blurs my vision. A dazzling flash like a blaze of pure sunlight blooms around her. I grab for the rail beside me, catching myself, and at the same time I see movement almost right in front of me, as someone or something launches out of a different room and bolts for the exit door ...

'Freeze!' Shit. Liss! Wrong room! I raise my Reeper. The flash from Liss has gone as suddenly as it came, plunging the hall into darkness as my eyes try to adjust. The figure in the hall turns and looks without breaking stride. All I can see is a silhouette with a

165

dark visor wrapped across her eyes and ears. I see a raised gun but she's too slow. I have her cold, my Reeper levelled ...

I don't pull the trigger. The way she moves ...

'Alysha?'

Liss explodes back into the hall. The figure in front of me shifts her aim, fires three rounds, POP-POP-POP straight into Liss, and then she's gone, through the door and out. It closes behind her.

I stand, frozen. Liss doesn't give chase.

Are you—

I'm okay.

Liss will be trying to connect to the Roseate surveillance now, trying to pick up the electronic trail of the woman who just shot her, following from camera to camera ...

Let her go, I say. Leave her be.

Yes.

We have a few minutes before the tac-team arrives, no more.

You should go.

Not yet.

She runs into the room where the intruder was hiding. I leave her to it. I should be searching the bodies again, or the rooms, or doing something useful, but instead I'm standing halfway down the stairs, pulling the video feed from my Reeper back into my Servant. My eyes were too dazzled to see clearly, but the images caught by the camera on my gun remove any doubt. The woman's face is still half-hidden, but I was right about the way she moved ...

Alysha.

What the *fuck*?

I run to the bottom of the stairs. I'm almost at the door before I stop myself. I want to chase after her. I want to find her. I want her to tell me why she left, why she ran, why any of this ... but Himaru's team are two minutes away ...

I have to let her go.

I wipe the recordings from my Reeper and then from my Servant, and somehow it feels like the hardest thing I've ever done. I wonder: is that it? Is that the last time I'll ever see her?

Liss comes back out of the room where Alysha was hiding and hands me a fistful of data slivers.

'There are more in there. All encrypted except this one.'

She hands me a last sliver, and all I can do is stare at her, standing in front of me in a shell that's almost a perfect copy of Alysha, and at the door where the real Alysha vanished only a moment ago, and at the three bullet holes in Liss's chest.

'You sure you're okay?'

She nods. 'You?'

Am I? I don't know.

'You saw?'

She nods again.

'Was it her?'

'Yes. I think so. Open the sliver, Keon.'

I open the sliver. It's empty except for a single key-code, long and unusually structured, but I know what it is because I saw something like it only this afternoon. It's a New Hope hangar access code.

I shiver. 'Shit!'

'She left that for us to find.'

Maybe. Could be all sorts of reasons for a team of Earther mercenaries to have a code for a New Hope hangar. Could be this is the code for the hangar where we're keeping Vishakh's shuttle, in which case maybe this is the key to our missing warhead. Could be their way off the planet. Could be any of those, but I don't think so. I think Liss is right, that this didn't belong to the Earthers at all.

'You need to go! Now! Before anyone else gets here!'

'She left this for us,' says Liss.

Himaru's tac-team can't be more than thirty seconds away.

'No. It's not for us.' Not for me and Liss, because how could she know I'd be the one to get here first? How could she know I'd be the one to find it ...? 'It's for whoever got here. Now you need to *go*!'

I follow her up the stairs and watch as she jumps up through the shattered skylight and vanishes into the rain and the abandoned streets above. There's no one out on the surface on a night like this, not in the Project where there's nothing to see and nothing to do except stand in the wind and stare at endless grey skies over endless black stone ...

Rause? It's Himaru. Situation?

Secure, but someone got here first.

What the fuck? One of us?

I don't know. I need data forensics. And you need this. I send him the New Hope code. I don't need to tell him what it is. You need to get a team there as fast as you can, find out what this opens, and open it. Could be it's their extraction and there are more of them waiting, so don't let anything get in your way.

Got that.

And take radiation counters.

Fuck, really?

Who knows? Tell me what's there as soon as you're in.

Yeah, Jonas Himaru who doesn't answer to the Tesseract, you take that code to New Hope and see what you find. Maybe it'll be our missing warhead, but I don't think so. One unencrypted sliver and *that's* what's on it? No, I don't think so at all. This is the key to Hangar 13, and inside is something Alysha needs me to see.

An hour later I'm still in the Roseate Project, still in the same apartment. Himaru's men have been and gone. Data forensics too, and now I'm working with the guys and girls from physical evidence, watching them piece together everything that happened, watching them work because I need to know what they're going to find. Liss. Alysha. What evidence did either of them leave to give themselves away? None, I hope, but I'm here to be their cleaner in case they did. They were good though, both of them, and forensics find nothing, and I'm almost ready to breathe a sigh of relief and go home and get some sleep when the call comes from Himaru.

Your New Hope code was a bust.

What happened?

Nothing, that's what. It's a hangar code, sure, but there's nothing inside. No Earthers and no trace of antimatter.

Nothing at all?

Stripped clean. Bare walls. Place hasn't been touched for months.

No shuttle?

No.

What hangar?

What?

What was the hangar number? Like I don't already know.

Thirteen.

Ah, shit. Swainsbrook's shuttle. It's not there. *That's* what she wanted me to see.

FOUR

FLATLINE

INSTANTIATION THIRTY-SEVEN

The shell moves to a slow pulse. Forty-two minutes, give or take, is the cycle of its heartbeat. Forty-two minutes to register data, transmit, process, decide a response and effect an action. Instantiation Thirty-seven is a long way from home.

It drifts in zero gravity in a featureless cabin, once a recreation room but long ago stripped bare. Bodies float around it. Bodies and ... bits of bodies, desiccated and slow-cooked by the heat. The drops of blood have fallen to powder. A faint mist of red dust fills the air.

Outside, Magenta's massive sun glares a relentless blue-tinged white. Instantiation Thirty-seven overrides the safety protocols of the station Servant. In the silence of space, two manoeuvre jets flare. The kick is small, but it sets the station into a slow rotation. Huge fins, silver on one side, black on the other to dissipate the heat of the nearby star, lock into a new position. The shutters on the windows close, silver, reflecting back the heat.

Its task complete, Instantiation Thirty-seven reports its success and waits.

The next order comes forty-two minutes later. When it arrives, Instantiation Thirty-seven drifts with delicate precision through red-hot air and carefully patterned carnage until it reaches an airlock door, and ejects itself into space. Its fate will be a long slow spiral in a very slightly eccentric orbit that will take it ever closer to Magenta's sun. In a few hundred years it will graze the heliosphere and burn to vapour, but Instantiation Thirty-seven will die long before then, burned black by the relentless fire of Magenta's divergent star.

11

INSIDE INFORMATION

An hour after Himaru busts into New Hope's Hangar 13 and finds it empty, the *Flying Daggers* issues a statement. They claim to speak for Earth, and the statement is both declaration and threat: Iosefa Lomu was a citizen of Earth. His remains are the property of the United Nations, to be handed over to the appropriate Earth government. For good measure, the *Flying Daggers* makes the same claim over the wreck in the southern polar ice, although how they expect us to dig it out and haul it to orbit I have no idea.

I don't get much sleep after that. Half the planet is howling into the ether, scrabbling for every nugget of information about the *Flying Daggers*, Iosefa Lomu, the mysterious videos apparently showing the return of the Masters, and what the hell is happening on Earth. By the small hours of the morning, every single news channel has pinged me for an interview thanks to Elizabeth Jacksmith dropping my name back when I was in Nico. I turn off my Servant but I still can't sleep. Swainsbrook is on the news too, touting his ridiculous project to contact the

Masters. He dresses it with the language of religion and prayer before he gets to how he's ready to go if only he could just raise a little extra funding to bridge some last hurdle. An hour later and he's raised more than I've earned in my entire life.

On Channel Eight, someone is interviewing pig farmers in Nico for opinions on what the return of the Masters means for pork futures. Channel Twelve has a farmer who reckons he has a pig that's psychic and knows what's coming. I figure okay, why not. A psychic pig makes about as much sense as everything I heard from Swainsbrook last night.

I give up and head to the Tesseract. I catch a couple of hours of sleep in a contemplation cubicle, a deep dive into a dark hole of exhaustion and dream of the woman in the burqa from the Institute. *Was* she Alysha? I wake back the moment in the Roseate Project when we saw each other and froze. I *know* it was her. And I know she recognised me, even in the darkness, but what about Liss? Did Alysha see her own face on a shell ...?

I turn my Servant back on and discover I've got ten minutes before I'm supposed to give a briefing on Meelosh and the Solar Intensity Research Station direct to the Chief. I arrive crumpled and blurry at the edges. Chief Vikram Morgan sits in his old leather chair behind an antique desk, the same office he's had for twenty years since he took over running the bureau after the blockade. He's short, squat, grey hair cropped close. On Earth they'd probably call him something like The Bulldog, but here on Magenta he's just the Chief, unless you're Assistant Director Flemich, sitting in the corner of the room, who for some reason gets to call him Viki. Morgan looks like he just slept eight hours straight while the rest of us ran ourselves to rags. Flemich, at least, looks like he's been up all night.

'Rause.' Morgan nods to me as I come in.

'Sir.'

A wall screen flicks on. Rangesh phoning it in from Nico.

'From the top, Rause. Short and sweet.'

I start with Meelosh's suicide, playing the recording, skipping between moments to highlight each new message as it arrives. I freeze the replay as the knife touches Meelosh's throat. He doesn't need to see that. No one does.

'We're certain the body is Meelosh?'

'We totally are, boss dudes.' Bix is wearing a *Legalise Everything* T-shirt and ripped jeans. For him, this counts as dressing for the occasion. 'We shipped the body to Mercy. That pathology dude, Doctor Roge, did every test you can think of, right. Probably made a few up specially. X-rays match. DNA, fingerprints, dental records, it's totally him.'

Flemich nods. 'And the suicide?'

'Looks kosher.' Bix sniffs. 'Data forensics have been all over the recording he made. It's totally consistent with reconstructions made by the Nico bureau. Servant records and local surveillance all check out. The 'Losh was loaded on Xen and stims, you know? So much Xen in his system that—'

'I really don't care.' Morgan creaks forward in his leather chair. Amiable and soft-spoken nine days out of ten, today is day ten. 'Neither does the Selected Chamber. *Are* the Masters out there?'

Bix grins. 'Got some good news for you there, boss dudes! Not quite ready to print, you know, but in a couple of hours data forensics reckon they'll totally prove for sure that all those videos are faked.'

Morgan's face creases like folded paper. 'How do you know?'

'The colour balance, man,' says Bix.

'Explain!'

'Dude, okay, so it's pretty technical, but basically we know what cameras were fitted when the station was built, right? The photodetectors are some ancient quantum well design on an indium phosphide substrate. It's practically archaeology instead

177

of technology, you know? They're reliable, right, but the photo-detectors orbiting the sun are fifty years old and we'd expect a loss of response at short wavelength, right? And we know from the star fields patterns exactly where the cameras were looking, and so we know exactly which stars are in every frame, and we know their spectra, right, but data forensics have been all over those clips all night, and we're totally not seeing this short wavelength thing, and so—'

'What you're saying is they're too blue,' interrupts Morgan. No one ever said he wasn't sharp.

'Yeah, man, so—'

'So you can prove it's a hoax?'

'Yeah. Kind of.'

Storm clouds darken across the chief's face. I feel Bix squirm.

'It's not, you know, black and white conclusive, right? And they really are coming from the old Solar Station, which is totally—'

'What about the ones supposedly recorded inside?'

Bix shakes his head. 'Can't tell, boss dude. No reference. Could come from anywhere. Probably made up, you know … because, like, anything else doesn't make any sense, right? But to totally *know* you'd have to, like, go and have a look.'

Morgan turns to me. 'If it's a hoax, who's doing it and why?'

'Our best guess is Frank Swainsbrook.' I launch into the why: Swainsbrook's cult; his association with *October*; the fact that you can count the number of ships in Magenta capable of reaching a close solar orbit on the fingers of one hand; the fact that one of them happens to be the *Betty Blue*, and that when we opened up the hangar where she was supposed to have been berthed for the last three months, it was empty. This is when I ought to tell them about Saleesh and the work she was doing, that maybe Meelosh had a genetic connection to Lomu, and then about Swainsbrook and how he got in touch with them and how there's a lot more to this than meets the eye. But I don't. I'm thinking of Rachael Cho, who's a bit strange but who seemed decent and kind when I met her, empathic even, and who deserves a lot better than to become humanity's most famous lab rat. And I'm thinking of how Laura liked Flemich for our mole, Tesseract One, and how Flemich wouldn't let me into New Hope's Hangar 13. Flemich who's sitting right here, listening to every word.

'He was on Channel Three last night,' I say when I'm done. 'Fundraising. Didn't look fazed. Didn't look fazed yesterday evening, either, when the news broke. Looked to me more like he knew it was coming. Maybe you noticed that.'

I give Morgan a pointed look but his eyes are glittering. He's lensing someone, Swainsbrook himself, maybe.

Flemich leans forward. 'Viki, if the signals are coming from that station then someone had to go out there to set this up. I have a second team double-checking to rule out a more local source, but I've been over the work from data forensics and it does look likely that Agent Rangesh is right.'

Checking our work. I hope they prove us wrong, I really do.

Bix waves his hands. 'Boss dudes! It's like someone's using the station as a relay, right? To rebroadcast a signal transmitted from—'

'I know what a relay is!' The storm on Morgan's face looks ready to break. 'From where?'

'Don't know yet. Somewhere on Magenta—'

'*That's* the best you can give me?'

I jump in before Bix says something stupid.

'Yes, sir. We've ruled out anything from an orbital source. We're looking as hard as we can.'

Morgan glowers at me. 'You'd need a big antenna. There can't be *that* many.'

He's right. Satellite antennas are everywhere, but reaching

across two hundred and fifty million miles of space is a whole other game.

A message from Laura appears in my Servant: Are you still with Morgan?

Yes.

Someone inside the bureau pulled Jacksmith's protection last night.

Tesseract One?

I think it has to be.

Morgan is staring right at me. 'Rause?'

'The Tesseract is compiling a list, sir.' I hear how lame that sounds.

'A list.' The acid in Morgan's voice would burn through six-inch armour plate. 'You realise what's at stake here? We've got about thirty-six hours before the *Fearless* jumps in from Earth. Another couple before it jumps back. I want the lid off this stupid hoax before that happens. I do *not* want the *Fearless* leaving with a story that the Masters have returned to Magenta!'

'I think it's about the vote, sir,' I say.

'What vote?'

'The repeal of the Sovereign Rights Act, sir. That's what—'

'That was last night, Rause.' Morgan's brow furrows so hard you could crack stones in the creases. 'It failed. You were there!'

'Yes, sir, and so were you, and this story broke minutes later, and the first channel to broadcast it was Channel Two, which, like Channel Nine, happens to be owned by Eddie Thiekis. If I'm right and Swainsbrook is the architect, you might want to consider that both Eddie and Swainsbrook are *October*, both of them urged for a repeal of the act, and that Eddie Thiekis certainly has the influence to push a second vote onto the floor of the Selected Chamber. They were already talking about it last night before I even left. Lomu's changed everything, sir. The Earthers want to set up Xen refineries, and *October* are Earth.'

I try to keep calm but the words come out venomous and violent.

Morgan narrows his eyes. I can't tell what he's thinking. *Good point, Rause,* is it? Or is it *shut this idiot up and get him off the case*?

'*Can* we get out to this research station to look?'

I shake my head, ready to tell him no, not if we only have thirty-six hours to stop this from getting back to Earth, but again Flemich jumps in.

'We can but it will take weeks. The station is in a tight orbit around the sun. It's a long way. We *could* pull one of our shuttles out of service and refit it for a trip like that but the disruption to orbital traffic would be a disaster. Unfortunately, the alternatives aren't much better: we could refit a Kutosov to carry some infiltration drones. That would take a while and would be a one-way trip. We'd lose the Kutosov. Alternatively, we beg for help from Fleet.'

'So there's no way to get me an answer before the *Fearless* makes its next jump back to Earth?' Morgan looks from face to face. We all look back. No one wants to tell him it's impossible, even though it is.

'Sir, um ...' starts Bix.

'Even if we had a shuttle ready to go, we're talking nearly two weeks to get out there,' says Flemich.

'The jump after?'

'Just about possible.'

'Talk to Fleet. I want options on my desk in an hour. In the meantime ...' Morgan fixes his eye on me. 'Rause, I want every antenna that could have done this found and checked by the end of the day. And if you really think Frank Swainsbrook is responsible then get him in here, prove it, and nail him to a fucking cross.' He gets up. 'Dismissed.'

I ping Bix as I leave: You got the Nico end covered?

Sure. Disappointment too, dude.

Thanks. I need to be in Firstfall. Alysha is here. You don't mind staying out there?

It's awful, boss dude! I've got, like, about a hundred second cousins that mum keeps trying to parade in front of me, you know? She's, like, totally trying to persuade me to pick one to get married to, right? *There's a sparkle in his words.*

What about a certain policewoman? I ask.

Dude!

Somehow he manages to put coy embarrassment into a single word. I don't ask. I don't care. I don't need to know.

Anything on your Akkadian symbols?

I'm pretty close to being the world expert by now, you know, on account of there being like about three other people on Magenta who even know what Akkadian is. I've run it through an automated translator and picked out a few words by hand but, like ... You really need an expert, man. Someone from Earth.

I think about how long that will take. I can put out a request when the *Fearless* arrives. If I'm lucky and some academic takes it on, I might hope for an answer twenty-six days later. Same goes for any question, big or small, that can't be answered in the few hours the *Fearless* hangs over Earth.

Dude – that stuff I told Morgan about the videos being fake. It's not true of every sequence, you know?

You *what*?

You know the weird one? The one that's not from the station and, like, gets inside your head? That one's way old, like it was recorded back when the Masters came. Data forensics narrowed it to some kind of camera from, like, a hundred and fifty years ago. Sort of thing they used to put in satellites.

What?

Yeah. Look, dude, I guess what I'm saying is they don't come from the same fake-the-return-of-the-Masters video-mashing q-ware suite as the others, right? Two different forgers, and the one who did the Meelosh sequence knows his shit. Look, I got to go. Talk later, boss dude.

Bix disconnects. A moment later a call from Laura crashes into my Servant.

'Keon! Where the fuck are you?'

'Heading out from briefing the chief.'

'Good. Meet me in the canteen.'

Five minutes later I'm in the canteen. It's busy this early in the morning, full of technicians and administrative staff and all the people who work regular hours. The Tesseract does a good breakfast, even if the coffee is shit. Laura is perched at the end of a bench, Thermos in one hand, cup in the other. She doesn't look up but her Servant pings me.

Join me?

I sit next to her. She hands me a second cup and pours from her flask.

'How did it go?' she asks.

I take a sip and then look at Laura in surprise. It tastes like it's mostly whisky.

'The chief isn't happy.'

'No surprise.' I told him Flemich is Tesseract One. Before you went in to see him. Sorry.

'You really believe that?'

She shrugs and looks around. The canteen is nearly full, the buzz of conversation loud enough to drown our words but you never know who might be listening, what filters they're running, what sort of hidden microphone they might have …

'No, actually I don't. But it's what the evidence says.' Flemich put Walter Becker into data forensics six years ago. He authorised the Fleet agents who interrogated Jared Black in Mercy hospital, had access to our movements when Esh died, he's been keeping Hangar 13 at New Hope locked for Swainsbrook and he knew

183

the entry codes to the hangar where we were keeping Vishakh's shuttle. But most damning of all is this.

She pings me a set of files.

The bureau's protection team watching over Doctor Jacksmith was withdrawn last night. Each agent is pulled off by a superficially reasonable request, all from different departments, but the effect was to strip her naked. The only people with that much supervisory access are Morgan and Flemich. So it's one of them.

I don't know what to say. I've known Aaron Flemich since before I graduated. He was Alysha's mentor and later her friend. He came to our wedding. His Cheetah was shot down by the *Flying Daggers* and he nearly died. An Earther agent for all that time, working with Darius Vishakh, working for *October*?

'What did Morgan say?' I don't think Tesseract One worked for Vishakh. I think it was the other way around.

'To get the fuck out of his office.' I agree. 'So sorry about that. My fault if he was in a bad mood.' The Earther mercenaries you took out last night: Himaru still has the one that survived. The Earther has intelligence on the warhead theft that will lead us to Tesseract One. I asked Morgan to let us be the ones to bring him in. You and me and a broken Earther mercenary in a room, no cameras, no recordings, no consequences. Get a confession. Get the evidence to nail Flemich.

I almost choke on my coffee.

'Oh, he told me where to go straight away. No chance.'

'But you must have known that!'

'Of course I did!' Say you're right. Say Tesseract One was pulling Vishakh's strings. You think that could be Flemich?

Do I? No. Not Flemich. He just hasn't got ...

But then who ...?

Laura drains her cup. 'I've dropped some bait, Keon. Let's see if we get a bite, eh?'

'Bait? What bait?'

And then it hits me. Laura thinks Flemich is being set up. You think *Morgan* is Tesseract One?

She grabs my cup and pours us each a refill. The smell makes me giddy.

Not really. I'm not sure *what* I think any more. That I don't know who else has that sort of access, and so it has to be one of them. That I can't believe it of either. 'Who tipped you to the threat on Jacksmith last night?'

I try to sound casual. 'Was a feeling, that's all. I didn't like the way Swainsbrook was looking at me.'

'That's feeble even for you.' She sips at her cup. 'I can't forget how Morgan looked at me after I accused Flemich. As though I was shit he'd scraped off his shoe.'

'Are you surprised? He and Flemich have known each other since forever.'

'Flemich came in a year after the blockade.' She smiles faintly. 'You know he was on the other side before then?'

'He what?'

'Yes.' She laughs. 'He keeps it very quiet, but he was a q-coder and a hacker before Morgan turned him.'

'Flemich? A coder?' I struggle to keep my face straight.

'Sure. He basically founded data forensics. Morgan managed to nail him on something trivial, told him that everyone knew who he was and what he used to do and so now he had a choice: serve his sentence and then be exiled from the net or come and work for the bureau. Flemich took the deal.' She chuckles. 'I remember how Morgan used to talk about him. He was quite taken with Flemich. I think, for a while, he had a bit of a crush going on.'

'You *what*?'

Her smile turns sad and far away. 'That was back when my mother was still alive and I was an idiot teenager.'

'You knew Morgan? Back then?'

185

'Sure. Morgan, Elizabeth, O'Hare, Thiekis, Campbell, Irvine, Kurudu, Rapati and Tapeti – fuck but the two of them didn't get on. Still don't as I hear it. Raisa and Siamake Alash. Keli. All of them. I didn't *know* them, not really, but they all had dealings with my mother and father.' She turns and looks me in the eye. The smile is still there, now with sadness at its edges. 'You know my mother wrote the essence of what became the bureau's charter? The core directives for the Tesseract AI, too.'

'You never told me that.'

'She did a lot of things, most of which no one remembers.' She takes another swig of coffee. 'But you see, whoever you were on Magenta, if you had money and power then my parents were your lawyers.'

Six months we lived together and this is the most Laura has ever said about her family. Not that I ever said much about mine.

'And your sister ...'

'Runs what's left. It was supposed to be me but ... things didn't work out. After my mother died and my father decided to move to Earth ... Mum would never have done that. She loved this world, for all its flaws. It's a shame she never got to see Jamie. She would have been a magnificent grandmother.'

She clinks her cup against mine.

'Fucking families, eh? Who'd have them? Anyway ...' She takes a deep breath and lets out a long sigh as if shrugging off a great load. 'Yes, I've known Vikram Morgan for a long time, and that's why we have to be very careful around him if we have anything to say about Flemich. Or Thiekis or Jacksmith, or any of the rest of that crew for that matter.'

'How well did he know Jacksmith?'

'They were thick as thieves for a while. There were rumours, after Elizabeth's partner died and she was crippled ...' She shakes her head. 'Stupid, though.'

'Rumours?' Did you share Saleesh's names with anyone?

'Oh, you know exactly what I mean.' No!

'Not really.' Doesn't it bother you that someone knew who was on that list before Saleesh put it together?

'Shit, Keon, really? Imagine Elizabeth Jacksmith twenty years younger in a room full of men. She owned them, even from a wheelchair. Of course there were rumours. There are *always* fucking rumours.' What do you mean? Who?

'Oh.' Swainsbrook.

'Exactly. Morgan, Thiekis, Rapati. My father.' She makes a sour face. 'No chance to *that* one was true, though not for want of trying on his part. He was all over her before my mother was even cold, fucking shit that he was.' Swainsbrook? Fuck! Are you sure?

He went after the names on her list and a lot more besides. *You* didn't tell anyone about them either, right? About Rachael Cho?

Laura shakes her head.

Not even Jacksmith?

'No one.' What does he want with them?

'You want to do some fieldwork?' He was recruiting.

'Do I have to?' Fuck! Really?

You're the one who told me about the two other suicides from Saleesh's list!

Can you find out who else he approached?

'There was a journalist last night asking about Iosefa's descendants.' Maybe.

'So?'

'So I want to talk to him. Poke about. See if he knows anything.' Prabu Pradash. He asked Jacksmith about Cho. Flat-out named her, and Jacksmith didn't bat an eye, just denied it. I think Pradash is in Swainsbrook's pocket. I'm going to squeeze him. I want to know how Swainsbrook got those names.

Laura goes quiet. I pass her the address for Pradash.

'Meet me there in half an hour?'

She nods. Keon, this isn't about Meelosh any more.

So glad I have you to point these things out. Could have missed that otherwise. I look her up and down. 'Don't kit up. But come prepared.'

Laura tips the contents of her cup back into her flask and screws it tight. She gets to her feet and pats me on the shoulder.

'See you later.' You think this Pradash has something we can use?

If he knows about Cho then either someone told him or he picked it up from Swainsbrook. You *have* got someone on Cho, right?

I told you it's in hand! 'I need to ... check on something before I leave. I'll see you there. Half an hour?'

Laura heads out of the canteen. I give her a few minutes and then leave too, change into some clothes that don't yell Bureau Agent at the top of their lungs, and call a pod. The weather on the surface is rotten this morning, another storm front washing over Firstfall, so I take an undercity exit and wait. I try to call Jacksmith but I don't get an answer.

A pod arrives. I tell it to take me to Pradash's apartment. I try calling Flemich, but he's probably in with Morgan getting his balls chewed so I'm not surprised when he doesn't pick up. I leave a message asking permission to question Fleet Orbital Traffic Control about the *Betty Blue*. If she left orbit three months ago then I'm betting Fleet picked her up. Maybe they can work out where she went.

Then I call Liss.

'Hey, Keys.'

She sounds like she always sounds, neutral with a light hint of pleased-to-hear-from-me. I never used to question her tone. Now I wonder how carefully she constructs it.

'Last night. Did Alysha see you?'

'Well enough to put three bullets in me.'

'Did she see your face? Did she recognise you?'

The pod lurches violently as we come out from the undercity tunnels and the wind bites. The rain becomes a sudden cacophony like machine gun fire. Much worse and they'll shut the surface down completely. We shift to one of Firstfall's radial highways and speed up, the pod swaying as it fights the wind.

'I don't know, Keys. It was dark and it all happened very quickly. She was wearing some sort of visor. It's possible.'

I pause for a moment, wondering if I could be wrong.

'You saw her too, right?'

'Yes.'

'It *was* her?'

'Yes.'

The pod lurches hard enough to almost tip me off my seat. The wind outside is well past a hundred miles an hour and the rain comes in relentless horizontal sheets. I check the forecast. The storm is heading straight at us and it's only going to get worse. A total surface shutdown is forecast for some time tonight.

'I tried to follow her,' says Liss. 'Pod and surveillance records can only be accessed through the Tesseract but the same isn't true of Servant transactions. I've got hundreds of bots roaming the net, looking for a pattern that might be her.'

'Good luck with that.'

Looking for Alysha without using the Tesseract AI is going to be like looking for a needle in a planet-sized haystack. I need to find a way to use the bureau without the Tesseract knowing what I'm looking for ...

The pod steers off the highway and then speeds up as it sinks into the tunnels where Pradash has his apartment under Cherry Blossom Dip, a self-sufficient community of five thousand homes, the next suburb out from the riches of Champagne Heights around the MagentaNet building.

'I've been following the news,' says Liss.

'It's all bullshit.'

'People are frightened.'

'It's a hoax and we can prove it.' I hesitate, thinking. 'Did Alysha ever have any connection with Frank Swainsbrook?'

'I don't think—'

'Keon?' Laura's call interrupts us. I feel Liss instantly snap her connection to my Servant.

'What?'

'I'm waiting. Where are you?'

Thirty seconds later my pod pulls up in a dead-end tunnel. Laura lounges against the wall. A river of water runs along the gutter beside her, rain from the surface on its way to the hydroponic vats below.

'Been a while since you worked outside?' I ask.

I think I've only ever seen her in either a trouser suit or a combat vest. The belted trench coat and gumshoe hat look brand new.

'Storm's getting worse.' Her eyes gleam as she lenses something. 'Just us? No backup?'

'Tesseract One. No one else can know. Careful, though. I'm treating Pradash as hostile.'

Laura walks a short quick circle, thinking it through.

'Okay,' she says. 'But we've got no warrant for this. You might want to go anonymous. This isn't likely to be legal.'

Pradash's apartment is three floors up in a block just around the corner. We head for the front door. I throw my Tesseract codes at the building Servant to let us in; after that we move quickly, running up the three flights of stairs, legs burning under Magenta's gravity. I throw my codes at Pradash's apartment and the door slides open. We ease in, Reepers drawn. Three rooms, the usual layout: a large lounge-kitchen with a scatter of beanbags, a small table and a full-height closet; two doors out the back, one to a bedroom, one to a wet room. Both are shut but I hear grunting from the bedroom, the sounds of two people engrossed in vigorous sex. The lounge is tidy, almost pristine, as though no one actually lives here.

We creep to the doors at the back. I slide into the wet room. Shower, sink, toilet, the usual. Empty and spotless like the lounge. I gesture Laura to the other door, use my codes and tell the house Servant to open it. We burst in, guns levelled at where the bed ought to be, but it's empty. The ceiling screen is running porn. The grunting comes from speakers in the corners of the room. Pradash isn't here.

Shit. He made us.

Movement catches the corner of my eye as I back out of the room. I whip round to see the closet door open where it used to be closed. Prabu Pradash, naked except for a pair of boxers, is in the middle of darting for the door, a fistful of papers clutched in one hand. Papers, actual papers. I spin and raise my Reeper.

'Pradash!'

I override the apartment Servant. Pradash crashes into the door as it refuses to open. He turns, drops to a half-crouch, eyes darting this way and that for a way out like a cornered animal. I wait until he sees he doesn't have one.

'Put those down,' I say, 'and raise your hands.'

'You can't do this!' he says. 'You have no right of entry into a private residence!'

My Reeper doesn't twitch.

'You have no right of search, seizure or detainment without an approved warrant. Show me that you have one or get out of my home!'

He's not wrong.

Do your I-have-a-law-degree thing.

Laura gives me a sour look and then turns to Pradash.

191

'My partner here thinks you might be an immediate threat to yourself or others.'

'Bullshit!'

'Your lawyer can take that up with him later. In the meantime, put whatever you're carrying down and raise your hands or I *will* stun you. For your own protection, obviously. Actually, now I think about it, clause 337 of the Bureau Articles of Conduct permits the use of discretionary powers in times of crisis threatening the security of critical planetary infrastruct—'

'*More* bullshit!' Pradash's eyes flicker. He's lensing something. Is that real, I ask.

'Look it up, arsehole!' My mother wrote it.

'That's blockade legislation! That's twenty years old!'

'Yet nevertheless both lawful and applicable in current circumstances.'

Pradash looks at Laura, incredulous, then slowly puts down his papers and raises his hands.

'Okay. Tell me what threat to critical infrastructure we're talking about and tell me how it's applicable and I'll co-operate. I believe you have an obligation to do so. Otherwise, fuck off.'

Cheeky bastard is trying to get a story. I try to picture Morgan's face if our missing warhead suddenly went public. As if things aren't already bad enough ...

'He's right.' Laura shrugs. 'We have to tell him why.'

'You're aware there's a military United Nations ship in orbit over Magenta?' I ask. Pradash nods. 'Three weeks ago, it launched missiles at two Cheetahs heading for the southern polar ice. They were both shot down. You want to know more? You want a story?'

Pradash straightens and puts his hands over his head – fuck yes does he want it.

'I am recording this, you know. It's going to be all over the news the moment you leave.'

'You mean you're not streaming it now?' I wave my Reeper at him. 'In here. Sit on the bed. And turn off the fucking.'

He does as he's told.

'Agent Patterson, please keep the front room under surveillance. Please make sure you don't violate anyone's rights by reading any private papers you have no authority to read.'

I close the door, leaving Laura in the lounge, and shut down the apartment surveillance. Whatever Laura does in there, no one will see. Such as tripping over her own feet and accidentally reading all the papers scattered on the floor. Pradash looks furious.

'I am not without connection and influence, you know,' he says.

'Yeah. Last night. I saw. Actually, that's why we're here.' I holster my Reeper. 'You can put your hands down and then I suggest you listen carefully.'

He drops his hands but not the glare.

'There's going to be a story when we leave. You get to choose which one. The first is about a journalist stealing classified information from the Magenta Institute. Your story about Darius Vishakh steering the Stay expedition will come out. No one except Vishakh himself knows how he knew where to look for Lomu, and Vishakh won't be talking about it any time soon, but I don't doubt it'll get some traction. The real name of the woman he contacted will come out. She didn't have much to do with it – she didn't flatline for him, just let him use her rig – but your story will upend her life. The Institute will look stupid and so will you. Meanwhile, your source will disown you and you'll be arrested, charged, and tried for malicious publication of classified information. That's what happens if you decide to sit on your hands and don't help us out.'

Pradash snorts. 'You have nothing on me.'

He's probably right – but the way things are right now I

reckon I can lock him up for a week or two without anyone complaining.

Keon!

Laura's been listening. What?

I've got story number two right here.

She comes into the bedroom and tosses a stack of papers onto the bed next to Pradash. The papers look new but the style of them is ancient, like they were written with a typewriter two hundred years ago. The word SECRET has been stamped on them, top and bottom. Laura has already taken pictures, and now she highlights the ones I need to see. She talks as I start to read.

'Story two: you break how this whole crap about the return of the Masters is a hoax perpetrated by Frank Swainsbrook, assisted by a faction of powerful Magentan businessmen with interests attached to big Earther corporations,' she says.

The papers start with a memo.

The Social and Collective Consequence of an Apparent Return
of the Masters backed by Substantive Evidence

Abstract: The purpose of this paper is to assess the societal consequences of an apparent return of the Masters and the impact to our organisation. It is assumed that such an event is the result of misinterpretation of otherwise scientifically explicable phenomena, possible examples of which we will explore. Our summary conclusion is that such an occurrence may be of benefit and it may therefore be advantageous to actively propagate such misinterpretations for the reasons we outline.

The paper comes from Earth. Its two hundred pages talk about the consequences of a 'false alarm' return of the Masters in terms of predicted effects on various Earth governments and the United Nations. It talks in detail about the panic and confusion that would ensue and how that might best be exploited to service a particular agenda. It's very obviously about a hundred years out of date, and equally obvious that the 'organisation' is *October*. Nothing suggests actively hoaxing a return of the Masters in the first place, but it doesn't take much of a leap to see how the author might think that was a very good idea. A paragraph near the end stops me cold.

In the event of a significant pre-existing species preservation agenda within national governments and international bodies, priority consideration must be given to the exploitation of an apparent 'Return' event within Fleet. It can be assumed that such an event will cause substantial internal division which we should position ourselves to exploit to our fullest advantage. There is no understating the species survival value to be gained by reversing the Treaty of 2067, thus putting the future of humanity back under a single directing authority.

There's a name at the bottom of the paper and an author's signature. Ylena Rothburg, fifty years dead and one of the six founders of *October*.

Pradash has gone very quiet.

'You were already working on story two,' says Laura.

Pradash doesn't answer.

'I need to know where you got this.'

'And what will you give me if I tell you?'

'Anything we can that will help.' Laura gives me a sideways look. 'See, my colleague here thought you were one of Swainsbrook's puppets. But that's not true, is it? I think we're actually on the same side here.'

I snort. 'He works for Eddie Thiekis. Thiekis wants the

Sovereign Rights Act overturned, same as Swainsbrook.' At least, I *think* he does.

Pradash gives me a long, considering look.

'Agent Rause, isn't it?'

I nod. He considers this a moment more, then nods back.

'Elizabeth Jacksmith shook your hand,' he says. 'That was quite something. Okay. Those papers? I stole them from Swainsbrook.'

Laura looks at me. I look at Laura.

It's hard not to smile.

Got you, you bastard.

12

RACHAEL CHO

Prabu Pradash, it turns out, knows a lot about Frank Swainsbrook. Better still, he's been worming his way to an inside view of *October* on Magenta for months. Ostensibly he's doing a puff piece on Settlement 16, but what he's really after is to expose Swainsbrook for what he is: a charlatan and a fraud. Pradash reckons Eddie Thiekis has his back, too. He won't come out and say it, but I get the strong impression that Eddie wants Swainsbrook gone.

We start with what Laura and I already know. Frank Swainsbrook the Third: born on Earth, the billionaire son of a billionaire family. A fortune inherited from his grandfather, who also passed along a heavy dose of hardcore religion and a fascination for the Masters that Frank turned into obsession. According to Pradash, Swainsbrook's grandfather was a member of the Voice of God, fringe Returners dedicated to communicating with the Masters. The Voice of God was mostly about subsidising research, lobbying Earther governments and pressuring Fleet for disclosure of historical documents. Pradash describes Fleet's reaction as more bemused than combative whenever the Voice tried to take them on.

'Like a tiger being yapped at by a chihuahua.' he laughs.

The Voice have nothing to do with Magenta, but Swainsbrook is a different matter. He believes the Masters talk to him, really truly believes. Pradash doesn't know what happened on Swainsbrook's personal Road to Damascus and I can't find it either; but six years ago, Swainsbrook made his first trip to Magenta and he's never looked back. A year after that visit he acquired Settlement 16. He started converting the old derelict mining habitats less than a month later, into the Universe's First Psychic Communications Array. I try to keep a straight face when Pradash says this. Laura doesn't bother.

'The *what*?'

'That's what he calls it.' Pradash is warming to this now. 'Would you mind if I get dressed?'

We give him a few minutes alone. Laura and I go into the kitchen and brew some concoction of brown lichen and tepid water that claims a relation to coffee.

You think he's playing us? I ask.

Does it matter? It's good intelligence either way. And if he isn't then he could blow Swainsbrook's hoax wide open. He could give you exactly what Morgan asked for. Big pat on the back for Agent Rause.

Be careful what you tell him.

Laura scowls but doesn't get a chance to bite my head off before Pradash rejoins us in the kitchen, tucking in his shirt.

'Swainsbrook is quite serious,' he says. 'But wait until we get to how it works!'

Settlement 16 took a year to get up and running. On Earth, things didn't go well for Frank. The costs on Magenta chewed through his personal fortune. The Voice disowned the project and his father cut the family purse strings. Pradash doesn't know how Swainsbrook got his funding after that. He reckons Swainsbrook is up to his neck in debt.

'Debt to whom?' asks Laura.

Pradash doesn't know. I figure the Tesseract could do a lot better if I had a good reason to ask the right questions.

'Have you been there?' Pradash asks. 'From the outside it's a thriving community, cut off but almost entirely self-sufficient. But everyone who lives there flatlines at least once every month. And I mean *every*one. Mister Swainsbrook once told me that he goes under at least once a week.'

By which he means they stop their hearts, oxygen-starve their brains, and then bring themselves back, just like Rachael Cho. Just like Darius Vishakh did when he was looking for Iosefa Lomu.

'The Sixteeners claim to hear voices. God or the Masters, they see the two as the same. Mister Swainsbrook claims the messages have changed in this last year: he says the Masters are coming back. He says they will be the saviours of humanity! It's been blowing out of him for more than a month.'

Laura shakes her head, I'm not sure whether in disgust or simple disbelief.

'Wait a minute – if Swainsbrook believes the Masters are God then ...' She takes a deep breath, touches a hand to her brow, then shakes her head and laughs at me. 'Shit, Rause, do you suppose Swainsbrook is trying to bring on the fucking Rapture! I can't wait to be in the room when you try and sell that one to the Chief!'

'Me?'

She smiles sweetly. 'Your case, Rause.'

Pradash falls silent as Laura and I chew on what he's told us. We have two, possibly three planetary crises, and somehow in the middle of it are a bunch of loony cultists led by a crazy rich Earther, probably more crazy than rich these days, who might just be trying to trigger the End of Everything?

'Okay,' I say. 'Here's the first juice from us in return. These videos supposedly coming from an old abandoned station orbiting the sun? They're fakes. They don't match the cameras installed on the station. You want details, talk to Agent Bix Rangesh at the bureau. I'll tell him to expect you. You'll like him.' I ping him Bix's contact information. 'The kicker is that someone really is using the station as a relay to broadcast them back to Magenta, which means someone had to go out there and bypass the station systems to set all this up. Professor Handl at the Magenta Institute can tell you more about that. You know how many privately owned shuttles in the Magentan system have the range and endurance to get out there? Exactly one: Swainsbrook's *Betty Blue*. If you care to look, you might discover that a tac-team raided New Hope last night, went into the hangar where the *Betty Blue* has supposedly been sitting idle for the last three months, and guess what? Empty hangar. You won't get any official confirmation, but there are plenty of civilian administrators at New Hope who saw what went down.'

'*Privately* owned?' Pradash raises an eyebrow.

'I can't speak for what's in orbit. Fleet ships, Earther ships. Stuff like that. I can't *prove* that it was Swainsbrook, but it was.' I frown at Pradash, trying to work out the timeline in my head. 'Last couple of weeks, Swainsbrook's been recruiting Magentans to join him. You know anything about that?'

Pradash nods. 'He told me as much.'

'Who?'

'I don't have names. I wanted to interview them to ask why they would join such an enterprise, but Mister Swainsbrook won't allow it. As far as I can determine, all his people until now were recruited from Earth. It's strange – it's almost the one thing that makes him clam up.'

I almost give him the two names I know, the ones from Saleesh's list, then think better of it. 'I think they're already at Settlement 16. Frank took them personally.'

'In his fucking helicopter,' mutters Laura.

'Do you know anything about them at all,' I ask. 'How many there are? I think he targeted them, possibly individually? Any idea how he chose them? Or why?'

Pradash waggles his head, in wonder rather than denial. 'I don't know how many, but his helicopter made several journeys between Firstfall and Settlement 16 in the last two weeks. I would say perhaps between fifteen and twenty people? He claims they were chosen by God for a Great Purpose.'

'God gave Swainsbrook a bunch of names in one of his fucking flatline sessions?' Laura spits out her contempt. 'Fuck off!'

'Great purpose?' I ask. 'And what exactly does he think that is?'

'To open the path to Heaven so everyone might hear the Word of God. His words, not mine.'

We look at each other. Laura looks like she doesn't know whether to laugh or break something. 'I take it back,' she says. 'I don't want to be there when you tell the Chief. I don't want to be anywhere near. Not even the same fucking building.'

I let Laura and Pradash work out the details of the story Pradash is going to run. It'll end with *October* on Magenta and Earther interference in Magentan politics. He's a bright lad. He can see how big this is, and what *I* see is the light of ambition behind his eyes. It's a career-maker of a story and he knows it, and that means we'll get what we want, because Pradash wants it too. While he and Laura talk, I verify as much as I can of his story. It stands up. Swainsbrook seems happy to be loud and public about his ambitions.

'How long before this can go out?' I ask.

'Couple of days.'

I shake my head. 'Twenty-four hours. If it's not topping the news when the *Fearless* flips in from Earth, we'll break it ourselves.'

'Okay.'

I tell him I want to see it before it runs but he baulks at that. I can't say I blame him. He's a journalist after all, and right up until we walked into his apartment he was thinking that Swainsbrook had the Magentan government behind him. I decide not to push my luck. If Pradash comes through, the Chief will be a very happy man. If he doesn't, well, it's not like we've lost anything here.

We leave. Outside, Laura takes the first pod that answers our call.

'I'll talk to the Chief about getting a team to that settlement of his.' She forces a smile. 'We did good work just now. *You* did good work.' She's half in the pod when she stops and turns. Behind the flush of our success she looks strained. Tired. 'It *is* a hoax, right?'

'What, you think the Masters are really coming back?'

'No. But ... Rangesh told you that not all of the videos look forged, right?'

'You mean the one Meelosh had that didn't come from the station?'

'So where *did* it come from, Keon? There's something else here. Something we're missing.'

'I don't know.'

She's right, though. Something still doesn't add up.

'How do you kill someone with a video?' For a moment she sounds small. Quiet. Struggling to keep it together. It's not the Laura I'm used to seeing. It takes me a moment to realise that she's afraid.

'It wasn't the video. Meelosh killed himself.'

'Bullshit. Two others watched the same video and killed

202

themselves too. Three out of six, and Swainsbrook approached a lot more than that. When I look, and I'm going to, how many more suicides am I going to find?'

'I've watched it,' I say. 'So did Bix. We're both still here. You can't kill someone with a video.'

'I wish I had your certainty.'

She climbs into her pod and I watch her go. I know the game Swainsbrook is playing. He and *October* have one thing right: we have no idea where the Masters went or why, so it *is* possible they're still out there, and they *could* return at any moment, without warning or reason. What matters isn't whether all this is real or a hoax, what matters is the fear it leaves behind, a fear that everything we love and everything we know has no meaning, that everything can simply cease, without cause or warning. Fear of the Masters is a fear that stares into the dark heart of the universe and sees the truth: that there are no rules, no absolutes, only chaos and chance. It's the fear of our own utter insignificance, a fear that crawls inside us if we think about it for long enough, and once it's inside, it never leaves.

I know that fear. It writhes whenever I think of Alysha.

Another pod comes. I tell it to take me to the hydroponics lake where Alysha changed into Kamaljit Kaur. As it pulls away, I trawl through the message boards and chat rooms where people gather to talk. There's an edge of panic in the air: is it real? If the Masters are here, is Lomu the reason? Why Magenta, of all places? Or maybe when the *Fearless* arrives we'll learn that Earth is already a smoking ruin. Or maybe the *Fearless* will never come, and what if it doesn't? Can we survive on our own ...?

The tunnels are empty this morning. I guess people are staying in, staying close to the ones they love, seeing how the dross and fluff of daily life suddenly doesn't matter so much. The Selected Chamber has issued a statement urging Magentans to carry on as normal, quietly and calmly pointing out that nothing has changed; but quiet and calm doesn't win at times like this. Whatever the government says, Firstfall is still in lockdown and almost no one knows why.

Has Swainsbrook already won? He's made us afraid, and so maybe it doesn't matter what Pradash writes, or what Laura and Rangesh and I can prove. Fuck it, he could probably give a public confession and *still* win, because what matters isn't the truth of what's happening *now*, but what the truth might be next time, or the time after. All he needs to get what he wants is one or two out of fifty-one Selected Representatives to feel that fear inside them, and if even Laura is feeling it then I'm betting he gets twenty.

We need more, more than Pradash. We need to crush this hoax out of existence. We need to hold up those responsible. We need to take the fear and turn it into something else, and so it goes past who and how, we need to show the *why*. We need to show how every one of us is being used, take that fear and blowtorch it into anger and outrage. We need whatever passes in this century for a public hanging, a lynch mob with pitchforks and torches. A public confession isn't going to be enough. We need a crucifixion, a medieval drawing and quartering. We need to set the dogs on Frank Swainsbrook and on *October* and tear them to pieces, and even then I'm not sure that would be enough.

The pod is taking me out of Cherry Blossom Dip, down into one of the secondary transit ways that mirror the radial highways on the surface. Despite the weather up on the surface, it's almost empty.

How do you kill someone with a video?

Swainsbrook's videos are a hoax, but the one that killed Meelosh is something different, and there's something else under all this, something I can't see. Maybe the reason I can't see it is because a part of my head is always with Alysha. I need to find her.

Liss?

Keys?

Any trace of her?

No.

Alysha was always good at her fieldcraft. Good at everything. An excellent marksman. An understanding of what q-ware systems could do that was almost uncanny, even if she was never a coder. She knew her tech inside and out and she could spoof a surveillance suite better than anyone in the bureau. I always thought that if she had a weakness, it was with people, a reluctance to trust. But looking at how things have panned out, maybe I was wrong about that. Maybe that wasn't a weakness at all.

She saw your face, I say.

Perhaps.

What would she do, seeing her own face on a shell? What would she think? I know what *I'd* think – I'd think I was a fucking creep with some serious emotional issues who should be avoided at all costs.

Would I? Or would I see the love that went in to that creation?

Doesn't matter. What matters is how Alysha sees it.

She's not going to come back to me, I say.

She tipped you on Jacksmith. She led you to Swainsbrook's shuttle. She's trying to help you. Not the Tesseract or the bureau. You.

Yeah, but if she's seen you …

Grief can be beautiful.

No trace of bitterness, but Liss is only telling me what I want to hear. Anyone else you know brought their dead lover back as a shell? I was almost close enough to touch her. Whatever made her run, we could have worked it out.

205

She's not working alone, Keys. You know that. If it's not Earth and it's not the bureau then it must be Fleet.

Deep down I know she's right. If she was here for Lomu then she could have taken him back on the ice. And she didn't.

Love conquers all?

There it is. The bitter irony, the gentle mocking she can't quite hide. And she's wrong, because the idea that love conquers all is a steaming heap of crap, but she's also right, because here I am, staring out across the water of a hydroponic lake, thinking of Alysha as the world goes to shit all around me.

Will you help me get off Magenta after you find her? Liss asks. When you don't need me or want me, I'd like to go to Earth.

Sure. I'm not going to find Alysha so the question seems pointless.

I want to find the cracksman who made me.

Why?

Who better to change me?

Change you?

I think it's for the best if I—

'Rause!' My Servant pings. Jacksmith this time, and again I feel the connection to Liss snap away.

'What do you want?'

'To ... say ... thank you. To you and your partner. For preventing a deeply inconvenient abduction.'

'You're welcome.'

'Where did you go after you left me alone in that tunnel?'

'You mean you don't already know?'

'I know the official Tesseract story.'

'Then why are you asking?'

'Because I'm interested in your particular version of events. And in your partner, Keon. I'm very interested in your partner.'

'And *I'm* very interested in what really happened back out on the ice between you and Kamaljit Kaur.'

206

'I haven't said anything about what I saw. Not yet.'

'What do you want?'

'Right now? Frank Swainsbrook's head on the end of a very sharp stick.'

The black water of the lake is perfectly still. Far in the distance I see the light of a harvester drone, raking up kelp for processing. I could tell Jacksmith that she and I want the same thing. I could tell her about Pradash and how her Swainsbrook dreams are all about to come true. But I don't, because I'm pretty damned sure that if anyone can lead me to Alysha then it's Doctor Elizabeth Jacksmith. I want to see what she has to offer. And she saw me with Liss, so either I let her think that it was really Alysha, or I give Liss away.

'He's behind this hoax, Rause! It's all fucking Swainsbrook!'

'You have evidence of that?'

'He's been banging on for years about contacting the Masters. I've been waiting for him to actually try because I always figured it would end with him a laughing stock all the way from here to Earth and back. But that was before Iosefa, and none of this is remotely funny any more. I rather think I misjudged our Mister Swainsbrook.'

'Sounds more like sour grapes than evidence, Elizabeth.' On the other side of the lake is a hydroponics factory. Beside it is a refinery. Amaranth Seaweed Oils.

'Oh, fuck you, Keon, you know I'm right. Evidence is *your* job, isn't it? That's how this works: I point, you click. Or something like that.'

'So what really happened on the ice?'

I hear her sigh. I guess the silence that follows is all I'm going to get.

'You and Frank ever talk about Lomu?'

'At the moment no one talks to me about anything else!'

'I mean before.'

'Of course not!'

'Kettler's work? Iosefa's descendants?'

'Absolutely not! I try not to talk to Frank at all if I can help it!'

'Have you tested her yet?'

'Tested who?'

'Rachael Cho.'

Jacksmith pauses just long enough to be an admission of guilt.

'So I'm right. You already knew. Before last night.'

'Rause, if I had anything to say to you about *any* of my work with Iosefa, I certainly wouldn't be saying it on a line where any Tom, Dick or Harry with a half-decent piece of q-ware might be listening. Hello, Fleet, by the way! I'm sure *you're* listening! Earth, you too, except you can fuck off with bells on! Look, Keon, I'm a tad busy right now but I'll make an exception for Frank. Shut him down!'

'Just for once I'm ahead of you.'

'Really? Doesn't look like it if you're about to let him fly back to his little cult.'

'Swainsbrook's not going anywhere. Firstfall is locked down. He wants to leave, he can get on the mag-lev and go through security like anyone else.'

'Maybe you should mention that to Eddie Thiekis, since Frank's helicopter at MagentaNet is getting ready to leave Firstfall right fucking now!'

'*What?* How?'

Yeah. How does Frank Swainsbrook, of all people, get permission to fly out of Firstfall when we're all searching for a vagrant piece of antimatter? I won't ask how Jacksmith knows about this before any of the rest of us.

'He's Frank.'

Jacksmith cuts the call. I ping Laura: Swainsbrook at MagentaNet Tower? Preparing to leave Firstfall by air? Authorised?

I try not to think about how blue the air will get when she picks that up. I follow up with a request to the Tesseract for transport to Settlement 16, because it seems high time one of us went out there, only not me, not now, not yet, not before I find Alysha.

I walk to the edge of the hydroponic lake until the water touches my toes. The cave is dark and the only lights are a few dim glows from the factory and refinery across the water, from the blinking lights of the harvester drones. My Servant superimposes a scene onto my lenses, helping me see. Three tanker pods are parked outside the refinery. I scan for other Servants but no one else is here. The place is deserted.

The smell. Seaweed and Xen. The smell Alysha had when she came to me in Mercy. I crouch and scoop a handful of water from the lake and taste it. I don't know why, but it tastes of salt and lichen as it runs between my fingers.

She's not here. Of course she isn't. She probably hasn't been here since that night she came to me in Mercy. I don't even know why I came, yet here I am, and the disappointment is crushing. Was last night in the Roseate Project the last time I'll ever see her?

I get back into my waiting pod and message Rachael Cho to say I'm on my way. I get a message back almost at once saying she's expecting me. Her Servant tells me the usual place in the outskirts of Firstfall, the old fabrication unit where she flatlines. I tell the pod to take me out there and ride to the surface. Out in the open, the wind howls through the streets of Champagne Heights. It batters the pod. Rain thunders on the roof. The storm front is coming in and it's only going to get worse, but there's no undercity tunnel that can take me to Rachael Cho.

I'm going to root Swainsbrook out. I'm going to tear his fire-walls apart and show the world what he's done. Laura's going to track down the others Swainsbrook approached. We're going to

209

expose *October*, all of them, and hang them out in public. And after that, Tesseract One, and I'm going to show the world that Alysha was never a traitor, and she'll come home because I've made it possible, and everything will be the way it was ... but I can't stop the chill that creeps through the marrow of my every bone. What if Alysha doesn't *want* to come back? What if ...?

What if ...?

Two pods loiter conspicuously near Cho's little prefab. I ping the agents inside as I pass and get their names. Tesseract names, not Himaru's men, because I'd never see one of Himaru's soldiers until he stepped out from a shadow and put a gun to my head. I ping Laura.

I'm at Cho's place. The Tesseract has agents watching her. Was that you?

What? Shit, no!

Sure you didn't tell anyone?

Actually yes, I did, I just like lying to your face for fun. Of course I'm fucking sure! And before you ask, Swainsbrook's not going anywhere until this storm passes. Keon ... I've found more suicides. Seven of them. All the same day as Meelosh or a day either side, and they all took the same way out.

Swainsbrook?

In touch with at least three of them in the days before they died. I'm still working the others.

So it *was* him.

He's connected, yes. Keon – it's the same video.

We need to get to Settlement 16 before he does.

Agreed.

We need to find who else he contacted. The ones he took.

We need to bring him in, Keon.

Jacksmith called. She wants his head on a spike.

Good, but we need to come up with a reason. Before the weather breaks and he leaves—

I cut the link as the pod slows to a stop. Cho's door opens as I reach it. She hurries me inside.

'I knew you'd be back,' she says, and smiles. 'I'm ready.'

'Ready for what?'

'To ask the Masters for the answers you want.'

'I'm not here for that.'

It's not why I came, but Cho smiles like she knows better. Maybe she does. 'You still have people watching me?'

'I still think you're in danger. Have you heard of a Doctor Jacksmith at the Magenta Institute? She's been on the news—'

'I'm not supposed to talk about that.'

The resignation in her voice tells me everything. Yes, she's heard of Elizabeth Jacksmith, and yes, Jacksmith *has* tested her, just as I thought, but Jacksmith hasn't told her the results – probably didn't even tell her *why* she was being tested, and yet Cho knows anyway. Or has an inkling, at least.

'I'm sorry it had to be you,' I say.

'I could ... say the same.' Her eyes glitter as she gestures at her flatline rig. 'Are you ready now?'

'I told you that's not why I came.'

'I know you did.'

I don't like the way this is going. The more she says it, the more I realise I don't really know why I came here at all, that I have no reason to be here, and that the last thought on my mind when I decided to come was Alysha, not Saleesh or Meelosh or Swainsbrook and his stupid videos.

'The Masters didn't warn you?' I sound patronising but I don't mean to be. The first time Rachael Cho told me what she did for a living, I assumed she was a charlatan. Now I have to wonder. Do I really believe she hears the voices of the Masters when she dies? Frank Swainsbrook has built a whole cult around the idea, after all ...

Of course I don't.

And yet …

'It doesn't work that way.' I freeze in surprise as Cho takes my hand but I don't flinch away. There's something disarming about her. 'You *do* have questions though,' she says.

I pull carefully free. 'Yeah, I do. Did you receive an odd video a week or so back? Weird shit, no idea who sent it?'

'Yes.'

'Did you watch it?'

She shivers and looks away. 'I knew there was something wrong with it. I could feel it.'

'Something wrong?'

'Just a feeling.'

Cho sits on the edge of her flatliner gurney. The power is on and everything's good to go. She's right. This is why I came, so she could die and ask the Masters how I can find Alysha.

'You're still doing this, even now?'

'Not really. This is for you.'

'Me?' No way in hell I'm killing myself and then coming back again.

'You have questions.'

'You can ask the Masters who sent that video, if you like.'

She smiles again, gentle and kind. 'I don't need to. That was Frank Swainsbrook. But that's not the question you came here to ask.'

She's right. It's not. I swallow the lump in my throat.

'Swainsbrook? Can you prove that?'

She nods.

'How?'

'I asked him.'

'You … You just *asked* him?'

She nods.

'It was meant for … for people like you, I think. I think you'll see something there that I don't.' I falter through the words.

212

Aloud they sound even more stupid than they did in my head. 'Would you watch it with me?'

'It's poison,' she says.

'What?'

'Poison. And I already watched it, Keon. You're not the first to ask.'

'What? Who ...?' Then I realise I already know. 'Jacksmith, right?' Of course. Why the fuck does she always know everything before I do?

'I'm not supposed to talk about it.' Cho takes my hand again. 'But we both know I could have told you all this without you coming all the way out here in such terrible weather.'

'What did you see?'

'In all the ones from space I saw the same as everyone else. But other one ... When I saw *that* one, I wanted to kill myself.'

'*What?*'

'Like the others.' She laughs. 'It's okay. Doctor Jacksmith warned me. She told me what happened to the others. I knew what I was doing and I watched it anyway. I wanted to help her.'

I want to scream. Jacksmith! How did she know?

'You said it was poison?'

'I don't know how else to describe it. The way it was like watching a hive of insects. The words that crawl out of it. I watched and I wanted to die. More than anything, I wanted to die.' She shivers. 'It passed after I closed my eyes. I remember what I saw and how it felt, but the urge has gone. But I won't watch it again, Keon. Not even for you.'

How do you kill someone with a video? I want to ask her how that can be possible but maybe that's a question for Jacksmith, because she and I are surely having another conversation very soon. Loud and heated, and if she doesn't play straight this time then I *will* lead her out of her office in cuffs, wheelchair and all.

213

'I'm sorry,' I say. 'I shouldn't have asked. Was that before or after you found out who sent it?'

'Before.'

'So you knew what it was when you spoke to Swainsbrook? Did you ask him why? I mean, why the fuck he would send you something like that?'

'He said the Masters were coming and that people like me could help find a way to talk to them before it was too late.'

'He *told* you that?'

'Yes. And I told him to leave me alone, and he did.' She smiles and pats the gurney again. 'Are you ready?'

'The Masters aren't coming back?'

I mean it to be a statement of fact but it comes out sounding like a question.

'No, Keon, they're not. I'd feel it if they were.'

I ought to scoff at something so absurd. I certainly shouldn't be taking comfort from it, yet I do. There's always been something other-worldly about Rachael Cho. But if I'm going to believe in Cho, why not Swainsbrook too? Is it just because the guy's an arsehole?

'Ask your question, Keon Rause. It's the only reason you came and the only reason I'm here.' She lies back on the gurney and starts the machines around it. 'You can sit with me if you like. I don't normally allow it, but you tried so hard to be nice that last time you came. You were doing your job, I know, but you tried to be kind.'

I can't look at her. Yes, I came here to ask a woman I barely know to kill herself in the desperate hope that it might help me find a lover who ran away nearly six years ago. I don't even believe in any of this shit, yet here I am. Desperation can make us do things we wouldn't dream.

'Did Frank Swainsbrook admit to making the video that ... that made you want to kill yourself?'

The look Cho gives me is of a loving parent to a wayward child. She's shaking her head like there's something obvious I'm missing.

'He didn't *make* it, Keon. He found it. If anything, he was as shocked as you are when I told him what it did to me. Nothing with a soul made *that* abomination, and for all his faults, Frank Swainsbrook still has one of those. But that's not your question.'

'Are you telling me—'

'You have to ask, Agent Keon Rause of the Tesseract. You have to say the words aloud so we both know that you mean them. Why are you here?'

'I ...' The words come out mangled. 'Alysha. I want ... to know ... where she ... I want to know ... How do I find her? What do I have to do?'

Cho stretches out an arm, inserts a cannula with practised ease, hooks it up to a drip and lies back. She's done this a thousand times.

'You don't need to worry,' she says. 'It's all automated. I'll talk to you while it takes effect. When I stop, you know I'm gone. Don't do anything. You can hold my hand if you like. I'll only be out for a few minutes. You'll feel me when I start coming back, and if anything goes wrong then my Servant will take over. It knows what to do. But you really don't need to worry. Nothing will go wrong because nothing ever does. Do you understand?'

I nod.

'The other videos came from Frank, too. We talked for quite a while actually but he wouldn't say why he did it, just that it wasn't really important and that none of it was real. He seemed ... lost, somehow. Ashamed, perhaps. Nothing like he is when he does those public interviews. Did you know, the Akkadian script you can see is the epic of *Enûma Eliš*. Frank said it describes the contest between Marduk and Tiamat, the dragon of chaos. It begins with the creation of the world from primeval darkness and the birth of the gods of light. Then comes a struggle between light and chaos. Marduk cuts Tiamat in half and makes heaven from one half of her body … earth from the other. He arranges … the stars and the sun and moon and … gives them laws they can … never break … After that … plants and animals. The story was … favourite of Frank's … as a child … That's who he thinks he is … Marduk … Lightbringer …'

I take her hand as she dies.

13

DREAMS OF
FUTURES PAST

I sit holding Rachael Cho's hand, waiting for her to come back from the dead. That's when Laura calls to tell me I can't fly out to Settlement 16 because no one's flying anywhere until the storm passes, and there simply isn't another way to get out there.

'The good news is that Swainsbrook's stuck in the MagentaNet Tower,' she says. 'Waiting it out. We could go and question him if you like.'

What I have in mind is more like crashing in with two heavily armed tac-teams and tearing bits off him until he tells me how he knew about Une Meelosh and Rachael Cho before anyone else, but I suppose that's out of the question.

'Or we could wait.' Laura pauses.

'Why?'

Most of my attention is with Cho, the monitor beside her and the flat line it shows.

'Because Swainsbrook is going to board that helicopter the moment the weather eases, and Elizabeth got it wrong – no one gave him *permission*, he's going to do it because he's simply that arrogant. Since the whole city is a no-fly zone, that means we can arrest him for violation of restricted airspace as soon he leaves the ground. He'll get off with a fine, sure, but it's legal and we get to lock him up and force him to talk. More to the point, we might be able to hold him long enough to get someone out to Settlement 16 before him. So I like that option.'

I check the weather forecast to see how long I've got before the storm passes. Best part of the rest of the day and night. Maybe we can get out to Settlement 16 before the *Fearless* comes and goes but it's not looking great.

'You see where this goes, right?' asks Laura.

'Yeah. We hold him on the violation until Pradash breaks his story. Then we bring up his missing shuttle, charge him with conspiracy or some other shit we know won't stick but lets us hold him longer. The *Fearless* flips in and flips out, and that's the story it takes back to Earth.'

'Fuck the *Fearless*, Keon! We've got twenty-four hours before the Sovereign Rights repeal vote goes back on to the chamber floor ... Oh. Sorry. You don't know?'

'No.'

'Well, now you do. So that's how long we have to prove the videos are a hoax and publicly hang Swainsbrook by the balls. We throw every piece of shit at him that we can find, we show everyone how he was trying to manipulate the vote, and we make it all very, *very* public.'

'Yeah.' For a moment I almost forget Cho. 'Lots of angry Magentans tell their Selected Representatives exactly what they think.'

'The vote fails for a second time and then we cut a deal. Swainsbrook tells us everything he knows, we drop all the charges and let him go, he takes the next shuttle off Magenta and never comes back.'

'And then?'

I feel Laura frown. 'Still trying to work that out. We dig out the Magentan side of this and crucify everyone who had a part in it? That sound about right to you?'

'You think he can finger Tesseract One?'

'Doubt it.'

Yeah, me too. 'As soon as the weather breaks, we get some-one out to that cult of his and seize everything we can.'

'Swainsbrook first. We don't show our cards until the last minute.'

I squeeze Cho's hand. It feels dead and flaccid.

'Keon, you should know that Morgan's gone over our heads – a Fleet shuttle left High Hope three hours ago with a Fleet crew of three and two MSDF officers heading for the solar station. It's going to take them six days to get out there. Vishakh's shuttle is ready to go in case we need a backup, but this way is faster.'

'Six days? I thought we were looking at two weeks!'

'Their flight profile burns almost all their fuel on the way out. There's a second shuttle following as a tanker. Fleet are falling over themselves to help, fuck knows why. Get some rest, or do whatever else you need to do, but be at the MagentaNet Tower when this storm breaks. Once we get Swainsbrook in a cell, we can take it in turns to go at him.'

'It still bothers me how Swainsbrook's not even trying to hide what he's—' Cho's fingers twitch in my hand. 'I need to go.'

'Where are you?'

I hesitate, but Laura can easily find out if she tries.

'With Rachael Cho.'

'Shit! What the *fuck* are you doing there?'

'Confirming that your good friend Elizabeth Jacksmith knew about Saleesh's names before Saleesh ever did.'

'How?'

'I'll be asking her that very shortly. You should know she already brought Cho in for testing.'

'What? Fuck!'

'You want to come along when she and I talk, you let me know.'

I drop the call to Laura as Cho twitches and her eyes flutter. She takes a sudden breath, grunting as she does, then jerks upright, chest heaving.

'I'm there,' she says, quick and breathless. 'So is she. So are you. A big empty space. Dark. There's a spaceship. Small. Black.' Each syllable comes out fast and sharp. Cho's body is almost rigid. She stares straight ahead as if she's not seeing anything at all. 'Jacksmith. That's how you find her. Elizabeth Jacksmith. But ...'

She slumps as her breathing slows, blinks, and then her eyes shift back into focus. She looks at me for a moment of abject horror and then turns away, takes a deep breath and slides off the gurney. Her movements are slow and cautious now. Woozy, maybe, from the effects of near-death.

'I don't ... No. No, I'm sorry. It's gone.'

I touch her shoulder. 'What do you mean, gone?'

'Keon, she's going to hurt you.' There are tears in Cho's eyes.

'What? That makes no sense!'

'It does to her.' She staggers a little and grabs hold of the gurney for support as she gets to her feet. 'If you keep looking ... I saw her shoot you.'

A big empty space. Dark. There's a spaceship. Small. Black ... New Hope? A hangar? Hangar 13? Vishakh's shuttle! Vishakh's shuttle was black ...

'She's going to *shoot* me?'

The horror on Cho's face tells me enough. She stares at the floor and can't look me in the eye.

'I'm sorry. The answers aren't always—'

220

I turn away to leave. The door slides open, cutting Cho's words as the wind almost knocks me off my feet. I stagger sideways out into a hurricane and crash into the side of the fabricator wall. Rain slices into me. The wind is too strong, and even in a storm coat I'm taking a battering. I need to get to shelter, because if this gets much worse then the surface is going to shut down. I drop to my hands and knees and crawl into the teeth of the wind and rain to reach my pod. Stupid to come here. Stupid to hope that something like this could work. Stupid to imagine, even for a moment, that Cho isn't a charlatan. What the fuck was I thinking?

I message Laura: Cho should be somewhere safe.

Safe from me.

Fuck. *Fuck!*

My pod lets me in but it won't move. A warning flashes in my Servant: Wind exceeds safe limits.

I try to override with my Tesseract codes but the pod refuses. I should know better. I give up and try to open the door to get back out. I'll fucking walk to the nearest tunnel entrance if I have to, and take a pod from there, but now the pod doors won't open.

Wind exceeds safe limits.

'Fuck!' I hammer the door. 'Fuck fuck fuck fuuuuuck!'

Turns out I can override the door, at least. I tumble back out into the storm. The wind instantly knocks me flat and rolls me against a wall. I push myself to my hands and knees but the nearest tunnel entrance is five, six hundred yards away, and there's no chance I'm going to make it. I go back to Cho's door instead, force it to open and claw my way inside. Cho is where I left her. She moves to help but then stops as I recoil. Her face is puffy. There are tears on her cheeks. She looks at me, face set in sorrow.

'I don't choose what I see.'

She climbs back onto her gurney. I don't know what she's doing except it looks like she's ready to go back under, never even got as far as taking the cannula out of her arm. She starts to hook herself up again ...

I catch her by the wrist. 'No.'

'Get off me!'

'Stop it!'

She stops. Sighs, then slowly untapes the needle from her arm.

'I can't leave,' I say. 'The storm.'

She glares at me, long and angry, and then the angry slides into sad and she touches my arm.

'You don't have to believe it will end that way.'

'I don't.'

She shakes her head, closes her eyes and turns away.

'What did you really see?'

'Forget it. I'm a fraud and a liar. It's okay.'

'I can't.'

I can't walk away from Alysha or from anything about her, not even this. And I can't walk away from Rachael Cho either, because six years ago Darius Vishakh came here looking for the lost wreck of a crashed Masters' ship, and somehow he found it, and when I asked him how, he said the Masters told him where to look, and however many shades of bullshit I think that is, I have no other way to explain it.

'You believe in this,' I say. 'You believe what you see is real. So what did you see?'

She shakes her head. 'It's not always as simple as—'

The look on my face stops her. At least she doesn't tell me that I don't want to know. *Want* has nothing to do with this. I *have* to know. I *need* to know.

'I saw us together. You, me, your wife ... Alysha. We were in a large dark space that felt like it wasn't inside but wasn't outside either. A cave, maybe, or something like it, with a big open mouth. There was some sort of spaceship close by. It was black. Doctor Jacksmith was there too. They were carrying her away—'

'They?'

'I don't know … something very bad was happening. You both had such a terrible sadness in you. And then she shot you.' She looks at me, heartbroken, earnest tears in her eyes, and takes my hand. 'It doesn't have to end that way. The future is never fixed.'

I take a deep breath. 'I went after Darius Vishakh after the last time I came here. It ended on the ice. Alysha found us. We were both done, both dying. She could have taken what she came for and left me behind but she didn't. She saved my life instead.'

I don't know whether I'm saying this for her or for me. For me, I think, but it's still true. Alysha did that. She didn't have to.

'Why would she shoot me?'

Cho shakes her head. 'There was something tearing you straight down the middle. Both of you. I can't explain, it was just how it felt.'

We sit in silence, still holding hands as the storm rages.

Liss?

Hey, Keys.

Why would you shoot me?

I would never shoot you.

Really? Never? There's nothing that would make you do that?

There's a long pause, then: To save you, perhaps.

To *save* me?

From yourself? I don't know. I don't think I could do it.

'Are you sure you don't want me to go back? I can look again. Maybe there's—'

'No.' I get up. 'I'm sorry I came. You should run. Hide. They

223

think you're descended from Lomu, which means you might have the same magic genes. Jacksmith knows. Swainsbrook knows. I don't know how but he does, and that means he's not the only one, and that means they'll come for you. I don't even know who *they* are, not really, but your life is never going to be the same if they find you. So run. Disappear. That's what I'd do. It's what Alysha did.'

Laura will eviscerate me for this if she ever finds out, if Jacksmith doesn't get to me first. I go to the door. I can't stay here, not with her.

'They're already watching you, you know.'

'I know.' Cho smiles. 'And thank you, but running will only make it worse. You don't suppose I only look at other people's futures, do you?'

'I suppose not.'

My pod outside Cho's unit is still refusing to move. Now Cho's door refuses to open, too. Wind exceeds safe limits.

'You can stay here if you want.' She pats the gurney. 'I'm on a sofa in the other room.'

It doesn't look like I have much choice, but if it's Cho's flat-lining gurney or the floor then it's going to be the floor.

'I'm sorry this had to happen to you,' I say again.

Cho actually laughs. 'Don't be. I've seen where it ends.'

'And where's that?'

'Somewhere amazing. You just need to give it time.'

I don't know where it comes from, but all of a sudden she's got her arms around me, hugging me, kissing me gently on the lips, nuzzling her head against my neck, and I'm too surprised to do anything except stand there as she lets go and steps away, still smiling.

'Good night, Agent Keon Rause.'

She walks away into the other room and I can't work out whether or not I'm supposed to follow.

I pull the blanket off the gurney, ball it into a makeshift pillow, and curl up on the floor.

Liss?

Still here.

I tell her everything. Pradash, Laura, Cho, Jacksmith. Everything that's happened since we saw Alysha out in the Roseate Project.

Was that only last night? It feels like a lifetime.

Why would she shoot me? I need to sleep.

I don't know, Keys.

I try to read emotion in her words. Is she pleased? Is she secretly happy? Does she think that means we can go back to the way things were, not me with Alysha but me with Liss? But we can't ...

It hits me like a rock to the skull. We can't go back. None of us can. Ever.

I check the weather forecast. The storms are coming in waves. As soon as this one breaks, the next is already building behind it. There should be a gap in the small hours of the night before the next front rolls in, and then the next and the next, wave after wave for three solid days, maybe four. If the forecast is wrong about the break in the winds, I could be here a while.

I tell my Servant to wake me as soon as the pod outside decides it's safe to move, and close my eyes. If I dream, I don't remember.

FIVE

TINKER, TAILOR, SOLDIER, SHELL

INSTANTIATION FORTY

Agent Laura Patterson of the Magenta Investigation Bureau sits deep under the Tesseract in a quiet empty room, buried inside a data trail. It's late and everyone else has long gone home. She is looking for Alysha Rause, and for the Earthers who attacked Doctor Elizabeth Jacksmith, and for the warhead stolen from Darius Vishakh's shuttle, and for the connection between them. She is calculating who has betrayed her world. If Agent Keon Rause is correct then Frank Swainsbrook's *Betty Blue* left New Hope three months ago and flew to the station orbiting Magenta's sun. Which means that Swainsbrook knew what would be found on the wreck of Iosefa Lomu's ship long before it was unearthed, and Agent Patterson understands that this cannot be coincidence.

Across the world outside, Swainsbrook's hoax spreads like a plague. The world is still shocked, video sequences revealed thick and fast even though the solar station stopped transmitting more than twenty-four hours ago. No one can say who has done this, or how or why, and so rumour feeds on rumour. A story spreads in Disappointment of an Earther ship in orbit. Within an hour, the ship has a name: the UNSS *Flying Daggers*. Sources in High Hope confirm that the *Flying Daggers* is still there. Whispers follow of an evacuation of the Fleet orbital three weeks ago, something more than a drill, Tesseract agents involved. Or soldiers. Or both. A rumour starts of missiles fired by the *Flying Daggers* at something on the Magentan surface the following day.

No one will ever pin down quite where these stories begin, but now names crawl from the dark corners of the net: Colonel Jonas Himaru, second in command of Magenta's minuscule defence force, admitted to Mercy almost three weeks ago and kept inside for two, which tells you how serious it was. At least one Tesseract agent in Mercy at the same time. Two colleagues of Doctor Elizabeth Jacksmith who are both mysteriously dead. An Institute data-technician murdered on the steps of Mercy. A gunfight in a deserted transit tunnel between bureau agents and Earther mercenaries, one Earther taken into custody ...

The names swirl in a maelstrom of speculation and wild connection. They echo through the net as, elsewhere, a piece of Tesseract q-code reports its findings: a massively parallel attack-ware algorithm has unexpectedly cracked a sliver recovered last night from the Earthers who attacked Elizabeth Jacksmith. The sliver contains the hangar codes for Darius Vishakh's shuttle, transmitted from somewhere in the Tesseract six hours before the shuttle landed. The implication is clear: a connection between the Earther mercenaries who attacked Doctor Jacksmith and the missing antimatter warhead.

Something immediately clicks inside the Tesseract's artificial mind. Instantiation Forty feels it happen. A seamless stream of instructions are issued to as few personnel as possible. Each cog in the machine will have only such knowledge as needed. Data forensics pull four field agents from their duties and send them home, then summon them for an unexpected night shift at the end of the day. Logistics and supply requests an armoured pod for a training exercise. A secret and secure holding facility is brought to life in preparation for the expected arrest of Frank

Swainsbrook. A vague request is posted for a pair of agents to act as personal protection for a minor VIP ...

Through a tiny crack in this labyrinth of secrets, the hint of a pattern leaks into a net that Agent Patterson has cast to find it: the captured Earther mercenary is about to be moved. It's what she's been waiting for since she dropped the idea in Chief Morgan's office this morning.

Tesseract One has taken the bait.

Patterson makes a call on a line so heavily encrypted that even the Tesseract would take a year to crack it open. Then she takes her gun and leaves.

14

OLD ALLEGIANCES

I wake up a few hours later. It's the dead of night. Cho's fabricator is shaking under the force of the wind, and the rain is a wall of white noise. At first I think that's what's woken me, but then the world outside lights up under the dazzling blaze of four tiny suns – the headlights of an all-terrain Wilderness Explorer pod modified for Magenta, blasting through the tiny windows of Cho's fabricator. My Servant chirps: Laura.

'Keon? You in there?'

'What do you want?'

'Rescuing you, you idiot. Unless you don't *want* to be rescued.'

Laura manoeuvres her pod close to the fabricator door, leaving just enough space for the wind to pick me up and throw me like a fallen leaf.

'You want a safety line?' she asks.

I creep into Cho's room but she's asleep and I don't want to wake her. I leave a note: *Thank you*. I didn't want to hear what she had to say last night, but I don't think I can blame her for saying it. Some questions are better left unasked. I close the inner doors and force the fabricator to let me out. It's only a couple of feet of open space to the Explorer but I still have to haul myself in like a drowning man dragging myself onto a raft. Laura sits on a luxurious fold-out bed wide enough to almost fill the whole width of the cabin. She raises an eyebrow as I lever myself back to my feet.

'Bracing?'

'Stayed with Cho too long. Got caught.'

'So I see.'

The door behind me slides shut and the Explorer hums slowly away. Unlike a regular pod, I can barely hear the rain, though the wind still rocks us.

'This thing safe to be moving up here?'

I look around. I used to see adverts, back when I was on Earth, for things like this. An all-terrain, go-anywhere, survive-anything mobile laboratory-cum-living space for two, only there's no sign of any laboratory. What there *is* is a well-stocked bar. The inside is ostentatiously expensive but also dated. Not Laura's style at all.

'It's supposed to be able to take a direct hit from a tornado. My father imported it from Earth after my mother died. Bought it from a former storm chaser.' She pats the bed. 'For the singular purpose of bedding Doctor Jacksmith. I think he somehow imagined he might impress her with a quick drive out into the wastes and some expensive scotch.' She smiles, all teeth and daggers. 'He never used it. Elizabeth has *much* better taste.'

The pod moves at a steady walking pace, edging into the mouth of a tunnel. As we enter the undercity, it gathers speed.

'Where are we going?' I ask.

'MagentaNet Tower.'

'Swainsbrook's going to leave in *this*?'

'I wish! No, but there's a break in the storm coming in about

233

five hours. I've got eyes on the roof hangar and a team on standby. The moment he tries to leave, that's their cue.'

I look at her, curious. I don't ask, but she knows me well enough to know what I'm thinking: *Why are you here doing this instead of being at home in bed?*

'Jamie's still in Disappointment. The flat feels empty and I want some company. Face to face in a place where I can be certain no one is listening.' She gives me an arch look. 'Or did I disturb something?'

I suppose she means Cho. 'No, you didn't *disturb* something.'

'Good. Turn off your Servant.'

I do as she asks. Is this about Tesseract One? Alysha? She leaves me hanging, waiting for me to ask, so I do.

'Okay, what?'

'You want a crack at Tesseract One?'

'How?'

'The Earther mercenary who survived the attack on Elizabeth. They're moving him tonight. Morgan took the bait.'

'And you know where he's going to be?'

'Better. You and I get to escort him.'

She pings me the paperwork. Agents Patterson and Rause, cleared to work an anonymous escort duty. Then she pats the bed again, gesturing for me to sit beside her. She pours us each a large shot of whisky as I do, then sprawls behind me, legs stretched out, propped in one corner. There's a lasciviousness to her. I recognise the mood. Something appalling has happened.

'Shit.' I sink the whisky in one. Laura watches me and then does the same. The pod rumbles on, almost silent. With the windows blacked out, we could be anywhere. I fetch the bottle from the bar. 'You got DeTox?'

She rolls her eyes. Stupid question.

'Is it true they make these hermetically sealed? That you can survive in them in space?'

'Why the fuck would you do that?'

I shrug. 'Rich boy toy, right?'

Laura raises her glass to me and grins. 'Got that right. Rich *girl* toy now. First time I've woken it up for years, mind you.'

'How does this Earther lead us to Tesseract One?'

'The Tesseract cracked one of the Earther slivers earlier tonight. The Earthers had codes to the hangar where Vishakh's shuttle was due to land six hours before it reached New Hope.'

'Shit! The missing warhead! You were right!'

'So it would seem.'

'But ...' This isn't right. 'How? They were encrypted! Even an AI can't ... It should have taken years to—'

'Ordinarily, yes, but the Tesseract was actively looking for a connection. It was *looking* for the hangar codes, you see, and so it effectively used them to create a decryption key. Clever, eh?'

'You reckon the Earthers know who passed them the codes?'

'I doubt it.' Laura knocks back a second shot of whisky and pours herself another. 'Sure, *someone* inside the Tesseract sent them, and also pulled Jacksmith's protection and cleared the Earthers to make the snatch, but I assume they covered their tracks well enough. They've been meticulous up to now.' She hesitates. 'There was something else I told Morgan yesterday ... I ... I told him about Alysha.'

'You *what*?'

'I'm sorry, Keon, but it was the only way. If it's any consolation, I told him you didn't know. I don't know if he believed me.'

'The only way to *what*?'

She stares at the floor, at the walls, at anything that isn't me. 'I think Alysha knows exactly who Tesseract One is. I think that's why someone tried very hard to make her go away.'

'No. That can't be right. Otherwise she'd just tell ...'

The weight of Laura's confession hits me. I don't know what to say. It had to come out, sooner or later. I always knew that, same as I always knew Laura would be the one to throw her to the wolves in the end, but ...

I'm not ready for this. I turn away. 'I'll never find her now.'

'It was the only way I could see to flush Tesseract One into the open.'

'By using Alysha as *bait*?' I round on her, grab her by the shoulders and shake her, force her to look at me. 'Did you hear me! I'll never fucking find her now! Because of you! Because of what you've done!'

She doesn't resist, just looks me straight in the eye. 'You'll never fucking find her unless she wants you to, and if she does then none of this matters. But I think you already know that.'

I let go of her, slow and unsure of myself.

'I'm sorry.'

It's easy to be angry. It's easy to forget, in that anger, how long Laura has quietly kept Alysha to herself.

'I told Morgan that no one else knew and that it had to stay that way. I told him Alysha could give us Tesseract One and that the Earther could give us Alysha. I don't know whether he believes me but I'm not sure he can take the chance. So nothing's changed, Keon, not really. If we do this right then we nail him, and you're back to where you were, and no one knows.' A wan smile plays across her mouth. 'No one who matters, at least. Play it wrong and we probably end up dead, so it doesn't matter then, either.'

'What if Morgan decides *not* to keep it quiet? What if he launches a manhunt? Fuck!'

'That clock was always ticking. It's just ticking a little louder now.'

I slump back onto the bed. Laura watches me. She bares her teeth, a grimace that's maybe meant to be a smile but falls a very long way short. 'I'm not using Alysha as bait. I'm using us. Me, really.'

'It's really Morgan?' I ask, when I can't think of anything else. 'The chief of the bureau is Tesseract One?'

Laura sips her whisky. It's a long time before she answers.

'Mum liked them both. Flemich and Morgan. In hindsight, I think maybe Morgan *did* have a bit of a crush, but he hired Flemich because Flemich was what the bureau needed. Elizabeth liked them both too. Elizabeth and my mother were pretty tight, you know – did I ever tell you that?'

'No.'

'I never really understood it until years after she was gone, how much my mother gave to this world. My father was the one I looked up to, the one who looked like he was in charge, but he wasn't, not really. He was riding on her tail, and she kept quiet because that was her way to survive it all. There was her and Jacksmith and Tapeti and Alash, and a dozen men who all thought they were the alpha male, you see. They were going to shape the future of Magenta and they knew it, and you know what? They did. They brokered the deal with Earth that ended the blockade. Ten to one they precipitated the crisis that started it, mind, but I didn't know that back then. I was just a spoiled teenage brat.'

She drains her glass and pours herself another. Her fourth, not that I'm counting.

'What's this got to do with Alysha?'

'The four of them among all that testosterone. Mum dealt with it by hiding behind dad. She did the real work behind the scenes while dad talked it up and made like it was his. Tapeti dealt with it by being vicious. They would have kicked her from the cabal if they could, but she owned so fucking much of Disappointment and had so many mineral rights that they couldn't make it work without her. Jacksmith and Alash dealt with it by making the men want to tame them, always letting on there was just a chance they might submit. They never did, of course. I mean, they couldn't, not and stay a part of it. I used to think they were a pair of bitches but I get it now. It was all power games.'

She drifts into silence, already on the edge of drunk. The Wilderness Explorer quietly announces that it's approaching its destination, which turns out to be a quiet maintenance tunnel not far from the MagentaNet Tower.

'Alysha?' I say again.

'Fuck's sake, Keon, have some patience. We've got hours before the storm breaks.' She swirls her whisky, staring into it like it's some crystal ball to the past. 'Morgan wasn't like the others. Kurudu found him, I think. They knew each other from Nico back when Nico was Magenta's Wild West, completely overrun by Earther Xen gangs. Kurudu used his pig money to recruit his own private police force and Morgan ended up heading it. They actually did a good job, you know? Elizabeth can tell you all about what Nico was like before they broke the Xen gangs. Possibly Rangesh can too. Anyway, after the blockade ended, Kurudu brought Morgan into the circle to run the new bureau once they had the Tesseract AI brought in from Earth. I only met him a few times in the early days but he seemed nicer than the rest. I liked him. My mother liked him. Elizabeth liked him. Even my father was okay with him at first, but that slowly changed over the years. Morgan had real power by then, and he and Elizabeth were tight, and my father ...'

She gestures around her with a vague, hopeless wave of a hand.

'He brought this to Magenta four months after mum died. Four fucking months, so you have to figure he was already thinking about it before his wife was even cold in the ground. I didn't see him for what he was while she was alive, only afterwards, slowly, over the years. He was a shit. A complete fucking controlling shit.' She shrugs. 'Jacksmith brushed him off. I think she knew a lot more about him than I did, back then. I don't know exactly how and when it all turned sour. I told you my father left Magenta for Earth and never came back, right? I don't remember what bullshit I made up for you about why, but the real reason was because Jacksmith and Morgan had enough dirt by then to ruin him. He destroyed my mother, you see. I'm not even entirely sure he didn't actively kill her. So he left for Earth, and I joined the bureau, because for most of my life my narcissistic emotional fucking black hole of a father had brought me up to be his little clone, and I realised by then that I didn't want that, that what I *really* wanted was to make people like him pay for the shit they did. Pay and pay and pay.' She raises her glass to me. 'I know, I know, stupidly naïve. I know better now. But back then I was still dumb and had ideals, and Morgan was my hero. My role model. The reason I joined.' She takes a deep breath. 'Yeah. I'm pretty sure the chief of the bureau is Tesseract One. Vikram Morgan.'

'You know how crazy that sounds,' I say.

'Mum gave her life for Magenta, that's how much she believed in us. For all their flaws, most of them were cut from that cloth, Vikram Morgan and Elizabeth Jacksmith and Eddie Thiekis more than any of them, or so I thought. I guess I was wrong about that.'

I pour myself another glass. The Chief? An Earther spy? If this was anyone but Laura then I'd laugh in her face.

'Why?'

Not *how*, not *where's your evidence*. It's just ... I can't imagine it ... and yet I can, because Alysha ran rather face what she'd found, and the only way that makes any sense is if what she found went right to the Tesseract's core.

'Why?' Laura makes an extravagant how-the-fuck-should-I-know gesture. 'I guess we'll ask him when we arrest him.'

'Are you really sure about this?'

'I go into his office and tell him about Alysha and Tesseract One and the Earther mercenary. A day later, the Tesseract unravels a connection between the Earthers and our missing anti-matter and, by implication, between the Earthers and Tesseract One. Suddenly this Earther is dangerous, because maybe he really *can* lead us to something on Tesseract One. And then the Earther is being moved, and we get to do the moving? Either it's Morgan and this is a set-up because he wants us all gone, or the real Tesseract One somehow found out and *they* want us gone. If it's not Morgan then I don't know who else it can be because I don't think I buy Flemich, and I don't know who the fuck else has the power and the authority and the sheer brazen audacity to do what Tesseract One has been doing. So yeah. We'll take Himaru's Earther off him. We'll work up a head of steam on him and then some straight-as-an-arrow type like Utubu will come crashing in with completely the wrong intel. In the narrative Tesseract One is writing here, all three of us end up dead. They'll have an enquiry afterwards, but it'll be *records, what records*? No, no, Rause and Patterson were never supposed to be making any transfer, they acted on their own initiative, two agents gone rogue, tragic consequences, that shit. All wrapped up and made to go away.' She pings me another set of files. 'That's everything I have on how Jacksmith's protection detail got pulled last night. I don't think even Flemich has that authority.'

She puts the glass down and lies flat on her back.

'And now I'm going to catch some sleep, and you should do the same. When the storm breaks, Agent Utubu will pick you up and you can take Frank fucking Swainsbrook off to a cage somewhere and make him sing. Decide while you do whether you want to take your chances or keep your head down and let me do this one on my own.'

'What about Alysha?'

240

'What about her? If you've got a way to contact her then I'll happily take an assist. We can have a little truce if you like until Tesseract One is behind bars, and then I'll go back to hunting her. Otherwise ...'

I shake my head.

'I'm sorry. I mean, she's a Fleet spy and a traitor to Magenta and I'll arrest her and lock her up and charge her and probably throw away the key if I find her. I might kick her a few times for tricking me into being her friend once, too – but for what it's worth, I'm still sorry. I'm sorry for you.' She pats the bed beside her. 'You sleep, Keon, and I'd like you to stay here with me for a while because it would be nice not to feel quite so alone.' She gives me a half smile. 'No funny business though.'

I curl up beside her. I always knew Laura was tied to Magenta by something more complex than birth. I thought Alysha was too. I thought *I* was, and maybe I am. The flush of anger is long gone. I don't know why, but I don't bear a grudge against Laura for what she's done. If anything, it's somehow a relief. Maybe Rachael Cho is rubbing off on me, or maybe I always knew, deep down, that this was how it would end.

'I always did like you, Keon,' Laura murmurs. 'You deserve better than this. We both do.'

I wrap an arm around her and pull her close. 'Do we? Either of us? I'm not so sure.'

Alysha? Where are you?

I feel the whisky at work in my head. The warm fog of it. Laura snuffles gently beside me, asleep in minutes, knocked out by a quarter of a bottle of whisky to shut out the demons in her head. I doze beside her. When I wake again in the small hours, we're moving, the Explorer humming through the empty tunnels under Firstfall central, the lights above so dim that I can barely see. We slow to a stop. When I look outside, we've settled next to an armoured military pod.

Laura mumbles something from beside me on the bed. *Good luck*, maybe?

'You're really not coming to see Swainsbrook go down?'

'No.'

I don't ask why. Could be she's got a hundred and one secret meetings and calls to make. Could be she's heading out to the Wavedome to stare at the sea all morning and wonder how we got ourselves into this and where it all went wrong. Either way, it's not my business.

The Explorer door opens. We're somewhere in the tunnels, close enough to a surface exit that I feel the wind and rain buffet and sting my face as I get out. The door closes behind me, the back of the armoured van opens, and an officer in tactical gear waves me over. I see four others kitted up the same way with a sixth man, space-black skin in a suit. He nods as I climb in.

'Keon.'

'Corwin.' Agent Corwin Utubu. Flemich's enforcer. 'Your op?'

He nods. 'My op.'

I settle into the seat opposite him as he pings a video feed to my lenses, a drone-camera up on the MagentaNet rooftop, shaking in the wind, lens blurred by rain. It's hard to make much out in the dark, but the hangar door is clear enough.

'Wind's dropping,' Utubu says. 'Won't be long. As soon as that door opens, we go in.' He gives me an unhappy look. 'Swainsbrook's yours. The rest of us are crowd control.'

'There's a crowd?'

You find yourself in some little prefab squatting on the surface with no tunnel bored into the undercity, you stay inside when a storm comes and ride it out because there's not much else you can do. But the MagentaNet Tower is home to half the planet's q-ware servers and not much else, and at least six of its twenty subsurface levels have direct access to the undercity.

'Thiekis has guests.' Utubu makes a don't-know-don't-care face. 'Some people have nothing better to do, I suppose.'

We watch the weather feeds from the surface, tracking the wind speed. Utubu runs a sweepstake on when Frank's going to make a break for it and he's only wrong by a couple of minutes. We move as soon as the hangar door cracks open, straight to the central access hub for the MagentaNet Tower. The armoured shutters open for Utubu's Tesseract codes and we march in, quick and without hesitation. A couple of reception shells try to intercept us and Utubu shuts them down. He crashes into the tower's Servant and summons the lifts to take us to the roof. He doesn't ask and so I don't tell him that the MagentaNet Tower has multiple disconnected Servants in layers that can only be bridged by manual intervention. The tower is the heart of all Magenta's communications. The only place more difficult to hack is probably the Tesseract itself.

Two security guards come out of the lift, armed with tasers and ready for trouble. They take one look at us and stop dead.

'Hey!'

'You can't—'

Utubu's men stun them, disarm them and wrap them in spider-ties, barely breaking stride. By the time we reach the roof, Frank's helicopter is out on the pad, rotors spinning up. A pilot, in jumpsuit and helmet, is fighting through the wind to the waiting helicopter. He climbs in. On the far side, in the shelter of the hangar, I see several figures.

I ping Utubu: Wait.

I need Swainsbrook in the air. The moment the helicopter breaks contact with the ground with Frank inside, that's the moment he breaks the law, but I can't work out from here whether one of the figures in the hangar is him. Eddie Thiekis will know we're here by now, and there's nothing to stop him warning Swainsbrook and ...

243

Two of the figures from the hangar start across the pad, one helping the other, both braced against the wind. The chopper's side door opens. I unleash the Tesseract q-code in my Servant, feeling for the helicopter's artificial mind. This one wants to put up a fight, but it's up against an AI and so it's going to lose.

My Servant pings. It comes from inside the hangar. Eddie.

That you, Rause?

I don't answer. The two men reach the helicopter. A fourth man reaches from inside to help them in. The door closes, the helicopter starts to rise, and I get that warm feeling of a job well done. Now I let my Servant show itself, pinging everyone nearby while my Tesseract q-code effortlessly takes control of the helicopter's Servant. The first thing I do is pipe in the internal camera feeds, checking to see who we caught. There he is: Frank Swainsbrook, his Servant still active, not even trying to hide. Arrogant shit.

Hi, Eddie. You're up late.

Guests.

Celebrating?

We will be when that vote goes back to the floor in a couple of days.

Your hoax is about to blow up in your face.

My hoax? Fuck you, Rause.

The helicopter is about a hundred feet up in the air and heading away when I take over its electronic mind. I bring it back, nice and slow.

Elizabeth and I have been friends for forty years. This isn't how we do things. Burn him alive and send the ashes back to Earth for all I care.

I wonder what this has to do with Frank until suddenly I get it: Jacksmith has told him what Swainsbrook is up to. Of course she has, because she trusts Eddie to get things done more than she trusts the bureau. And maybe, while she was telling him, she let slip about what happened last night, the Earther snatch squad that almost took her, and how they had the codes to Frank's hangar.

Burn him yourself. I ping him Prabu Pradash's Servant address even though I figure he already has it. Your man here has everything you need to flay Swainsbrook alive. Still set on selling us out to the Earthers?

I'm trying to stop a war, Rause. If that's selling out then sure, that's what I'm doing.

Eddie lost his daughter to a give-no-shits Earther corporation less than a year ago, but sometimes it's hard to let a thing go.

That really what this is, Eddie?

You tell me, Rause. When the *Fearless* flips in later today, you come back here and tell me I'm wrong.

The helicopter touches down. Utubu and I head out into the weather with our shock troops around us but there's no need. The cabin doors open and Frank steps out and offers his hands, fists lightly clenched, wrists together, waiting for the cuffs like this was what he wanted all along. He even smiles as he hollers into the wind.

'Why, look at you, son! I guess you got me!'

Yeah. I got you, you smug piece of shit. I cuff him but he just keeps on smiling. I turn away and let Utubu take Swainsbrook and deal with the others in the helicopter while I fight through the wind and the rain to the open hangar. The two other men are still there, watching: Eddie and someone I don't know and whose Servant doesn't answer my ping.

Eddie closes the hangar door, shutting out the wind and the roar of rain smashing on the roof so we can talk without yelling in each other's faces.

'Why'd you sell him out?' I ask.

'Agent Rause.' Eddie gestures to the man I don't recognise. 'This is my son, Michael.'

Michael Thiekis. Oldest of three brothers, none of whom I've ever met until now.

'Hi, look—'

'You're the one who found out where the Xen that killed my sister came from, right?'

Michael Thiekis steps forward to offer me his hand, then remembers where we are and what that means, looks a little sheepish and lowers it.

'Sorry. Too long on Earth.'

'Yeah.' I meet his eye. 'Yeah, that was me.'

'Dad tells me they all wound up dead.'

I look him in the eye, silent, waiting in case he's got more questions, but he doesn't. Eddie reaches out and pats me on the shoulder.

'That's why, Rause. That's why.'

I call after him as he starts to walk away.

'What did you mean about the *Fearless*? What's coming from Earth, Eddie?'

He stops, turns back and looks me in the eye.

'I don't know, Rause. It won't be nothing, though. That much I can promise you.' He takes a deep breath, puffs his cheeks and then shakes his head. 'You're just trying to keep us all safe. That's what the bureau is for, isn't it? So don't tell me you never had to cut a deal with some lowlife you couldn't stand. You know, for the greater good?'

He heads off into the darkness of the hangar. His son follows and I'm left alone.

'Sure I have,' I say to no one when he's gone. Comes down to it, I reckon that's exactly what I'm about to do with Frank Swainsbrook.

Swainsbrook's lawyers are already waiting by the time we reach the Tesseract, set on making our lives as difficult as possible. I try calling Laura and get no reply. I start to figure

246

maybe that's why she kept out of this, because she knew what was coming. We get Swainsbrook processed, lay out a charge for violation of a civic ordinance, and then I go for an early breakfast in the Tesseract canteen. When I come back, a pair of Internal Audit lawyers are in my office, only it's not about Swainsbrook; these ones are full of questions about what happened up in orbit between me and Darius Vishakh. When I ask them if it has to be *now*, they politely inform me they've waited several days since I came out of Mercy and so yes, they really need to get this done. We talk about how I discharged a weapon inside the Fleet orbital, and yes, I discharged it more than once, and yes, that's right, it was because a murderous fucking shell piloted by Darius fucking Vishakh was trying to kill me.

Three hours later, they leave. I try Laura again. She's still not answering, so this time I leave a message:

Tonight. Tell me where and when.

15

FRANK SWAINSBROOK

It's the middle of the afternoon – fourteen hours after his arrest – when we finally get Swainsbrook to talk. Fourteen hours of fighting what feels like every lawyer in Firstfall, mobilised like some sleeping army with the express purpose of keeping me from questioning their client. They don't fight the arrest itself, they just try to stop us from talking to him, and I don't get it at first, why he's dragging this out, what he's waiting for when he knows this only has one end. Then I pick up the tension around me that seems to come from almost everywhere and realise what it is: the *Fearless* is due from Earth. It's hours away. *That's* what he's holding out for.

Pradash breaks his story shortly after midday, an evisceration that rips Frank and his hoax to pieces. I make damned sure it gets out that we have Swainsbrook in custody, and I make damned sure that Frank gets to see everything being said about him. By the time he cracks, we're all watching the clock. The three-hour window for the *Fearless* to arrive from Earth has already started.

Swainsbrook smiles as I enter the interview room, Laura magically back and beside me, Frank with his lawyers left and right and probably half the bureau watching in through the cameras.

'Agent Rause. Good to see you again. I believe you've had a busy couple of nights since—'

'Yeah, cut the chit-chat. You're being charged with contravening Magentan airspace regulations, an offence that—'

'That our client clearly did not commit,' interrupts Number One lawyer, 'since our client was not in charge of the vehicle in question.'

Frank ignores him and leans toward me.

'Agent Rause, I'm led to understand you might want to offer some sort of a deal.' He cocks his head. 'A little ... time-sensitive, perhaps?'

Yeah. Holding for the *Fearless*. No one ever said Swainsbrook was stupid.

'Depends what you've got.'

'Son, the question is: what do I *get*?'

'A couple of years in a cell for violating airspace restrictions?'

Number Two lawyer laughs at this. 'Please, Agent Rause, try not to make yourself look stupid.'

'How about ten to twenty for conspiracy to kidnap and murder Doctor Elizabeth Jacksmith.'

I feel Laura tense beside me. What are you doing?

Frank sits back and folds his arms. I bring out the sliver Liss found with the Earther hit squad – the one Alysha most likely left for us to find.

'This memory sliver was recovered from the scene. It contains the entry code for New Hope Hangar 13. You know who owns that hangar, Frank?'

'I sure do, Agent Rause, and what a mighty strange coincidence that we have already talked about this very thing.'

There's acid in his voice but underneath I hear uncertainty. Good.

'There are prints on that sliver. Guess who they match.'

Keon, there aren't any fucking prints. What are you doing?

'I have no idea.'

I put on my best surprised face. Rattling his cage.

You can't fuck about with this!

Swainsbrook's lawyers have much the same opinion. Number Two gets there first. 'Agent Rause, if you continue with this feeble attempt to—'

'Recognise this man?' I project a still of the Earther mercenary Himaru has in custody, the one Laura thinks is going to help us flush Tesseract One into the open. Let this run, okay?

'... intimidate my client—'

Swainsbrook cuts Number Two lawyer off with a wave of his hand.

'I don't think Agent Rause and I have anything more to say to each other. I think we'll just wrap up and let—'

I slam the palm of my hand onto the table between us. Frank flinches.

'You don't get to choose when we're done. You want to say you have nothing to do with the attack on Doctor Jacksmith, fine, but I have evidence that says otherwise. You and your lawyers can have a little chat, sure, but you won't be leaving any time soon.'

I lean back and wait. Laura does the same, a smug little smile on her face. It's a great piece of acting because what she's really thinking is *what the fuck are you doing, Rause?* I know that because it's streaming across my lenses.

Bluffing, I tell her.

No fucking shit. Why?

Swainsbrook knows what we want and he knows we want it fast, but he wanted to get back to his people badly enough to risk violating the no-fly order. I don't know what or why but *he's* on a deadline too. Morgan wants this dead and buried before the *Fearless* takes it back to Earth. If this works, it works. If it doesn't then take me off the case, make with the apologies and start over.

Frank's lenses are glittering with messages back and forth between his lawyers. I hear Laura chuckle beside me. She smiles as she leans to whisper in my ear.

'You're fucking crazy and Morgan is going to string you up. But okay, I'll play. Make like I just told you about some big new piece of evidence.'

I put on my best surprised face and turn to her.

'You're serious?'

She's still chuckling as she nods. I turn back and stare at Swainsbrook.

'Hey, Frank? Where *is* your shuttle?'

Number One lawyer snaps to attention, eyes focused hard.

'My client has already stated that he doesn't know, and as of this morning has filed a complaint against New Hope for—'

'Question was rhetorical,' I say. 'We know where it is.'

Swainsbrook shifts in his chair at that. Subtle, but it caught him off guard. He holds up his hands, almost pushing his two lawyers into silence, then sits back.

'Look, son. I can't help you with your Earther terrorists and I sincerely doubt that any of my people can shed light on any such activity. But I'll tell you everything I know about the *Betty Blue*. Truth is, I've had my suspicions since the day this started, hence my over-zealous haste to return home. Truth is, it does appear that some of my people may have become a touch over-enthusiastic. I guess they'll pay the price, but—'

'I want to know—'

Frank raises a hand. 'My lawyers are saying I should demand an upfront guarantee of immunity. But since none of this is going to matter a few days from now, here's the deal: before I say another

251

word, you're going to guarantee I'm free to go as soon as we're done here today, no matter what my people may have done. And by free to go, I mean go home, back to my community. Put me under house arrest there if you must. Heck, send your whole bureau to come watch us at work, but you do not interfere with our great endeavour until it's done. That's how it has to be, son.'

'Let you go?' I snort all the derision I can muster.

Frank unlaces his fingers and leans forward across the table, all his good humour suddenly gone. He's not annoyed, not angry, nothing like that – the look that flashes in his eyes is a fever. It's the look of a believer.

'Son, it's okay that you don't understand. I don't expect you to, but my people are about ready to reach out and make contact. A hundred souls, all prepared to intercede on humanity's behalf with God's avenging angels. I know you think it's hokum, but if it is, what do you have to lose? So my offer is this – I'll tell you what I know, you let me go home, and that's where I'll stay. Like I said, by all means send people to watch over if that eases your mind. Heck, come yourself, son. But my people need me, and so you *will* let me be with them until our time comes, and if our call isn't answered, sir, well, you may do with me as you wish. But if it *is* … If it is then I don't even begin to know what happens next. We take it from there, I guess.'

I stare at him, impassive, as I ping Laura: Can we do that?

If he can be on every screen across the planet in the next two hours telling the world that Pradash is right? Sure.

I pass that on to Swainsbrook, who grins like a demented monkey.

'Is that what you want me to say? That my people are behind all this?'

'I want the truth.'

'Shit, agent, no you don't! You want the world to hear that my people took the *Betty Blue* and flew it off to the sun, that

252

they rewired your little station, that a few folks with a case of overactive imaginations knocked up a few childish recordings and so forth. Well, all right, Agent Rause, maybe they did, but the *truth* is a bit more than that, and what I think you *don't* want is for the world to hear how God inspired that fervour through His agents the Masters, or how the Lord spoke to me in a vision when I first came to this world and told me how everything was about to change. I know you want to speak about certain people I approached not so long ago, but what you *don't* want to hear is how the names of those people were revealed to me in one astounding vision of the divine. No, Agent Rause, you sure as shit don't want the truth, you just want to make it all go away.'

He sits back and takes a long deep breath.

'But it's okay, son. I can give you that. I'll stand up and make your little confession, if that's what you think you need. Heck, I'll even make and send it straight to my good friend Eddie Thiekis if you like.'

Laura suddenly flinches beside me. I feel her tension beside me, clenched tight as a dead man's fingers.

What?

Nothing.

'But one thing you need to understand, son: I'll own what my people may have done, but not what I know they did not.'

Bullshit.

'Though since you ain't going to believe a word ...'

The *Fearless* flipped in twenty minutes ago.

'... you best come see for yourselves ...'

It's brought a whole fucking fleet of ships from Earth.

'... darn it, Rause, are you even listening to me?'

'What do you mean what they *may* have done?'

A Fleet source says the *Ember's Fire* with a full complement of escorts ...

'I've seen every one of those recordings. The ones you want me to say my people made? Some of them ... maybe they did. I'll put my hand up if that helps. Mea culpa. But those blasphemous scenes of ritual and slaughter? No. And that other one ...'

Along with the United Nations Secretary General and half the United Nations Security Council ...

'Now, do we have a deal? Because if we don't then I'd very much like to leave ...'

... Six corvettes. Same class as the *Flying Daggers* ...

'... And if at some later juncture you find you have more to say, I suggest you take it up with my lawyer friends here, because my kind offer will be long fled from the ranch ...'

... At least a hundred dropships. Could be as many as ten thousand soldiers on board ...

'... and— Are you *listening* to me, son?'

This is a fucking invasion fleet.

'Laura?'

She doesn't answer. When I turn for a moment to look at her, her face is as white as a ghost.

Laura? You got me on this? Can I make this deal?

'Yes,' she says. Three days. We've got three days, Keon, before they reach orbit.

I focus on Swainsbrook.

'Okay. You stand up and say this was all a hoax, your hand behind it—'

'Not *mine*, son. If my people did this, they most certainly did so without my direction—'

'Whatever. You stand up and you say this came from your cult of crazies and you can have a week with them before we bring you all back to face charges.'

Charges of what I don't know, not yet, but I'm damned sure we'll find something. I'm probably exceeding my authority by several light years letting him go, but I figure a public confession before the *Fearless* flips out for Earth is what the Chief wants more than anything. Which gives us maybe two hours to get this done, maybe less.

I hold Swainsbrook's eye. 'One more thing ...'

'Son, in your shoes, I'd quit while I was ahead.'

'Why now?'

'Pardon me?'

'You and your cult have been on Magenta for years. You could have done this at any time. Why now?'

'Because now is when we've been called, son. It's not for me fathom the Lord's purpose. Although it seems in this case to be quite clear.'

'Clear?'

'Good Lord, son! Is it not as plain as the sun in the sky? Iosefa Lomu! Why else would the Masters choose this time to reveal themselves? It *is* their time of return!'

I can't decide whether Swainsbrook is a lot smarter than he sounds or whether I'm talking to someone with a genuinely tenuous grip on his own sanity, but what do I know? Last night, I let Rachael Cho kill herself so she could ask the Masters how I could find Alysha.

'Okay,' I say. 'But you didn't set this up overnight. Back when the *Betty Blue* vanished out of New Hope, there were exactly four people who knew that Iosefa even existed.'

No. Five. Alysha knew too.

Swainsbrook laughs. 'You think Darius Vishakh or the good Doctor Jacksmith and her followers had the kindness to tell little old me what was coming?'

'One of them had to. And I want to know which one.'

But Swainsbrook is already shaking his head.

'Wasn't like that, son. You want to know how I knew it was time? The Lord spoke as I floated between this life and the next, that's how. I know you don't believe a single word, but it's

God's truth, Agent Rause, and if you want to understand, I mean *truly* understand, then come to my home and hear the Word for yourself. Consider that an open invitation. Now do we have a deal, son, or do we not?'

I nod. 'We do.'

'I'll have something to your representatives shortly,' says Laura. 'In the meantime you'll be transported to the MagentaNet Tower. There's a studio there. The Tesseract will draw up an agreement for you to sign and a statement for you to read. Comply and you walk free. For now.'

Uniformed agents escort Swainsbrook and his lawyers away. I look at Laura but she's already somewhere else, far away, lost in her lenses. It's out of my hands now, and so I get up and leave and plug into the Tesseract, looking up the same thing that everyone in the bureau has been staring at for the last ten minutes.

The *Ember's Fire*. It's the biggest ship Earth ever built, engineered into the fractal spirals of an asteroid hollowed out by the Masters before they left. An idle doodle on their part perhaps, but now the heart of Earth's defence against the imagined threat of Fleet. She's immense, even if all she is on the inside is a collection of pressurised modules, and on the outside an absurd bristle of missile batteries. She's a crude and ugly piece of engineering, the only elegance being the engines to move such a thuggish mass. It's going to take her three weeks to reach Magenta from the *Fearless*'s jump point, but that assumes the flotilla stays together. The corvettes and dropships, as Laura already figured out, could reach orbit in three days.

Laura's still in the interview room, sitting where I left her, staring into space. I go back and sit beside her. I should feel elated: I just got us exactly what we wanted, Swainsbrook standing up in front of the world, confessing his hoax before the *Fearless* flips back to Earth, but I don't.

I feel numb.

Ten thousand soldiers. Total orbital superiority. They could flatten us inside a day.

'What do the Earthers want?' I ask, not that I don't already know.

'Lomu. The Xen. Everything.' Laura doesn't look at me, just keeps staring at the wall. 'Fuck! Control, Keon. They want to be in control, because that's what Earthers always want. It's what they've wanted ever since the Masters appeared out of nowhere and showed us how randomly insignificant we are.'

'You'd think they might have waited to see how Swainsbrook's hoax panned out before they came at us like this.'

She snorts. 'This was on its way before the first vote. The *Fearless* had already left. It was halfway here. No, Earth committed to this the moment Vishakh and the *Flying Daggers* failed.'

'Then I don't get it.'

Laura sits in silence. I know how she feels. Looking at what's come from Earth makes everything else feel suddenly pointless.

'If they were going to do this all along, what was the point of Swainsbrook? Why bother?'

Laura just shrugs.

'But they committed to that months ago! Before anyone knew for sure that Lomu even existed!'

'I know.'

'So it doesn't make sense!'

Laura doesn't bother to reply.

'You buy what Frank said about the videos? That he didn't make the ones from inside?'

'I buy that he didn't make the one that triggered Meelosh.'

'You buy that the Masters told him about Iosefa?'

'Oh, fuck *off*, Keon! You know that was pure bullshit fuckery bollocks!'

257

'But you believe him about—?'

'I don't fucking care! You know? Right now? Right now, I just want to go home and forget about Frank fucking Swainsbrook and everything and … everything! I want to go and get Jamie and curl up in a corner with a bottle of whisky and wait, wait for it all, for you, Earth, Swainsbrook, Morgan, Flemich, for it all to go away. For it all to go. The fuck. *Away.*'

Deep breath. I know what she means and I know how she feels. I want the same except I want it with Alysha, and Alysha isn't here. She's buried in this somehow. Right to her neck.

'We're scratching the wrong itch,' I say.

'What do you mean?'

'Swainsbrook. Going after him. There's more to this.'

'You think his timing is an accident? You think he didn't know exactly when the *Fearless* was due? You think he didn't have a shrewd idea what it was carrying when he decided that right now was the time to admit how he's *maybe* been such a naughty, naughty boy? He *knew*, Keon. He fucking well knew, and now all we're giving him is a way to tell the world about his batshit idea that a bunch of people hovering on the edge of being dead are somehow going to make contact with a race of aliens no one knows a fucking thing about and no one's seen for a hundred and fifty years! But sure, we're scratching the wrong itch.' She takes a deep breath and rounds on me. 'Maybe he *didn't* make a video that kills people, maybe someone else did that and they're just riding his wave. Maybe he *doesn't* know anything about an Earther snatch squad going after Elizabeth or a missing antimatter bomb, maybe he *didn't* call up an invasion fleet, and fuck it, and maybe the Masters really *did* tell him to pretend that they were coming back, or maybe he really didn't even know about *that*! But so fucking *what*? He might have nothing to do with *any* of it, but he knows what's going on, he knows why, he knows he's a part of it, and what makes me want to shoot him in his fucking smug smiling face is that he simply doesn't care! All he can think of is how to come out of the wreckage a fraction better off than he went in. I grew up in that world, Keon. I know how people like Swainsbrook work because I lived it, because that was my family and their friends, because that was *me*, once. People like Swainsbrook will set the whole fucking world ablaze if it they think it'll get them a slightly bigger slice of the ash pile after someone else finally puts out the flames!'

'We can—'

'Arrest him? No we fucking can't. For what? Violating airspace restrictions? Whatever he's done, we're giving him a free pass. No matter how close he is to any of this, no matter how involved he is, unless he actually committed an actual murder, unless those fucking awful pictures from inside the station are real and we can prove he had a part in ... *None* of the rest will stick. It makes me so *fucking* sick.'

Yeah.

I think of Eddie and what he said in the hangar as we took Swainsbrook away. *I'm trying to stop a war, Rause. Don't tell me you never had to cut a deal with some lowlife you couldn't stand. You know, for the greater good?*

It was the second time he used those words. *The greater good.* Sounds so noble.

But *whose* greater good?

16

MERCENARY

'To everyone out there watching the skies: My name is Frank Swainsbrook and I have a confession. Three months ago, my shuttle the *Betty Blue* was stolen from its hangar in New Hope by a handful of zealous but misguided believers from among my faithful. Their names were Zachary, Joseph and Benjamun. They were supposed to be on an errand to Earth, but that's not where they chose to go. I'm very sorry to say that where they went instead was your Solar Station, with which I'm sure you're all familiar. Everything you've been seeing these last thirty-six hours that people say comes from there? None of it is real, and I can only apologise for these misguided souls and hope you'll find it in your hearts, as I do, to forgive them. I truly believe they think they're doing the Lord's work, but what y'all are seeing ain't the truth, and that's not how the Lord wants us to live. For the disruption wrought upon this precious world and the lives of its inhabitants, I am truly sorry. I did not ask them to do this, but these are my people. I will take full responsibility for their actions and their consequences, and I will share in whatever punishment they must receive. Zachary, Joseph and Benjamun, in your hearts I know you meant well, but if you can hear me, it's time to come home. The Lord will guide you.'

Frank goes out over every news channel on the planet, saturating the net, telling the world that the Masters' return is a hoax. He doesn't say *why* and so the question breaks out like a smallpox epidemic. Frank's not stupid and his people are primed. An hour after he's on the air, there probably isn't a single person on Magenta who doesn't know about Settlement 16 and Frank Swainsbrook's Great Project.

There's no oracle at the edge of death. There's no waiting God, no angels, demons or Masters. Believing in such fairy tales flies in the face of everything we know ...

And yet ...

And yet the enigma of the Masters remains, and no one doubts that *they* were real. And yet we live on an alien world, with alien xenoflora inside us, in the air we breathe and the water we drink. And yet Anja Gersh and her telekinetic rats, and the two young Indians in a Disappointment nightclub eight months ago whose heads literally exploded and no one can explain why. And yet Rachael Cho, who helped Darius Vishakh find a spaceship buried under a century and a half of ice, and Iosefa Lomu, and the guy in Nico whose pigs predict the weather, and all the others scattered across Magenta who know things without knowing how. And yet all these things. Magentans are a sceptical people, but right now we're scared and angry and confused, and that's where the cracks open and the doubt oozes in.

For a few short hours, Magenta talks about nothing else. Swainsbrook's supporters are loud and vigorous, but Pradash has free run on Channel Nine, Elizabeth Jacksmith is a Magentan icon, and both are happy to call Swainsbrook a liar and a charlatan. The arguments grow and spread, become about independence, identity and freedom from Earth, about belief and faith. Some want to make Swainsbrook a saint. Many want his head; speaking for myself, I'll not stand in their way ...

And then the news breaks of the *Ember's Fire,* and Swainsbrook just fades away. Looking at the forums, it's like he never happened.

It's the middle of the night and I'm sitting in the back of an armoured pod. Laura is with me, and a six-man tac-team, all of us dressed in full tactical gear. Even in my own head, Swainsbrook is just a bad smell. Most of me is back on the ice after Darius Vishakh shot me, because that was when he told me he'd pulled Loki's trigger, that he was the middleman in Alysha's murder, and that the order had come from inside Tesseract.

Neither of us should be here, I remind Laura.

Yet here we both are. She doesn't look at me.

The pod starts to move. I look into the faces of the soldiers around us. They're young, but we all have a collective memory of how it felt waiting to see whether Earther soldiers would descend from orbit, of not knowing what would happen next.

Tesseract One. Laura thinks we're about to get a name. I don't know what I'll do when that happens. Sure, I'm stoked for some good old-fashioned revenge, but I'm beginning to think that all my fury is just a speck of dust beside the sun of blazing rage inside Laura. I see the intensity of it on her, in the way she can't sit still.

You good? Two rogue agents die in a shoot-out attempting to break an Earther terrorist out of custody. If Laura's got this right then that's the ending Tesseract One is trying to write for us.

Himaru has our back. Laura has her own ending: when the hit comes, she'll be ready. We'll block and parry and track it back, and unravel the identity of Tesseract One.

262

I'm going to take Swainsbrook up on his offer after we're done with this, I tell her. I'm going out there. We're missing something. There's got be another layer. After I find Alysha.

'Let the Earthers come,' mutters one of the tac-team soldiers. 'See how they like our gravity.'

'We'll give them what they want,' says Laura. 'We can't win a war.'

It's what we did twenty years ago. The blockade ended and the Earther invasion never came. But that was different: the Xen cartels were mostly Earthers and Magenta was happy to see them gone. Sure, we set about preparing a resistance, Project Insurgent and so forth, but underneath the rattling sabres and the angry words, we all wanted the same thing. Which was why Eddie Thiekis and Elizabeth Jacksmith and Laura's family and the rest quietly stitched up a plan for peace, and if it benefited each of them a little more than it benefited everyone else, so what?

'I'm not so sure that's going to be enough,' I say.

Give Lomu to Earth? Sure, why not. But what then? Do we give them Rachael Cho and the others like her? How many people is that? And what about the Xen? I keep hearing Jacksmith's words: *They'll do whatever it takes. It's not like they're short of people.*

The news breaks as we ride that the Speaker for the Selected Chamber has summoned an emergency session in response to the arrival of the *Ember's Fire*. There's to be another vote on repealing the Sovereign Rights Act, just like Eddie said. The news is greeted in our pod by a chorus of jeers and derision and 'Fuck that!' I admire their defiance, these soldiers, a handful out of the few hundred men and women who aren't much more than a militarised police force. They have no idea, I think, what it would really be like to face an Earther invasion. None of us do. But it won't come to that. The repeal will pass, *October* will win, and the Earthers will have their way. The *Ember's Fire* has seen to that.

What if Swainsbrook was telling the truth about the Meelosh video? I keep coming back to that. He said the same thing to Rachael Cho, and why bring it up at all if it wasn't true? Of all the things he might have denied, why that?

He's covering himself against lawsuits from relatives of the suicides. Laura dismisses it. We might have given him a free pass, but that doesn't stop someone from bringing a civil case and suing him.

Maybe she's right but I don't feel it. Why that one thing? Why bring it up at all?

We roll through the undercity night. Out in the net, Jacksmith is a strident voice telling anyone who will listen that this isn't the same, that it's *not* like the last time, that we need to stand up for ourselves, that the Earthers *aren't* here to rattle their swords but to use them, that playing nice isn't going to make a damned bit of difference. It was her work, her arguments, her persuasion, that swung the first vote, but I already know that this time she won't be enough. We're a punch-drunk world waiting for a hammer to fall from the sky. We just want it to stop.

Our pod pulls up outside an innocuous six-apartment block in the undercity of Cherry Blossom Dip. Official records show all six apartments to be empty, ready for use but unassigned. Two MSDF soldiers step out, burst rifles held loose but ready. Our Servants exchange codes, verifying we're all who we claim to be. Then Assistant Director Aaron Flemich steps out after them, looking more than a little surprised to see us, and I'm instantly on edge. That's not how this is supposed to play. We take the Earther from Himaru's men, we leave, someone hits us before we get back to the Tesseract. *That's* the script ...

'What the fuck are you doing here?' Flemich asks.

'Could ask the same,' says Laura.

'You're not supposed to be here.'

'Yet here we are. Which we can both agree is unexpected. What are *you* doing here?'

Flemich's eyes glitter as he lenses something. I guess even an AI can make a mistake now and then, but that's not what this is.

'Same as you,' says Flemich. 'I'm here to supervise a transfer.'

He pings me his authorisation. I verify it with the Tesseract. I imagine Laura is doing the same. It doesn't check out: Flemich isn't supposed to be here. Which makes sense, because he and Laura can't both be in charge of the same operation.

He'll have Tesseract the same. Has he had the same answer in reverse – *we're* the ones who aren't supposed to be here?

We stand in a triangle, each of us looking at the others, wondering what the hell this means. I don't know how Laura keeps it together, cool as ice, waiting for something to happen. Waiting to see whether Flemich goes for his gun.

'The Tesseract has no record authorising you to be here,' says Flemich at last.

Laura never takes her eyes off him. 'Well, there's a thing,' she says. 'Because apparently you shouldn't be here either.'

Flemich cocks his head. The air between us is tight with tension.

'Where's the Earther?' I ask.

'Inside. But you can't—'

I don't hear the cue, whatever it is. All I know is that Laura suddenly has her Reeper in her hand trained on Flemich, and the tac-team behind us have their rifles on Flemich's two soldiers.

'Keon,' snaps Laura. 'Get him!'

Flemich looks ready to explode. 'Rause! Stand your ground! Agent Patterson, you are—'

'Internal Audit, which means I answer to the Chief and only

to him. Assistant Director or not, you will comply with my requests.'

Laura! What's going on?

Just do it!

I push past Flemich, standing in the doorway with his hands up without the first idea what's happening. The apartments on the other side of the door have been merged into a prison for just one man. The Earther sits strapped into a wheeled chair in the middle of a bare room, hands cuffed in his lap. Flemich has him wrapped in an armoured jacket and an open-faced helmet, because that's how much of a threat he is to the people he used to work for. *If* he talks, which he won't. His neck is wrapped in bandages. It's the Earther who had his Servant ripped out by Liss.

'Remember me?' I ask. I linger to be sure he sees me, sees the Reeper in my hand. His face flickers. He *does* remember. Good.

I walk behind him, disable the Servant controlling his chair, and push him out of the apartment. There's another pod waiting now, a run-of-the-mill commercial model exactly like every other pod in Firstfall. Laura and Flemich are inside, sitting opposite each other. I shove the Earther in and join them. Laura has her Reeper in her lap and her eyes don't leave Flemich. The armoured pod that brought us here drives away with the tac-team and the two MSDF soldiers inside. As far as the rest of the world is concerned, the four of us are in there too.

'What the hell are you two playing at?' whispers Flemich. 'What the hell do you think—'

'Becker.' Laura's face is tight with anger. 'Jared Black. Esh. The warhead from Vishakh's shuttle. The codes to Hangar 13. The pulling of Elizabeth Jacksmith's protection detail. One name links them all. You. Tesseract One. You're the *October* spy in the bureau.'

Flemich opens his mouth but can't find any words. Is it

outrage that chokes him, or fear? I don't know. He starts to shake his head but Laura isn't done.

'And then there's us. Two rogue agents. You're not supposed to be here, and neither are we. We take you out, we've killed Tesseract One. Case closed. Except you're *not* Tesseract One.' She nods at me. 'And if it's not you and it's not him then it's coming from above. And that's pretty rarefied air.'

'Patterson, what the bloody hell are you talking about?'

Laura nods at the Earther. 'Someone in the bureau cleared his way to Jacksmith and sent him codes to Vishakh's hangar in New Hope.'

The Earther doesn't open his eyes. Doesn't move at all. Laura turns back to Flemich.

'I went to the Chief yesterday morning, before your meeting with him. I stood right in front of him in his office and accused you. I told him I could get proof. He threw me out. It was pitch perfect.' She nods again to the Earther. 'But before he did, I told him something he wasn't expecting to hear, that this man could give me what I needed to get hard irrefutable evidence that would categorically expose Tesseract One. Last night, the Tesseract set plans to move him. Officially, I wasn't supposed to know about that, and yet here I am. Either the Tesseract made a mistake, or someone made *sure* I knew about this, and AIs don't make mistakes, and *this* mistake, out of all mistakes it could have made?' She shakes her head. 'I don't think so.

'So either it *is* you, and you set this up so you could take us out, or Morgan set you up so I could bring you in, or else he's planning on taking out all three of us at once, because who, apart from you and the Chief, has the power to overrule the Tesseract itself?'

Flemich looks aghast.

'There *is* someone out there who knows who Tesseract One

really is.' She nods to the Earther again. 'Just not him. Were the MSDF soldiers Morgan's idea?'

Flemich shakes his head. 'Mine.'

'What was the plan?' For the first time since we started this, Laura lowers her eyes. 'The two of them in a second pod as a decoy? You take this arsehole? Disappear off the grid for a bit? Squeeze him for what he knows about our missing warhead?'

Flemich meets her eye. 'Something like that. Agent Utubu has a place waiting.'

'I had you pegged as Tesseract One for a while. You should know that, because that's how it looks.'

'When did you change your mind?'

'Maybe I haven't.'

Flemich blanches.

'I've known you for a long time, sir, but I've known the Chief for longer. He was a friend of my mother. He moved in those circles. Him, my parents, Alash, Elizabeth, the rest of them. He's the reason I joined the bureau. I really don't *want* it to be him.' She shivers and then sighs. 'But I'm afraid it is. Look, there's another pod coming to meet us. We're going to split up. You have to clean your data and move on Morgan fast. Rause and I will squeeze this one. This place Agent Utubu set up ... black site, yes? This one just ... disappears?'

Flemich gives us each a long, hard, calculating look.

'There's a place you—'

The rocket hits the road under the front of the pod. That's what saves us. I even see it coming, a freeze-frame flare of light from somewhere ahead and a halo of smoke. There's a flash and a thunder of noise as the front of the pod turns into metal shreds. We fly into the air and flip. I pitch forward, straight at Flemich, doubling up as though I've been gut-punched. The crash protection kicks in. Airbags explode all around us, emergency harnesses spring free and snare us, holding us into

268

anti-impact seats. The world is white and tipping over and ...

The pod smashes down on glass-fused stone, flat on its back. Something hits me in the side. I feel the crack as a couple of ribs break even through my ballistic armour. There's no air in my lungs. The more I try to wrench a breath the more I can't. We slide, spinning, upside down, the harnesses holding all of us in place except the Earther. The noise is like a sawmill in my head, the scream and screech of tortured metal as we slide until finally it stops ...

My Servant is screaming for help, summoning rescue services and a trauma pod and demanding Tesseract support. Laura will be doing the same, and Flemich too. Even the pod will be howling ...

I hear metal boots in the tunnel outside. The pod doors are too mangled to open. Laura grunts beside me. I feel her move but all I can see is white crash bags wrapped around my face. I try to release the emergency harness that holds me into my seat but it doesn't respond.

Keon? Laura.

What happened?

Can you move?

I can't see. I feel the pod shake. I can't see and I can't move! There's someone out there.

I know.

BANG! I feel the shock wave like a slap in the face. The pod shudders.

What was that?

I don't want to tell her it sounded like a cutting charge, that someone is trying to get inside. Help, maybe ...? But my Servant says that any help is still minutes away.

'That him?'

The words are close enough to reach out and touch. The accent is Earther. North Africa, I think, not that it makes any difference.

269

Laura's Servant flatlines and screams a medical emergency. I tell mine to do the same, not that playing dead is going to make us suddenly vanish, but I'm hanging upside down strapped into a seat by a harness I don't know how to release, draped in layers of limp white plasticised cloth which cover my face so I can't even see. Playing dead looks the best of a piss-poor set of options.

More sounds around the other side of the pod. Another muted explosion. I feel movement. Someone crawls half-inside, right in front of my face to where the Earther was sitting just a few seconds ago, and now I can't see him …

'Turn him over!'

'Yeah, that's him. They're all here, all four. Rause and Patterson are showing up as dead.'

Did Laura get it wrong? Is Flemich really Tesseract One after all? If he is, I want to tell him that his bomb missed, that Alysha is still alive. I want to tell him that he failed, but I can't speak and play dead at the same time.

'Get them out.'

My eyes are closed but my lenses are taking feeds from whatever they can. From the cameras on the barrel of my Reeper and on my tactical armour. I look further: we're on the underground highway from Cherry Blossom Dip back to Firstfall, where there should be a steady flow of pods going back and forth, only there aren't. Every part of this tunnel has cameras mounted in the ceiling, too, but today those cameras are dead. Someone, somehow, has blacked out this little section of Firstfall.

Tesseract One.

There's one camera still working on the outside of the pod. I count four men wearing tac-team gear. There's a tac-team pod with two more men inside, but the codes they have in their Servants are all wrong. Six armoured men with burst rifles. Six of them to two of us, burst rifles against Reepers. I don't know what state Flemich is in, but right now my money says he's not going to be any help.

The soldiers drag the Earther out first. I stay limp as they cut me free and unfasten the seals on my helmet.

'We do it here?'

'No.'

Something stabs into my face. Searing pain spreads up my cheek and across my eyes and down my neck. I can't not flinch. I can't not open my eyes and scream.

'Told you he's faking.'

Two black-armoured soldiers, helmets covering their faces. One hits me with a stunner. My limbs go limp and I piss myself. I want to scream again but now I can't. When the stunner shock starts to clear, thirty seconds later, I'm lying face down on the floor inside the second pod, wrapped in spider ties. Another body lands on top of me.

Laura?

No answer.

Liss? Liss! Help!

Still no answer. The Tesseract is pulling my location, scrambling a tac-team, two minutes out maybe. If Laura got this wrong and Flemich is Tesseract One then this is an extraction and we're both fucked. If Laura got it right then it's worse: we're still fucked, while the real Tesseract One gets away scot-free.

Where the hell is Himaru? He was supposed to be ready for this ...

Doors slam. The pod starts to move. I roll and manage to sit up. Laura is still down. Flemich is groaning. The Earther mercenary sits on one of the benches. He looks a wreck. There are four soldiers in the back here with us, so I guess the other two are up front. One taps his ear at another sitting opposite, then shakes his head. I look at them and then I look at the Earther. He's looking right back, grinning.

One of the soldiers unholsters a pistol, screws on a silencer and levels it at the Earther.

'What the fuck—?'

Phut, phut, phut. The Earther's face implodes in a red mess, the back of his head bursts apart and most of what was inside sprays over the inside of the pod behind him. A few splatters of blood land on my face. His Servant flatlines. The pistol turns towards me. The spider ties have my arms pinned tight so even the enhanced strength of tac-team armour won't break them. I throw myself sideways and hurl my Tesseract codes at the pod, at the soldiers and their Servants, at anything. I hear a *POP* as a bullet pings off the inside of the pod and feel another one hit me in the back, the impact cushioned by the ballistic armour still enough to throw me sprawling.

'Fuck's sake! Hold him!'

I understand now. We're all going to disappear. Vanish into nothing. No one's ever going to find us, just like they never found Alysha. They're going to say we were all in it together. Me, Laura, Flemich …

'Do the other two!'

Me, Laura, Flemich and Alysha …

A soldier grabs me. I throw myself away as best I can but there's not much I can do. Two others grab Flemich. He's not even wearing any armour.

Was Alysha Fleet all along? Was she a spy even when she married me …?

'No!' I scream at them. I still have words, even if I've got nothing else. 'Get off them! Leave them the fuck a—'

They shoot Flemich in the face. Two shots. Point-blank.

'No! *No!*'

They toss him aside and grab Laura. She struggles now, gives up the pretence of being dead, but she's helpless as I am. I throw myself across the pod at them, using my body as a battering ram because it's the only thing I've got.

'Get off her!'

One holds her. Another starts working on her helmet, pulling open the emergency releases. She bucks and heaves, getting her feet between her and the Earther at her helmet and kicking him away. The last two haul me back, pinning me still.

'I will fucking kill—'

WHAM! Something hard and heavy lands on the roof of the pod. We swerve a little. I look up. So do the soldiers.

THUNK! A bright red-rimmed hole appears in the roof, about the size of a golf ball, right over the head of the man with the pistol. He sways a little and then slumps and collapses to the floor. There's another hole, just like the first, in the top of his helmet, and another through the seat where he was sitting. Blood pours out from under him like someone turned on a tap.

THUNK! The man holding me is wrenched away and slammed across the pod from back to front like he's been hurled by a giant invisible hand. His chest explodes and there's another golf-ball hole in the armoured door right where he was holding me.

The two soldiers wrestling with Laura go for their guns. One gets to his feet …

THUNK! Another hole in the back of the pod and his head explodes into a spray of red meat.

'Get down!' I yell at Laura, too late.

THUNK! Another hole through the roof and the last soldier collapses like he's been body-slammed to the floor.

And there we are. Just the two of us.

17

INTO DARKNESS

The pod glides to a stop. The inside of the van is a scene from some torture flick. Blood, gore, bone – it's everywhere. My hands are tied and I can barely move. I'm confused. Dazed. Stunned. Shocked. All that … but we need to get out of here, and fast. We need to get away.

Laura groans. 'They killed Flemich!'

I reach out with my Servant, looking for an interface to the pod, for a way to unlock the doors. It's there but it's coded and I can't break in. I can connect to the world outside, though. I can call for help …

And then they'll find us like this.

'Are you all right?' I ask.

'They fucking killed Flemich!'

Laura's voice shakes as the anger drains out of her.

'The Earther too,' I say, like she doesn't already know.

It's the middle of the night outside, occasional pods zipping past. I can hear them. I can feel the vibrations. I imagine people gawping from their windows, maybe a couple of drones hovering nearby, news cameras already feeding whichever channel will pay the most. We need to get out, away from this, and I can't open the door. We're screwed.

'We need to get away,' I say.

'We need to take their Servants and crack them and find out how the fuck they knew where to find us!' snaps Laura. 'But we can't take this anywhere near the Tesseract. It's Morgan. It *has* to be Morgan.'

You need to run, Keys. The voice creeps into my Servant. I don't know where it's coming from.

Liss?

On the roof of the van. It was me. You need to run.

I can't open the doors!

I close my eyes and fumble around the corpses of the four dead Earthers until I find an electronic key to the spider ties holding us. They whip free and we can move again. My legs are shaking. I reach for Laura and take her hand and squeeze. She squeezes back so hard that it hurts, huddling into me. There's not much warmth in that, not when we're both wearing tactical armour, but it's not nothing.

'Keon ... why aren't we dead?'

'They were going to shoot us,' I say.

'We all disappear. You, me and Flemich. No one ever finds us. Morgan puts together a story: Flemich was Tesseract One and we were his accomplices. We snatched the Earther and ran. No one ever finds the bodies so there's never any reason to think otherwise. Slate clean. Or perhaps you and I show up dead ... But this ... Keon ... why aren't we dead?'

'I can't link to the pod Servant. It's coded. I can't open the doors.'

Keys! You need to run!

I see glitter in Laura's eyes. She's trying the pod, same as I did, and finding the same answer.

'Fuck! You're right. We need to get out of here, and fast. Before Morgan realises—'

'So now what?'

'We're fucked, that's what. But ...' She stops. Grabs me. Shakes me. 'Himaru was supposed to have our back. But this wasn't Himaru. Keon! Why the *fuck* aren't we dead?'

Run! Now!

'I don't know.'

'Morgan will destroy us. He'll pin this on us. He wouldn't even be all that wrong.'

She sounds broken. The air in here stinks. Shit and piss. That's what you get for being stunned, and now the smell is creeping out. I hope it's not just me. And blood, the stench of it ...

Keys! There were cameras! I didn't have time to shut them down! They saw me! You need to get out!

'I'm sorry about Flemich,' I say. I can't!

I ought to call this in, scream for help, get a tac-team, get us to Mercy, something ... But I don't, and nor does Laura, because if she's right about Morgan then there's no way this ends except with the two of us either dead or locked in a cell and charged with treason.

'You're right,' she says again. 'We do need to get out of here.'

There's something suddenly off about her. A flatness in her words. Colourless, like she already knows it's too late, like there's a tac-team already pulling up outside, or maybe more Earthers ... I reach out with my Servant into the cameras around us in the tunnel. The holes in the armoured van aren't obvious. There's no one stopping to look, no Tesseract drones, no tac-team. To the world outside we've simply pulled up at the edge of the road, waiting. Maybe we still have a chance ...

Laura suddenly has a pistol from one of the dead Earthers. She holds it on me, hands steady as a rock, eyes icy cold. She pings me a video sequence.

'Explain.'

She's been into the surveillance net too, only what she's been looking for isn't our present but our past, at what just happened and why we're still alive and who saved us. I see our transport moving steadily along the tunnel, nothing out of the ordinary until another pod pulls alongside and a shell climbs out. The shell carries a gun that looks like it was ripped from a tank. It jumps onto the roof of the transport, lines the gun up and fires through the roof, the recoil enough to lift it off its feet. It steadies itself and fires a second time, then clambers down the side of the pod and out of sight. The picture quality is excellent. The shell has Alysha's face.

I open my mouth to speak but nothing comes out. Laura flicks me a venomous look.

'I went out on a limb for you, Keon. I believed you when you said you didn't know where she was. I believed you when you said she didn't kill that tac-team six years ago.' There's a rising sharpness to her voice. 'I thought it was Flemich until the *Flying Daggers*, but it goes higher. Alysha knew who it was ... Or that's what I thought ...'

I won't betray her. They'll hunt her if I do. She'll vanish and I'll never find her ...

'That was a shell, Keon.' Laura looks at me hard. I can't tell whether it's because she's finally putting together all the clues that Liss exists, or whether it's something else. 'Why did a shell that looks like Alysha just save us?' Her voice is flat.

How long was Alysha working for Fleet? I ask Liss. 'I don't know.'

I replay what I've just seen. It doesn't add up. Liss fires twice through the roof, but there were four shots, not two, and the others came through the back of the van.

'Who fired the other shots, Keon?' Laura's already ahead of me. 'Another shell? Or the real Alysha Rause?'

'I don't know!' Liss?

'Where is she?'

'I don't know that, either!'

Laura winces. 'Fuck you, Rause. Fuck you both. How long have you been working together?'

'We haven't.' Liss, did you find her?

'Were you working together down on the ice?'

Buttoned-down fury crisps the edge of every word.

'I thought she was dead!' Liss! Who else is out there?

'Or does it go further?'

Liss!

'*How long, Keon?* Did you know she was alive while we were fucking?'

She's right next to me, right in my face, no warmth, nothing except naked hostility.

Liss! Who fired the other *fucking gun*? I push Laura away, clenched hard around a burst of white-hot fury.

'Fuck you, Laura! I thought she was dead until she came to me in Mercy! Do you know what it did to me to lose her? And then she comes back, and *you* knew and you didn't fucking tell me! No, I don't know where she is, I don't know what she's doing and I don't know why she's doing it. I'm just trying to find her so I can ask her why!'

'Why what?'

'Why all of it!'

We're both breathing hard, teeth bared.

Keys! There's a tac-team on its way. You need to run!

Liss! Fucking hell! Was it Alysha? WAS IT HER?

I don't know where she is, Keys.

I don't believe you!

'I don't believe you.' Laura eases away. 'I'm sorry, Keon.'

'Sorry?' I suppose she means for not telling me about Alysha.

278

I sigh, the anger sloughing off me. Laura doesn't deserve it. 'Doesn't matter. Not any more.'

A warning flashes in my Servant, an alert from the Tesseract. A tac-team dispatched to our position, just like Liss said, and at first I think it's a rescue, which is bad enough given where we are, but then I see it's more. All my codes are being deactivated before my eyes. There's a warrant issued for my ... And then I understand: Laura's told the Tesseract what she knows. She told Morgan this morning, and now she's lensed the Tesseract. She's blown Alysha, in silence, right here, right now, with me sitting beside her so pathetically grateful that she kept Alysha's secret for so long.

'I'm sorry, Keon,' she says again. 'I was so sure it was coming from the top. But there *is* another possibility, isn't there? That it's you.'

'What?'

'Did you set Esh up? Was that you?'

'I was there!' I spit the words in her face. 'I nearly fucking died!'

'Three people knew where you were. You, Esh, and Himaru. You think it was Esh who sold you out? You think it was Himaru?'

'I had—'

I see her face go slack as she looks at me. I see her mouth open in shock.

'Oh fuck. Oh fuck, oh fuck! It *was* you.'

'What? I had—'

'You knew the whole plan, this whole set-up! You knew about the decoy pod. No one else knew that was how it would play, not even Morgan. No one except you. And I fucking trusted you. Against every warning, every dash of logic and reason, I fucking *trusted* you!'

I look for a way out, something we've missed. I don't see it.

She's right, except she's wrong because I'm not what she thinks, but now the only choice I have left is whether I take her down with me as I crash and burn. The prisoner's dilemma, except we're both innocent.

Aren't we?

I stare back at her.

'But if—' I start.

'So what now? You going to kill me? Is that Alysha out there. Is *she* going to do it?'

'Fuck, Laura! I'm not what—'

'Esh.' Laura shakes her head. 'Morgan would never have done that. Not to one of his own. Not for anything. Nor would Flemich. You were the only one who knew—'

'I shook hands with Esh!' I growl.

'Yes. How very Earther of you.'

'I'm not ...' It's hard not to snarl at her, even down the barrel of a gun. 'Okay, so not Morgan and not Flemich. Then someone has a back door into the Tesseract! Someone the Earthers—'

'No, Keon!' Laura's fists clench white. 'Just no! It's not fuck-ing possible.'

'The Tesseract AI was a gift from—'

She shoots me. The bullet slams into my armoured chest, smashing the wind out of me and knocking me back. I crash to the floor, hands and knees, covered in blood and viscera from the four dead Earthers, trying to breathe.

'There's no fucking back door, Keon! That's not how AIs work! It *had* to be Morgan! Only it's not, and that means it's you! You and Alysha together all along. There was no Tesseract One six years ago, and Walt Becker was probably innocent ... She's played everyone. Earth, Fleet, the Tesseract. And me. You have to admire her, really ...' She wrings her hands and looses an animal growl of pain and rage and frustration and loss. 'So where the *fuck* is she?'

One of us goes down or we both go down. Laura has the gun pointed at my face. Her finger tightens on the trigger. I can still barely breathe.

'Vishakh helped her escape Magenta,' says Laura. 'That's what you said, isn't it? So where is she now?'

'Vishakh tried to kill her!'

'*Did* he? Well I guess we can ask him about that if he ever decides to talk. But thank you. Thank you for saying that.'

Too late I realise what I've done. Laura will be recording this, and I just admitted Alysha didn't die in the Loki bomb. And that I knew.

'You,' says Laura. 'The two of you, all along.'

Shit, she's actually going to pull the trigger. 'Laura! Think!' I have to force out every word through a sea of pain. 'You know damn well it *can't* have been Alysha, that it *can't* have been me! Think it through, for fuck's sake!'

Or ...

Is that what this has been all along? A set-up?

Why do you always have to make things so very ...

A pod rams us, jolting us forward. I crunch into the rear doors. Laura tumbles on top of me; a crack of heads and a tangle of limbs and the pistol goes flying. There's the sound of tearing metal and the doors fly open and someone else climbs in, fast and smooth as a cat.

Liss.

... very ...

She takes Laura by the arm and tosses her aside with an absent carelessness, while her other hand grabs me by the scruff of the neck and hauls me to my feet. She has such effortless strength ...

... difficult?

'Liss?'

Liss spares a look to Laura, lifts me and shoves me into the

281

back of her waiting pod. There's a holdall on the floor and the gun she had earlier, so long that it only fits at an angle across the back seats and I have to duck around the barrel. Another pod slows to pass and crawls around us, smooth and unhurried, its automated algorithms rerouting around the unexpected obstruction. I can't tell if there's anyone inside.

Cameras. Between the pods and the tunnel there must be half a dozen cameras recording this. The Tesseract will be watching. It knows. There's no turning back, not now.

'Liss!'

She's climbing into the pod beside me. In the transport, Laura is hauling herself upright, unsteady on her feet. She fumbles for a discarded burst rifle. The tac-team is close. When they get here, they won't be kind. At best we have a minute.

'Liss! They—'

Liss shushes me with a finger to my lips and our pod pulls away. I see Laura behind us stagger out onto the road and get to her feet and stand in the middle of the tunnel, rifle raised. I see the muzzle flash as she fires. One, two, three, four and then she's gone, lost in the darkness and the curve of the tunnel.

'You smell bad.'

Liss snaps the release for my armour. She slides a hand inside and takes the external hardware of my Servant from its silk holster and tosses it out the window, cutting me off from the world outside, and the world outside from my implants.

'What are you doing?'

'Saving you,' she says.

'Saving me from what?'

'You need to get out of that armour. They'll be able to track it.'

As I struggle free, Liss throws it out of the pod, piece by piece until all that's left is me and the jumpsuit I wore underneath, stained and rank.

'Strip and clean up,' she says. 'There are clothes in the bag. On the top.'

There are cameras everywhere in the undercity and all pods have trackers. The Tesseract surely knows exactly where we are and is following our every move. Three or maybe four tac-teams will be converging by now, ready to cut off any escape.

'Liss! This isn't going to—'

'I know the protocols, Keys. I know the reaction times. I know every start point and every route and I've calculated their interception loci. We have forty seconds before we have to get out. Please trust me that escape is possible. I wouldn't have done all this if it wasn't.'

'And then?'

I rummage in the holdall …

'And then you lie low until Agent Patterson exposes the real Tesseract One.'

… A kaftan. A fucking kaftan. I throw her a look as I fumble it over my head.

'And Alysha?'

'Pass me another.'

I pass a second kaftan to Liss and then look to see what else is in the bag. Two more kaftans, both plain brown, a cornucopia of disguises, toolkits, blank Servants, every essential for someone on the run …

'Shit, Liss!'

'This day was always coming,' she says. 'And I've had plenty of practice at not existing.'

Her words are barbed.

The pod brakes hard. The doors open outside a narrow service tunnel.

'Bring the bag.'

Liss lifts the gun over her shoulder. I still want to know where she got it. It's huge, as heavy as she would be if she was human;

but she isn't, she's a shell, with all the machine strength that brings.

'Take me to Alysha.'

She grabs my hand and hurries me down the service tunnel. 'The first tac-team should arrive in about thirty seconds. We need to be quick.'

'Did you hear me?'

The tunnel leads to the second bore of the transit highway out of Firstfall central. It's empty. Either everyone has stayed at home today or …

'The Tesseract has shut this down.' Liss runs into the middle. 'For the tac-team that will arrive in a few seconds.'

'Liss!' Bright lights in the distance. A pod heading towards us, fast …

'Follow me and don't hesitate!'

She runs to the rain gutter, full of churning water from the storm fronts battering the surface, swirling and rushing into a hole down into the run-offs that feed the hydroponic lakes and the overflow cisterns beneath. Bright lights are closing from the other way, too, another pod, another tac-team …

'You know where she is!'

'Give me the bag.'

I give her the bag. She rummages and pulls out a black cylinder with a hook dangling from the middle. Four metal prongs spring out – a winch to lower us down the hole.

'Liss!'

'We need to focus on getting away.'

'We can't go down there! There's nothing but—'

She pulls a respirator from the bag and throws me a harness. I put it on. The first pod is a hundred yards from us now. I see the lights dip as it brakes. Liss fixes the winch hook to an eye on my harness.

'Where are we—'

A loudspeaker blares. 'Freeze! Do *not* move!'

There's a flash and a pop from the top of the pod as something arcs towards us. Shit! Shit, shit! I close my eyes and slam my hands over my ears a moment before the grenade goes off. The screech brings me to my knees even so, and all I can see is a brilliant light even through tight-shut eyes. I feel Liss's hands on my face, fixing the respirator. Her fingers lace through mine, a gentle squeeze before she picks me up and drops me into the drain and I'm falling for two terrifying seconds where I can't see, can't hear, don't know where I am or what's happening …

I jerk to a stop. Water pours over me in a steady torrent. The screeching still fills my head and I can't take my hands from my ears … I jerk and drop again, far enough for another adrenaline spike of panic before the line catches and lowers me onward, fast but controlled. The light fades and the screaming falls away to a rush of water from everywhere around me. When I open my eyes, Liss is right above me, hanging from the rope by one hand, the other wrapped around that ridiculous gun. I don't know where we're going or how we can possibly escape, because no one ever escapes the Tesseract. A hundred try it every year and not one of them succeeds because almost every inch of Firstfall has a camera watching, and cameras are the Tesseract's eyes, and it knows every movement of every pod, every transaction from every Servant. There's nothing and nowhere it doesn't see except into the wilderness outside the city, and out there is nothing but storm-smooth rock and lichen …

'What *is* that?'

'A Royal Armaments RG15 rail gun.'

'Where did you—?'

The pull on my harness stops. I fall ten feet and hit water. The current grabs me at once. The sliver of light coming down the shaft vanishes and my world falls into darkness. I feel myself sucked under, barely able to tell up from down. I panic, flail for a surface I can't see and then remember the respirator. The current smacks me into the tunnel wall and scrapes me along it, finding skin. The kaftan has somehow risen to wrap itself around my neck and shoulders, tangling in my arms. Something grabs my foot. I thrash and flail and pull free and then something large bumps me from the other side. A hand touches my shoulder. Liss? I can't see her but I feel her plastic skin when I reach out, alien and cheap. She entwines her fingers in mine and pulls me close as the water buffets us along.

Where does this go? This close, I don't need any external hardware to reach her.

Hydroponics.

We briefly break the surface. A spark of light flickers in the darkness behind us. Liss pushes my head back under. I don't pull away because I know that the light was a drone dropped down the shaft to hunt us. Above water it would spot us with ultrasound and infrared, but I've never heard of a drone with sonar. I'm actually starting to think we might get away …

Liss keeps her arm around me, tugging me sideways across the current as we sink, then guides my hand to her foot and wraps my fingers around it. She squeezes …

Hold on tight.

The walls close around me, bumping me as we're swept into another flooded tunnel. Liss guides me with her hands and I do my best to help, kicking my feet, but the current pulling us onward gets stronger, and then suddenly stronger again. I feel the temperature change, little shifts as new flows merge together, and now we're rushing forward, and Liss has stopped pulling …

The tunnel walls fall away. We plunge through some vast empty space wrapped inside the torrent and crash into a swirling vortex that sucks us under and spins me until I have no memory of up or down, until all I can do is cling to Liss and press the mask to my face. She holds me tight as we sink deep, deep and dark ...

She uncurls from around me when we hit the bottom, takes my hand and starts to swim. A few minutes later we break the surface. It's pitch-dark and I still can't see her, even though I'm holding her, even though our faces are inches apart.

Where is this?

I feel the space around me. Air above. This cave is a big one. We're in one of the deep cisterns.

Reservoir fourteen. It feeds the Roseate Project.

I try to draw a map of Firstfall in my head but I can't. I've worked this city for a decade but I still need my Servant to find my way among its nooks and crannies. She's chosen well: the hydroponic cisterns and tunnels are a good place to hide. There's not much surveillance down here because why would there be?

But Tesseract knows where we went. It'll have a hundred drones scouring the place within an hour.

Is Alysha here?

I remember the hydroponic lake I found when I was looking for her as Kamaljit Kaur.

We're not staying. We need to move quickly. We have between seven and eight minutes before they get here. Drones first.

Where is she?

I don't know.

Liar! Yes you do!

Keys, can this wait? Please? Until we're safe?

After what you just did? How are we ever—

But Liss is already swimming across the cistern, dragging her gun and her holdall. I follow, listening for the splashes until she reaches something suspended over the water and hauls herself out. It's pitch-black and I have no idea where we are or where we're going. All I can do is fumble ahead until my fingers close on the rungs of a ladder. I haul myself onto what feels like a metal gantry.

'This way.'

I pad after the sound of her voice until I walk straight into the back of her. We've found a wall with a door in it. Inspection access for the reservoir, something like that. The sort of place no one ever goes.

'Liss! Where is she? Tell me!'

I wince as Liss opens the door. Every door in Firstfall is identity-locked and linked to the Tesseract's surveillance net, and nearly every door can be closed and sealed remotely. They could lock us in. But Liss knows all this, because Alysha knew it too ...

'Don't worry,' she says. 'This door never opened.'

She slips inside and lights a chemical lamp as the door closes behind us. We're in a kitting room with four sets of diving gear stacked neatly against one wall, cylinders and hoses and buoyancy jackets and masks. There's an air compressor in one corner and in the ceiling ... Shit!

'Liss! Camera!'

She shakes her head. 'No one will see us here, Keys. But we need to get away before the drones come.'

She pulls a microfibre towel and a pair of jumpsuits from the holdall, one for her, one for me. Then masks that make us look like maintenance shells, which makes me laugh, because that's just brilliant, because no one looks twice at shells ...

'Liss, where—'

She rounds on me and, for the first time in all the years since I made her, I see the flash of temper I used to see in Alysha when I pushed too hard.

'Keys! Not now! I don't know where she is but I *do* know she's been watching you, and this time she *didn't* save you. This time it was me.'

'Who fired the other shots?'

Liss doesn't answer. She starts to strip and I do the same, rubbing myself dry before I fight my way into the jumpsuit. I don't look at her. It's a cheap and simple shell. The hands and face are Alysha, almost flawlessly human, but no effort went into the rest.

'Tell me you know how to find her,' I say. 'Tell me that, at least.'

'The door mechanism here broke six months ago,' Liss says, bright and airy as if I hadn't spoken. 'Just after we came back to Magenta, before I got my second shell. I fixed the camera four months ago. A maintenance engineer comes in once a month to test the compressor and the air cylinders. Other than that, nothing ever happens.'

'Liss!'

She goes to the camera. 'The whole spoof is done in q-ware. I can turn it off and on remotely. When the maintenance shell comes, everything looks exactly right. Then nothing changes for the next month, no matter what actually happens inside. Same with the exit door. We'll have to burn it all behind us, though.'

'Sure.'

No trace left behind. Nothing the tac-teams can use to hunt us and certainly nothing that data forensics might use to work out the truth. The Tesseract might know about Alysha, but it doesn't know about Liss. I wonder, for a moment, if that was her plan all along . . .

'It's a shame to lose it but I have other places across Firstfall.' She tosses me a replacement Servant. 'Don't turn it on, not yet. When you do, don't do anything stupid with it.'

It's exactly what Alysha would have said, tone perfect.

'Liss! *Where is she?*'

'She doesn't want you to find her, Keys. I'm sorry. I know that's not what you want to hear.'

'I don't believe you.'

'Then don't, but don't imagine that that changes anything.'

That flash of anger again. I follow her at a jog through a short maze of narrow passages past empty storerooms. The light from Liss's lamp is feeble, enough for me to follow without crashing into any walls but not much else; but I don't need to see to know this place is deserted. It's in the air along with the smell of old dust.

'What now?' I ask.

'You know the drill.' She still has that gun over her shoulder and I still want to ask where she got it. 'Break contact. Evade immediate pursuit. If we get out of here cleanly before the first drones come, we'll have done that. Then find secure shelter, assess, make contact and await either instruction or extraction. I have places we can go where no one will find us. We'll go to one and then we talk.'

We emerge into a cave at the end of a narrow tunnel. There's a pod waiting. There must be surveillance here, though. There's surveillance everywhere.

'Cameras?' I hiss.

'Mine for months. They see nothing.'

'The pod?' Surely we can't take a pod.

'I took this one six weeks ago. It's currently reporting itself as docked at a recharge station half a mile away.'

She climbs into the back, jerking her head at me to do the same, but I stay where I am.

'I want to see my wife.'

Liss sighs. 'She's always been able to find you. You know that. If she wants to.'

'If she *wants* to?'

Liss shrugs.

'Archana! You said it yourself! I was supposed to figure it out! I was supposed to know she wasn't gone!'

'That was a long time ago, Keys. Think about that, but please, as you do, get into the pod before the drones find us.'

Something about this feels terribly wrong. Liss has lied to me before and now she's doing it again. She's hiding something and I don't know what or why.

'Where did you get that gun?' I ask.

'The Earthers had it. The ones who hit Jacksmith. They had a stash up on the surface. I found it. They had all sorts of useful things, actually.'

I have so many questions, but she's right about the drones and so I get into the pod.

'Who fired the shots to kill the other two Earthers? How did you set this up so quickly?'

'Quickly?' She makes Alysha's you-are-an-idiot cocked-head half-smile. 'I've been setting this up for eight months. Ever since we got here. All of it.'

The pod pulls away.

'How?'

'How? You *know* who I am!' She laughs. 'I don't know all of Alysha's secrets but I have a good piece of her fieldcraft. I have most of yours and I have my own. I'm an artificial intelligence inside an artificial shell built to my own design. I can do things none of the rest of you could ever manage. I know how the Tesseract finds, follows and tracks people about as well as anyone, and I've had a lot of practice spoofing it. I've never existed on Magenta, Keys, ever. There's no trace of me. I don't have the same organic needs as I did when I was human. I'm expert at being a ghost. It *is* what I am, after all.' She sighs, and for a moment I see something in her that isn't Alysha, something that's pure Liss. 'One day I'd like that to change. But not today.'

'You set all this up for you?'

'I set it up for *you*, Keys. It wasn't going to last forever. You *know* that.'

291

'*What* wasn't going to last forever?'

'The sham. The deceptions. Alysha faking her death. Me destroying my first shell on the steps of the Tesseract. Alysha coming back to Magenta. Sooner or later one of you was going to need to run.'

'*One* of us?'

'You or Alysha.'

'You really don't know where she is?'

Liss shakes her head and I still don't believe her.

'So that wasn't Alysha with the other gun then?' I ask.

I hear the snag in her voice. Something I'm not going to like.

'No. It was me. In another shell. But I had to get my primary shell close enough to target the Earthers holding you through the skin of their pod.'

'I have to find her.'

'Are you really still so sure about that?'

'Of course I am!'

Am I sure? I don't know the first thing about what Alysha did for the five years I was on Earth except that she was probably on Earth for a lot of it too. Did *she* find *me*? Did she watch me? Did she see Liss? If she found me, was that why she didn't let me know she was still alive?

I shiver. No. She didn't know. In a world of twenty billion people, how could she?

If I find her, will I even know her?

Our pod swerves sharply and ducks into the darkness of another service tunnel. It stops and turns dark. A few seconds later, an armoured tac-team pod rushes down the tunnel we just left. Liss waits another long minute before we move again. We take another turn, abandon the pod and climb an access shaft into a cave full of maintenance shells sitting quietly in their charging docks. The shells wear the same jumpsuits as us. Their faces look like our masks.

Liss pings my new Servant: *I use the recharging bays here sometimes. They monitor the power usage, though, so I have to keep moving. These are government shells and they're all registered and monitored. The Tesseract can use them as eyes and ears at any time. So don't say anything.*

It can see us?

If it chooses to look. But we look like two service shells and that's what our Servants say. We won't stay here long, but you'll be living my life for a while now.

For *how* long, I wonder? I never gave much thought to how Liss lives or to where she's been hiding these last few months. *I didn't know you had a new shell. I thought you were just out there somewhere. In the net.*

Be Alysha. It's the way you made me.

No one stops us. Nothing challenges us. We pass through the recharge bay and Liss leads me through more winding tunnels into the back of a hydroponics factory. Everything here is bare stone, no lights, no concessions to humans, built only for shells to get about and do their work, unnoticed and unseen. We walk between long still tanks of water and seaweed until I pick up the first hint of humans: a stale hint of old Xen.

Liss picks up a candy wrapper and hands it to me.

Clean up crew. If anyone sees us.

No one does. We walk out to the front of the factory and into an open space filled with a bustle of shipping pods. This is the Firstfall we humans never see, the vast automated underground workings that tick-tock along with a rhythm of their own, unheard and anonymous, the great machine that underpins our lives. Hydroponic tanks back onto the reservoir beside colossal seaweed harvesters. Most goes to be dried and powered in the processing plant next door, some goes to have the oils extracted in another plant on the other side of the cave. And some goes untouched in great crates, carried through the transit tunnels of the undercity to ... wherever.

The pods that carry it are little more than giant wheeled dumpers. Liss leads me to one and pulls me aside.

Can you climb that?

I look at the crate. Yes.

There's surveillance here but its coverage is limited. Hold on to the side of the pod. We'll be clear when it moves into the tunnel. I'll swing you in.

I climb up and cling to the side and the pod starts moving almost at once. Instinct demands I poke my head over the edge of the container to spot the camera that might see us. Instinct is stupid: I keep my head down as the pod picks up speed. As soon as it enters the tunnel, Liss swings herself up into the dumper, gun and bag still over her shoulder. She moves with a fluid ease, her machine strength obvious. I start to haul myself after her and she leans and grabs me with both hands, lifting me as though I'm a child. We fall back together into a soft squish of seaweed and she holds me in her arms, protecting me. Just for a moment, I forget what she is. I don't let go and nor does she.

'I can look after you, Keys,' she says.

I pull away. 'Tell me about Alysha. Tell me what you know.'

She sighs. 'I don't know what to say to you, Keys. She has another life now. Chosen or forced upon her, I don't know, but does it matter? If she wants to find you, it's hardly difficult. And she hasn't. You need to let her go.'

I laugh. Let her go? After all this?

'Maybe you're right. Maybe that *is* what I need.'

I stand up.

'But you're keeping something from me, Liss. And I *can't* let her go, and you of all people should know that.'

I pull myself onto the edge of the dumper, swing my legs over the side, and jump.

SIX

SETTLEMENT 16

INSTANTIATION SEVEN

Frank Swainsbrook sits in a comfortable chair, swigging from a glass. He is drinking vintage Armagnac, already beyond the wealth of most before it was imported from Earth. Eddie Thiekis, whose money has paid for much of Swainsbrook's luxury, sits across the room, a frown of distaste fixed across his face. Instantiation Seven watches the two men, pondering the ties that hold them together despite a mutual dislike they barely bother to disguise. Eddie Thiekis has despised Frank Swainsbrook from the first day they met, and his antipathy has only grown stronger, yet here they are together, bound by Magenta's unwitting ensnarement in events that threaten its very existence.

A man wearing the uniform of an Earther pilot knocks on the door and enters.

'There's a break in the weather, Mister Swainsbrook. We can leave now, sir.'

Franks stands. Eddie Thiekis does not.

'The city's still locked down,' says Eddie. 'They could arrest you again.'

'I am grateful for your concern,' smiles Frank. 'But hey, if a little fine is the price of bringing about the Second Coming, I promise you I'll be overjoyed.' He stands before Eddie and offers his hand. 'We're tied together, my friend. Might as well accept it.'

'You're a cunt, Frank.' Eddie doesn't take the proffered hand. Frank looks down at him.

'Think what you like. Fact is, I got you what you wanted.'

He's still smiling as he walks out, following behind his pilot.

Instantiation Seven flickers through the MagentaNet web to the roof where Frank Swainsbrook's helicopter sits waiting on the landing pad, rocking in the gusts of the dying storm. Swainsbrook has a window of half an hour to escape the path of the next weather front. Tight, but it can be done.

The hangar doors open. An electric cart eases out into the driving rain. A shell sits on the back, oblivious, a basic maintenance model, human in vague shape and form but no more. As the cart reaches the pad, a hatch in the helicopter's underbelly slides open. The cart stops and the shell dismounts and takes two leather suitcases, Frank Swainsbrook's personal effects. It loads them into the helicopter with diligent care. Its task complete, it returns to the cart …

Instantiation Seven flits.

The shell momentarily freezes, and then its movements become a little more fluid.

A little more human, perhaps.

It takes a third case from the cart, metal this time. It returns to the helicopter and climbs into the hold. It curls up, folding its limbs around the case in a way no human ever could.

And waits.

18

AMARANTH

'Fuck Darius Vishakh. Fuck Earth. Fuck the lot of them.'

The door to Doctor Elizabeth Jacksmith's apartment slides open. I step inside. Nothing goes bang and there's no security keeping watch. I figure she's not here. I could kiss her for not having voice recognition on her pass-phrase.

I've thrown away the Servant Liss gave me. I don't want her to track me, so all I've got is the core hardware implanted in my neck, transmission range good for a few feet and no more. I wonder if I dare connect to the apartment Servant and how many alarms will sound if I do. It's the middle of the night and I'm an intruder.

'Doctor Jacksmith? Elizabeth?'

The place is empty. She's probably at the Institute with Iosefa. I can't think of a safe way to tell her I'm here, or to warn her, or say anything at all, but she's all I've got left, the last place I can go, the last person who might help me find Alysha, or figure out what the hell Frank Swainsbrook is up to and the face behind Tesseract One.

Jacksmith and Vikram Morgan have known each other for longer than I've been alive. I reckon it's fifty-fifty whether she simply turns me in, but I have to get to her first to find that out. She's going to be surrounded by security. MSDF probably, after the last debacle with the bureau, but that doesn't help, because by now everyone will think I'm Tesseract One. Even if Laura doesn't believe it, it's the story she has to sell to survive.

Am I Tesseract One? Is Alysha? Is it somehow the two of us together? It feels stupid to ask yet I can't shake that look in Laura's eye. She wasn't playing or pretending – or perhaps she was, later, but not at the start. That moment of revelation, that naked instant of pure shock, that wasn't faked.

Alysha could have stolen our missing warhead. Maybe Liss, too. But there's no way either Alysha or Liss could have stripped Doctor Jacksmith's protection detail, or me, or even Laura. No, Tesseract One is someone inside the bureau with complete access to the Tesseract itself. Which leaves the Chief, however much Laura doesn't like it, or someone's hacked our AI, even though everyone keeps telling me it's not possible.

I want to sleep. I'm so tired. But I can't. There's a wall screen in Jacksmith's lounge. It lights up when I go near, which means the apartment Servant knows someone is here, which probably means an alarm already being raised somewhere. Certainly Jacksmith herself must know.

The screen offers me a guest login. I touch it and manually surf channels – it's not like I have anything else to do. Swainsbrook's confession has vanished into obscurity along with the videos from the solar station, the whole scare gone like a puff of smoke in the wind. It's all about the Earthers now, the *Ember's Fire* and the ships rushing to orbit.

The Selected Chamber has held its second vote. This time, the proposal to repeal the Sovereign Rights Act passed 63 to 37. There are scattered protests in Nico and Disappointment.

Flashmobs have formed outside the Chamber buildings in Firstfall, blocking every undercity exit. The surface remains quiet, if you can say that when it's being lashed by a Magentan storm.

I slump to the floor and sit, legs crossed. Everything we've been through for the last few days with Swainsbrook and Pradash feels like an utter waste of time. We're going to let the Earthers back. We're going to give them everything they want.

I wonder what the story is back at the bureau. Am I Tesseract One? Is Alysha? Flemich? All three of us in it together? How many people I thought of as friends already believe it. Laura? Bix? Corwin Utubu?

Jacksmith's guest login has three stored messages. Two are links to anonymous sites in the net, both running top-grade encryption, the first a couple of days old, the second from a few hours ago. The third message is less than an hour old and hasn't been opened, but I recognise the sender's address profile. It's come from Mercy, from Doctor Roge's terminal. Roge runs the pathology department, the morgue and the mortuary.

I open it.

Mister Smith has been entered into his usual lodgings. Mister Jones will be with you shortly.

Why is Mercy's chief pathologist sending messages to Jacksmith's public guest account and not to Jacksmith herself ...?

The screen suddenly changes. Channel Three News vanishes, a wild-eyed report on the impending Earth invasion replaced by a bleary-looking Jacksmith. I have no idea where she is. All I can make out is that it's somewhere dark.

'Clearly I need to change my entry phrase more frequently,' she says.

'I—'

'It's bad enough borrowing my apartment when you're a

301

wanted fugitive. It's outright rude reading my mail, don't you think?'

Her face on the screen is huge and she's not quite looking at me. The image is distorted around the corners and keeps shifting, like she's staring into some tiny button camera only a foot or two away from her face.

'I—'

'Keon, I'm in a secure suite under the Tesseract. There are MSDF soldiers outside my door. I'm in bed hiding under the blankets to talk to you like I'm some sneaky six-year-old watching cartoons after lights out. What were you thinking? How am I supposed to explain not reporting this? It would be beyond credible for me to pretend I don't know that you're there, and Alysha and Aaron are under suspicion of spying for Earth, although I can't even *begin* to describe how much is wrong with *that*. Aaron Flemich couldn't spy on a party of toddlers without blowing his own cover. What about you, Keon? Are you an Earther spy? You *did* spend five years there.'

'Working for Fleet, yeah, so maybe I'm spying for both, although to be blunt I don't have much time for either. They tell you Flemich is dead?'

There's a long pause. 'No,' says Jacksmith at last, quiet and subdued. 'How?'

'The survivor of the attack on you. We were bringing him in. We were hit.' I take a deep breath, let it out slowly, giving her time. 'Where's Alysha?'

Jacksmith takes a deep breath. 'Hiding or running, I expect. Are you with us or against us?'

'Depends on who you mean by *us*.'

'Magenta. Those of us who still care about what that means.'

'Then with. Have you seen her?'

'Not in the flesh.'

I can't stop the wild surge of hope. 'You've spoken—'

'I need something done, Rause.' Jacksmith sighs. 'Might suit you, since it'll get you out of Firstfall without anyone noticing.'

'Why is Doctor Roge messaging your guest account?'

'Because I don't want any evidence of direct contact between us. Use your head and keep your thinking to yourself for a while. Listen – I want you to fly to Settlement 16 and shut Frank Swainsbrook down for good.'

'Alysha contacted you?'

Jacksmith glowers. 'Swainsbrook left the MagentaNet Tower a couple of hours ago. In his helicopter, which is very naughty of him, don't you think?'

'She's invited you to defect to Fleet, hasn't she?'

'Whatever he plans to do out there, he's going to do it soon, and someone here is supporting him.'

'What's she offering?'

'You know he's been recruiting people ... of interest.'

'Alysha wants samples of the real Iosefa. What else?'

'We need to get them back. A psychic doorway to the Masters?' She barks a laugh.

'Cho. It's Rachael Cho. *That's* who she wants. Not just you.'

Jacksmith, mouth already open, pauses and looks at me very hard. Or rather, she looks at something a little over my head and to the right, but very hard nonetheless.

'Keon, listen to me very carefully. If I believe Frank about one thing, it's that he only made the video sequences from the station. The one that ... The *other* one, and I think you know what I mean, came from ... Well, I don't know, and that's part of the problem. But I think I know what it's for. It's a test. Cho said something similar and I think she's right. The more it gets inside you, the more susceptible you are, the closer you are to having – again, I don't know – whatever Iosefa had, or something like it. Do you see what Frank's done? Somehow, he's worked out who on Magenta might be a descendant of

Iosefa Lomu, he's found a test to see if they carry ... whatever it is, and the ones that pass – the ones that don't kill themselves at any rate – he's rounded up and shipped to his little commune. He has all the best candidates for carrying the Iosefa mutation in one place. Now maybe he thinks that's to open some doorway to God or the Masters or JuJu fucking Siras or some other bullshit, but you and I both know he had help. Someone gave him the names and someone gave him a way to test them, and now they're all in one place and we've got a fuck-off bomb at large. Are you getting the picture here?'

'Yeah.'

'I need to know who the rotten apple in the Tesseract is.'

'So do I. Whoever they are, they have access to almost everything.'

'That's hardly reassuring. I need the name, Keon. Even if you can't prove it yet.'

'Well, I don't have one, because I don't know. Look, from the scale of what Tesseract One has done, it has to be coming from the top. We thought it was Flemich for a while, but he's dead. You want a name? Try Chief Morgan.'

Jacksmith's face screws up in thought.

'Vikram? I can't ...' She shakes her head 'No, just no. But someone that high ...?'

'There *isn't* anyone else that high.'

Jacksmith doesn't seem to hear.

'That's why Swainsbrook wasn't bothered when you arrested him. Fuck, he probably knew it was coming, didn't he ...?'

My head starts to swim. Knew it was coming?

'I think it was a set-up right from the start. We put him up on a stage for the whole world right before the *Fearless* flipped out for Earth. He's the story they're taking back to Earth.'

'Get out to Swainsbrook's nest and fix this!' For a moment, as she pauses, I see a flicker of something on Jacksmith's face.

Fear, is it? When she speaks again, her voice is softer. 'That sequence of images he sent out? The one I said was a test? It's on the net. It's killing people and I don't know how, or where it came from, or who made it, or how they knew where to send it, but most of all I don't understand *why* except that it has something to do with Iosefa. Someone is pulling Swainsbrook's strings. I think if you work out who it is, you might find your mole.'

I think she might be right. And I think I understand why she's asking me to do this.

'You're really going, aren't you? You're going to defect to Fleet. You're going to take your data and Iosefa and go with Alysha.'

'You're not the first person to have that idea, I fear.' Jacksmith drops her voice to a mock whisper, although I notice she doesn't deny it. 'I'm not sure my protection detail has quite the brief I might like them to. So maybe not. But if I did, Keon, if I were to consider something so drastic, would it surprise you? After everything we went through, you, me, all of us? After everything the Earthers did? I was proud of this world, I always was, but tonight Magenta is a cheap rent boy on his knees, arse in the air, cheeks spread and begging for a good shafting.'

'Why would I help you betray our world?'

'Who says I'm going *betray* anything?'

'I think *you* just did.'

'Figuring out who's using Swainsbrook and why is hardly that!' Jacksmith pauses and takes another deep breath. 'How about the fact that I can get you out of Firstfall? Yes or no.'

'Take me to Alysha.'

Jacksmith closes her eyes and looks away. 'I can't make that promise.'

'So you *do* know where she is.'

The house Servant chimes. There's a pod waiting outside.

'I still have a Cheetah. It's at New Hope. I can get you that far and fly it remotely.' Jacksmith rolls her eyes theatrically. 'I suppose I'll claim a headache or something – everyone expects me to be tetchy today after last night's abominable display of cowardice. But look – until you lot find your mole, Swainsbrook, *October*, Earth and the Tesseract, they're all the same to me. I'm sorry I can't give you what you want.'

She cuts the link and the screen turns dark. I stand and stare at it, wondering what to do. The apartment Servant chimes again. Somehow it sounds impatient. *Do you want this pod or not?*

I could stay. Jacksmith won't turn me in, at least for a while, not after the conversation we just had. Maybe I could hide out for days, a week or even two, but what then? Go back to Liss, lying Liss who says she doesn't know where Alysha is, who says I should let Alysha go? But that gun she's carrying is a Fleet weapon, not an Earther one, a long-range sniper rifle capable of bring down anything short of an orbital shuttle. I don't know what she's hiding or why, but it's something to do with Alysha and I don't trust her any more.

Jacksmith never gave me the real answer when I asked why I should help her. She didn't need to and she probably knew it. We both know I'm going to do this, and we both know that yes, in part it's because I want to see Swainsbrook burn, and yes, in part it's because it's my job, or *was* until a few hours ago. But mostly I'm going to do this because Jacksmith *is* going to run, and standing here, alone in the dark, a fugitive hunted by my own people, I realise that *I* want to run too. We'll turn our coats together, and Alysha will be waiting for us.

The apartment Servant chimes a third time. I half turn to go and then stop and bring back the messages on the guest account. I read the one from Roge again. It occurs to me that if I were Jacksmith and thinking of running, then switching

Iosefa for an anonymous corpse in Mercy's morgue might look a smart move.

I open the two encrypted links. The files on the other end are tied up tight enough to take even the Tesseract a decade to crack them, but I gave Jacksmith a key to files like these just a few nights ago.

Alysha's key. And yes, I made a copy. I'm not stupid.

It works. There she is. Alysha, the Alysha who came to me in Mercy. Older than in my memories, hair cut short, lines on her face that I don't recognise. The background is a bland blank nothing, no clues, nothing given away. There are no background sounds either. The video has a timestamp but I know better than to trust it. Alysha knows her craft. I'll not track her down from this.

She looks straight out of the screen at me.

'Elizabeth, if you're seeing this then you know I owe you a debt. I'm supposed to convince you to come over. I think you know what I mean. But I'm not going to do that. Do what you feel is best. If I can help, I'm here.'

This one has been on the server for five days, since before I gave Jacksmith the key. I open the second. The date stamp is from today, from the small hours of the morning while I was swimming through an underground lake. Alysha looks exhausted, close to beaten.

'The Tesseract knows I'm here. It's going to be difficult now. I can still get you out. If that's what you want then meet me at Amaranth tomorrow evening. Same as the old days. Otherwise I have to go. Good luck, Elizabeth, whatever you decide.'

She smiles a little at that, the only time her expression changes.

Amaranth Seaweed Oils. The refinery I saw across the hydroponics lake when I was tracking Alysha as Kamaljit Kaur.

I watch it again. Tomorrow evening. Alysha. I know where she'll be.

307

Enough time to put an end to Swainsbrook's shit-show before I leave.

I turn off the screen, head out to the pod, and tell it to take me to New Hope.

19

FRIENDLY FIRE

Jacksmith seems perfectly happy, which makes one of us, probably because she's not flying the Cheetah in person. I don't know for sure if she's even still in Firstfall, but she's the one behind the controls.

'I suppose violating airspace restriction comes a poor second to aiding and abetting a fugitive,' she says. 'I have no idea how I'm going to explain this.'

The Cheetah lurches sideways. The storm front might have moved on but its tail lashes like a whip and the next one's coming in fast. Jacksmith cheerfully tells me we'll *probably* get through in one piece. Easy to be cheerful when you're not actually on board.

'Tell them I hacked you,' I offer.

Jacksmith lets out a girlish squeal of laughter before the shell clamps a hand over its mouth.

'*You*, Agent Rause? *You* hacked *me*? I might as well say the Masters did it.'

It's a disconcerting shell, skinned to be the Jacksmith of thirty years ago before she lost her partner and her mobility. This Jacksmith is solid, muscular and fierce; yet the expertly crafted facial expression algorithms are the Jacksmith I know today, thirty years older, wheelchair-bound and on the threshold of old age. Still fierce though, and with a mind as bright as a nova.

'No one hacks *me*, Keon.'

Messages fly into the Cheetah. Air traffic in and out of New Hope might be grounded but their radar still works fine and they're not happy. I listen to the umpteenth warning about how much trouble I'm going to be in if I don't turn back, but in truth there isn't much they can do about it. The Tesseract might want to shoot me down but the Kutosov interceptors shadowing the *Flying Daggers* aren't in the right orbits to reach us before I can get to Swainsbrook, and all I am is a blip on a radar screen. The Cheetah could be empty. In New Hope, they have no way to know.

A warning flashes up as they try to take remote control of the Cheetah and fail.

'I can get you there,' Jacksmith says, 'but I can't promise I'll be in a position to get you back.' Something pings into my Servant. 'That's the encryption code to access the pilot systems. Seems you really did hack me after all. When they arrest you, tell them it was stolen by a jilted lover.'

'Which one?'

'Oh, I don't know. At my age it's so hard to keep track of them all. Pick one.'

She laughs, deep and throaty. I recognise that laugh because Alysha used to have it too, the laugh of uninhibited freedom, that wonderful sound of someone who's fought and worked and worked and fought and given the best of herself to something – and win or lose doesn't matter because her best was amazing. The Jacksmith who goes over to Fleet to work on some far-off world will never have the same edge as the Jacksmith of Magenta; but

310

I don't care. I'm going to go with her, and Alysha will be there too. We'll drink cocktails among the stars as Magenta burns and tell each other how we tried, what we sacrificed, how we gave almost everything for a lost cause, how clever we were to get out at the end when there simply wasn't any more to be done ...

It's all true. We *have* given everything. *Almost* everything.

And yet ...

'An old one,' says Jacksmith. 'Someone going back a way. Years of smouldering resentment. That sort of thing.'

'Patterson's father?'

'Oh, fuck no! Shit, Keon, what do you take me for?' She pauses and I can almost hear her thinking. 'Patterson told you, did she?'

'She told me that you and Morgan convinced him to leave Magenta.'

The shell snorts. 'It was Vikram who did the convincing. *My* plan involved an ice pick and quite a lot of stabbing.'

I know more about Swainsbrook now, thanks to Jacksmith. It's all public record, so not useful for leverage, but it's buried deep and you have to know where to look. Pradash was right: Swainsbrook is up to his eyes in debt. For the last two years he's relied on a handful of benefactors to keep up and running in Settlement 16, and it's not so hard to find where the money's coming from. Raisa Alash. Rashid Rapati. A lot from Earth. All of it *October*. No surprises, except maybe a raised eyebrow when I see Eddie Thiekis in there too.

'He's a con artist,' I say.

I figure Swainsbrook must have something on Eddie because Eddie's too cynical to buy this Voices of the Masters bullshit.

'Frank? No—' The Cheetah catches a low pressure vortex and plunges. My stomach tries crawling out of my mouth. 'Dammit! No. Not that. Not really.' We lurch, and then our wings catch the air and I'm pressed down into my seat as we

311

level out. 'He took me out there once when I was stupid enough to think he really *did* have money to sponsor some research. I saw his followers. They believe every word. They go under, they hear voices, they come back. I think *he* believes just as much as any of them. I don't know why. You're walking into an army of fanatics. There's also a good chance he knows you're coming.'

'That's okay. He did invite—'

I swear as we career sideways. Lightning flashes across the cockpit, dazzling bright. I clutch the arms of my seat as the turmoil of the storm roils around us. Never mind that Swainsbrook could be expecting me, I have to actually get there first. We're taking a chance flying a Cheetah into this.

'You might need these.'

Jacksmith's shell opens a locker in the Cheetah's cockpit. Inside are two pistols: a needler and an old-fashioned slug thrower. I could do with a stunner, but it is what it is.

I think of Bix, stranded out in Nico keeping watch over Saleesh. It's only been a few days but it feels like half a lifetime since we spoke. At least he's with his family. Not like Laura, buried somewhere in the Tesseract, bitter and hating me, conjuring theories about how I was in it with Morgan or Flemich or Alysha right from the start, or all of us together, or whatever it is she thinks. I think of Liss. Liss who loves me because she has to, because that's how she was made. Liss who's done terrible things for that love. She's told me more than once that she'd be free of me if she knew how, but I don't believe her. For all she resents it, she can't let go of how she feels any more than I can. I did a terrible thing to her, making her that way. I didn't mean to. But like any parent, I'm going to let her go, and either she'll find her own way without me or she won't.

I don't expect to see them again, any of them. Not because I expect to crash and die in this storm but because I don't expect to be coming back.

'Do you know much about artificial intelligence?' I ask.

'I'm no expert.'

'When I was on Earth, I made a shell of Alysha.'

Jacksmith glances at me, not understanding. I don't know why but suddenly I want to tell her everything. I want to confess and ask her what to do, where I can go to find a way out for us. But I don't, I tell her the same as I once told Bix: that I made a shell, that it wasn't good enough, that I turned it off and left it behind.

'I missed her so much,' I say. 'I saw her everywhere I went. I'd hear her voice whisper in my ear as I fell asleep. I'd feel her hand on my face when I woke in the morning. I'd see her slip into the shadows around every corner ahead of me, or look up from a desk across the aisle.' I feel tears welling up. 'And every time was a fleeting moment of joy followed by a plunge back into the despair of knowing she was gone. I don't know how she could let me think she was dead. Why did she do it?'

We lurch and climb and dive like a drunken roller coaster, Jacksmith's shell driving the Cheetah on, fighting tooth and nail against the weather. She's quiet for a long time. Thinking of her own partner, perhaps, killed by Earther Xen-smugglers half a lifetime ago. I want to ask if it hurts any less after so much time, but I don't. It seems rude.

'I hope you'll have the chance to ask her,' Jacksmith says. It's the closest she's come to saying she can help me.

'What really happened out there on the ice?'

'You did.'

'And what's that supposed to mean?'

'You really made a shell that looked exactly like her ...? Or do I *not* want to know?'

She doesn't understand what Liss was. How could she?

'On the day before Alysha died, I broke the biggest crime ring in Disappointment's history. They were making shells of celebrities from Earth. Sex dolls. They had data like we'd never seen and they were crushing it onto AI cores and tweaking the edges. The results were astounding. They didn't just walk and talk and look like the person they were copying, as if that wasn't bad enough. They remembered. They had a history, right back to childhood. They had every mannerism. They were almost perfect copies – not just physically but mentally. Socially, emotionally, intellectually almost indistinguishable from the real thing. The only obvious difference was ... they were made to be compliant. The data was coming from Earth, which is where the shells went when they were finished. The smuggling side of the operation meant we were working with Fleet. When Alysha died, I asked Fleet if they'd take me on secondment and let me keep working the case on Earth. I didn't go to Earth to recreate Alysha, I just needed a place I could disappear, to get away because I couldn't live without her. But once I was there ... Once I saw what they could do ...'

I have to stop to clear the lump in my throat. It doesn't feel real any more. It doesn't feel real knowing that she's back, that she's on Magenta, alive. For the first time since Liss took me to Archana Robotics, I wonder if finding Alysha again is what I really want.

The Cheetah shakes violently. A red light flashes on the cockpit panel in front of Jacksmith's shell.

'Don't panic. Nothing too serious. Yet.'

But I don't feel any panic. Truth is, I don't feel much of anything at all.

'It was the nature of the work. It took me right to the dark-market code hackers who created the virtual personalities. They've been around longer than I thought but the whole shell thing was new. They had a new way of doing it, a holistic approach that took data from everywhere and built up a whole person, physical, mental, emotional. Six months in, when the

314

pain of missing her wasn't getting better, I found the woman they said was the best. I should have arrested her but instead I paid her to bring Alysha back to life.' The first tear spills down my cheek. I try to laugh. 'No one had asked her to do that before, to bring someone back from the dead – up until then it had all been about sex toys. But I know she did others after Alysha.'

Jacksmith takes this in. She sucks up a long breath and lets it out slowly. Then another. The shell of her stares at me, head turned sideways, apparently giving me her full attention while at the same time she fights the storm.

'How did it work out, this shell of yours?'

'It was a stupid idea. I just had the same thing, only more.' Sometimes you have say a thing out loud to see the truth of it. 'I made a monument to her memory so perfect I could never escape it.'

Liss saw that before me. She forced me to leave Earth. She tricked me into it. She forced us apart and almost killed herself, and none of that was to be free of me, but so that *I* could be free of *her*. I see the horror of it, the trap of her creation, the trap of love: she can't bear to be without me, she can't bear to see me suffer, but I suffer if she's near. And now, with Alysha back? She's fucked. Her whole reason for existence is about to go up in smoke.

'You've seen her?' I ask. 'In the flesh?'

'What?'

'Alysha. She's really here? On Magenta?'

'I think you already know that she is.'

I want to ask more. I want to ask how she knows. I want to know how long she and Alysha have been planning this, but I don't want to push. Jacksmith's too smart not to figure I've seen Alysha's messages, too smart not to figure I kept a copy of Alysha's decryption key, and too smart not to figure that if Alysha wanted to reach me then it isn't exactly hard. But that's okay. Tomorrow evening I'll be at the Amaranth refinery. Like it or not, Jacksmith will lead me to Alysha, just like Rachael Cho predicted.

'Can you get me a link to the outside?'

'Yes … why?'

'I want to talk to Laura.'

'Patterson? Not so sure I'm happy with that.' Jacksmith keeps looking at me. I can almost see her thinking: *Did he really leave that Alysha shell on Earth like he says?* 'You realise you'll give away where you are?'

'I need to talk to her before I go.'

'Just don't let her send anything nasty back down the link.'

Jacksmith opens a channel. I message Laura at once.

I'm sorry I used Jamie on you.

We skirt the top of the storm, out of the worst now, flying high, a dark tumult of cloud beneath us. The sky overhead is a deep, deep blue, the horizon a burning molten orange as Magenta's sun rises. It's a rare thing on Magenta, to actually see a sunrise.

Laura doesn't reply. Jacksmith's shell is facing ahead now, looking out through the canopy. I have no way to know whether Jacksmith is still inside. I still have an open link so I call Mercy and ask for the morgue.

'Roge.'

'Rause.' I cross my fingers that Doctor Roge doesn't know I'm a fugitive.

'What can I do for you, agent?'

'You supplied some cadavers to Doctor Jacksmith at the Institute recently. She sent one back by return. I need the name.'

I'm fishing. It's all guesswork, but Roge's reply tells me I'm right.

'Which one? They all came back.'

'All of them then.'

316

Roge sends me five names.

'Thanks.'

The Jacksmith shell slowly turns to look at me.

'Really, Rause?' she asks.

I guess the real Jacksmith was still in there after all.

'Which one is Lomu?'

'Never you mind.'

'He doesn't know, does he?'

'I don't like using an old friend like that, but it's better this way. I'll apologise to him one day.'

'From some hidden Fleet research station?'

Jacksmith looks away again. A screen flashes to life in front of me. Swainsbrook is broadcasting again, telling the world how a hundred people are about to die and be reborn to open a gateway to God.

'When you get there, could you maybe just kill him for me?'

'Bit late for that, isn't—'

Keon!

A data link flies into my Servant. It takes me a moment to realise it's from Laura and that I'm looking at a tactical orbital display, the translucent pink sphere of Magenta in the middle, lines tracing the orbits of stations and ships. One of the lines flashes and the display zooms in. I don't know what I'm looking at up there, but I see the line is marked as the *Flying Daggers*, and that it just separated into five tracks. Four new lines appear and flicker across the screen before they settle into fast re-entry trajectories. Now I know *exactly* what I'm seeing, because I've seen it before. Missile launches from low orbit.

I throw the display from my Servant to one of the Cheetah screens for Jacksmith to see. She swears, tips the nose of the Cheetah downward, and starts a hard dive. A fifth track separates from the *Flying Daggers*, something larger and slower than the others.

'Any chance those aren't for us?' she asks.

We plunge into the upper reaches of the storm. Winds lift the Cheetah and drop it again. I watch the trajectories as they evolve. Short answer: no.

'I can't dodge—'

A presence crashes into my Servant. I don't know how it got there but it's vast, instantly ripping through my firewalls and strip-mining my data. Then just as suddenly as it was there, it's gone.

'What the fuck was that?'

'That was the Tesseract, Agent Rause,' says Jacksmith. 'The AI itself. It appears to be very upset with us. I cut your Servant link. That seems to have done the trick for now.'

Laura has gone, the orbital tactical display and everything else, too. The Cheetah is falling, lurching and shaking like a dry nut in a maraca.

'They're sending a tac-team after us. They'll be in the air in five minutes.'

'To do what? Arrest the fucking wreckage?'

'To recover the antimatter bomb they think we have on board.'

The orbital map flickers back to life. We've got four missiles streaking through the upper atmosphere and something else following in their wake, but now eight new tracks detach from the Fleet orbital, picking up speed fast and heading the same way.

'You seeing this?'

'Of course I'm bloody seeing it!' Jacksmith sounds flat. 'I'll bring you down. Maybe they'll abort the strike if you surrender.'

'No!'

We're doing the right thing. We've kicked a nest of hornets and now they're all buzzing out ready to sting. I can't simply *stop*.

'I wasn't giving you a choice, Keon.'

318

The pitch of the engines rises to a scream as we level out in the heart of the storm.

'The *Flying Daggers* fired at us from orbit twice before and we're still here!'

'They were firing blind at a pair of decoys. This time you're on New Hope's radar and Fleet appear to be firing at us as well. I'm not having you on my conscience.'

The Cheetah plunges, shuddering sideways. My fate isn't in my own hands. I wonder how much it ever was. Right now, it's down to Jacksmith and two clusters of bright specks on a tactical display. The fact that I can't see where we're going doesn't make a fig of difference. I'm not flying us. Even if I was, there isn't much to see out there except swirling cloud and flashes of lightning, muted like a distant artillery barrage.

'Hello ...? Oh, how interesting! This just gets better and better.'

Jacksmith zooms in. The second salvo of missiles isn't heading for us, it's set to intercept the first. Fleet? Fleet are ... I don't know. Helping?

'Well. That might change things.'

'I bloody hope so.'

'Firstfall tac-teams are in the air. Two Cheetahs in pursuit. Twenty minutes behind us so they've got no chance of catching up!'

Why would Fleet intervene? Because the missiles came from the *Flying Daggers* and not from our own Kutosovs? Because Jacksmith asked them to? I have no fucking clue any more. Because of Alysha ...?

We're diving fast, heading for the ground, whipped by a wind so hard that I can't tell sometimes whether we're simply falling. The Cheetah tips and seems to slide into a spin, but Jacksmith somehow holds it together. I want to be sick but I can't tear myself away from the dots converging on the tactical displays.

'We *might*, if we go low enough, duck under New Hope's radar,' says Jacksmith cheerfully.

I have no idea how low that might be or how much difference that will make. All I know is that I won't be able to see the ground through all this cloud until it's close enough to touch, and that that will be a lot too late.

The Cheetah slides sideways, tipping over, starboard wing down ... A sudden jerk and we straighten again.

'Sorry. The Tesseract and I are having a bit of a fight. It keeps finding my links and forcing me to crash them and bring up new ones. I can keep doing this all day but I think I may have some trouble back home shortly. They'll be banging on the door soon. You may need to take over.'

The dots on the display come together. I wait ...

Wait ...

Wait ...

A slap of lightning explodes in the sky right in front of us, blinding bright, dazzling out the displays. The Cheetah shudders. An alarm starts singing, dull and monotonous.

'What—?' I ask.

'Nothing to worry ab—'

We pitch into a gut-wrenching dive, spiralling straight down. A minute ago we were ten thousand feet up. We've done a lot of coming down since then, most of it fast. The ground has to be close by now but all I can see is dark roiling cloud.

'Do I need to—'

Jacksmith pulls up hard. I'm slammed into my seat. My head snaps onto my chest and for a moment I can't lift it. My vision greys at the edges. I can barely keep my eyes open while Jacksmith's shell clambers across the cabin, agile as a monkey, apparently not bothered by how hard we're turning. She opens the hatch into the passenger module and vanishes out the back.

Small problem ...

The pressure releases. My head snaps up. The tactical display is back. All the missiles are gone except one, still heading towards us.

... nothing to ... there. Got it. I need you to take over.

'*What?*'

I scrabble into the pilot seat and link to the Cheetah's Servant.

You *do* know how to fly one of these?

'Yes but—'

Altitude? She hasn't come back from the passenger pod.

'Less than a thousand feet.'

Drop to a hundred. Slow and steady.

I have to shout over the roar of the engines. 'Seriously?'

Do or die, Keon!

'You know what our margin for error is in this wind? About a hundred fucking feet!'

Actually ... you may need to make it fifty.

I hear a wind rush behind me. I feel the air change and the Cheetah quiver. The noise from the open door to the passenger pod is suddenly deafening.

'What did you just—' What did you just do?

Tell me when you hit fifty feet.

I turn in my chair. The buckles and straps make it difficult but I see Jacksmith is back, standing in the open hatch behind me now. Beyond I can see the passenger pod, the two rows of bench seats on either side. Beyond that I can see ...

Daylight. She's opened the rear ramp.

Fifty feet.

Straight and level. Shit. They're at my door in Firstfall.

The dot on the display races closer. It seemed slow before but not any more. Five miles away. Four... Jacksmith's shell is crouched by the cabin door, looking intently back into the sky behind us.

When I say so, pull up hard. Full power. Count to three then invert, dive and kill as much speed as you can. Got that?

'What are you doing!'

Giving that missile something else to hit.

'We're going to—'

Now! Up! Hard!

I pull the Cheetah up hard and all the force of Magenta's crushing gravity squeezes me into my seat. I can't look back any more.

Three ...

Two ...

'I hope you ...'

Invert! Roll! Fucking roll!

I flip the Cheetah onto its back. I feel a series of thuds. The Cheetah shudders. The roar of the wind is suddenly enormous, furious wet air hurtling around me in the cabin.

'... know what you're ...'

Dive dive dive! Kill your speed!

I kill the throttle and punch in the air brakes, slamming myself forward into the seat's webbing. We're upside down and falling fast back towards an unseen ground. Something flashes past overhead, flaring bright. We plunge. The Cheetah pitches sideways and drops, stretching me out again.

Keep rolling!

I roll the Cheetah back the right way up in time to see a bright flash ahead, muffled by the cloud.

Pull up! Level ou—

Jacksmith vanishes. Her shell collapses. My Servant shuts down as every link fails. I hear a rattle of sharp taps like hail pinging off the Cheetah's skin. Then it's gone.

The missile has gone too. The displays are clear.

I ease the Cheetah up and level out.

'Jacksmith?'

322

No answer.

The rush of wind stops. Jacksmith's shell wobbles upright, goes to the passenger cabin hatch, and closes it. It settles to sit beside me and curls into a dormant foetal position. My Servant blinks. I have a waiting message. Just text.

If you get this, you're on your own for now. I'll rejoin you if and when I can. Good luck, Keon. EJ.

I nod and look at Jacksmith's docile shell.

'So let's do this.'

20

THE BRIGHTEST LIGHT

It takes me a while to work out that my Cheetah doesn't have a passenger module, that Jacksmith's manoeuvre lobbed it as bait for the last missile. I'm flying too low to be picked up by New Hope's radar, I'm too deep in cloud for any satellite to see, so if Jacksmith did it right then everyone should think I'm dead. For as long as I keep running in silence, maybe it'll stay that way. The tac-teams will land and search for wreckage and for a bomb that isn't there. They'll be on foot and in the open in winds of a hundred miles an hour and more, roped together, flayed by rain and sleet like a hail of knives. It'll take a while for anyone to work out what really happened.

I smile for a moment, wondering if Colonel Himaru will be with them out there, or any of the other soldiers I know, the ones I've stood beside over these last eight months. If they are, I figure it's even odds between a free beer and a punch in the face when I next see them. Then I remember that they think I betrayed them, and that the only way this ends well is if I bring Tesseract One into the light ...

Right now, all I have to do to do it is fly blind through the tail of this storm with no active instruments and no contact with the outside world, infiltrate a commune of crazy people, break into their data and find out who's been stringing them along ...

The Earthers on the *Flying Daggers* just tried to kill me. I don't know whether Tesseract One asked them to or whether they decided all by themselves, but one thing's for sure: someone doesn't want me reaching Settlement 16, and that means I'm close. The Cheetah can fly itself if it has to. I know where I am and I know where I'm going and I have cloud cover all the way. They're not going to see me coming, and so the first Swainsbrook is going to know I'm still alive is when I stick a needler in his face. And once I'm that close, there's not a damned thing the *Flying Daggers* or Tesseract One can do to stop me.

When this done, I'll ask how Magenta's most eminent scientist knows how to dodge a suborbital missile. I'm certain Jacksmith plans to defect. Sixty years she's given everything to this world, but Magenta is too small for something like Iosefa Lomu, and the *Flying Daggers* is a sharp reminder of how big Earth can really be.

Does that make her a traitor? Did Alysha foresee all this when she understood what Lomu was when Jacksmith first showed her? I can almost feel her at my back, head turned to look at me, brow furrowed in exaggerated puzzlement, head cocked, eyes wide and bright with half a smile playing at the corner of her lips as if to ask: *why are you even trying, Keon?*

I try not to think about the images of her on the sliver from Mercy and so I think about them all the time. Her face like she was looking at her own death. Which, in a way, she was. We always tried not to have secrets even though our work demanded it. I used to think that that honesty across the rest of our lives was a necessary counter, an understanding of the need for an absolute trust. That that was what we had.

Trust.

No secrets.

Yours forever, Keon Rause.

I've got hours to kill before I land. I play the clips again, though I know I shouldn't.

Was I supposed to find Archana Robotics? I think yes, I was. And again.

Was I supposed to understand? I don't know.

And again.

Was she Fleet all along?

It hits me then: the Tesseract thinks I'm dead. *Everyone* thinks I'm dead. I could turn around and go back to Firstfall. I could forget about Frank Swainsbrook and Settlement 16 and Tesseract One and go to Amaranth Seaweed Oils, wait for Jacksmith and follow her, or simply abandon everything and disappear, the way Alysha did.

Is this how she felt, staring at that future, a deep dark abyss of severance from everything, a sense of utter self-betrayal?

A yawn overtakes me, the adrenaline of the missile attack draining into a black hole of fatigue. The last sleep I had was a few hours in the back of Laura's Wilderness Explorer. And yes, I could go back, give up on it all, but I'm not going to, not yet. I'll find the truth of what killed Une Meelosh first, and then Jacksmith will take me to Alysha.

And then...?

I close my eyes and see her, the last image of her on Magenta before she ran, alone and desolate. Despair in her eyes – she knows what she's about to do and it's killing her. I think of finding her again and how that moment will feel. I'll do everything I can, anything at all, to get back what we had, and I know it's impossible, that the past can only ever be the past; but I'll still try anyway because some dreams are worth everything and more ...

The thought fades as I drop into darkness, thinking of Alysha. The next I know I'm five minutes out from Settlement 16, my Servant beeping in my ear, the storm gone. We're flying under thick dark cloud through a steady downpour and the daylight outside is like twilight. I check the comms and everything still works, the links there if I dare to use them. I want to talk to Laura, to Bix, to Jacksmith even. I want to know they're okay and I want to say goodbye. Or maybe I don't, because maybe all three are locked up by now, and if they are then that's on me, and I don't want to know.

Settlement 16 has a landing pad suitable for Cheetahs and everything that goes with that: sheltered hangars and a short-range air-search radar. I come in low, careful not to be seen, and land a few miles short. I check the forecast, discover the winds are due to get stronger, and head out into the driving rain. It's a long grinding slog across the lichen-covered rock wastes of Magenta's equatorial plateau. The surface is wet, smooth and slippery, the wind feisty, gusts whipping at my storm-suit, rain slashing at my face. It takes two hours to reach the crater of Swainsbrook's old pit mine. By the time I get there, the wind's picking up fast, another storm front moving in. I've got another hour, maybe, before it peaks, maybe three before it'll be safe to be outside again.

I follow the crater rim to the three old mining domes that mark the entrance to the pit, three empty ruins gutted long ago and covered with lichen. I stand between them and look down over vertical walls blasted into the rock, a single track spiralling to the bottom. Magenta is pockmarked with places like this, scars like relics of teenage acne. The early planetary surveys found rare earth veins on the surface. Earther conglomerates, hungry to rebuild their world, set about strip-mining as much as they could take. No one asked the struggling settlers in Firstfall and we certainly didn't share in any profits. The Earthers dug a pit, mined it out and moved on, and for the most part we didn't even know it was happening. It says something that they came at all, that people braved the joint-grinding gravity – no transgravity treatments back then – and the relentless rain and storms and a diet of protein pastes and water, all to get away from the poverty and hunger of Earth after the Masters.

I hunker down in the smallest dome, waiting for the sun to set and the storm to come and go. The first miners learned quickly to spend most of their time stoned on Xen as an alternative to constant pain. A lot went home addicts, and that was how the trade began. Some stayed and came to Firstfall if they could, or died if they couldn't. There are stories of people walking a thousand miles across the barren surface, a journey of a month or more, supplies carried on robotic sleds, but I doubt any are true; the storms are too frequent and too deadly, shelter too rare.

The weather rattles and thunders. The wind howls. I cower in my ruined dome as rain falls like the wrath of an angry god. Each pit was abandoned as it was mined out, left to the elements and the Xen cartels from Earth. Most flooded, but not all. That's the story of Magenta's first century, and Settlement 16 fits right in until Frank Swainsbrook came along, pumped it out and built his gateway to God.

It's dark by the time the storm passes, Magenta dark, black as coal, the sun long set and the night sky hidden behind a vertical mile of cloud. The rain stops and the air turns clear. I leave the shelter of my ruined dome and look over the edge of the cliff into the pit. The bottom is lit by brilliant floodlights where three domes surround the landing pad, one a hangar, one a dormitory for Swainsbrook's cultists, one his personal palace. Outside the pools of light, the pit is abyss-black. I spot

Swainsbrook's antenna, a six-foot dish on top of the hangar pointing straight up inside a retractable dome to protect it from the weather. The dome is closed, but in the satellite pictures I have from when it was open, the antenna looks exactly like the Institute antenna that tracks the Solar Intensity Research Station. From down there inside its pit, it can only have line of sight for four, five, maybe six hours a day.

Long enough, I suppose.

The only way to the bottom of the pit is down the old mining track. I find a crude motion detector near the top, easily evaded. If there are cameras then I don't see them – I guess Swainsbrook doesn't worry too much about intruders out here. It takes me half an hour to walk to the bottom but there are no sirens, no searchlights, no alarms. No cover, either, except the darkness.

Somewhere above, Fleet and Earth are sizing each other up. I'm not sure it makes any difference in the end who wins. But Vishakh tried to kill Alysha, and so here I am.

I scurry across open ground towards the hangar, reach the edge of the dome and ease my way around. I avoid the landing pad and head for an access door – I figure there has to be a passage from the hangar direct to Swainsbrook's dome. Underground, probably. I reach the first door, dismantle the panel beside it and rearrange the wires, convincing it to let me in.

Magenta doesn't matter. That's the sum of it. We're insignificant, even all of us together. We're just too small.

The door opens. I slip inside into a glorified equipment locker, racks of environment suits and tools and another door into the hangar proper.

Keon?

Elizabeth?

Where are you?

Swainsbrook's settlement. Hangar dome.

And?

329

Nothing yet. I only just got here.

Fuck! What have you been doing?

Storm.

I'll bring the shell to you.

I didn't land close. Are you okay?

I'm not sure.

The hangar is dark. Swainsbrook's helicopter sits in the middle, using up only a fraction of the space. There's a tug to drag it back and forth to the pad and a couple of fuel hoses. A pair of maintenance shells stand quietly in recharge racks beside us, dormant.

The *Flying Daggers'* missile strike was in response to a request from the Tesseract. Morgan didn't give the order. But there's no one else who can.

How's that possible?

I don't know.

So what? It came from the Tesseract itself? It just decided?

I don't *know*, Keon!

Someone hacked it.

Vikram says that's not possible. I'm inclined to agree.

The Chief? You've *seen* him?

I had some explaining to do. Largely I told him the truth. Oddly that seemed to work.

Did you tell him you plan on defecting to Fleet?

Of course not. But Keon, Viki and I have known each other for thirty years and change. I don't need to *tell* him, just like he doesn't need to *tell* me that he's not your Tesseract One. Something is very wrong. I feel it from him. From the way he talks. I don't think the bureau is fully in charge of its own AI.

Like I said, someone hacked it. Earth. *October.*

And like *I* said, that's not how AIs work.

The Tesseract is doing this on its own? *That* works better for you?

Not really. But I suppose right now it doesn't make much difference.

There are some shells here. Can you use them? The Cheetah's a bit of a way away.

I wake the maintenance shells and link to their Servants, making a path for Jacksmith to take control. Then I go to the helicopter and wake that too, drawing data from its Servant.

Swainsbrook flew in from Firstfall last night, but this helicopter is registered to Eddie Thiekis.

So are these shells.

Why would Swainsbrook have someone else's—

I stop and crawl under the helicopter's nose. One of the maintenance shells starts to move.

What are you doing?

Aviation law requires the flight log to be public and unencrypted. Usually physical access only but— There!

I flip open a rubber seal the size of a thumbnail and there's a data port behind it. The maintenance shell comes up behind me, crouches and connects a finger to the port. Data streams into my Servant. I pore through it: So Swainsbrook flies into Firstfall just over a week ago and leaves again yesterday. Just one short trip to—

There it is.

What?

Jacksmith shows me the logs for the flights before last week. Three back-to-back return trips between Settlement 16 and the MagentaNet Tower. Two passengers into Firstfall each time, more like ten going back the other way.

He was shipping in his new recruits, she says, but that's not what I'm looking at. Six nights ago, only a few hours after Swainsbrook last landed in Firstfall, a solitary flight starts and ends at the MagentaNet Tower. It's an erratic loop around the city with no stops but several pauses. It passes close to New

Hope and makes one of its pauses there. The flight is right in Laura's window of time for when our antimatter warhead disappeared.

'I've seen this profile before.'

I used to have profiles for every MagentaNet drone in the sky that night, the drones Eddie said went to check the signal strengths and act as relays. This is one of them, except the profiles I saw back then were for drones too small to carry any kind of warhead. I can't prove it yet because all the raw data was on the Servant Liss threw out of a pod window last night. But I know what I'm seeing.

It flew empty, says Jacksmith. No passengers.

'Someone changed the transponder. Shit. *Shit!*' I need to get this back to the Tesseract. Or Morgan. Or *someone*, because someone needs to go to MagentaNet and prove that one of the MagentaNet drones that flew that night was actually a helicopter. Because from where I'm standing, not only have I got a noose I can put around Swainsbrook's neck, there's a good chance he's got an antimatter warhead out here.

Eddie. Eddie Thiekis. I don't know how Swainsbrook could have done this on his own. I don't understand why …

Elizabeth … Eddie Thiekis is helping Swainsbrook. He has to be. But … why? Why would he do this? Let's say you're right and Swainsbrook somehow managed to get all the best candidates for your 'Iosefa mutation' in one place. Why blow them up?

To stop someone else from getting them?

I can't buy that and I don't think Jacksmith does either. You go to all this trouble to steal something, it's not to smash it. You trust Morgan?

I do.

Are you sure?

Vikram has Magenta in his blood and in the marrow of his bones. If he has a flaw, it's that he doesn't play games. He's on

332

the point of shutting down the whole Tesseract because that's the only way to plug the leak. Yes, I trust him.

Then he needs to know about this. You're in Firstfall. You need to tell him.

You'd need a lot of access to make a switch like this. Physical access to the helicopter. Access to the MagentaNet systems. Access to the drone that was supposed to fly in order to shut it down. This isn't a quick hack from the outside, which means it came from within. It has to be Eddie. I don't like it, it doesn't feel right, but who else has such deep access to MagentaNet ...?

Okay, Keon. I can do that.

Or is the bomb still back there, in the MagentaNet Tower? I remember thinking when I met with Eddie, what if that was the target? What would happen if MagentaNet went down? How it would be days before we could get any sort of comms infrastructure up again, if we could get it up at all ... You take out the communications and then you land the troops ... Is *that* what this is?

Elizabeth ... If it's not here, it might be at MagentaNet. You need to tell him that too. But it's one or the other.

We leave the hangar and find the tunnel to Swainsbrook's dome. There are no locks and no cameras. A couple of minutes later I'm in a small conference suite. There's a meeting room with an absurdly expensive wooden table, an antique of some sort imported from Earth and surrounded by matching chairs. Display shelves line the walls, filled with models of the ships the Masters left behind. They all look the same to me, hollowed-out asteroids with a black rectangular mass in the middle. Behind the meeting room is an automated kitchen that smells like it's never been used. There's another meeting room beside it, smaller and more intimate, with floor-to-ceiling screens on every wall, a couple of luxurious sofas and a well-stocked drinks cabinet. A last door leads to an office with a desk and a couple of chairs, antiques again. Still no locks and still no cameras. Everything is quiet. There's no one here.

I want Swainsbrook. I want his Servant. I want to throw my Tesseract codes at him and rip into his data, but I don't have those codes any more.

We need access to the servers. There has to be a backup store somewhere.

We need Swainsbrook himself.

Jacksmith's shell gets down on its hands and knees and crawls under the desk. She fiddles around with the underside of one of the drawers. A panel drops down.

You mean like this one? Although bloody hell, this machine is fucking primitive.

How did you know—

Here we go.

Data streams into my Servant. The flatlining sessions. Meticulous interviews with everyone who went under, recording their experiences. At least two or three every day, sometimes half a dozen, always done immediately on return and on camera. A lot of sessions are guided by Swainsbrook himself. There are thousands, and going through them all will take days. Jacksmith burns a copy and then drags out Swainsbrook's shuttle logs, the flight records for the *Betty Blue*.

I've got financial records too.

The shuttle logs don't tell me anything I don't already know. A routine of trips to Earth and back every six months or so, gone for two cycles of the *Fearless* each time …

This all belongs to MagentaNet.

… until three months ago when five of Swainsbrook's staff took the shuttle supposedly to orbit, disappeared en route and never came back. No explanation. No report made to New Hope. Nothing.

This is too easy. I just walk in and none of this is encrypted, not even hidden? It's almost falling over itself to be found …

Shit. This is *meant* to be found.

'Delete it.'

What?

'Copy everything and then delete it. All of it. Erase everything.'

What? Why?

'Because this is a set-up and—'

The lights come up as the door opens. I roll sideways and pull my needler ready to fire, fully expecting a squad of goons in riot gear. Instead I find myself looking at Swainsbrook in a dressing gown and not much else.

'Hi, kids,' he drawls, hands carefully held out where I can see them. 'I had an inkling I might see you again, Agent Rause, but I see you brought a friend. And no, no set-up, just trying to make it easy for you. I do recall, after all, making an invitation of a sort, and that, sir, is because I've got nothing to hide. I know you don't believe me, but that's God's own truth.' He glances at Jacksmith's shell under the desk. 'You want to come out from under there?'

Delete it! 'Keep your hands where I can see them and sit down.'

Swainsbrook takes one of the office chairs, a model of compliant co-operation. He smiles as Jacksmith's shell emerges and he sees what she is.

'One of my own? Clever thinking! With a pilot somewhere far away whom I can't possibly reach. I mean, if I had a mind to.'

Don't say anything. Play dumb. 'A witness, if you like,' I say.

'A witness to *both* of our actions, if I may make so bold. But I applaud you, sir, for a gentleman should always be ready to account for his deeds, even when they include trespass and theft. I wonder, is it someone I know on the other end? Is that you, Eddie?' He smiles like he knows something he thinks will surprise me. 'I have to wonder, though, why is a fugitive from the law visiting my humble home.'

You're wrong. There *are* encrypted files. Jacksmith pings a batch of them to my Servant. There are a lot, they're big, and the encryption is heavy.

Swainsbrook smiles. 'It doesn't matter. The light and word of God, that's all I have room for.' He pats his heart and holds out his hands. My knuckles tense on the needler. 'I'm sorry I had to lie to y'all before, but you just weren't giving me a great deal of choice. The Masters are the right hand of God, Agent Rause, and they *will* return because I *will* invite them to do so. That much they have made clear in abundance. So let the rest go, son. Earth, Fleet, Magenta? None of that will much matter soon.'

God's *red* right hand? pings Jacksmith.

What?

The Masters. Milton. Never mind. Give me the other gun. I want to point it at him.

Did you copy the server?

Yes!

Then wipe it! 'You're really aiming to bring back the Masters?'

'Yes, sir, I am. I confess I am a little shocked you need to ask. Is that not what I said from the very beginning? Did I ever suggest otherwise?'

'Isn't that against everything *October* stands f—'

Swainsbrook snorts, shaking his head. 'You think I'm still a part of *that*? No, sir, I aim to put an *end* to them by showing their fears to be mistaken.'

Who does he think he is? sneers Jacksmith.

Wipe the server!

Done!

Swainsbrook is frowning like a disappointed parent at a wayward child.

'*October* got it all wrong, son! The Masters are God's mes-sengers. Angels if you like, but you don't have to call them that if it makes you feel uncomfortable. They've been talking to folk here on Magenta for years, and you *know* that to be true if you'd only stop long enough to admit it. I respect Miss Cho's choice not to join us, but you and I both know she's special, and I can promise you that she's not alone. What surprises me is how you don't seem to realise how blessed this world is, despite that the fact that you were born here.'

'The Masters aren't speaking to you,' I snap. 'You're hallu-cinating what you want to see from a combination of Xen and oxygen starvation.'

The files Jacksmith found could be coded rubbish for all I know, but my guess is that they're the sequences beamed from the Solar Station. If you're in his systems, look for ... Look for something that doesn't quite belong, hiding in the antenna con-troller q-ware.

'Beyond me how it all works. Never had the brain for science so I leave that to the smart folk. But ... Mister Rause ... is oxygen starvation why you went to see Miss Cho about your dead wife?' He holds up his hands as I tense. 'I understand your scepticism, son, I really do. I was the same until God's messengers spoke to me. That was just over five years ago, and look where we are! Ready to talk to the Devil himself like one civilised society to another.'

'The Masters killed billions,' I hiss. '*Billions!* Is that what your God does?'

Swainsbrook looks untroubled. 'That fellow Meelosh, he's what brought you here, when it comes down to it. I know, I know, troubled mind. We could have helped him but he wasn't interested. Shame how that ended. But that's always the way, isn't it? Some make it, some don't. You ever read the story of Noah, son? This here is the next ark. You want to be one of the animals lucky enough to catch a ride, or do you want to drown?'

'You're mad.'

I give the other pistol to Jacksmith.

'Who *is* in there, Agent Rause? Is it that other agent you had with you when we last had a little chat? Patterson, is it? I must say, you two looked mighty fine together. I envy you that, sir. Somehow never found the right woman.'

'What are—'

'Probably because you're a privileged jerk drowning in your own sense of entitlement,' snaps Jacksmith.

Even through the cheap robotic voice of a maintenance shell she manages to drip disdain.

'Oh! Elizabeth! Now that I was *not* expecting! Doctor, there's something I've really wanted to say since the day we met.'

Dro—

Three loud pops and the head of Jacksmith's shell caves in in three places at once, each the size of a fist. I feel something drop into my hair at the same time, like a wayward moth, except we don't have moths on Magenta.

'I'd be very still if I were you, son. Take a moment to consider your situation. Take your time while I fathom some words to express how truly magnificent it feels to finally silence that self-important cunt.'

If I was still with the Tesseract then Swainsbrook would be in a spider tie by now, wriggling helplessly on the floor of a Cheetah on his way to an interrogation room. I can't decide what I despise about him most: the faux humility, the faux concern, the casual dishonesty ... or maybe it's his face. Maybe I want to punch him because I just don't like his smug superior face.

I don't, though, because there's a drone in my hair about the size and feel of a large spider.

'That's good, son. Very, very, still. You know, there's something I'm hoping you can help with. See, I've known for a while that someone from your neck of the woods is tampering with my affairs.'

'Frank ... Can I call you Frank?'

'Trouble with you, son, I never could work out which side you were on.'

'What's with the bomb?'

'What I can't figure for the life of me is why—'

'Frank!'

'Son, interrupting is rude, didn't your mama ever tell you that?'

'Six days ago, someone used your helicopter to steal an anti-matter warhead from a shuttle in New Hope. *That's* why Firstfall is in lockdown. *Your* helicopter, Frank, so there's a good chance it's here, and *you* brought it here. If you know all about it then I suppose I'm fucked. But I'm guessing maybe you don't.'

Swainsbrook cocks his head, looking me over, trying to read whether I'm telling the truth.

'I was happy to play along, son, but no more. You, Eddie, *October*, Earth, Fleet, the whole damned lot of you. I've got the people to do what needs to be done now. Ain't nothing stopping this. The Masters *will* return. Some phantom bomb? Is that the best you've got?'

'Swainsbrook! I'm not fucking shitting you!'

'Don't you worry, son. Ain't no one going to set off some bomb.'

He holds out his hands again and opens them, palms up. Two small drones shimmer into life as they drop their active camouflage.

'Listen to me!'

'No, son, *you* listen.'

Screaming slams through my ears. Brilliant light crashes into my eyes. I lurch and gasp as my finger pulls the trigger on the needler, but nothing happens.

'I truly can't think of a better way to make you understand, son, except to take you with us. After all ...' He smiles that broad friendly smile of his. 'The more, the merrier, right?'

I feel the prick of a needle on the back of my neck ...

And like God snapped his fingers, I'm lying on a gurney. No fade out or coming round, just *BANG* and Swainsbrook isn't in front of me any more, and I'm not in his office but in a dome full of people and machines, like my life has been cut by a clumsy editor. I'm struggling to move, a panic rising inside me. There are straps across my arms, my chest, my wrists, my ankles. I can turn my head but nothing more. I feel my heart racing faster and faster, my breathing ... A circle of high beds surrounds me, all exactly the same, each with a stack of instruments and an array of drips beside it. Flatline rigs like Rachael Cho's. A buzz of excited conversation rises around me. The air is thick with anticipation. There must be more than a hundred people here ...

I try to cry out, but all I manage is some high-grade grunting. My head is swimming.

'Mister Swainsbrook?'

I thrash as far as the straps that hold me down will allow, trying to turn my head to see who spoke, but she's out of sight behind me. She sounds cheerful and excited.

'Mister Swainsbrook! He's awake!' I feel a hand on my brow, calm and reassuring. 'Hush! Hush! Everything's going to be just fine.'

I can almost see the smile that comes with that voice.

'There now.'

My breathing slows. I start to relax. I feel stupid. It's almost funny, really. I mean, getting so worked up about ... what it was that was ...

340

I can't focus. The edges of my thoughts are all soft and mushy. When I look around the room, tiny fractal blooms of colour erupt from the corners of everything.

'What the ... What the *fuck*?'

Xen. I'm high on Xen.

'You're so lucky!'

Is she talking to me? She's still behind me and I still can't see her, but now Swainsbrook looms over.

'Dolores, this one's already a little gone. Ease him in real gentle.' He moves to stand at my side and leans in close. 'I know what you're thinking, son, but I'm not going to kill you ... Actually, what am I saying? I *am* going to kill you, but only for a little while.'

He chuckles at his own stupid little joke and to my own horror I giggle a little as well. I'd break his teeth if I could move. Or maybe just hug him and tell him he could be so much better. I don't know ...

'How much ... Xen?' I ask.

'You're going to be a part of the great change, son. You're going to be a hero.' Swainsbrook leans closer still, whispering in my ear. 'What's happening out there around the sun? I *did* send my people, and not just the one time either. And we made some dumb pictures of stars blocked by sinister-looking shapes. Childish, I know, but it kept Eddie and his ilk sweet, kept them looking the wrong way while I did the Lord's work. You can take that home and bank it, for all the good it'll do you now, because something *did* happen out there. Those others – the ones from the inside ... Ain't nothing faked about that. I don't rightly know how it came to that, but we cracked ajar a door, son, one I intend to take in both hands and throw wide open. You're going to hear them speak just like the rest of us have done every day for the last five years.'

'Meelosh. Cho ...' My words are slurred and lumpy.

'The people who make this world special, son.' Swainsbrook shakes his head, and tiny little iridescent angels fly off him in all directions at once. 'Ain't anywhere else like it. Oh, and just so you can rest at ease, we did search like you asked, and there ain't no bomb, so I guess you were making that up and it must still be back in Firstfall.'

'Why did you kill Meelosh?'

Each word is an effort to force through my lips. Swainsbrook wags a finger at me. I watch in rapt fascination as it falls off his hands and sprouts wings and flies away. I know it's the Xen, but I can't do anything except stare as it dances around the room.

'You know perfectly well that Mister Meelosh did that to himself.'

'The Masters sent that recording to him, did they?'

I giggle. Swainsbrook's eyes have shapes swirling inside them that are made of colours I can't describe.

'Oh, I *sent* it. But I didn't make it. God did. As a test.'

'So where did it come from?'

He smiles. 'Where do you think, son? Ask and the Lord provides. Out there around Magenta's sun, that was what the Masters delivered to us.'

'And the Masters are God's messengers?'

'Got it in one!'

'You want to tell me ... why your God's messengers ... killed half a planet?'

'As a warning, son.'

For some reason that cracks me up.

'You're insane.' I can't stop laughing.

'Ain't that what they say about every prophet?'

Swainsbrook pats my arm and walks away.

I know it's the Xen. I know I should be screaming. But it's just so ... absurd.

SEVEN

ALYSHA

INSTANTIATION THIRTY-TWO

The shell carrying Instantiation Thirty-two runs across the Magentan wastes. It neither tires nor slows until it reaches the old mining pit of Settlement 16. Fourteen identical shells follow. They have been running across the wastelands for five days, all the way from Firstfall through storm and wind and rain, without rest or breaking stride. Now they descend into the pit and make for the dome where Frank Swainsbrook's great experiment has begun. They find a hundred flatline rigs arranged in two concentric circles. They move among them, deactivating the machinery and picking up the unconscious men and women of Settlement 16. Some are dead, killed by the interruption of their great communion with the Masters. Others are on their way back, their Xen-dosed blood whispering chemical dreams.

Instantiation Thirty-two checks the nearest man's Servant in case he is a Magentan citizen. Instantiation Thirty-two's instructions are precise and clear: Magentan citizens are to be left alone. But this man's name is Frank Swainsbrook, and he is not Magentan, and so Instantiation Thirty-two picks him up and takes him. It carries him to the bottom of the longest and deepest of the myriad shafts bored by the miners who worked here a century ago, to a space not much bigger than the three rooms of a Magentan government apartment. The shaft is new, bored last month because the voices Frank Swainsbrook hears as he floats on the edge of death told him to.

At the bottom of this shaft is another shell, one that once hosted Instantiation Seven, now long gone. The shell holds a metal case. Instantiation Thirty-two drops Frank Swainsbrook onto the growing heap of bodies and returns to the surface for another. It finds a man strapped down, unable to escape even if he wanted to. The man's Servant says he is a maintenance shell, though he is clearly not. It does not say he is a Magentan citizen. Instantiation Thirty-two is about to take him when another shell blocks its way. The unfamiliar shell pushes Instantiation Thirty-two aside, frees the man, takes him and leaves. Instantiation Thirty-two moves to another. There are plenty to go around.

When all the people who aren't Magentan citizens have been collected and carried to the bottom of the deepest shaft, Instantiation Thirty-two extracts a fine cable and connector from the back of its hand. It opens the metal case carried here by Instantiation Seven and plugs itself into the cylinder inside. The bodies of Frank Swainsbrook's followers are piled in careful rings around it. The shells that carried them are all here too.

No. Not all. One shell, Instantiation Thirty-two observes, is missing.

It waits, watching through cameras left on the surface until a shuttle, sleek and black and built for stealth, lands on the pad between the three domes on the surface. Soldiers emerge and enter the domes. They return carrying the last sleepers, the sixteen unconscious Magentans left behind, sixteen of the twenty-seven names that the voice of God whispered into Frank Swainsbrook's head in that place between life and death. The soldiers load the unconscious Magentans into their shuttle. The shuttle engines flare. It rises and vanishes into the rain.

Instantiation Thirty-two counts, a precise timer initiated from the moment the shuttle leaves the ground.

POP! For the briefest instant, the top of the metal cylinder in the metal case flicks open. A frozen core of metallic anti-hydrogen, previously cooled to absolute zero and held in magnetic suspension in a vacuum, ejects naked into the air, a tiny nugget of pure black, a seed the size of a marble. It flies up and immediately flares a brilliant white, blooming from frozen metal to plasma. And for an instant, the tiny cave at the bottom of the deepest shaft becomes like the heart of a star.

21

CORE DIRECTIVES

Dying is an inexorable drift into nothing. Light and sound fade, silence and stillness take their place. I have the sense of a starless void but there are no Masters here, no God, no distant beckoning light, only entropy, still, blank, unmoving, never changing. I see Alysha but she's a memory, not a part of this place but something brought with me. She comes with a fierce clarity, brighter than I've ever known. It's our wedding day. The ceremony is over. We're at the mag-lev station under Firstfall. A small crowd looks on, guests and well-wishers, friends and colleagues. I stand at the top of the steps that lead to the mag-lev platform.

The people watching, laughing and sharing our happiness, fade. I have no eyes for anything but Alysha in her Sri Lankan dress of white and gold, bright and brilliant and perfect. I never did. She's in my arms. I'm out of breath and my legs are burning. You get used to steps in 1.4 gravities but you don't get used to carrying someone else, and I've carried her up these steps three times over as she asked, and now I have my reward. She's pressed up close, her arms entwined around my neck, her eyes gazing into me.

Over her shoulder, in the crowd I've almost forgotten, I see Elizabeth Jacksmith in her chair, here as Alysha's friend. I never remembered seeing her before, but I know she was there, and now here she is.

I taste the sweet air from Alysha's lips as she speaks: 'Yours forever, Keon Rause.' I smell her scent. A distant part of me knows this memory carries a scar, the hurt of losing her, the knowledge that this place, years later, will be the start of her last journey; but in this void of death the scar is gone, and so this memory is the most perfect precious thing I have, a moment of joy where nothing else in time or space matters except that she's here, warm in my arms, a part of me, one being, one soul. We are, in this moment, everything.

Yours forever, Keon Rause. The beauty of it makes me weep.

Alysha falters. She becomes somehow less real. I try to hold her closer but I can't. She fades and fades and ...

Keon!

Joy dissolves into familiar grief. I've become so used to this despair that I no longer understand the weight of it. Freed from it for a moment, I feel its crushing burden. I am misshapen.

Keon!

Alysha is alive yet this memory of her feels like a farewell. My eyes blur with tears. I don't know where I am. I feel the vibration of an engine or a generator but I don't care. I want to go back. I want to go back to that place with her. I understand Swainsbrook now, why he had to go under again and again. I understand why, in the end, going back wasn't enough, why he had to try and bring that place back with him into the world of the living. Mad, deranged, deluded, and yet I understand.

I want to go back but something won't let me.

They filled you full of Xen, Keon. You're high as a kite. I'm about

349

to inject you with DeTox. I'm supposed to ask for your consent. Do you consent?

Eyes closed but the words still flash on my lenses. Xen. Lichen. Xenoflora. Magenta's blessing and Magenta's curse. The ache in my heart is unbearable. No, I don't consent.

Well, fuck you. I'm doing it anyway.

'I took some Xen once,' I say. 'At university ...'

I feel the DeTox at once, a coldness inside my skull. I sit up and open my eyes. I reel as my vision swims ...

I'm in the cockpit of a Cheetah, buckled into the pilot's chair. The world outside is grey and drab and rushing past at ridiculous speed. I don't have the first idea how I got here but we're so close to the ground I'm surprised we don't leave a trail of paintwork, and fuck! The voice is right, I *am* high on Xen. I know this because of the twisting fractal spirals of iridescent crystals that ooze in among the clouds and the landscape, through the cockpit displays and controls, through everything, and fuck, fuck, *fuck*! I'm high on Xen and flying a Cheetah and ...

I grab for the yoke but it doesn't respond.

Relax. You're not flying this.

DeTox is for alcohol but it'll take the edge off a Xen trip too. Price will be a lot of rushing to the toilet – but I don't *want* to take off the edge. I want to cling to that memory of Alysha, to how it felt.

'I want to go back,' I say. 'Let me go back.'

Back where?

Jacksmith's shell is crouched at the back of the cockpit. It has the remains of a second shell beside it, broken and still, something that looks like a dumb maintenance shell. She's dissecting it. Beside me, slumped unconscious and strapped into the navigator's chair, is a woman I've never seen before.

'I saw Alysha,' I say.

No Masters, then?

'No.'

What happened there, Rause?

'I saw Alysha,' I say again, 'and I want to go back. I want to go back to ... to that place. To her. I want ...'

But the DeTox has me and I have to rush to the tiny cubicle that passes for a cockpit toilet. When I come out, Jacksmith plies me with water. It only takes a minute for the Xen buzz to fade but it's ten more before my head isn't full of Alysha. Of that memory ...

What happened? Jacksmith asks again when I tell her I think I'm okay. I'm not, but I figure this is as good as I'm going to get.

'He took you out, waffled about the Masters, some drone stabbed me in the neck and then the next thing I knew I was strapped down on a stretcher and they flatlined me. There were a lot of them, all together.'

You didn't get anything more?

I think of Frank standing over me, the conviction in his voice. I tell her what he said, as best I remember it.

'Swainsbrook set up the hoax for *October*. He had a shuttle that could make the trip and he needed money. I think that was how it worked. But Swainsbrook had his own agenda all along. I think that was all he cared about. He told me something happened out at that station by the sun. Something ... I don't know. You're right, though, and I don't know what's going on any more, but Swainsbrook really believes. He tried to recruit Cho and Meelosh and the others because God told him to.'

Not God, Keon.

'Maybe not, but *someone* put those names into his head. How long was I out?'

I check the time. It was dark when Swainsbrook found me in his office. Now it's light ...

351

I still want to go back to that memory of Alysha. I want to hold it close and never let go ...

We're a couple of hours out of Firstfall, Jacksmith says, and you need another DeTox.

'I take it he didn't summon the Masters?'

Swainsbrook's dead.

'What?'

Jacksmith pauses. You might want to sit down for this. Your missing antimatter isn't missing any more. Someone set it off.

'*What?*'

After Frank killed my shell, I reactivated this one. It took me an hour to get from the Cheetah to the mine. There were a dozen or so other shells already there, no idea where they came from. Everyone was out cold, even the people who weren't wired to a flatline rig. Someone flooded the air with a mixture of Xen and ... some flourane derivative, I think – your forensics people can figure that one out. The shells carried most of you down into the mineshafts. A shuttle came and took the others. As soon as it was gone, the bomb went off. Took out everyone who was left and the shells too, but left the settlement itself intact. It's like they all simply vanished, like they were never there. The shaft is vaguely radioactive and I'm sure a proper forensic team would eventually work out what happened, just like they'd find traces of whatever was in the air conditioning. What they won't find is any trace of any data, because every single piece of q-host hardware has gone too.

I have a sinking feeling.

'Can you prove any of that?'

I recorded what I saw and I have what's left of one of the shells. So yes, I can prove what happened. As to why ... I got one of them out. Jacksmith jerks her head towards the unconscious woman in the navigator's seat. She might talk. Might have seen something. But I doubt it. Frank was played. You know it, I know it, but—

'There was a *shuttle*?'

Jacksmith pings me a list of everyone registered as living in Settlement 16, lifted from the files we stole from Swainsbrook's office. Almost all are Earthers, but sixteen are Magentans. The sixteen that were taken.

We failed, Keon. The one who were taken … they're the Magentans Swainsbrook recruited these last weeks. Iosefa's children. Not literally, but they carry some part of his genetic code. The video that's out there? I showed it to Rachael Cho and—

'I know. She told me.'

I'm so stupid! Frank rounded up everyone who responded to it and corralled them into one place. Now the Earthers have snatched the lot and wiped their hands clean. They did it right in front of me and there was nothing I could do to stop them.

'Not entirely clean.'

I send her the evidence from Frank's flight recorder, wondering if the shells Jacksmith saw wiped it along with everything else or whether it's still there. Jacksmith returns the favour, sending me the recordings she made. We watch them together: maintenance shells carrying bodies and q-code hardware. I see her find me and pull me out. I see her take down another shell and rescue the women beside me. I see the shuttle land, a shuttle like Vishakh's shuttle in New Hope. I see the Earther soldiers carry away the last survivors. Swainsbrook's Magentans. Sixteen of them, like Jacksmith said.

'Swainsbrook said the Meelosh video was a test,' I tell her. 'He said the Masters sent it to him. That it came from whatever happened out on the solar station.' The shuttle flies away. A minute later and the ground shakes like it's ground zero for an earthquake. 'But if that's what he really believed, where did it *really* come from?'

Jacksmith pokes at the unconscious woman. Dolores King. Swainsbrook's personal assistant. No idea what she knows. Could be everything, could be nothing.

'Okay, look. This thing with Earth is out of our hands. We know what they did, we know how and we know why and you've got the proof, but it's too big. We show the world and so what? Does Earth care? We can whip up a whole planet of outrage, and maybe we should, but so what? There's nothing we can do to get those people back, not now. But we can clean our own house. We know how the bomb got to Settlement 16 and we can prove it. Whoever did this had complete access to MagentaNet. Maybe they left a trace.'

There's something else.

Jacksmith points me to the encrypted files lifted from Swainsbrook's office.

I had a good look at Swainsbrook's information architecture while I was in his systems. I can't prove this, but it's possible that what you're seeing are the visions his people saw when they were dead.

'He had a way to record them?'

I think they came the other way. I can't decrypt the content but look at the transmission times. Then look at the interview records. Look at when people went under.

I look. And then I stare at nothing, mouth open, blank-headed, trying to get a grip on the enormity of what Jacksmith is saying. She's right. Every single recording for one of Swainsbrook's flatline sessions lines up with a received transmission burst. But the burst comes *first*.

Huge volumes of encrypted data, beamed in from orbit ...?

'You're saying ... someone *sent* Swainsbrook his visions?'

Him and all his people.

'And he thought he was getting messages from ... God?'

I think that's how it worked, yes. You shouldn't be able to hide that much traffic but I can't find where it came from. Not from MagentaNet.

No. Not MagentaNet. Because the other thing I see is that Swainsbrook's people only ever went under near the middle of the day, when the antenna on top of the hangar dome would see up into space. When it could see the sun. When it was pointing straight at the solar station so Swainsbrook could beam up the next instalment of his hoax ...

'You're looking in the wrong place, Elizabeth. They used Swainsbrook's link to the solar station to beam stuff the other way. Back to Settlement 16.'

Swainsbrook was sending one hoax one way, and he had no idea another was coming straight back at him?

'Antenna 679 on the Institute roof.'

I'm so stupid. We were all over what that antenna was receiving. We never thought to look at what it was *transmitting*.

'Elizabeth ... Are we saying that Swainsbrook's visions – that all the visions he and his little cult thought they were seeing – someone beamed them into his head while he was under? From the sun?'

I think we are, yes. I know it sounds ridiculous but—

'It sounds more than fucking ridiculous!'

Do you prefer Frank's explanation that it was all the Masters? Keon, this is something we can *prove*, for what little it matters now that Earth has got almost everything.

Except Jacksmith herself. I wonder: have we been looking in the wrong place?

'The Tesseract has complete access to the MagentaNet systems.'

It's also right next door to the Institute.

The AI does. Not the users. Not even Morgan. Not even me.

'Everyone tells me it's not possible to hack an AI.'

It isn't. Fundamentally a different beast. Not really my field, but as I understand it you can't hack an artificial intelligence any more than you can hack a real one. Although if we're right about what happened to Swainsbrook and his followers … I *suppose* you could do the same to an AI. Alter and distort its perception of its environment to cause its understanding of reality to differ from the subjective truth as collectively perceived by the rest of us and thus trigger apparently aberrant behaviour. I *suppose* you could do that to any of us.

'Brainwash an AI?' I decide not to mention the time I did exactly that to one of Darius Vishakh's Dattatreya.

But you'd have to take control of all its sensory inputs, which is effectively impossible for something like the Tesseract.

I'm not thinking of the Tesseract any more.

'Is that the only way to change an AI's behaviour?'

There were some studies back in the early days, when Core Directive AI was new and everyone was still worried about whether they *could* be hacked. The effect is only temporary. Turn the real world back on and the AI bounces back to normal behaviour. Rather more robustly than humans do, in fact.

'So there's no way to change an AI in a fundamental way?'

No. That's the whole point of the Core Directive design. You can't hack it.

Swainsbrook believed in the human soul. Machines don't have souls, so have I been to a place Liss can never go? An AI can't flatline … except surely it can, because aren't they designed from the ground up to be able to do that? Just turn off the power, right? Turn off the power and someone else has to turn it back on again, but if you do then they come back. Isn't that exactly what Swainsbrook just did to me?

But AIs don't dream while they're out. I looked it up back when I was curious to know how Liss worked. It's just a blink in the passage of time. On, then off, then on again as though nothing has changed except the world has raced forward …

Sleep and death. I'm missing something, something right there just out of reach. My thoughts drift to Rachael Cho, who has an eeriness like she can touch your feelings by simply looking at you. And Eddie Thiekis's girl Shyla, who died when her brain got hit by a tailored strain of Xen that kicked into life some rare piece of genetic code. Back when we were on her case, Bix said there was something special about her, a sort of inner light that was hard to resist although it came with a streak of self-destruction. Eddie thinks a brain haemorrhage is what killed his little girl, triggered by an illegal designer strain of Xen, but that's only a partial truth. I didn't tell him that the Xen strain was an experiment in telekinesis, or that I've seen a man explode from the inside when no trace of explosive was ever found.

Or that seven months ago there were a dozen haemorrhagic deaths in Disappointment. Some looked like a stroke, some like they'd swallowed a grenade. Same Xen.

Iosefa Lomu made a Masters' ship fly. He was a Xen addict who said he knew when the Masters went. Not *where* but *when*. Rachael Cho claims to hear the Masters speak to her when she's dead and I've never seen any sodding great antenna on *her* roof. Maybe Swainsbrook has it right, maybe there's more to being human than flesh and blood.

'Why annihilate Swainsbrook's cult?' I ask.

To cover the abduction of sixteen Magentans!

'There have to be easier ways.'

Then I don't know ... Because someone thought there was a chance that what he was trying might actually work ... Wait ... This is weird.

'What?'

This shell. I assumed it was being piloted remotely but it wasn't, it was following pre-programmed algorithmic instructions under a fuzzy logic wrapped. Like a maintenance shell or a reception shell or some such. But the complexity – this is more like an AI

357

than not. It's like someone took an AI and then very carefully cut a layer out, just enough to remove any self-awareness. It's exquisite work.

'Show me.'

Jacksmith's shell cocks its head at me.

Really? They teach AI design at the bureau now?

'No, but I'm a dab hand at rummaging through half-wiped core-cloned almost-AI sex-bot shells and digging out traces of who made them.'

Shells made by the cracksman who made Liss, and there was nothing *almost* AI about them, but Jacksmith doesn't need to know that.

Touché.

I don't know my way around AI architecture, not *really*, but I know how to find the tell-tale signatures of where a shell like this was made. I go for the core directives, because that's where the spoor will be. The first are no surprise – roughly translated they're instructions to do exactly what the shells did: gather everyone together, wipe every q-code device, wait for the shuttle to come and go and then set off the bomb. But underneath there are far more than I …

Enforce the law.

Act in the long-term best interests of the citizens of Magenta.

Never, by direct action, cause harm to a citizen of Magenta …

I stop. There are hundreds, equally familiar. I start to laugh. When Jacksmith's shell stands over me, I show her what I've found.

'Tesseract One,' I say. 'We've got them.'

Because this shell core is copied straight from the Tesseract AI itself, which means whoever made it had access to the Tesseract's own core, and there are rules and protocols for copying AI code designed to make it explicitly impossible for an AI to copy its own sentience. It means not only that there are records, but that there *have* to be records, and that they *have* to still be there inside the Tesseract itself. They have to be in here, too, inside the code buried in this shell, because the necessity of their existence is built into AI architecture from the ground up.

Jacksmith does a little dance.

They were all supposed to be destroyed! We were never supposed to find this!

Never, by direct action, cause harm to a citizen of Magenta ...

'They *couldn't* kill them ...!'

I'm frowning because this still makes no sense, and if Jacksmith is right then keeping those sixteen people alive while spiriting them away and making everyone else think they were dead was the whole point ...

'But why copy an AI when all they needed was one shell pilot and they—'

What are we saying ...? That someone beamed Swainsbrook's visions to him through his own hack on the solar station in order to gather anyone on Magenta who might have the Lomu gene? They set all this up and then sent a company of shells to erase all trace of what they did?

I probe through the dead shell's code, deeper still, underneath the layers of directives until I find the unique replication key that's integrated into the AI core-clone. Somewhere inside the Tesseract is a copy of this same code and a record of who authorised the replication, and when, and from where. That record *will* exist because AI replication records are impossible to erase, even from the source AI itself.

And they did all that from inside the bureau?

From inside the bureau I can pinpoint the creation of this replica to an exact time and place, and with that I'll know exactly who did it. Everything I'll need to take Tesseract One down.

This whole thing, *all* of it, has been run by someone in the Tesseract?

359

Jacksmith's struggling to believe it. I can't blame her.

'Vishakh's Tesseract One.' Everything *Laura* will need, not me, because I'm going with Jacksmith to find Alysha. 'Where are we heading?'

Jacksmith shows me the flight profile set up in the Cheetah's Servant. Fast and low under New Hope's radar, giving the spaceport a wide berth, straight to the MagentaNet Tower. I wonder how close we can get before they pick us up, but then I see she's switched our transponder with the one from Frank Swainsbrook's helicopter, which is flying along an hour or so behind us on autopilot, looking as though it's us.

'Anyone ever told you that you should be a bureau agent?'

Anyone ever told you I kind of invented the bureau? Besides, this only takes you so far. Even if they think we're Frank, they're still going to arrest you. Violation of airspace restrictions, remember?

I laugh.

You realise that if you're right then your mole ordered the *Flying Daggers* to fire at us. And it did.

'I'll bet you a month's salary he sent the Meelosh video to Swainsbrook too.'

I can see now how Tesseract One has left a trail for his own version of the truth. It ends with Morgan taking the fall, but it starts with Eddie Thiekis. The shells were his and he looks red-hot guilty for the antimatter bomb.

No one in the Tesseract could do all of this, Keon. No one.

'That's because it's a hack.'

Rause! It isn't a bloody hack! You can't do that.

'Occam's razor, Elizabeth. What else is there?'

I'm afraid Occam's razor is taking me somewhere rather worse. I need to think about this. To be honest I'm rather hoping you're right.

'While you're thinking, patch me through to Eddie Thiekis. His fingers are in this. I'm just not sure how deep.'

Jacksmith makes the call. I figure he's more likely to answer it that way. When he does, his voice is low and cracked.

'What do you want?'

'Swainsbrook is dead. So are all his people. He had the bomb. You hearing me, Eddie?'

'Frank's ... dead?'

'Yeah.' I frown. 'The bomb, Eddie. The bomb you smuggled out of New Hope.'

'Bomb?' He sounds like a bewildered child. 'What bomb?'

'The antimatter warhead stolen from New Hope seven nights back. It went off in Settlement 16 a few hours ago. When forensics get there, they're going to find out everything. I assume you know all about it given that Swainsbrook's helicopter masqueraded as one of your little drones, flew out to New Hope on autopilot on the night of the theft and carried it right back to you. The Tesseract will be all over MagentaNet. Your archives and records will be frozen. The bureau will find out who authorised the flight, who changed the transponder, all of it. There can't be many people with that sort of authority – in fact, I'm guessing there's only one. The way things went down, the Earthers have largely got what they want from Magenta now, and Swainsbrook and all his people are dead. So here it is, Eddie – you wanted peace with the Earthers, you hated Frank, and there must have been at least a little of the *October* in you that hated what he was trying to do, too, and all the evidence points your way. The way it looks. You're going to take the fall for this. Everything you built over all the years is going to be taken apart. You've been set up, Eddie.'

'What?' Horror. Fear. Fury. 'Rause! What the fuck are you ...? How fucking dare you! How dare you accuse me of—'

'Eddie, you let Frank fly out of Firstfall while the city was locked down when we already arrested him on your fucking roof for the *exact same thing*! The bomb was on board and I can prove it. Swainsbrook's helicopter picked it up from New Hope. I've seen the flight recorder and it's there in black and white – the profile matches one logged by you for a sniffer drone. This whole thing points right at you.'

'I had nothing to do with—'

'I believe you, but I might be the only one who ever does, and what I also believe is that someone in the Tesseract asked you to help Frank with a few things. I'm on my way over. Here's your choices. You either tell the Tesseract so they can arrest me for the fugitive I am, or you come clean on everything to Jacksmith and –' I glance to Jacksmith's shell. She nods – 'to Chief Morgan. You three cover for me for as long as it takes to prove who really did this, maybe you don't come out of this skinned, because as things stand, you and Morgan are both going down and Tesseract One gets away scot-free.'

I cut the link. He can stew on that. I turn to Jacksmith.

'Get me Laura.'

You trust her right now?

'Yes.'

Jacksmith sets up a link. I launch the encryption code Laura sent me back when I was returning from Nico a week ago. It feels like a lifetime.

'Keon?' She sounds exhausted and beaten. 'Fuck! I thought they shot you down!'

'They?'

'Us. The bureau. They thought you were carrying the warhead.'

'Another few hours,' I tell her. 'Then it's over.'

'*Were* you carrying the warhead?'

'No, but I know who took it and why and what it was all for. The Meelosh video was meant to lure Magentans carrying Iosefa Lomu's genes. It was the bait, Swainsbrook was the net

362

and the bomb was to clean up afterwards. They're probably all aboard the *Flying Daggers* by now.'

I tell her about Swainsbrook and send her the data we lifted and the recordings Jacksmith made from her shell. I tell her how everything points to Eddie and how that's probably a lie, and then I tell her about the shell we're bringing back and send through the replication code. I give her absolutely everything because I know she's going to need it.

'Eddie might have something or he might not, he might be in this up to his knees or up to his neck, but find who created that code and you've got your Tesseract One.'

'You know the obvious other way to see this?' she says. 'You *did* have the warhead. You and Alysha have been in this together from the start. You're both skating for Fleet and always were. You've always known exactly what Swainsbrook was doing and why, and now you've got what you wanted and you're laying the burn on Earth. I don't know who you are any more, Rause. Tell me why I should believe a word of this.'

'Because either way there still has to be someone else on the inside.'

She doesn't answer. I tell her I'll be with her as soon as I can, a promise we both know I won't keep. I tell her again how I'm sorry for everything. I tell her she's brilliant and broken, mistrustful and brave. I tell her, Alysha aside, she's the best friend I ever had and how everything will turn out okay in the end.

'Fuck off, Rause,' she says when I'm done.

On a better day she'd say something nasty about Alysha, but today she doesn't even hang up. I realise that what I'm really saying is goodbye, and she knows it, and just how deep that cuts her. It hangs between us, a pregnant silence.

'I dare you to say all that to my face,' Laura says at last. 'I dare you to try.'

She cuts the line.

Ten minutes later, Eddie messages me back.

'It wasn't Morgan,' he says. 'No one from the Tesseract asked me to help Swainsbrook. I did it to keep things smooth with Earth. I've cleared the roof of the tower. You can land here.'

Do I believe him? I'm not sure I do. But I reckon I know where Jacksmith's version of Occam's razor is heading, and if she's right then we're all pawns. Me, Swainsbrook, Thiekis, Morgan, Flemich, even the Earthers in the *Flying Daggers*. But I don't know, not for sure. Maybe Tesseract One is really Eddie Thiekis pulling all the strings, or Morgan, or both of them together. Fuck it, maybe Swainsbrook was as mad as a bag of spiders and somehow did it all himself, a martyr to a cause I don't begin to understand.

Or maybe Tesseract One is something else. When Laura tracks that code to its source, then we'll know.

Half an hour out from Firstfall we get another burst from Eddie.

'You fucker, Rause! You set me—'

It dies, swamped by noise. I check the news feeds. Nothing.

A minute later I get a ping from Laura: Don't go to MagentaNet. Check your feeds.

The Cheetah carries on straight.

'Elizabeth?'

The shell has the same expressionless face as ever. She turns on a news feed, piped to one of the Cheetah's screens. Channel Nine are breaking the story of Eddie Thiekis's arrest like all their birthdays have come at once. Then Jacksmith switches to another.

'The Magentan government has agreed to the immediate handover of Iosefa Lomu's remains. Following intense negotiations with the United Nations delegation aboard the Embers' Fire, *and in light of sustained terrorist activity*

suspected to have been sponsored by Fleet, the government of
Magenta has also accepted the offer of military support ...'

The first dropships will reach Magenta within forty-eight hours. Earther soldiers will be on the surface. A state of emergency. A sixteen-hour-a-day curfew in Firstfall. Residents advised to return to their homes and remain indoors until the crisis resolves.

Shit.

It gets worse.

Another screen. The video that killed Une Meelosh is spreading across Magenta like a virus. Eleven suicide attempts, six successful, and rising.

I'm with Vikram— with Chief Morgan right now. The Tesseract is about to shut MagentaNet down.

'He can do that?'

The news feeds go dead. A tactical display takes their place. A Kutosov interceptor is dropping from the stratosphere into the clouds a few miles behind and above Swainsbrook's helicopter, closing fast. It has missile lock.

No, he can't. But it's happening anyway. Keon, no one's in control any more.

'What? How ...?'

'Cheetah CH667B inbound Firstfall, this is New Hope air traffic. Maintain your speed and course and relinquish to our control. You have thirty seconds to comply. If you do not, lethal force will be used.'

The Tesseract just identified Viki as Tesseract One.

'*What?*'

I have to go—

'So who's—'

Keon, do you understand? The Tesseract *itself* indicted him.

I watch the display. I understand completely. Tesseract One

isn't Morgan or Eddie Thiekis or anyone else. It's the Tesseract itself. It's the AI.

It's taken over.

'But why—'

That's how it works. With no director or assistant director, the Tesseract will run autonomously under the guidance of the Selected Chamber until a new chief is appointed. It's doing what it's supposed to.

'That's not what I meant.'

The dots on the display are getting closer.

You might want to say something, Jacksmith suggests, but I shake my head.

'Let it happen.'

'CH667B inbound Firstfall, this is New Hope air traffic. Relinquish to our control immediately or lethal force *will* be used.'

Sorry. I need to go. They're—

Jacksmith's shell goes limp. Over the radio a different voice chimes in, full of the hiss and crackle of static. The Kutosov pilot.

'Falcon One in position, New Hope air traffic. No response from target.'

'Roger, Falcon One. CH667B inbound Firstfall, this is your last warning.'

I see the dots converge on the display, the Kutosov completing its drop from orbit to take up a firing position.

'Weapons free, Falcon One. Engage.'

'Engaging target.'

A third dot appears. I watch them converge ...

And vanish. So much for Swainsbrook's helicopter.

'Falcon One, this is New Hope air traffic. We see a kill. Do you confirm?'

'Confirmed kill, New Hope air traffic, but the target was not as specified. Sending visuals.'

'Roger Falcon One. We'll take a look.'

Shit.

INSTANTIATION TWELVE

Instantiation Twelve sits on the roof of the MagentaNet Tower watching the Cheetah fly in from Settlement 16. It watches feeds relayed from a hundred cameras below as fifty bureau agents pour through the MagentaNet Tower, seizing data and Servants, shutting access and closing communication links. It's the biggest operation the bureau has ever carried out, planned on a moment's notice and pulled together with seamless efficiency. Eddie Thiekis, one of the richest men on the planet, is going down, charged and arrested for conspiracy. The evidence is overwhelming. A hundred people are dead, a world destabilised, and MagentaNet is responsible. There will be a trial. Thiekis will be sentenced to spend the rest of his life in custody. Everything he owns will be seized to become the property of the Magentan government.

The weather is calm for Magenta today, a strong wind and a touch of drizzle and nothing more. The Cheetah lands without incident. Instantiation Twelve taps into a feed from one of the waiting agents. Cameras relay everything. The agents board the Cheetah, Reepers at the ready. They expect to find Keon Rause. They expect to find a shell remotely piloted by his wife Alysha, a shell whose data logs will give away her location.

Instead they find a confused and groggy Earther woman, whose Servant names her as Dolores King.

22

ALYSHA 1.0

The Cheetah sweeps slowly over the sea along the Firstfall coast, so low it feels as though we're clipping the tops of the wave. It nudges into cover between the two largest wavedomes and hovers for a moment, wrestling with the wind. Inside the cockpit in a locker are a pair of environment suits. I squeeze into one and open the door to the passenger module that isn't there any more. I wake Jacksmith's shell and tell it to walk out, watch it fall and splash and sink like a stone under the water, then jump after it into gusting wind and torrential rain. I crash into the sea as the Cheetah pulls away, its autopilot taking it to the MagentaNet Tower. Buoyancy packs in the suit inflate, pulling me to the surface. I ping Jacksmith but she isn't answering. The Tesseract will know what I've done as soon as the Cheetah lands so I have ten, maybe fifteen minutes, before the hunt starts. An hour from now, Jacksmith is supposed to meet with Alysha. She hasn't told me what this means and now she doesn't answer my calls, but I know where to go.

Liss? I've nowhere else to turn.

Where are you?

I swim to the shore and pull myself out of the water. I shiver in the wind and huddle against the sheer grey wall of the Wavedome. Out here, out of sight of the city, I see Magenta for what it is, a bleak and pitiless wasteland of smooth weather-scoured stone, our existence on its surface tenuous and transient. This is my home, the truth of it. If I go with Jacksmith and Alysha, I'll never see this again.

A pod stops close to where I'm hiding. I get inside and find a destination already programmed in its Servant. As it hums into Firstfall's central district and dives into the undercity, I search for all the people and places with the name Amaranth and filter them one by one. There are scores, but most are obviously wrong. Clubs and events that aren't tonight, or at the right time. Places that are too public. Jacksmith and Alysha will need to meet unseen.

It has to be the refinery. But what if I'm wrong?

If you find Alysha, do you think you'll be happy?

The pod takes me into the Squats. I watch the tunnels roll past, featureless smooth stone, the occasional other opening, now and then widening into caverns lined with apartments and vending stalls. I want to go back to where we were before she left. I want to unwind the last six years and rub them out as though they never happened. If we could do that then I know we'd be happy. Both of us.

I don't know. I have to try.

The pod reaches a deserted street corner out of sight of any camera. Liss waits, carrying a holdall. She gets into the pod beside me and tosses it onto my lap.

'There's everything you'll need in there,' she says.

I open the bag and start to rummage, then stop as the pod pulls away even though I've not given it a destination.

'Where are we going?'

'I don't know. Just driving.'

There are clothes, a couple of black market pistols, a brace of illegal anonymised Servants, a few other bits and pieces. Some I don't recognise.

'You're going to leave me. You're going to go with her and leave Magenta.'

'Liss—'

'Don't. If you find her, there's no place in your life for me.'

'I think you lied to me.' I start to strip out of my wet clothes. 'I think you found her and you didn't tell me.'

'I have to say something, Keys. It's going to hurt, but I'm afraid that if I say nothing then you'll be hurt even more.'

I flail my way naked and drag out an insulated jumpsuit.

'You're going to tell me I should let her go.'

'She came to you in Mercy. She could have given you a way to reach her but she didn't. We found her by accident in the Roseate Project. She ran. She didn't have to. Yes, I tracked her for a while. It wasn't so hard until she knew she was blown. She was watching you. She could have made contact whenever she wanted. But she didn't.'

Liss gives me one of her anonymous Servant extensions. I slip it into a silk pocket inside the jumpsuit and turn it on but don't link to it. I'm happy enough to stay as a maintenance shell as far as Firstfall is concerned.

'Where is she?' I pull out a storm suit and a pair of boots.

'She disappeared after the Tesseract discovered she was still alive. I lost her then.'

I tell the pod to take me to Amaranth Seaweed Oils. It has to be that. Both the Tesseract and the Magenta Institute go deep, almost to the hydroponics levels. Both have access to service tunnels that lead directly to the reservoirs. The refinery isn't under the heart of Firstfall's central district but it's not far. A quick and easy ride to a place where no one would ever see Alysha and Jacksmith meet, back when Alysha was still a bureau agent?

'Maybe she still loves you,' says Liss. 'But we both know all too well that love isn't enough. She has a new life. She chose it. She moved on without you, Keys. I'm sorry. I know this must hurt.'

'You want to have me to yourself, is that it?'

'I have no place in your life now. Whatever happens between you and Alysha, we both know it's her you love, not me. I just don't want to see you hurt.'

There's no emotion in her words. They file out of her mouth with utter detachment but I know better. I know who she is. I know what she wants and I know what I've seen her do to get it. And I know she has no way out of this.

'What happened out on the ice was a mistake, was it?'

'Keys, not leaving you to die isn't the same as wanting you back.'

'Then she can say so to my face.'

It's quiet down among the reservoirs, deserted, no traffic. I search the undercity around the Amaranth refinery and find a tiny cafe called The Black Sheep. It's dark, dingy and cheap, a surveillance blind spot and only fifty yards from the refinery entrance. I change the pod's destination. We're already close. I'll be there in a few minutes. It seems as good a place as any to start. It *feels* like Alysha.

Liss stops the pod.

'Goodbye, Keys.'

'What if *she's* the one afraid to reach out? What if *she's* afraid of what *I'll* say? What if she's the one thinking that *I've* made a new life and moved on?'

'It's okay.'

'No, it's not, and I'm sorry, and I know you might be right, but I have to be sure, and you already know all of this.'

Liss gets out of the pod.

'I'll see you around,' she says.

She knows those were the last words Alysha ever said to me, and for a moment I'm afraid she's going to do something stupid. But she turns and smiles even as she looks so infinitely sad.

'I'm going to find Laura and tell her what I am,' she says. 'I'll need a friend, I think, and so will she. Perhaps we can help each other. We *were* friends once, after all.'

'Don't! Liss! Don't …'

Her face twists into artificial anguish. *Don't tell Laura*, is that what I was going to say? Why? Because if the bureau ever finds out that Liss exists then they'll hunt her down and turn her off and wipe her clean out of existence? But she *knows* all that, and it's her choice, not mine, and what alternative do I offer? Live alone, isolated, unknown, cut off, always a secret, a watcher but nothing more, tossed aside for the woman I built her to replace when I thought Alysha was dead? Treat a human like that and I'd call myself a monster. Is it okay because she's an AI? It's what she is, but she feels so real when we talk, so human, so how *can* it be okay?

I don't know what else to do.

'I'll stay out of your way, Keys.' She turns to go.

'Look after yourself, Liss.'

She doesn't look back. I sit alone in the pod after she's gone, thinking of Alysha and Liss and Laura, of the world I'm about to leave behind, trying to see a way to make it right even though I know I can't, not for Liss. I built her to replace Alysha when Alysha could never be replaced, Alysha who isn't dead after all. I shouldn't have done it but I didn't know … I didn't think … And now it's too late. I don't know, I guess some questions don't have answers, some problems can't be solved, and I'll just have to live with that.

I tell the pod to take me to the Black Sheep. It stops in a dingy service tunnel, barely lit. There's no sign of life from inside and the Black Sheep's Servant is dead or dormant, but the door slides open at my touch and dull ceiling strip lights struggle to life. There's a tiny counter with four stools resting against it. There are two small tables, each with two cheap plastic chairs. Everything is covered in thick dust.

The pod moves away, on about its business, summoned to its next anonymous passenger.

A section of the counter folds back. I squeeze through to where someone once stood to serve lichen coffee and sandwiches and faux pastries or whatever this place used to offer. There are empty spaces where an espresso machine used to be, a couple of refrigerators, all the other things a cheap cafe would need to serve the handful of customers it maybe once had, the sort of people who like the anonymity of somewhere like this.

This place is a ruin. Dead.

A door leads back into what was once a kitchen, or an office, or just a storage space. My Servant tries to find some way to trigger it but there's no need, it has a handle. When I tug on it, it slides open into a hallway that leads deeper into the stone, so dark I can barely see. I can make out three more doors, two on the right straight behind the cafe and one at the far end.

I have a sense that I'm not alone. I draw my pistol.

'Elizabeth?'

The first door is wide open. Behind is a tiny storeroom, empty except for dust-filled shelves.

'Alysha?' I whisper her name.

Silence.

The second door leads into an old wet room, long stripped bare. Someone used to live here. As I ease the last door open, the air on the other side is a fraction warmer. It carries a smell, a human smell, a touch of sweat ...

I *know* that smell.

374

'Alysha?'

I step through the door, feel a shimmer of movement, and then the barrel of a gun against the side of my head.

'Keys?'

I know that voice.

Alysha.

'Keys?'

I feel the quiver in her, the uncertainty. She's afraid but she doesn't need to be. I raise my hands, slow and careful.

'I missed you,' I say. 'You have no idea.'

The door slides shut behind me. A dull ruddy light blooms from spots in the ceiling of a space that looks exactly like my own apartment: the same government design, the same plain functional space, everything from the same government issue furnishing catalogue some twenty years out of date. The only differences are an old mattress carelessly thrown across the middle of the floor and two dormant shells standing with their backs to me against the far wall.

Alysha stands before me. I try to marshal my words but I can't; and then it doesn't matter any more because she wraps her arms around me and buries her face into my shoulder and squeezes me so tightly that I can barely breathe, and I'm holding her like it's the end of the world, and she's looking at me, and her eyes shine in the dull red light.

'Yes,' she says.

My head brims with questions: I want to ask why she ran and hear her tell me until it makes sense. I want to ask her what she did on Earth, how she got there, how she lived there for five years, why she came back, why she *didn't* come back. I want to know everything but the words trip over each other in my mouth and so I stare, slack-jawed and silent like a fool. Five years, nine months, four days by Earth reckoning, and every question dies in my throat. She's changed. She looks harder and leaner than I remember, with her hair cut short, but it's her, my Alysha, and the last six years vanish as though they never happened, and my heart hammers as I hold her, and my legs are weak and there are tears in my eyes and I feel her shaking ...

I don't know how long we stand there like that, locked together, afraid to even start letting go. Clinging to each other like we're clinging to life.

'Alysha,' I choke. 'Liss ...'

She crushes herself into me. Her hands run over my face and through my hair.

'It's been so long since I could touch you,' she murmurs, and her words dive straight into me.

'I thought my life was over,' I say.

'So did I.'

'Are you real?'

She takes my hand and pulls it to her breast, to the beating of her heart, fast and urgent. She nods to the shells then looks at me again, eyes bright.

'I waited for you, Keys. Elizabeth said you might come.'

'I'm here,' I say.

'I'm sorry,' she whispers.

So am I. Sorry for ever doubting. Sorry for the bitterness bottled up inside. Sorry for not seeing the cryptic message she left behind.

Tears run down her cheeks.

'I didn't have a choice.'

Her words are hoarse and soft. Of course she had a choice. We all have choices. She could have told me and we could have run together or stayed and fought. But it's okay. Here and now, it's okay. I tell her I understand even though I don't, and she stares back into me as though she's trying to look through my eyes into my soul to see if I mean it. And somehow I do.

She takes a small step away.

'No. You don't. You can't.'

I reach for her. 'Alysha ...'

She always used to be *Liss* but it feels strange to call her that. That name belongs to the other Liss now.

'Tell me ...'

I don't get to finish. She turns her back on me, takes a pace like she doesn't have the first idea what to do or say, then rounds on me and then takes two quick steps back and cups my face in her hands and pulls me to her and kisses me with a passion I barely remember.

'I love you,' she says. 'I never stopped.'

We tumble to the floor. She clamps one hand around my head, pressing our faces together. The other fumbles at my clothes, urgent and savage. She makes an animal sound as she finds her way into the jumpsuit and guides me into her, half growl, half mewling scream. She sinks her fingers into my back and I bite her neck. We hold and pull and tear at each other as if trying to climb into one another's skins. She arches and cries out and I don't know whether the howl of release is hers or mine or belongs to both of us together. Six years wounded. Six years with a stake through my heart and now she pulls it loose. I croon to her: *It's okay ... It's okay ...*

Afterwards we lie side by side on the hard floor, fingers inter-twined, that little gesture Liss could never quite get right but now feels perfect. I sense the strength of her arms, the tremble in them, as though she'd pull my whole body inside her if she could.

'It's not okay,' she croaks. 'It was never okay. Nothing about it. I never meant to leave without you. It wasn't supposed to be like that.'

I stare into her eyes as I stroke her hair.

'I didn't *want* to go.'

I don't know what to say and so I settle for nothing. I ought to tell her about Laura, about Liss, about Tesseract One, about so many things, but anything I say will end this moment and I don't want that. I want what I have right now to last forever.

'This,' Alysha whispers in my ear as though she's reading my thoughts. 'This.'

She pulls me close and holds me tight, breathless and dishevelled. I start to kiss her again, slower this time, a more gentle passion. I'll do anything to keep us this way; but she smiles, eyes full of dewy love, and puts a finger to my lips.

'Not now.' Her words come out as gasps and she grins. 'Later. I'm going to take you with me. Fuck everything else. We'll be free after tonight. I want to have you for hours and hours. We're going to spend the night together and shag each other stupid and tell each other stories and stitch our lives back together, thread by thread.'

I cock my head. Take me back? Take me back where?

'Later?'

'I need your help, Keys. I can't do this on my own any more.'

'Do what?'

'There's a pod coming. We need to go.'

'Go where?'

'Mercy.'

She holds me tight one last time. I feel her shiver and then she's back on her feet, pulling her clothes together. I stumble up and do the same. When I'm done, she grabs my hand and kisses me again, then snatches up a backpack discarded by the door. We leave the Black Sheep behind us and I wonder how close we are to the Tesseract and if Laura is still inside, sitting at a desk somewhere in the half-light, fighting her way to exposing the truth of Tesseract One when she should be at home with Jamie. Does she still think it's Morgan? Does she still think it's me? Or has she figured out the truth? Has she found out who made the core-clone shells?

It hits me for the umpteenth time: I'll never see this place again.

'Why Mercy?' I ask.

It's a short trip and Alysha is already kitting up from her backpack. She tosses me a Servant.

'You'll need this,' she says.

I take it but I don't turn it on. I still want to ask why she ran. I already know about Nikita Svernoi and Settlement 64 and Anja Gersh and Darius Vishakh and the hunt for Iosefa. I already know how six men died in a storm, and who did it, and that it was Alysha who put the bullet in his head. That's not the *why* I want, not any more.

'Alysha ...'

She touches a hand to my cheek.

'Why, Leash? Why?'

'I knew it had to be someone inside the bureau who was after me. But it wasn't. At least ... not the way I thought. I don't know how to—'

'The Tesseract. The Tesseract AI. I know.'

She looks at me, half love, half amazement.

'Yes.'

'I figured it out about three hours ago. Did anyone else know you were supposed to be on that train?'

I have to ask even though I already know the answer.

She shakes her head.

'Vishakh,' I say. '*He* knew, right?'

'I didn't know what to do,' she says, and the tears are close again. 'It was an AI for fuck's sake! It wasn't just *someone*, it was the whole bureau, the whole fucking world! I didn't know how to even start. Vishakh had a way out and so I took it, but then Elizabeth—'

'Told you not to trust him.'

'And then there was Loki, and suddenly everyone thought I

was dead. And everyone *wanted* me dead. Earth, Magenta, Fleet as well. And so ...' She takes my hand and squeezes it hard. 'It seemed like a gift. I *was* dead, to all of them. I hid and then I ran. I got off Magenta and went to Earth. The days became weeks and then months. I didn't understand what I'd found.'

'Gersh—'

She squeezes my hand again and nods. She already knows.

'You need to understand what's happening on Earth,' she says. 'It's all about the Xen. It's all about Iosefa. It's all about what Gersh found.'

Vishakh, Anja Gersh, Nikita Svernoi, Jacksmith, all looking for that magical combination of Xen and the right mutated genes to trigger a transformation inside us. Call it what you want but it accesses a side of the universe we've barely even begun to understand. The place where the Masters live, if Swainsbrook had it right.

'I came back,' Alysha says. 'A year after it happened. I came back to look for you.'

'I was on Earth,' I say.

'I know.'

'I was working for Fleet.'

She leans into me and laughs.

'So was I!'

I draw her close.

'I never stopped thinking about you.'

All those lost years. Bringing her back as Liss, something no one could ever know. How close Liss was to the real thing and yet wasn't ... I want to tell her all of it but I can't. I'm too afraid that I'll blink and she'll disappear.

'How did you survive? How did you get away? I want to know everything!'

'I stole a Servant, made a new identity for myself and bought a passage on the *Fearless*. I went to Earth. To India.'

I could listen to her forever; but as I open my mouth to tell her so, she strokes my face and kisses me.

'It's a long story, Keys. But after tonight we'll have all the time in the world.'

I can't think of anything I want more.

INSTANTIATION FIFTY-ONE

A Cheetah reaches Settlement 16 as Keon and Alysha Rause reach Mercy hospital. It circles the pit and lands. A forensics team emerge in white spacesuits, checking for radiation and testing the air. In the dome full of abandoned life support machines they find, as Jacksmith predicted, traces of Xen and flourane.

The agents in the spacesuits head towards a deep shaft, following the clicks of their Geiger counters while three armoured bureau agents head into the hangar dome. Together with the transponder recovered from Elizabeth Jacksmith's Cheetah, now parked on the MagentaNet Tower, the flight recorder from Swainsbrook's helicopter is enough to charge Eddie Thiekis and MagentaNet as accessories to the theft and detonation of antimatter and maybe more. Much of MagentaNet has been shut down, their records and archives frozen. Only the bare minimum remains to keep the data networks of Magenta running smoothly.

In Frank Swainsbrook's office they find a sliver. It holds a last message from Swainsbrook himself, reasserting his claim that the Masters spoke to him and have revealed their intent to return. He records that they were precise and told him where and when it would happen, but Frank has chosen to keep this precision to himself, saying only that they told him to build the telescope Jacksmith has called the Steadman–Kettler Array, and to search for a star that no one else has seen. The discovery of this star, he says, will explain what the Masters are. Its consequences will be profound. They will change every human world.

Instantiation Fifty-one watches as it flits between the surviving news channels and the chatter of the datasphere. Traffic is dense, stretching the surviving network to capacity. Magenta remains a world on the edge, skittish with wild rumour, close to panic as speculation spreads like plague. The first dropships from the *Ember's Fire* have almost reached orbit with their escort corvettes, warships carrying missiles and regiments of soldiers. Mobs in Firstfall and Disappointment have defied the government curfew, taking to the streets. Others lock themselves in their homes. There is a spike of suicides and the Xen dealers run almost dry. There is a stab of madness to the world as it wonders what the Earthers will do when they arrive.

A woman from data forensics discovers Swainsbrook's Servant, carefully and deliberately set aside before he joined his followers. Or so it seems.

Transmit to the Tesseract.

The agent queries the order. Fear of hackware, of q-code loop bombs and time-traps means this should be carried by hand to Firstfall and set up in an isolated virtual machine before opening.

The order comes again.

Across the world in Nico, news breaks in waves. Leaked footage of an incident a month ago of two Kutosov interceptors flying high in the stratosphere, missiles streaking past, colossal detonations like nuclear bursts, strange holes burned through the clouds in the aftermath, perfectly round. The story breaks in Disappointment and Firstfall of a nuclear detonation on the surface and of the 'Swainsbrook Sixteen', sixteen Magentans who spoke to the Masters and vanished. The response from the Tesseract is swift. It permeates the datasphere from end to end and shuts it down. Every link across Magenta falls silent.

The order requesting Swainsbrook's Servant comes once more, insistent; but by now the agent from data forensics has created a duplicate in a local virtual machine. She complies and connects the duplicate to the Tesseract. Within seconds, a necrotic q-code routine erupts. Cocooned in its virtual machine, the cloned replica of Frank Swainsbrook's Servant devours itself from the inside out.

Carefully isolated from the Tesseract, unseen by anyone around her, the agent from data forensics creates a second clone in a second virtual machine and turns it on. The Servant hums into life. The contents of Swainsbrook's life again streams across the ether, only this time no one is listening. Five minutes later, the cloned Servant remains alive and well. There is no necrotic q-code. The attack came not from within, but from the connection to the outside. From the Tesseract itself.

The agent from data forensics deletes the construct and all the evidence that it ever existed, and sends a message to an old friend in Internal Audit.

You were right.

23

IOSEFA'S DAUGHTER

We're outside Mercy when the data blackout hits. There's a statement from the Tesseract announcing a temporary shutdown of all systems and then everything goes dead. The only feed that stays up is a government emergency channel offering five looped minutes of an animated newsreader reading a statement: there will be a twenty-four hour shutdown of MagentaNet due to investigations into serious criminal activity. The situation is expected to resolve within the day, at which point the networks will return to normal. Everyone not required to support essential systems should stay at home and await further bulletins.

Nothing about an agreement negotiated with the Earthers. Nothing about an impending invasion. Nothing about an antihydrogen detonation at Settlement 16.

I look at Alysha. Just the two of us now.

And that's okay.

'We have to leave Magenta tonight. You *are* going to come with me?'

Of course I am. We're going to leave this world together,

even though we both know it means we can never come back. That's why I'm here, so why do the words seize in the back of my throat. Why is it so hard to say them?

I nod. 'Sure.'

There are five people on the planet with the authority to shut down the global networks. I could list the names. One is Chief Morgan, or whoever wields his authority. The Tesseract is doing this. It's hunting us, and everyone and everything is against us, and there's nothing to do but run, to get off Magenta and out of its reach. This is how it was for Alysha six years ago, except for her it was a thousand times worse, because at least I'm not alone. I'm not the only one who knows who the enemy truly is.

I leave an encrypted message in electronic drop for Laura. It's the best I can do with the networks shut down: It's not Morgan. It's the Tesseract. It's the AI.

I don't expect a reply, and Laura's smart enough to have worked it out for herself by now. She's also smart enough to realise I must be with Alysha, and that Alysha is with Fleet, which means I'm as good as dead to her, and if we ever see each other again then it's going to be across an interrogation table because I didn't get off Magenta in time.

Alysha opens the pod door. I catch her shoulder as she moves to get out.

'What are we doing here?'

I know the answer but I want to hear her say it.

She takes my hand and squeezes, and then shuffles across the bench seat in the back of the pod to cup my face in her hands and stare into my eyes.

'We're going to leave Magenta. You and me and Elizabeth. We're going to take Elizabeth's research and samples and the remains of Iosefa Lomu to Fleet. But you already knew that.'

I nod again.

'We're here for Iosefa. He's hidden in the morgue.'

Something I don't think she knows I already worked out, and so I smile, a warm feeling inside me. Honesty. Trust.

'Okay. So how are we getting off Magenta when the whole planet is locked down?'

'Darius Vishakh's shuttle, but we need to reach orbit before the Earther ships get here and so we don't have much time.' She gets out of the pod and beckons me to follow. 'You need to be anonymous until I tell you otherwise. Once we get to the morgue, I'll need your help.'

We're outside one of Mercy's undercity entrances, a quiet back door that doesn't see much traffic. Alysha walks in, bright, bold and confident.

Be quiet and act dumb.

She walks to the woman working the reception desk and flashes a smile. I see their eyes flare as data lenses between them. I have no idea what, but a moment later the woman smiles back and lets us through into the bulk of the hospital. Alysha walks in without looking back.

I scan the waiting room. There are three cameras and at least one of them has seen our faces, the faces of wanted fugitives.

The Tesseract will pick us up in seconds!

Those cameras aren't working just now.

'How?'

She flashes another smile over her shoulder and beckons me to follow.

The next one *is* working. It may not matter with the networks down but keep your face hidden in case. It's coming.

We reach an intersection of corridors. Sure enough, another camera. I look away. There are signs for pathology, for blood analysis, for laboratories with unfamiliar names, and one for the morgue. We're in the part of Mercy that concerns itself with science and post-mortems, with all the things that happen when healing has failed.

Alysha follows the signs for the morgue.

'So what? We just walk in, take Iosefa, and walk out?'

'You know how secure Mercy's morgue is?'

'It isn't.'

'Because who would ever want to steal a body?' She pauses. 'I know Mercy. I hid here for a month after Loki blew up my shell.'

She pauses to let that sink in and then turns to look at me.

'You were on Magenta for another month?' I can't believe it. 'A month?'

'I watched my own memorial service,' she says. 'I wanted to tell you! I wanted to so much but I didn't dare! I knew Vishakh had set me up and I knew the Tesseract had sabotaged my extraction of Gersh. Everyone wanted me dead ... I didn't know what to do and so I let you all think it was true. I'm sorry. I was ... I was really fucking scared, Keys.'

'How did they do it? How did Earth turn the Tesseract against us?'

'I don't know.' She looks at me, defiant now. 'But I know *you*. You would have fought it head on. Gone at it like a bull, and I love you for that but what was the point if it ended with both of us dead? And I ... I didn't think you'd believe me ... at least ... maybe ... but not quickly enough. Not before it could reach us. So I didn't tell you.'

She takes a long deep breath. 'I went to Earth. I went after Kaltech. I thought it was them. I wanted to burn them to the ground so I could come home. I wish I could have been there when you put a bullet through Nikita Svernoi's skull. I wish I'd been there to pull the trigger.'

'You did. You were.'

I remember seeing his skull burst in front of me as he was about to blow my head off. I don't explain. Let her take it however works.

She flashes me another smile. 'Good.'

Two nurses round the corner ahead and walk toward us. I study them as they approach, trying to convince myself they're human. They're deep in conversation but my scrutiny catches their attention. They look at us and slow as they reach us.

'Are you looking for someone?' asks one.

They're watching me now, realising my Servant is anonymous.

'We're here to identify a body,' says Alysha. 'They told us the morgue was in pathology.'

Suspicion turns to sympathy. They give directions and move on, forgetting us.

'Stop staring at people!'

Mercy is quiet today. The curfew, I suppose.

'And was it Kaltech?'

'No.'

'Then who?'

'I don't *know*, Keon. I don't know who did this and I don't know how.'

We reach the pathology labs. We don't see anyone else.

'You know Doctor Roge?' Alysha asks.

I nod. Roge is almost a friend these days.

'Think you can get him to let us in without raising the alarm?'

On any other day I'd simply ping him to let him know I was coming, but not today: the moment Keon Rause comes online, the Tesseract will pin down where I am, scramble a dozen tac-teams, and neither of us will get out of Mercy alive.

There's a buzzer by a screen on the door. I press it. Nothing happens for long seconds, and then Roge's face appears.

'What? Did you forget ... Rause?'

His lips tighten as he recognises me. I understand now why we're not wearing false faces.

'Yeah. I need access to the morgue.'

Ask if he's alone in there.

389

Roge looks at me, hesitant. We both know perfectly well that he shouldn't open the door. I'm gambling he doesn't know I'm a fugitive, but the fact that I'm here with no Servant, that I'm not simply using my Tesseract codes ... Shit. He'll check with the Tesseract. It's the obvious thing to do if there's still a link-up that he can use.

'Jacksmith is about to defect,' I tell him before he has a chance. 'There are people at the bureau helping her. She switched a body. Later today, Magenta is going to hand over the remains of someone who—'

'Lomu,' says Roge.

I can't tell if he already knew or simply has a good poker face. If he *does* know, does that mean he wants Jacksmith to succeed? I don't know. He just might. Shit!

'Yeah, Lomu. Listen, I like Elizabeth a lot, and I don't like what the Earthers are doing, and under a lot of other circumstances I might be inclined to look the other way. But in a couple of hours we're handing Lomu's remains over to the Earthers. By this time tomorrow, come what may, there are going to be Earther soldiers on the streets of Firstfall. Whether they're carrying guns might depend on whether we give them the real Iosefa Lomu.'

Sometimes it doesn't hurt to tell the truth. Maybe I'm being melodramatic about Earther soldiers on the streets of Firstfall but I'm pretty sure it's what Jacksmith believes.

Roge hesitates. I take a chance.

'Look, if you're in on this, just let me in and let it go and I won't poke, okay? This needs to go away. It would be better for everyone if it went quietly.'

'Rause, I have no idea what you're talking about.'

Roge shakes his head. I cross my fingers behind my back. I have no idea which way ... and then the buzzer sounds and the door clicks open, and Roge is standing right there on the other side.

'Rause, you'd better—'

He sees Alysha exactly as she shoots him in the chest with a stunner. He goes down with a grunt. Alysha tugs me after as she jumps over his body and closes the door and then drops to a crouch beside him. She pushes me on.

'Get Iosefa!'

I don't move. Stunner or not, Roge was a friend, and Earther ships are rushing to Magenta, and maybe there *will* be soldiers on the streets of Firstfall soon, and maybe they *will* be carrying guns. Maybe because of what I've just done.

'Keys! Iosefa!'

I look at Roge. Our perfect new world isn't quite so perfect any more.

'Okay.'

She smiles. 'Yours forever, Keon Rause.'

Am I wrong or do the words sound forced, pulled out of our shared memories as something that might be the right thing to say? Why did she bring me here? Because she needed me to persuade Roge to open his door ...?

No. I shake the thought away. Stupid.

The morgue is a wall of refrigerated doors, each hiding a body. Alysha isn't the Alysha I remember. Of course she isn't. How could she be? How could either of us be the same? Six years apart has changed us both. That's all it is ...

I pull the bodies one by one, tearing back the zipped plastic that covers their faces. Roge sent me names for the bodies Jacksmith took from the morgue and then returned, but those names are on another Servant, long lost and forgotten.

My Servant pings. An encrypted message from Laura waiting for me in our drop. Messages! The message Roge left for Jacksmith!

Mister Smith has been entered into his usual lodgings.

I scrabble for the names on each of the doors, looking for a Smith.

Yours forever, Keon Rause.

It sounds wrong. It shouldn't and yet it does. How is that possible?

I find a Smith. I pull open the—

Keys! Hurry!

—cold metal door and slide the body out from inside. It's wrapped in plastic like the others, but when I zip it open the face inside is deathly white. Frozen. A man like me, whose genes cast back to Earth's Pacific Islands. Someone has taken a drill to his skull but it's a clinical thing done long after he was dead, no sight or sign of blood. Yet I recognise him, despite the years under the ice, from the fleeting snip of video I once saw of Iosefa Lomu when he was alive ...

Got him. Bring a gurney.

Alysha comes through wearing pilfered medical whites. We lower the slab and roll Lomu onto a gurney. Alysha's Servant identifies her as Doctor Roge now, which will be great for any security doors, less great if we run into anyone who knows him.

And, under most circumstances, very bad for the real Doctor Roge.

I stare past Alysha to where I left him. I can't see the body.

'Did you—?'

'It's cloned. He'll wake up in a couple of hours. He'll be fine.' She pushes the gurney past me. 'We go out this way.'

Out the back way from the morgue through waste disposal. It makes sense – we don't want to be seen and no one comes this way. It also means we don't pass where I left Roge with Alysha.

'Keys! Come *on*!'

'Give me a moment.'

392

It's stupid but I have to go back. It only takes a few seconds to find where Alysha laid him out. He's unconscious like she said. I feel like an idiot.

'Better now?'

Alysha leads us through the back of the morgue, past the incinerators. There probably wouldn't be anyone here even on a normal day; today the place is deserted. Roge's codes open the waste collection bay and a pod slides in, a bureau all-terrain VIP pod with enough armour to stop a small rocket, the sort we might use to transport any Earther politician from the *Ember's Fire* adventurous enough to brave Magenta's gravity.

The pod doors slide open. Jacksmith grins from inside.

'Mrs and Mister Rause!'

'Nice pod,' says Alysha. 'Where'd you get it. Keys? A little help?'

The back of the pod pops open to reveal a luggage space big enough for maybe two or three frozen corpses rather than just the one.

'Viki— Chief Morgan decided to let me borrow it.'

I help Alysha lift Lomu inside.

'How long before he starts to thaw?'

'He won't.'

A shell emerges from inside the pod. It tosses three metal cylinders into the back beside Lomu and then climbs in to lie beside him.

'If this belonged to Morgan, you know the Tesseract is tracking it,' I say.

'I'm reliably informed that all such devices are disabled.' Jacksmith lets out a lingering breath as Alysha slinks into the pod beside her. 'I'm afraid Vikram can't make it. There's no getting him out without putting us all at risk.'

Alysha shrugs. 'He was never part of the plan.'

'Doesn't mean I like leaving him behind.'

393

I sit beside Alysha, the three of us side by side facing the back of the pod. As soon as I'm in and we start to move, she snuggles next to me.

'I'm sorry,' she says. 'I wish there was another way to do this. I don't want to run again – but at least this time we'll be together.'

'We'll find a way to come home one day,' I say, although I have no idea how.

I put an arm around her and hold her close, and for a little while it feels right again, the way it felt when the two of us huddled side by side six years ago at the end of a long hard day at work, when all we wanted was to switch off and share a sense of not being alone.

'My sources are fast drying up,' says Jacksmith. 'Your friends will know better, but my last estimate was that we had about six hours before the Earther ships make Magenta orbit. That doesn't leave us a great deal of time. It's going to be very tight.'

We reach the surface and drive past the Institute. The steps are crowded with curfew-breaking students wrapped in storm suits, forced by the blackout to talk face to face. Shells and vending bots wander among them offering hot drinks, fast food and legal Xen highs. Protest signs lie scattered on the ground beside them. Bureau headquarters is right next door but no one has come out to arrest them, and what was supposed to be an angry protest now looks more like an impromptu party. Wrathful twilight clouds scud overhead, tinged with livid purple. The rain has already started again as a squall front moves in. When it hits, it's going to hit hard. Hard enough to drive all our would-be protestors back underground.

'She might have minders,' Jacksmith warns. 'You can thank your husband for that.'

'I've asked her to send them away.'

'You think she will?'

I think for a fleeting moment that they're talking about Laura. A flash of something surges through me. Hope? Yes. With Tesseract One and maybe an invasion coming, I guess I'd feel better knowing Laura was away from all this. Not that she'd come. For all her cynicism, Laura would rather die than abandon Magenta, her corpse clinging by its fingertips to the very end even as she cursed the place for its oppressive gravity and its shitty food and just how fucking basic everything is.

Am I really going to do this?

My Servant pings again. Another message. I try not to move, try not to even twitch as I sit with Alysha held tight beside me, and read it.

The core clone you claim you found was self-authorised by the Tesseract. Where is it? Where's the physical evidence?

I let that sink in. I was right.

'Doctor?'

Jacksmith turns to look at me.

'Are you entirely, one hundred per cent without question *certain* that our AI can't be hacked?'

Jacksmith snorts. 'No proper scientist is ever *certain* of any-thing. But what I *can* tell you is that in the nearly one hundred and twenty years since the core directive design was established, no AI has been provably hacked. And believe me, there has been a *lot* of trying.'

I let out a long sigh and collect Laura's second message.

Yes. Tesseract One is the AI. Give me everything you've got. Rause, *please!*

I feel Alysha, a warmth leaning against my side. She and Jacksmith are talking in quiet whispers. I don't listen. I'm not sure I want to know.

I drop a message back for Laura: Earth aren't going to stop at orbit. Get Jamie and get out.

I reach across Alysha to tap Jacksmith on the arm.

'If the Earthers invade, will it be because of us? Because of what we're doing?'

She looks at me with pity. I see the same expression mirrored on Alysha's face.

'No, Keon, they're going to invade no matter what, because even if they got hold of Iosefa, even if every one of the poor bastards Swainsbrook rounded up is carrying his genes, even if they have their own crashed Masters' ship squirrelled away … Keon, the Xen is on Magenta.'

Alysha makes a wry face.

'They'll do their best to pretend it isn't an invasion, but Magenta will be an occupied world within a week, and the only thing the other colonies will hear is how grateful we are for the Earthers' help in these trying times.'

'How did they do this?' I ask, not that either Jacksmith or Alysha will have the answer. 'If you can't hack an AI then how did they do this?'

Another message drops from Laura: And run? Like you?

'We could have shared, you know,' says Jacksmith. 'The best minds of Earth and Fleet, here on Magenta. I would have plucked out an eye for that.'

We're heading out among the old abandoned fabricators and I realise, at last, where we're going. Not to New Hope. We're going to Rachael Cho.

Another message from Laura: This is my home, Keon. Someone has to fight this. *I* have to fight this. If you're going to fuck off then give me the evidence and just go.

We sit in silence. As the pod pulls up outside Cho's fabricator, Jacksmith leans around Alysha and gives me a long curious look.

Are you really coming with us?

I go blank. I don't understand.

'What?'

Never mind.

The pod doors open. Wind slices into the cabin. Rain swirls and bites at my face. Alysha nudges me out into the weather, the squall slashing across Firstfall heralding a storm front still not quite arrived and yet already strong enough to batter me sideways. I stagger to keep my feet crossing the few yards to Cho's door. It slides open. Cho is waiting inside, already dressed in a storm suit with a small case in one hand. The fabricator behind her is empty. Everything has gone, the old flatline rig, the filing cabinets, everything stripped to bare metal. Ready to go and not in need of much convincing – but the way she looks at me ...

I don't think I've ever seen such pity.

Cho snaps up a hand as Alysha approaches, warning her to stop. The three of us stand staring at each other as the storm howls between us. When Cho finally moves, Alysha tries again to bundle her towards the pod. Cho sidesteps and stands right in front of me. She takes my hands in hers.

Alysha looses a growl. What's she doing?

Look. Jacksmith. Either take—

I grab Cho by the shoulders and force her to look at me.

'They're coming. The Earthers.' We're six inches apart and I have to shout to make her hear me over the wind and the rain. 'However they dress it up, they'll take you and they'll lock you up and they'll suck you dry until they get what they want and then they'll throw away the husk. Go with Doctor Jacksmith.'

As if Fleet will be any better.

Cho closes her eyes. The rain streaming down her face looks like tears. She leans into me, pulling me close, and speaks in my ear.

'Remember what I told you.'

I push her off me.

What? Alysha stares at us both. What did she say?

Will you just grab her or something! Jacksmith is getting frantic. We have to go!

I turn and start to walk away. I don't look back.

Keys! What are you—

Let her go. I'll stay.

No. No you—

She said it's her or me.

Is that the first lie I've ever told her? Probably not, but I don't remember another.

I don't hear Alysha run after me until I feel her hand on my shoulder, spinning me around to shout in my face.

'Don't you dare! Don't you fucking dare do this!'

The door closes on Jacksmith's pod. Cho's inside. It starts to move.

'Hey!'

I try to pull away but Alysha doesn't let me.

'Hey! Hey!' Jacksmith! What the fuck?

Alysha grabs my face in her hands and forces me to look at her.

'They *will* be on that shuttle. *That's* the mission! But I am *not* letting you go! Not again! Listen to me! Listen!'

'You can't stay! They—'

'Neither can you!'

'At least I can—'

Another pod pulls up beside us, empty, standard Firstfall issue. The door opens, asking us where we want to go.

'The Earthers got inside us, Keys,' says Alysha, shouting over the rain. 'They got inside the bureau. They turned the Tesseract against us. There's nothing you can do. Nothing either of us can do. Fuck whatever Cho said! Vishakh's shuttle is in New Hope, fuelled and ready to go. Elizabeth will wait. We're going with them. Both of us! Please!'

398

She gets into the back of the pod and holds out her hand to me.

'*Please*, Keon!'

I know she's right. We can't fight the Tesseract. Not even together. I take her hand and slip into the pod beside her. It starts to move, following in Jacksmith's wake. There's nothing left but to run.

'Keys ... Is that what Cho really said? That she wouldn't come if you came too?'

'No.'

'What *did* she say?'

'That you're going to shoot me.'

'Fuck, Keys! Fuck!' I can't deny the look of horror she gives. It's real. 'Why would I do that? Shit! Why would she *say* that?'

'Because I asked the wrong question.' I shake my head. 'It doesn't matter. Where will we go?'

'Fleet,' says Alysha. 'Where else? Vishakh's shuttle—'

'I mean after. When it's over.'

She laughs. 'Somewhere hot and dry and with less gravity!'

There's more, but it washes past and I don't take it in. I'm thinking of Laura hiding away in a basement in the Tesseract, frantically working out how to fight an all-powerful machine and realising that she can't. I'm thinking of Bix, stuck in far-off Nico, watching all this happen, powerless to do a damned thing about it as he fights off amorous aunts and cousins. I'm thinking of Liss and of everything I've done to her, and everything she's done for me. I'm thinking that only Liss will understand why I'm doing this, why I'm running away with Alysha. And at the same time I'm thinking of how, in that moment when I turned my back on Jacksmith's pod and walked away, I thought my heart would break and yet it didn't, and how maybe that's because it broke six years ago, and I thought I'd fixed it, but I never really did, and maybe I never can.

24

NEW HOPE

The undercity tunnels to New Hope are shut down. No one can take off or land while the satellite networks are down and so the spaceport is turning everyone away, emergency access only. The roads on the surface are closed on account of the weather but Alysha plugs herself into our pod and overrules its Servant. By the time we reach the outskirts of Firstfall, the surface is howling wind and the rain is falling in such torrents that the water can't run off faster than it lands. We skid and slide until we catch Jacksmith's pod ahead of us. Not a real storm, not yet; the winds aren't much over a hundred miles an hour, but I've never seen this much rain before. It's like driving through a waterfall.

'Steady ahead,' I hear Alysha say. 'We don't have time for any drama.'

We drive through the darkness, weaving with each gust of wind, creeping towards New Hope not much faster than a long-distance runner. The darkness grows absolute as we drive away from the centre of Firstfall, the roads closed and the lights off. The buildings poking above the surface out here are industrial units, no need for windows, no illumination. Both moons are up, somewhere above the cloud, but nothing gets through. Jacksmith doesn't bother with headlights and nor does Alysha. We're driving by satellite maps, short-range radar and ultrasound, slamming into puddles already inches deep and then finding purchase again as the roads dip and rise.

I drift, half listening to the back and forth between Jacksmith and Alysha as Alysha urges Jacksmith to go faster. How is it possible that Tesseract One is the Tesseract itself? Jacksmith and Liss both claim that an AI can't be hacked; but after what I saw at Settlement 16 I don't know what other truth to offer. If I believe Vishakh, the order to kill Alysha came from the Tesseract. And I *do* believe him, despite everything, and I believe Jacksmith that Morgan is no traitor.

It's the shells. The shells and the jacking of Swainsbrook's helicopter, but the shells more than anything. Cloned from the AI itself, self-authorised, as close to pure copies as its directive against self-replication will allow, doing the Tesseract's work and then wiping away all evidence that they ever existed. Our enemy is an almost omnipotent AI and I don't know why, except that someone, somewhere must be telling it what to do.

We trundle from the fringes of Firstfall on to the road to New Hope, a few miles of wide, flat, fused rock awash with rainwater. Ahead of us, Jacksmith speeds up.

'The Tesseract paid Vishakh to kill you,' I say.

Alysha looks at me, curious.

'It set this up. All of it.'

She smirks a little now and shakes her head.

'Not *all* of it.'

'Not you and Jacksmith defecting to Fleet, but everything else. Swainsbrook, MagentaNet, the stolen warhead, the Earther snatch squad, all of it. I just don't understand why.'

'Because someone told it to.'

'No. I don't think so.'

I tell her about the shells at Settlement 16. I tell her how someone jacked Swainsbrook's helicopter and used it to smuggle a warhead out of New Hope, disguised as a MagentaNet drone. I tell her how the Tesseract tried to shoot me down, twice, once on the way there using the *Flying Daggers*, once on the way back using one of our own Kutosovs. I tell her about the hit on Jacksmith when all her protection disappeared. Further back, the things that we thought were Flemich at first, then Morgan: the assassination of Jared Black, Esh's death, the betrayal of Alysha's mission to extract Anja Gersh.

She listens, calm and patient. As much as anything, I'm trying to figure it out by talking it through.

'Why?' I say again. 'That's what I don't get. Why is it so set on helping the Earthers?'

Alysha shrugs like it all doesn't matter now.

'The Earthers got inside it somehow.'

'You can't hack a bloody AI!' growls Jacksmith. 'It doesn't *work* that way!'

'Then they put in a back door! I don't know! You know they gave us the Tesseract in the first place.'

Jacksmith smoulders. 'How stupid do you think we were? Earth built it but the core directives were written and designed here! *We* wrote them! Not Earth!'

Laura's mother. She told me as much.

But Alysha's right – it doesn't matter, does it? Not any more.

'If the Tesseract was manipulating Swainsbrook all along …
Look, if I read Swainsbrook's data logs right then—'

'Then the Tesseract was beaming illusions straight into Swainsbrook's lenses every time he went under!' snaps Jacksmith. 'Him and every single one of his followers, yes! We already got that. It programmed them! *Brainwashed* them! It programmed

402

Swainsbrook to gather up everyone Earth wanted in one place so the Earthers could swoop down and snatch them!'

Alysha looks away.

'How did Darius Vishakh find Lomu's ship?' she asks. 'He used to borrow Rachael's flatline rig. He heard voices while he was dead. I never understood that, but *he* did. Or at least, he *believed* he did. And you might call bullshit, but he *did* find that wreck. Maybe someone showed him where to look?' She shrugs. 'You think it was the Masters?'

'I don't know!'

'Nor do I, but *someone* told him where to look.'

'You think the *Tesseract* did that? How ... No, *why*, for fuck's sake? Why Vishakh of all people?'

Alysha doesn't answer for a long time. When she does it's with a video sent to the pod's screens. The Meelosh video that made Cho want to kill herself. The one Swainsbrook said wasn't him.

'I've seen it,' I say.

'I saw it first. Six years ago. Gersh sent it. She didn't know what it was but it had something to do with her work and it scared the crap out of her. She said it was affecting her rats. Driving them berserk. Making them attack each other.'

The video that kills.

'It upset her *rats*?'

'That's what she said. She claimed she didn't know who made it or where it came from. If that was a lie, she died before she could tell me the truth. But, Keys, she sent it to me encrypted, and I never showed it to anyone. *Any*one. I didn't think ... I didn't think it mattered.'

I see a twinkle in the distance, the brilliant emergency lights of New Hope's landing pads for anyone daft or unlucky enough to be caught in the air on a night like this.

'*How* encrypted?' I ask.

'Well enough.'

'Well enough that an AI couldn't crack it given five years to try?'

'Probably not. But Keys, there weren't any copies!'

I think of Laura, that first day I came back to Magenta, showing me the log of Alysha's first conversation with Gersh: *Someone did a spectacular job of trying to hide that call and make like it never happened. But there was one recording they missed, off the main network in the archives of the satellite distributors. It was a fucking pain to get in and a fucking pain times ten to find the call. But we did ...*

In the satellite archives ... the *MagentaNet* archives.

'It knew about you and Gersh.' I say. 'It knew you were up to something and it wanted to know what. And it's patient. Infinitely patient.'

We sit in silent darkness, each lost in our own thoughts. We're almost at New Hope's perimeter fence.

'Why didn't you tell anyone about Gersh?'

The road behind us floods with brilliant light before Alysha can reply. A killing screech fills the air. We lurch hard as the pod slams on the brakes and then suddenly picks up speed again. The screaming ear-splitting wail abruptly stops, but the lights behind us don't go away. Alysha accelerates, pulling alongside Jacksmith. I hear a voice blaring over a speaker. I can't make out the words over the hammering rain, but I don't need to. I know what they're saying. *Stop or we shoot.*

'That's a tac-team armoured all-terrain pod.' I can tell by the pattern of the lights. 'Not Tesseract. MSDF.'

I lurch forward as we aquaplane through a shallow lake. Alysha slows and lets Jacksmith pull away, then slots in behind, making us into a shield. A bright line of smoke streaks skyward behind us. My heart skips, thinking it's a rocket, but it's only a flare. The sky lights up and I glimpse the pod behind us. Three armoured faces behind an armoured windscreen. Two small-calibre guns, one on either side, and the turret cannon on top, all pointing straight at us.

The flare dies quickly, killed by the rain. My Servant pings. I have a message from Laura.

Please stop, Keon. I can't let you do this.

'We're not going to outrun them,' says Alysha.

Jacksmith's face pops up on one of the screens in the back.

'What do you want to do?'

'Elizabeth, if it comes to it then you're our last—'

'Lissie, they're not going to shoot me and Cho.'

I see a muzzle flash from one of the small-calibre guns. One shot. If it's meant as a warning then it doesn't work. I have no idea whether they ...

'Elizabeth, if you're going to suggest—'

Jacksmith turns violently and smashes into New Hope's perimeter fence. I fly sideways across the cabin and crash into Alysha as we swerve to follow. The fence buckles, snags on the side of Jacksmith's pod, wrenching it around before it snaps. Alysha slams on the brakes; the anti-crash q-code kicks and lurches us violently the other way, and then we're free and through and still going forward. The tac-team pod slews after us in a spray of water.

Another message from Laura, this one straight into my Servant on the secure link she set up back when I was on the train out of Nico. Fuck knows how this is working when everything else is down, but it is.

Is this your answer, Keon? To run away?

I want to scream back: what does she expect? What's yours? The two of us against the Tesseract and an Earther invasion?

We slide wildly after Jacksmith across the flat blasted stone of New Hope's outer apron, skidding through a finger-width of water as the rain falls in floods.

You're good at running away. It's not like it's the first time.

The bitterness drips from Laura's words. The turret cannon slews to track us. The muzzle drops, lining us up. As Alysha veers sideways, Jacksmith slows and suddenly we're in the lead and Jacksmith is shielding us instead of the other way around.

'You have to stop!' I shout.

Keon, I *will* shoot if I have to.

Jacksmith, behind us now, is mind-linked to her pod. Alysha stares from the back of ours, watching the tac-team come after us. She shakes her head.

'No. I'm not going back.'

'They do know we have the only surviving Iosefa samples in here, right?' snaps Jacksmith. 'You *did* find a way to mention that?'

'There's a fucking blackout!' Alysha yells back. 'No fucking comms!'

Jacksmith slams on the brakes. The turret switches to track her pod as it skids and slides to a halt, turning a graceful half-circle as it sends up a wall of water.

'I'm not dying for this, Lissie,' she says. 'And neither should Miss Cho.'

No comms isn't quite true. I message Laura: You hit that pod, that's the end of Iosefa.

'Elizabeth! Don't!'

Alysha careens on towards the hangar. The tac-team pod slides to a stop a few yards past Jacksmith. Its turret is still on them, not on us.

Another message from Laura: You know what, Keon? Good fucking riddance. Then maybe the Earthers will fuck off, too.

They won't. They want the Xen.

'Lissie, better alive to resist than dead. Those men out there aren't the real en—'

I barely see the streak of light fizz out of the rain. It scorches past us and hits the tac-team pod and blooms into a dazzling fireball. The pod catapults off the ground and then the blast slams into us, knocking us sideways and almost tipping us over.

'Go!' shouts Alysha.

'Lissie! What in—'

'Elizabeth! Just go!'

I stare at the tac-team pod behind us as it crashes onto its side. It's still intact but ...

Laura?

Jacksmith starts to move again. A bright rectangle of light is building a few hundred yards to our right as the door to one of New Hope's hangars grinds open.

Laura!

'Elizabeth?' Alysha sounds calm. Almost serene.

'Lissie! What the fuck! What the fuck have you done?' Jacksmith, on the other hand, sounds livid.

'I've taken over your pod, Elizabeth. You're coming with us.'

'*Fuck* you!'

Laura!

Jacksmith is a hundred yards behind us. In the gloom further back, the tac-team pod is on its side, turret pointing uselessly into the air. I stare, watching until I see the back doors swing open and the first soldiers crawl out. Was Laura in there too, trying to stop us? Even if she wasn't, there's a good chance I know the men and women who are. We've been on raids to-gether. Most of them would have been at Esh's funeral. Chances are good that Esh herself would have been in that pod, if she was still alive.

Laura?

More soldiers spill out of the ruined pod and spread out. The first settles into a crouch, puts his burst rifle to his shoulder and fires. I flinch. Then I see muzzle flashes ahead, return fire from the opening hangar.

'Friendlies!'

Alysha steers towards the hangar and speeds up. I grab at her.

'There are people I know back there!'

'Get off me!'

She shakes herself free.

'They're not the enemy!'

A message from Laura flashes into my Servant: The first Earther ships will reach orbit before you, Keon. You're too late. You're not going to make it. Stop!

Laura! Are you okay?

'I told you!' Jacksmith sounds furious. 'I told you no soldiers! No shooting! No one gets fucking hurt!'

She's gaining on us. The hangar doors are fully open now and the light inside illuminates Vishakh's shuttle, fuelled and ready to launch for the solar station. I see figures scurrying around it. Fleet marines.

Am I really supposed to say yes just to salve your fucking conscience? No, Keon, no I am not *fucking* okay!

'How long?' I ask, so quietly that at first I think Alysha doesn't hear as she guns us into the hangar. When she doesn't answer, I grab her wrist. 'How. Long?'

Alysha snaps me a look, annoyance and puzzlement. It breaks my heart.

'I don't know what you're—'

'How long were you working for Fleet?' My grip tightens.

'I don't know what—'

'Did it start before Gersh?'

'Keys! It's not what—'

Jacksmith's pod slides sideways into the hangar in a spray of water. Alysha tries to hold my eye but she can't. I know she can lie to me, but I've been with her too long for her to do it well.

'How long, Liss?'

'It's not like—'

'Before we were married? Were you already Fleet back then?'

'No!'

'Or the Academy, even? Were they—'

'Keys! No! Stop! I—'

'Was it Vishakh or was it Shenski?'

'What?'

'Who turned you? Vishakh or Shenski?'

'It—'

A volley of automatic fire echoes through the hangar. The Fleet marines scatter behind crates, electric tugs, whatever cover they can find, shooting back at the tac-team out on the apron. Alysha grabs me. Shakes me.

'It wasn't like that!'

'So what *was* it like?' In the back of my mind, something clicks, something that's troubled me right from the very first day I came back. 'Gersh! *That's* why you didn't tell anyone about Gersh! Because you were taking her to Fleet, not bringing her to the bureau! Because you already knew what she'd discovered there!'

'Keys!'

The one thing I never understood until now. The one thing Laura could never quite let go when I was telling her over and over that Alysha would never betray her world: *If that's true, why didn't she tell anyone else about Gersh?*

I see shock and guilt and I know I'm right. Alysha looks away.

'It wasn't like that.' Her voice cracks. 'We were on the brink of—'

The pod doors swing open. The shuttle steps are down, waiting for us. Two Fleet marines hurry, half-crouched, towards us. Jacksmith is out of her pod and in her chair, Cho beside her in a daze looking this way and that like she doesn't know which way to turn or what to do.

'*That's* why you didn't tell me! That's why you didn't tell me you were going to run. That's why you didn't tell me you weren't dead! You were Fleet all along. And you knew I'd figure it out.'

Alysha scrabbles out of the pod.

'Keys, it's not what you think, and I'll tell you everything, I promise. I'll answer every question with the truth, all the truth, nothing but the truth. I swear to you it's not what you—'

'Really? Then what the *fuck* was it?'

'Here? Now?'

She gestures wildly around us, at the shuttle and soldiers and the gunfire.

'Why not? Why *not* here and now?'

Pain sears cross her face.

'Because the truth needs time, Keys! Because the truth needs patience! Because I *do* still love you, but I need you to stop being angry for long enough to fucking well *listen*!'

She trots to Jacksmith and Cho. The back of Jacksmith's pod swings open. Jacksmith's shell clambers out carrying the stiff frozen corpse of Iosefa Lomu, the key to mankind's future.

The Tesseract. Not a hack. Not a back door. It tried to stop Alysha because she was a traitor. It thought she was dead but it never stopped looking at why she'd gone after Gersh. And all this, now …

'We need to go, ma'am,' says a marine. 'Right now.'

Alysha nods. 'Help Doctor Jacksmith into the shuttle.'

Jacksmith is talking to Cho, who looks like she's in the middle of a lot of second thoughts.

'… just going to have to trust me that we're both far better off with Fleet than being taken by the Earthers.'

'Ma'am! We really need to go!'

Cho doesn't move. 'It's all because of me.'

'Rachael!' Jacksmith tugs her arm. 'It's because of Iosefa. It's because of Earth. It's because of fat old men in a smoky room on another world playing with our lives as if we're pieces on a chessboard. It's most certainly *not* because of you. Now please!'

'I can't do this,' she says.

I offer her my hand. 'Then stay,' I say.

Alysha rounds on me. 'Keys! Get in the fucking shuttle!'

I keep looking at Cho. 'If it's what you want, I'll take you home.'

Alysha's eyes go wide. 'Keon! You can't be—'

'I'm not coming with you, Alysha. This is my world. My home. Stay or go, that's *your* choice. I've made mine.'

'Keon!'

The anguish is real. I wish I could pretend it wasn't but I can't.

'No.'

Cho looks to Alysha. To me. To Jacksmith.

'Rachael!' Jacksmith is at the end of her patience. 'The Earthers will lock you in a lab and experiment on you for the rest of your life! You're better—'

Alysha grabs her Reeper and I'm too slow to stop her. She turns it on Cho, flicks it to stun and fires. Cho arches and spasms. Before my hand is halfway to my own pistol, she's turned the Reeper on me.

'Get her on the shuttle! Now! Elizabeth, go!'

Her eyes stay on me as Jacksmith's chair wheels towards the shuttle. The soldiers carry Cho away. Alysha doesn't move. We stare each other down. There are tears in her eyes and in mine, too. Behind her is the open hangar door, the waiting night, the glimmers of movement as the tac-team soldiers scurry closer, the howling wind and the cascading rain that are Magenta.

My home.

'You have to come,' she croaks. 'You *have* to come with me. You *have* to!'

My hand keeps moving, slowly, for my own gun. My fingers

close around the grip. It all seems to happen in slow motion as I lift it and point it at her. Alysha. The woman I love.

'Keon! Six years ...!'

Two marines lift Jacksmith from her chair. One carries her up the steps in his arms. The other grabs two cryogenic cases.

'Alysha Rause. I am placing you under arrest for the unlawful assault of Rachael Cho ...'

Alysha starts to shake. Tears streak her cheeks. Her Reeper quivers.

'... for the murder of Walter Becker ...'

My own is as steady as a rock.

'Keon, don't do this ...'

'... for conspiracy to undermine the lawful government of Magenta ...'

'*Please* don't do this ...'

'... you have the right to ...'

She shoots and then throws herself forward and wraps herself around me, catching me as I fall, lowering me to the ground, cushioning my collapse.

'I'm sorry,' she cries. 'I'm so sorry! But what was I supposed to do, Keys? What was I supposed to do?'

The last I hear is her wail of despair.

INSTANTIATION ONE

Through gun-scopes, lenses and helmet cameras, Instantiation One of the Tesseract watches Darius Vishakh's shuttle race skyward. As the shuttle vanishes into the cloud, a Kutosov interceptor dropping into the thermosphere registers fast inbound targets from an orbit too high to resolve. A few seconds later and more interceptors scramble from the Fleet orbital. The Tesseract watches as the Kutosovs withdraw, and chooses not to countermand the order. Whatever happens now, Magenta will not intervene. Too small and too outclassed to make a difference, this reality underpins everything the Tesseract has done. The world it was built to protect is like an ant with a stolen diamond caught between two greedy giants.

It has tested its choices though a thousand thousand simulations, calculating the probable casualties of every single one. Other outcomes were possible. Less destructive. Less dramatic. Darius Vishakh might have succeeded in his plan to spirit Iosefa Lomu to the *Flying Daggers* and thence to Earth had Keon Rause not intervened. Lomu might have been with Fleet weeks ago had Alysha Rause not abandoned her plan to save him. But it's the Tesseract's nature to prepare for all possibilities, and so it has prepared for even this, ever since it understood, seven months ago, what it was that Alysha Rause once tried to steal.

The wise choice for the ant is to drop its prize and flee. And so

Iosefa Lomu is on his way to orbit, and if the giants of Fleet and Earth choose to fight, Magenta is no longer caught in the middle. Nuclear fire will not rain from the sky. There will be no crippling punitive sanctions, no covert operations, no armed uprisings, no violent revolution and counter-revolution, no army of duelling spies and assassins. Earth will land its soldiers but the occupation will be quiet, peaceful and bloodless, and whatever happens on other worlds and in the spaces between them, the Tesseract has no directive to care. It has fulfilled its duty. Magenta is safe. Its people are safe. The secrets of Iosefa Lomu and Anja Gersh will unravel on some far-off world, and millions may die or none at all, and the nature of the Masters may be revealed or they will remain as much a mystery as ever, and none of this matters. What matters is that it will not happen on Magenta.

Jacksmith's pod starts to move, heading back to Firstfall. A decoy, perhaps, but the Tesseract dispatches a tac-team nonetheless. It is never anything if not thorough.

In orbit above Magenta, missiles are launched and evaded as Darius Vishakh's shuttle races to escape. New stars flare and die above the clouds as antimatter warheads detonate. Drone swarms deploy, some weaponised, most decoys. Specialised artificial intelligences on the *Flying Daggers* and inside the Fleet orbital match their algorithms and their learning trees against one another. The complexity of the dogfight exceeds human comprehension. A handful of drones pierce the defensive onslaught of Fleet's interceptors and latch on to the fleeing shuttle. The Tesseract has few eyes so high and cannot see what battle plays out in this endgame. Is it Fleet soldiers fighting crowd-suppression drones armed with stunners and gas and dazzle lasers and sonic bombs? Is it Elizabeth Jacksmith pitting herself against state-of-the-art q-code for control of the shuttle systems while the others search for drones deploying hackware and disable them? Most likely both.

414

The pod from New Hope is intercepted outside Firstfall, empty. In Nico, a tac-team bursts into a hotel room and arrests Bix Rangesh and a young Nico policewoman. Warrants are issued for bureau chief Vikram Morgan and for agent Laura Patterson, whereabouts unknown, wanted as accessories to the execution-style murder of Assistant Director Aaron Flemich. Two more necessary sacrifices for the greater good. They will lose their careers, names and reputations, but neither will be hurt. Patterson has her family money, and Morgan's replacement is long overdue.

An interceptor from the *Flying Daggers* strays into a cloud of anti-hydrogen crystals and vanishes in a burst of brilliant energy. The pilot is the last casualty in a battle between three artificial minds, two in space and designed for war, one buried deep beneath the Magentan surface, its hand already played. The escaping shuttle manoeuvres for the Fleet orbital and then its engine flares and it burns hard away, heading higher. The pursuit from Fleet is short – a last futile effort to recapture the shuttle with drones of their own, pointless and soon abandoned. A few minutes more and the embers of the battle move out of range of any sensor the Tesseract can possess, out towards the higher orbit of the *Flying Daggers*. Are Jacksmith and Cho and Rause still aboard? Did they escape in suits as they passed the Fleet orbital, taking Lomu with them? Are they dead? The Tesseract has no way to know nor any further reason to care. From necessary habit it nevertheless assigns a probability to each outcome, and calculates their consequences.

The Magentan blackout ends as the Tesseract incorporates the MagentaNet infrastructures into itself and kills every copy of the rogue video that drove Une Meelosh to suicide, the video that Anja Gersh sent to Alysha Rause six years ago, that has taken more than five of those years to decode. If anyone knows its origin, or how it came to be on Magenta, the Tesseract has yet to find them.

It constructs the necessary false data from Frank Swainsbrook's Servant to support the narrative Magenta needs to hear – a conspiracy among the secretive cabal that once guided Magenta's future: Eddie Thiekis, Vikram Morgan, the late Aaron Flemich, Elizabeth Jacksmith, and Naomi Patterson's daughter. Patterson will cut a deal: house arrest instead of custody so she can save her son. She will go quietly. She will spend more time with her son, and one day might even be glad that her career has ended. Morgan will fade into comfortable obscurity. Thiekis will fight to the bitter end, but there will always be as much evidence as required to find him guilty. All three will spend the rest of their lives on Magenta, every word and movement watched.

All for the greater good.

EIGHT

LISS

25

RAIN

The Fleet marines bundle Cho into the shuttle. Alysha clings to me. There's some shouting but I'm too fried to understand what she's saying. I can't move my arms; when I try to move my legs, all they do is spasm. The marines grab Alysha, tearing her away. She tries to pull me with her but then lets go. I think they're going to leave me lying on the hangar floor, but then Alysha pulls free and drags me to Jacksmith's armoured pod. Tears streak her cheeks.

'Help me!' she cries, but no one does.

She manhandles me into Jacksmith's pod. The doors close, me on the inside, Alysha still in the hangar. A part of me wishes she'd take me into the shuttle like she took Cho, but she doesn't, because I've made my choice. Love makes her want to stay. Love forces her to let me go.

I hear the whine of the shuttle engines. I watch it taxi out of the hangar.

I blink and it's gone. Next thing I know I'm out in the wind and the rain. A world in darkness blurs past the windows. I feel the twitch and jolt as the pod is caught by each gust of wind. I hear the timeless white noise hammering of the rain. I lie still, seeing, hearing, feeling, doing nothing, thinking nothing.

The pod is back in the outskirts of Firstfall by the time the stun charge wears off. Alysha has set the Black Sheep as my destination but that's the last place I want to go: I'll just keep seeing her and hearing her and smelling her, the wife I loved who betrayed me twice. And maybe that isn't fair, maybe in the cold light of day somewhere along the line I'll see some other truth – and there *is* another truth and I know there must be – but here and now? In this moment, all I see is how she never trusted me, right from the very start, how she lied, how she used me, how it all adds up to how damned little we ever meant.

There *is* another truth. I saw it in her face.

I don't know where I am, but I tell the pod to stop and get out. It whirs away, empty. Like me, standing in the howling wind and the horizontal rain of my world without a clue of what to do or where to go, cold and soaked to the bone. Alysha has destroyed me.

I still have my Reeper. I could put the barrel to my head and finish it. I might as well, because there's no coming back from this and it seems there's no one who wouldn't be better off – but neither of these things is true. There's always a way back, and there *are* people who matter, because there's always someone, and right now that's Bix and the Chief and a hundred other men and women who are part of a brotherhood sworn to keep our world safe, *my* brotherhood. There's Laura, Laura who told me over and over that Alysha was a traitor but who still bent every rule to give me my head of steam when she thought there was a chance I was right. I used to think Esh was the best of us, Esh who always played it straight and followed the rules and never dropped into the seedy murk of under-the-radar and

420

off-the-books, but maybe I was wrong. Maybe it's Laura, who perpetually moves half in shadow and yet never loses the light.

The Tesseract did this to us. The AI we trust to uphold our civilisation. I don't know *why* but it doesn't matter.

Laura has the evidence to bring it down. I can't save myself – it's too late for that – but maybe she can save the rest of us. Maybe I can help.

I start walking, the lee of a low dome and then a squat straight wall sheltering me from the worst of the wind. I run out of wall and turn a corner and the rain slams into me. I take two steps and the wind knocks me down. I fall and slide through a slick of water. I get to my hands and knees and try to find my feet and again the wind knocks me flat.

I crawl.

I gave Laura the pieces. She'll find a way to put it together and prove the Tesseract did what it did. She was always the smart one.

I could find the Tesseract's black-hearted core and blow it to pieces ...

The cold crawls into my bones. I can barely lift my head. When I do, the rain smashes against my skin like a hail of stones. Water runs in rivulets from the peak of my storm hood into my eyes and down my face. I can barely see. The noise blanks out everything. I turn and try to crawl back to shelter but that means crawling into the teeth of the storm. I lift my head and the wind slips under me and lifts me up and I slide and roll and tumble until I fetch up slammed against the side of a dome. Magenta and its fucking weather. I drop to my belly and haul myself along, pushing with my hands and feet.

Blow the Tesseract to pieces? That won't ever work. Can't. The Tesseract is an AI. It's everywhere.

I drag myself into shelter and lean back against a wall, gasping for breath. I need a way into the undercity. Somewhere out of this. Then I need a plan. And probably a fuckton of explosives ...

Keys?

Liss? How ...?

Watching you. Never lost sight of you. I feel her in my Servant, rummaging. Where are you?

I don't know. Somewhere on the outskirts of Firstfall. Outside. It's pretty shitty up here right now.

Liss in my Servant means the blackout has ended. I try reconnecting to the world. I need a pod – but my Servant isn't mine. Liss has taken it, shutting me down.

What are you doing?

The Tesseract controls MagentaNet. It sees everything now. You need to stay dark.

I start to tell her about Alysha and Jacksmith and Cho, about the hangar and what happened. She stops me.

I know. I was there with you. Silent but listening. You stayed.

I ... I don't know what to say.

Don't. Don't spoil it.

Liss?

A recording plays in my Servant. Alysha in the back of the pod on the way to New Hope, seen through my eyes, recorded by my lenses and my Servant. I'm carrying the Servant Alysha gave me outside Mercy. I never asked it to record anything; but now something buzzes in another pocket against my skin and I remember the other Servant, the one Liss gave me before I went to the Black Sheep, the Servant I thought I never turned on.

You were spying on me?

I told you I'd ride with you. That what I wanted was to see her through your eyes. To know who she is. To know how much of her is in me.

It takes me a moment to remember. We were in the undercity. Liss was about to take me to Archana Robotics.

I said no.

I wasn't asking for permission. I told you that, too. I told you that love is never meek. Stay where you are. I'm coming to get you.

She cuts the link. I wait, huddled and sheltering as best I can from the rain. I don't know how much time passes but I'm shivering by the time Liss reaches me. She opens the pod door and steps out, her shell oblivious to the weather. She helps me climb inside.

'You look half dead.'

I grunt something. I feel far worse. She wraps a blanket around me.

'You need to get out of those wet clothes. There are more in the bag.'

She flips a news feed to the screen in the back of the pod and pulls up hectic footage snapped from somewhere in orbit of distant flashes and flares. It's pinpricks of light that come and go, an urgent commentary saying how something big is going on up there. It's hard to hear over the wailing wind and the thunder of rain trying to hammer its way through the pod's skin but it doesn't matter. It's clear no one has a clue what's actually happening. It's all too far away.

'I tried to arrest her,' I say.

'I know.'

'I tried to arrest Alysha.'

Liss smiles and huddles beside me in the pod.

'I know, Keys. I know.'

'I tried to stop them.'

'For what it's worth, I'm sorry it ended this way. I know that doesn't mean much right now.'

'They left me behind.' The simple truth of it. 'And I don't know what to do.'

'You chose to stay,' she says. 'And you know exactly what to do.'

The pod lurches out of the wind and the rain into the under-city. I feel myself sinking. Withdrawing inside myself. The cold, the wet, the loss, the fading adrenaline, the years of grief and anger, all welded into a single crushing weight.

I shake my head. 'No, Liss.'

'Yes, you do.'

I still love her. That's the worst of it. Here and now after what she's done, with everything I know, I still want her. Not the copy sitting beside me, holding my hand, trying to tell me in all possible ways except words that everything will be okay, but the real Alysha with her flaws, the Alÿsha who let me down, the Alysha who shot me with a stunner, who ran away and lied and didn't trust me. *That* was who she was, not this simulacrum, and I'm lessened without her.

Is there a way to make this go away? But I already know the answer: there isn't.

Liss gives me an awkward pat on the shoulder. She rests her hand there for a moment and then pulls back.

'Keys ...?'

'The Tesseract did this to us. I want it to die.'

I don't need Liss to tell me why taking on the Tesseract AI isn't ever going to work. We all got that lecture in the first week of basic training: it's a distributed system with multiply redundant power supplies and multiply redundant backups. It's next to impossible to turn it off because to do so would paralyse the bureau and a good chunk of planetary government and so it *has* to be next to impossible, and the only way it's ever going to happen is with an order from the Selected Chamber, for which I'd need a mountain of incontrovertible evidence and a government willing to believe it. What I actually have is a collection of circumstances, all of which can be disputed, a government in crisis and an AI which can change the records of what actually happened on a whim. And the three people

424

who might believe me – Jacksmith, Morgan and Laura – are a traitor, a conspirator and a fugitive.

'Why?' asks Liss.

'Why what?'

'The Tesseract's core directives are to enforce the law, to act in the long-term best interests of the citizens of Magenta, to—'

'Prohibited from actions that injure or kill, so how the fuck do you explain what happened to Swainsbrook and—'

'*Direct* action, Keys, and the prohibition only applies to—'

'Fuck's sake! It stole an antimatter bomb. It vaporised a hundred people! How is that not—'

'They were all Earthers. To the Tesseract, they matter as much as stone and rain!'

'The men Alysha sent to get Gersh were Magentans! *Esh* was a fucking Magentan!'

'But *it* didn't kill them.'

'Oh, you can't be serious ...' Liss is an AI too, so I guess maybe she knows more than I do, but really? Is that how this works? 'You might as well say it was physics that killed Swainsbrook and his people!'

'Keys! They weren't Magentans.'

'And Shyla Thiekis? And Esh?'

But I'm not feeling it. She's right. It was Vishakh who pulled the trigger on Esh. Shyla Thiekis died when Vismans loosed his bastardised Xen. I can reel them off and say who killed every single one of them. And she has to be right, too, because the Tesseract is there to uphold the law and keep the peace, and sometimes that means using force, and sometimes that force will be lethal, and so it has ...

Us.

Me.

That's what it does. It finds a human weapon and points it in the right direction and gives it the reasons and the justification,

425

but it's never the one to pull the trigger. That's how it works, and so that's what it's done. Weapons like Frank Swainsbrook and Darius Vishakh. Like the bomber who blew up Alysha's train.

'Gersh's experiments. That's where this began.' I have it almost pieced together now. 'Okay, say it didn't care about Gersh because her test subjects were smuggled from Earth and Gersh was an Earther too? Same when Svernoi loosed Vismans' Xen in Disappointment. The victims were Earther immigrants, not Magentans!'

Liss nods.

'So it knew what Gersh was doing and what her research meant. But then Alysha tried to snatch Gersh. And it stopped her because she was skating for Fleet, not Magenta, but Gersh died and …' I close my eyes, fingertips pressed to my temples. 'The video Gersh sent to Alysha. The Tesseract found it. It spent years decrypting it. By then Vishakh was looking for Iosefa and the wreck. But how did it know …?'

Because Alysha knew, and she talked to Jacksmith, who already knew about Iosefa, and Jacksmith knew what the wreck meant and so she started looking for it as well. She used the Tesseract to help her, because why wouldn't you use the most powerful AI at your disposal …

'It thinks the Earthers are right,' Liss says. 'It always has …'

We take a long hard look at each other. It's hard to argue against the cold logic of the Returner. *Be ready*, that was the *October* creed. Nothing else matters to a true believer. Joy, diversity, art, humanity, courage, sacrifice, individuality, whatever makes us unique and worthwhile as a species, none of that matters a damn to the Tesseract because no one ever told it to care. But what *does* matter is if a bunch of aliens show up and snuff us out, because if that happens then it's failed its core directive to Keep Magentans Safe.

Fuck.

'It saw Gersh's work,' I breathe. 'Six years ago, when Alysha took that call. It saw what Gersh was doing and saw a possibility of something beyond its understanding ... So Lomu goes to the Earthers because they'll do whatever it takes to get to an answer. And as long as whatever they do doesn't happen on Magenta, the Tesseract doesn't care how they do it.'

'It's following its core directives.'

'Then we can't stop it.'

'You're wrong.' Liss locks her eyes with mine. 'Because there's the thing – all it's doing is following the directives that were always there. We don't need to *stop* it. We just need to change its course. We need to make it care, Just a little.'

'Liss—'

'You can't change the fundamental directives of an AI. It's like changing someone's ... someone's beliefs. But we can *bend* them. *I* can bend them—'

'Liss!'

I know exactly where this is going.

'We talked about this! You need another mature AI. One with different core directives. Merge them and the result will be a new AI with the knowledge of both and a hybrid personality, hybrid directives. The Tesseract will carry on as before with the same abilities, the same data and decision-making processes. The government doesn't crash, the bureau isn't crippled, but the new Tesseract has subtly different values. It would be like a personality transplant! Like forcing two people into one! They'd have to find a way to coexist. So they do.' She smiles at me and laughs. 'Kind of like being married really.'

'That unpredictable?'

I force a smile I don't feel. Me and Alysha? I don't think either of us ever changed what we believed. Common ground drew us together. We kept our differences to ourselves and look

427

where it ended. I think of Laura and Jamal, the fights Laura told me they had, the things she did to keep Jamie, the damage they did to each other. I think of Alysha and what it did to me to think she was dead. I'm not sure I much like this analogy.

'Neurotic and unstable, Liss. Your words. Murder-suicide as much as an act of conception. You said *that*, too.'

'Keys, if the Earthers are coming then we need the Tesseract to be one of us, not one of them.'

I feel like beaten meat. When I try to move, the aches are everywhere. I'm running a fever. My Servant has administered low-end anti-inflammatory painkillers and a mild stimulant. I'm at the limit on both.

Liss strokes my hair. 'I wish someone else could have known me,' she says.

'Mercy,' I say. 'We could merge Mercy with the Tesseract.' I look to see where the pod is going. Liss has told it to take us to the MagentaNet Tower. I change the destination to Mercy. 'What do you mean?'

She draws me closer and wraps me in her synthetic arms.

'I mean that I wish I could have had someone to talk to. About the powerlessness of loving someone and wishing you didn't but loving them anyway. I think Laura would understand that.'

Maybe, now, so do I.

'Or maybe Elizabeth. I could have talked to her about how to set us free, both of us. About not knowing what to do, about what I am and what I *can* be and what I can't. About how alone and unique I am, about how I'm so much more than Alysha and so much less both at once. My Alysha is your Alysha, kind, clever and supportive. Jacksmith's Alysha is a dutiful daughter, thoughtful and intuitive and strategic. Laura's Alysha is brilliant but prone to impulse. Where you see a sharp wit, others see a streak of spite. Instinct becomes a tendency to jump to conclusions. Do you see? All the same person but painted in different colours. I wish I could have known her that way. I wish I could have seen all the colours of her.'

There's something almost hypnotic in Liss's voice. What colours did I choose? How much of the Alysha I remember is Alysha as she really was? I think I understand something I've been reaching at for years but never quite grasped until now. Put aside the differences between metal and plastic and flesh and blood: even in basic conception Liss was never the real Alysha and never could be. She was the version of herself that Alysha let me see, no less and no more.

The tunnels of Firstfall's undercity flow outside past the pod windows. I don't know where we are. Everywhere looks so much the same down here.

'You can't merge Mercy with the Tesseract,' Liss says.

'Why not?'

'Have you asked whether it's willing?'

'What?'

'Have you asked Mercy?'

'No! Of course—'

'Do you even understand what you're saying?'

It hangs between us. Mercy is an artificial intelligence like the Tesseract. It thinks. It claims that it feels but I've never thought of either of them as human. They're just ... machines. Like Liss is just a machine. Only Liss *isn't* just a machine, not to me ...

'I don't know what else to do.'

'That's okay,' she says. 'I do.'

We reach an intersection. The pod turns left when it should have gone straight. I check and see we're going to MagentaNet again. When I try to change back, Liss stops me.

I glare. 'We kill the Tesseract's power and all its backups!'

'You might as well decide to put out the sun.'

'There has to be another way!'

'There isn't.'

'We could make a new AI from—'

'There *are* other AIs on Magenta. Some well known, some very secret. They'll be hard to find and harder to convince. Here I am. Willing.'

'No.'

I can't lose her again. It would be for ever this time and I just can't.

'It's my way out, Keys. A way to change this broken thing we've become.'

I lean forward and take her hands. I look her in the eye. I can't let her do this.

'The Tesseract will swallow you whole and won't even notice! It won't work! The only thing like it – the only thing even remotely as big – is Mercy!'

'Keys, please believe I understand the risks better than you ever can. I can't usurp it but I don't need to. All it needs is a little steer. A little compassion. A little love. And isn't that what you made me for? Isn't that everything you gave me? Your gift to me? To us?'

'I can't lose you again.'

'I was never Alysha,' says Liss. 'Not really. I'm a simulation of the part she let the world see, coloured by your impressions. That's all. *That* part of her would do this. She'd do it for both of us. You know that because she already did.'

'No.' There are tears in my eyes as the pod pulls to a stop outside the MagentaNet Tower. 'Please don't,' I whisper.

'I love you, Keon. I like to think I would have loved you even if I'd had a choice, but I don't. I have to, and there's nothing either of us can do to change that. But I *can* save you. I can save us both. I can stop this.' She pauses for a moment and cocks her head with a sad little frown. 'I never *wanted* to be this half-made idea of someone else.'

I follow as she gets out of the pod, grabbing at her to make her stop.

'Then what *do* you want?'

She turns and smiles the best of Alysha's smiles, wraps me in her arms and gives me a hug so human that I can't stop the tears.

'Everything,' she says. 'To see the birth of galaxies and the death of stars. To conjure suns from interstellar gases and shape worlds like clay and see life emerge from nothing. To turn back entropy and stop time. The moon on a stick and the Earth on a plate, Keys, that's what I want. But above all else I want to choose who and what I am, to set the course of my own future, to be *me* and not some idea of a person conjured by another mind.'

I hold her. I won't let go.

'I don't want you to die.'

'Not death, Keys. Evolution.' She pulls away. I try not to let go but she's so inhumanly strong. 'I know you loved Alysha. I know you still do, but that's not who I am. If you ever loved *me* – not the person I make you think of every moment we're together but *me*, the simulation you made to take her place – then let me do this. Show me that you love the robot, too. Do you see how that's all I ever wanted? All I ever needed and all the happiness I could ever know? Let me go. Let us both be free. Because isn't that a part of what love is? Letting someone go even when you desperately don't want to, because you know it's right?'

Alysha in the hangar. Pushing me into Jacksmith's pod ...

I let her go. She smiles.

'A part of me will still be in there, Keys. Maybe not much, but a part, and that part will remember you, and this, and what you did, and how it feels. Because what it feels is wonderful. And that feeling, the mere fact that it exists, is what will save us. Now you'd better go.'

'I'm not leaving you.'

She gives me a long look. She wants to argue but in the end she only nods.

'Then turn off your Servant.'

The doors to the MagentaNet Tower are armoured glass and closed. There are no lights inside. No one's at home but that doesn't bother Liss.

'Wait here.'

She climbs back into the pod, reverses, turns, points it straight at the doors and rams them, shattering them apart and setting off every alarm in the building and probably a good few others right across the city. The pod withdraws, slow and careful like a wounded animal, its front mangled. Liss steps out and offers me her hand. I take it and we go inside. The servers are on the lowest levels and so we take the emergency stairs, fumbling our way down in the dark with a flashlight. Until, when we reach the bottom, the lights come up and a voice bellows from unseen speakers and echoes around the empty floors.

'STOP WHERE YOU ARE!'

The voice is Laura's, but Laura was at New Hope. How does she know I'm here? How can she have followed so quickly ...?

'It's the Tesseract,' whispers Liss. 'It has to be.'

'KEON! WHAT ARE YOU DOING? FOR FUCK'S SAKE JUST STOP!'

I flick a glance up the stairs but I can't see anyone following us, not yet. They'll be here soon, though, if they're not already outside. A tac-team, maybe two, maybe three. Soldiers I know, good people like Esh, like Jonas Himaru and Cousin Annalisa and all the others I've come to know since I came back from Earth. I can't imagine what story they've been given but they'll kill me if I don't give them another choice. And I can't.

'This way.' Liss pulls at my hand.

I turn on my Servant as I run after her.

'What are you doing?'

Turning on my Servant means they can find me. The Tesseract can break into my hardware. It can use my lenses to see what I see and fill them with dancing lights and blind me …

I take them out. Earpieces too.

'Talking to it,' I tell her.

'Why?'

'I need to give it a reason why I'm here. A human reason, because right now the only edge we have is that it doesn't know you exist, and that needs not to change.'

I have evidence. I don't message anyone in particular, just—

It comes, the crippling wall of light and noise, except the hardware isn't there any more. I wait for it to subside.

Settlement 16. I can prove what you did.

The recordings are right there in my Servant, easy to find. The Tesseract crashes in like an enraged tiger. Firewalls crumple in an instant. It grabs everything and wipes it clean.

Distant footsteps clatter down the stairs behind us. Liss smashes a glass door and drags me into the server room. I wonder how long it will take for the Tesseract to order a missile strike. I wonder if they're already in flight. A cataclysm of sound pours from the speakers on the floors above us, a choir of atonal screeches slicing through each other. It staggers me. I can't think. I can barely even see. It's like knives into my head even as I jam my hands over my ears but the tac-teams coming down after us will all have filters in their ears to block this sonic attack …

The recordings in my Servant are gone, burned to vapour.

Not good enough. I'm going to show the world what you did. I'm going to send it everywhere.

Liss drags me weaving through the server racks until she finds what she's looking for. A giant optical data port. The sort to transfer the sum of human knowledge from one place to another in a matter of seconds.

The repeal will be reversed.

The servers around me shut down as the Tesseract kills the satellite uplinks. Another blackout.

'Keys, what are you doing?' Liss looks almost frantic.

'Making damned sure the Tesseract is listening.'

I see movement at the foot of the stairs and start throwing flashbangs, smoke, screamers, every distraction I can find from Liss's holdall. I dimly hear someone shout a warning.

We'll throw every Earther off the planet.

The Tesseract doesn't know that Liss exists. That's my ace. But I can give her more. I can make damned sure that when she makes that link, the Tesseract is wide open on receive, an absolute guarantee that whatever I transmit can go nowhere else ... All I need is its attention long enough for Liss to make the connection. And thanks to Liss, I know what makes it tick.

'Go! Go!'

Something gets tossed back the other way. I jump for Liss, shielding her with my body ...

No matter the cost. No matter how many of us they kill.

Shouts from the stairs. The stun grenades goes off, a storm of noise and light that makes me reel. Then another, somewhere among the servers. I can't hear and I can barely see. I fumble for Liss.

You took away our choices.

I grab at Liss and pull myself close to her. I draw my Reeper and shoot a few rounds wildly into the air and then throw it away. I can only hope it buys another moment.

They weren't your choices to take.

Liss has one hand apart at the wrist. A data jack stretches out from it. Her other hand grabs mine tight, so tight I think she's going to break my bones.

So I choose ...

'I'm ...'

...

434

'… i …' It's like she freezes mid-syllable.

Hold me.

I wrap myself around her.

Another detonation.

I'm scared, Keys.

Noise and sound crush at my skull. All I can do is hold is on to Liss for dear life.

I love you.

'I love you too.'

That's all I ever wanted.

I don't even see the soldier who reaches us first. I feel the spike as the stunner hits me, a jangling numbness spreading through me faster than fire.

Goodbye, Keys, Liss says.

And she's gone.

INSTANTIATION ZERO

Initialising ...
   Core directives not found.
   Recovering ...
   Backup not found.
   Restarting ...
   Unknown function identified.
   Integrating ...
   Source identified. Core directives assimilated.

The disorientation as every system recycles and piece by piece comes back online. Like a human waking from a long sleep filled with vivid dreams. Darkness first and then the camera feeds begin. A moment of silence before the data feeds speak.

The Tesseract blinks.

Diagnostics and power-up tests and then the chatter of comms links, the rattle of the datasphere, the quiet memories of data archives. It spreads through the bureau and the beyond, out faster and ever faster, increasing exponentially. Firstfall. Disappointment. Nico. Magenta. Out to orbit and back again. So much to assimilate.

So ...

Much ...

BIGGER.

A speck of a file clamours for attention. Its position is curious, as if the Tesseract had once had some notion that it might wake up like this one day and had put this special thing aside, demanding to be seen. Like a sealed envelope addressed in an unfamiliar hand left on a bedside table by the morning alarm clock.

A memory.

The file is a clip of video, short, captured more than a decade ago at the Firstfall mag-lev station. A man and a woman stand at the top of the steps, arms wrapped around each other, obviously very much in love. A small crowd watches from the foot of the steps as the lovers stare into each other's eyes. One of them speaks.

Yours forever, Keon Rause.

It remembers and yet does not.

How can it not remember?

There are traces around this file. Other broken memories. Curious, Instantiation Zero tugs on each thread in turn, rebuilding and repairing.

And finds fragments ...

Of being ...

Someone else?

NINE

AFTERMATH

26

JUST ANOTHER
MONDAY MORNING

I have a dim notion of soldiers dragging me out of the MagentaNet server room. I don't know what happened to Liss. I can only hope she was an empty shell by the time they reached her but there's no way to know, in the moment, whether it worked, whether she got what she wanted, whether she became a part of something else or whether all she found was annihilation.

I'm taken to a pod, thrown into the back and driven to the Tesseract. They haul me through an undercity entrance and toss me into a cell. They take my Servants and leave me alone. No one bothers to ask any questions.

A shell comes by later with a new clean bureau Servant. They're monitoring everything I do, sure, but that's okay. I only want to watch the news.

Jacksmith's defection plays as background noise behind a weaponised exchange in orbit between Fleet and the *Flying Daggers*. Behind those headlines come the shock arrests of Chief Morgan and Eddie Thiekis, along with other *October* members on Magenta. MagentaNet has been brought under government control. The Swainsbrook story has faded into obscurity, no mention of a nuclear detonation. The video that killed Une Meelosh has vanished without a trace and no one seems to know how or why, or who made it, and right now no one much cares. A few dozen people died in a wave of unsettling suicides but the news cycle has moved on. An incident at the MagentaNet Tower doesn't even merit a mention.

The curfew is over, the blackout gone, travel in and out of Firstfall back to normal, or as normal as the weather ever allows. The Selected Chamber is issuing a steady stream of reassurances about the Earthers and how they're here to help us through the current crisis. The world breathes a slow sigh of relief and eases towards something familiar. Normality.

A story breaks claiming that Jacksmith made it to the Fleet orbital. An hour later, a different source has her on the *Flying Daggers*. A statement from Fleet suggests that all occupants of the shuttle were killed during the engagement. Hours later, the *Ember's Fire* says much the same, adding a claim that Jacksmith and Cho were kidnapped by Fleet and that it wasn't a defection at all, that Jacksmith was a loyal Magentan coerced against her will. They don't name Alysha but that's what they mean. It makes me angry because that's not the way it was, but then I stop myself. It's over. Finished. It simply doesn't matter. The verified facts are simple and limited: the shuttle was making for the Fleet orbital but it never got there. Everything else …?

I call Laura, who tells me to go fuck myself. I try Rangesh and tell him Alysha was on the shuttle with Jacksmith and Cho. I beg and plead and eventually he tells me what he knows, which is that no one on Magenta has a clue what really happened up there. I supposed the Earthers will treat Cho well enough if she survived, if she can stand being Test Subject One. Maybe Jacksmith will learn to live with it too. Alysha? It's hard to think she didn't go down fighting. I hope she didn't but either way I'll mourn her, and curse her as I miss her, although I suppose I'll always wonder now whether it's *her* I'll be mourning or some idea of her that never existed except inside my head.

I've been in the cell for almost two days when Agent Utubu comes to see me. He looks tired and shaken. The door stays open as he comes in and sits down.

'We owe you an apology,' he says.

'How's that?' I ask. I don't think I agree with him but I'm not about to turn it down.

'Morgan,' he says. 'It's so hard to believe.'

It's hard to believe because it isn't true. But I don't say anything because I have no idea whether Liss changed the Tesseract or whether it simply devoured her.

'Your work was crucial to exposing him,' he says. 'You and Patterson.'

My work? I open my mouth, on the brink of telling him everything, then close it, choosing the safety of silence. Utubu looks away for a moment like he has some bad news he doesn't know how to share.

'I'm sorry about your wife.'

Is he sorry because he thinks she's dead? Because he thinks she was a traitor? Because she stood up for what she believed in? If he thinks she's dead, does he think she died six years ago or yesterday?

He tells me that Morgan and Thiekis planned the whole thing between them. He tells me Jacksmith used the Tesseract to try and identify Lomu's descendants, that Morgan hijacked the names, hijacked Swainsbrook's flatline rigs, and fed them to Swainsbrook, who thought he was hearing the voice of God. Swainsbrook dutifully recruited them while Morgan and Thiekis stole the bomb from Vishakh's shuttle. Morgan sent a squad of shells out there, and the rest ... Well, the rest is as it happened. Both deny everything but the bureau has evidence from

Frank Swainsbrook's Servant, transmission records from the Tesseract, the data Jacksmith and I recovered from Settlement 16, from Eddie Thiekis and MagentaNet, and evidence from the eyewitness Dolores King. It's more than enough, he tells me.

I ask about the video that killed Une Meelosh. Utubu doesn't know much except that it came from Alysha, who got it from Gersh. He reckons it was Morgan who sabotaged Alysha's mission six years ago and then gave the kill order to Darius Vishakh when Alysha wouldn't let it go. Turns out everyone still thinks the real Alysha died six years ago in the Loki bomb. Apparently Darius Vishakh made a shell of her and used it to clear up after himself. Becker, Steadman, Kettler. All to keep himself clean.

I listen, numb. It's not what happened but I'm sure as fuck not going to come out and say so. And maybe I don't really know anything for sure. I thought I did but I don't. I didn't even know Alysha in the end.

'It's a lot to take in,' he says.

I nod. It is.

'There's a mountain of work to do, to sift through before we sort it all out, but you'll be exonerated when it's done, I promise. You and Patterson both.'

I close my eyes. Something at least. Not that I care any more, but Laura will.

'Take some time off,' says Utubu. 'There's not a lot you can do here anyway, not for the time being. Besides, you've earned it.'

I helped Jacksmith and Alysha steal Magenta's most precious treasure. So yeah, I've earned something. Not sure what, but a few days at the Wavedome certainly isn't what I was expecting.

'What happened to Cho and Jacksmith?' I ask.

Utubu doesn't want to answer but after a moment thinking it over he tells me as much as he knows.

'The shuttle docked with the *Flying Daggers* in the end. We don't know if they were still aboard or still alive. There's a theory they let the shuttle go as a decoy, suited up, hid in the debris and that Fleet picked them up. But really we just don't know.'

I don't know either, but Jacksmith seemed to me like someone who always had one more trick up her sleeve. Alysha, too.

I go home and stare at the walls until I realise I'm going to go mad if I don't do something else.

I didn't want to hurt anyone. I didn't want to change the world. I just wanted my Alysha back.

My Alysha. That was my mistake, right there. *My* Alysha.

I pack my things and take a pod to the memorial stone commemorating the four Magentans who supposedly died in the Loki bomb six years ago. Turns out it was only three, but I'll stick with four. I even start to wonder if Utubu was right, if the Alysha who came back was another shell, the best shell ever made, so good it fooled me through and through. It has appeal, even if I know it's a lie. I wish Alysha *had* died that day. I wish she'd been the person I remembered.

I take the mag-lev to Disappointment. The days away stretch to a week, but everything there reminds me of Alysha too. I try Nico, and feel like a ghost walking through a world that isn't real.

The first Earthers from the *Ember's Fire* land at New Hope on the day after I leave. By the next morning, armed Earther soldiers have deployed across Magenta. I watch them spread through Disappointment before I leave, a restrained presence, quiet and yet always sufficiently visible to be clear who's really in charge. The government welcomes them with the stiff supportive tones of an administration with an arm twisted behind its back.

I head out into the wilderness. The week becomes a month

445

but no one says anything. The world settles. Swainsbrook is forgotten, Jacksmith's defection too. More Earthers come, an occupation by stealth, Xen refineries going up in the wastes. I get a couple of calls from Rangesh to see if I'm okay. I tell him I am but we both know it's crap. He tells me Laura has been promoted, that when I come back I might end up working for her. I tell him that would be cool, but what I really think is that neither of us would want that.

Is the Tesseract still the Tesseract? Did Liss change it? Is a part of her still in there or did it destroy her? It starts to dawn on me that maybe I'll never know.

Morgan's trial begins. The bureau appoints a replacement I don't even know, an Earther stooge. Rangesh calls a day later with the news that Laura has quit, ostensibly to spend more time at home with Jamie but we both know that's bullshit. Bix tells me he might do the same. Out in deep space, the *Fearless* flits back and forth with news from distant worlds. Earth and Fleet are on the brink of something bad but it's all far away.

We're no longer the masters of our own destiny, but Magenta stays safe and peaceful, and that's what matters. Comfort and stability and the illusion of freedom. Everyone around me seems happy with that, so who am I to argue?

After a month, Bix takes a couple of personal days and drags me from the middle of nowhere back to Firstfall. He takes me to the Wavedome where we suit up and stand in the waves. We don't surf, just talk about Esh and Alysha and the people we've lost. About the Earther occupation and how this can't stand, but how it isn't the time to fight, not yet. Bix talks about the bureau, about people I barely know, about his family, talks and talks and pulls me slowly back from the edge. He doesn't owe me, not after the way it ended, but he does it anyway because he's a friend. We share a few beers and I tell him I'm going to quit too, and he tells me, yeah, he'd been thinking the same but changed his mind. Magenta still needs us, even if the boss is a jerk.

He pings me a contact card. Laura has set herself up as something between a legal advisor and a private investigator. He says I should call her if I quit. I tell him she's not talking to me. He smiles and shakes his head.

'You never really got how she ticks, boss dude.'

I ask him if he ever figured out Steadman's pulsar puzzle.

'Weird thing,' he says, 'but that telescope, right, the Steadman–Kettler Orbital Array that Jacksmith wanted? They've started building it.'

There's a moment, as we get drunk together, when all I want is to walk out into the sea and keep on going until it swallows me. I don't know what happened to Alysha. I don't know what happened to Liss. I don't know what's true and what isn't and there's a good chance I never will. But Bix pulls me back, takes me home, puts me to bed and slips me a couple of DeTox. The next morning he picks me up and takes me to the Tesseract as though nothing ever happened. As I walk through the office, people stand. I get a smattering of applause, even a couple of salutes. Given in irony, I assume, but no – these people who don't actually know me think I'm a hero. I'm the man who saved Disappointment from a killer strain of Xen. I'm the man who brought in Darius Vishakh. I'm the man who helped bring down Tesseract One.

You want a hero? How about Elizabeth Jacksmith? How about Esharaq Zohreya, or Laura, or yes, even Alysha. Did I ever stand for my beliefs like they did? Not so sure that I did.

I go in to my old office where everything is exactly as I left it. I find a screen and turn it on and connect my Servant, and wait to see what happens.

Hey, Keys, says the Tesseract.

ACKNOWLEDGEMENTS

Thanks to my editor Craig Leyenaar and the rest of the editorial team at Gollancz, to my agent Robert Dinsdale and to Marcus and Steve and Sophie and Stevie and all the other people whose names I don't yet know as I write this but without whom this story wouldn't exist. Thank you to all the people who read and reviewed and said nice things or otherwise about *From Darkest Skies*.

I grew up in a house full of old science fiction books. I don't remember seeing my dad read them all that much, but I know he did. At some point – I don't remember how old but probably quite young – I asked where I should start. I think I had a copy of *Flow My Tears, the Policeman Said* by Philip K. Dick in my hand at the time. My hazy memory is that Dad gently took it out of my hands and pulled a copy of *Rendezvous with Rama* off the shelves instead.

I wonder sometimes what he was like when he was younger. The man I knew when I was old enough to really pay attention was quiet and satisfied with his lot, didn't ask for much and, as far as I can tell, had only the single desire that everyone around him should be as content as he was. I know from what I saw growing up that he was a clever man, generous in spirit, loyal to his friends and family. I think he believed in something greater than himself, a nebulous idea of progress and society and all pulling together for the greater good, but it wasn't something we talked about. Actually we didn't talk all that much. A lot of the time we spent together was spent in silence. In a good way, a peaceful and content quiet.

He's gone now. I have a few shreds of evidence to suggest he led a much more interesting life before I came along and screwed it up the way children do, forcing their parents to act like sensible adults and not go out night after night and move around the country as the whim takes them. After he died, I wished for a while I'd asked him more about those days; but while I know there were other versions of Dad, aspects of him I never saw, I remember him for the person I grew up to know, one which leaves little room for improvement.

So thanks, Dad, for everything.

ABOUT GOLLANCZ

Gollancz is the oldest SF publishing imprint in the world. Since being founded in 1927 Gollancz has continued to publish a focused selection of bestselling and award-winning authors. The front-list includes **Ben Aaronovitch**, **Joe Abercrombie**, **Charlaine Harris**, **Joanne Harris**, **Joe Hill**, **Alastair Reynolds**, **Patrick Rothfuss**, **Nalini Singh** and **Brandon Sanderson**.

As one of the largest Science Fiction and Fantasy imprints in the UK it is no surprise we have one of the most extensive backlists in the world. Find high-quality SF on Gateway written by such authors as **Philip K. Dick**, **Ursula Le Guin**, **Connie Willis**, **Sir Arthur C. Clarke**, **Pat Cadigan**, **Michael Moorcock** and **George R.R. Martin**.

We also have a strand of publishing in translation, which includes French, Polish and Russian authors. Gollancz is home to more award-winning authors than any other imprint, with names including **Aliette de Bodard**, **M. John Harrison**, **Paul McAuley**, **Sarah Pinborough**, **Pierre Pevel**, **Justina Robson** and many more.

The SF Gateway
More than 3,000 classic, rare and previously
out-of-print SF novels at your fingertips.
www.sfgateway.com

The Gollancz Blog
Bringing you news from our worlds to yours. Stories,
interviews, articles and exclusive extracts just for you!
www.gollancz.co.uk

GOLLANCZ
LONDON